Praise for "Among

"With language as beautiful as it is riveting, ***Among Other Edens*** is a wonderful tapestry of gothic sentiment and modern day culture. The story is steeped in haunting imagery so vivid you'll feel the dread and longing right along with Evie, page after page."

-***Rebekah Hunter Scott***, author of ***Motherhood Is Easy...As Long As You Have Nothing Else To Do For The Next 50 Years.*** **www.MotherhoodIsEasy.com.**

***

"***Among Other Edens*** mesmerizes and compels the reader to fall soul-first into another world – a world of intrigue, passion, danger and fear. Guinevere Edern's writing harkens to the days of flowing literary prose, a welcome respite from the terse language generally spewed by fiction writers today. A must-read for lovers of the English language."

-Michael Ray King, author of ***Loves Lost and Found,*** and, ***Fatherhood 101:Bonding Tips for Building Loving Relationships.*** **www.ClearViewPressInc.com.**

***

"***Among Other Edens*** is an edgy, urban-gothic tale told by a very talented story teller. With a literary blend of contemporary and medieval voice, Edern leads readers through time and place at a rapid pace, visiting past, present and alternative time with grace and color. Urban legend fans will love this fresh new voice in the genre and will wait on the edge of their seats for the next book by this gifted author."

-N. L. Quatrano, Author/Editor, **www.NLQuatrano.com.**

"*Among Other Edens* is a modern-day gothic tour de force that takes the reader on a thrilling journey through the troubled mind of Evie, whose dark family history holds mysteries both horrific and magnificent. The author brings a beautiful, melodic literary voice to every page and breathes life into a stale genre with a unique character and concept."

-**Jeff Swesky**, ghostwriter of
Flight from Fear: A Rabbi's Holocaust Survival Story.
jswesky@yahoo.com

Among Other Edens

By

Guinevere Edern

Richardson Publishing
Altamonte Springs, Florida

Among Other Edens
by Guinevere Edern
© 2010 All rights reserved.

Richardson Publishing
PO Box 162115
Altamonte Springs, FL 32716

www.AmongOtherEdens.com

ISBN: 978-1-935683-01-8
LOC-PCN: 2010929524

Editing by: Nancy Quatrano / Nancy@NLQuatrano.com
Rik Feeney / usabookcoach@gmail.com

Cover & Graphic Design: Rik Feeney

Cover Photograph Credit: dundanim|dreamstime.com

Graphic Photographic Credit: freud|dreamstime.com, igordutina|dreamstime.com, & saniphoto|dreamstime.com

For additional information, please visit:
www.AmongOtherEdens.com

Acknowledgments

To both my parents who walked me through some of the oldest and best parts of Liverpool, telling stores of the working people who lived through those times. For the endless hikes through the hills and valleys of Wales, for allowing me to explore abandoned Victorian hunting lodges, and run up hillsides thick with bracken.

For my mom who fed me poetry and stories so I could read by age two. Who took me to the old graveyards, museums, art galleries and old bookstores of Liverpool. For submitting my ghost poem to the 'Liverpool Echo' for publication when I was seven.

In memory of my dad, world traveler and one of the best undiscovered inventors and Storytellers who ever lived. For all the theater auditions you told me about, and for all the times you drove me to those same auditions.

In memory of Dawn Hallowell of the 'Elliott Clarke Theatre School' in Liverpool. For your capacity to teach theater and literary history, for being my mentor and friend and who never stopped believing I could and should write. For all the cream teas at end of term and for telling us not to slouch.

To Gene, for all the books, paper, and my first desk. Because of you I didn't quit!

In memory of my grandmother who gave me a little apple pendant before passing away.

Thanks to my publisher and friend Rik Feeney of Richardson Publishing who took a chance where others feared to tread. For your vision, patience and belief in me.

My editor Nancy Quatrano who has an amazing capacity to understand where I am coming from.

For Michael King, Jeff Swesky and Tom Wallace. You are amazing, intelligent writers and I will never forget the kindness, support, advice and friendship you each have shown me.

To my sister Louise, for keeping the home fires burning....

To T...
Forever my Knight....
For being unafraid.....
For taking me by the arm...
For mending me.....
For leading me back toward Eden.

G

The Prologue

April 30th 1984

The glittering sandstone of the Liverpool Cathedral bore a gothic presence across Liverpool's River Mersey, while below, the polluted little river sparkled beneath the high afternoon sunlight. Slipping into the building's cool interior, Evelyn Edern trailed behind her twin Elaine and their father.

From inside, they began the long ascent toward the vestry tower. Dragging the palm of her hand against the rough salmon-pink wall running up the side of the stone steps Evie enjoyed the cool, abrasive texture next to her skin. A detractor also from the pressing headache.

"Almost there."

He sounded jubilant and Evie, counting the ninetieth stair out of one hundred and eight buckled beneath the terrible ache in her legs. A small opening stood at the top, casting light toward the trio's feet. It meant they could stop soon.

Two steps behind her father.

"You can see all the way to Wales from up here." He walked across the vast tower rooftop, the city, winding river and countryside exploding on all sides.

"Way over there." He pointed to the left, black suit jacket punching a hole in the blinding sunlight.

"Ringo Starr lived over there." He meant the Beatles drummer and continued stretching his arm toward the Dingle, a series of Welsh named streets winding toward the Albert Docks and the river.

"Your mother grew up around the corner from him. He had a yellow front door." Still he talked about Ringo.

Breathless, Evie took her father's hand, wishing her head did not hurt quite this much.

A feather brushing the side of the girl's face teased a peculiar airborne lavender scent.

She pulled away.

"Happy Birthday Evelyn and Elaine, this is for you!"

She didn't know what he meant. Clutching the feather, the child caught the bewildering sight of her father and Elaine climb to the very top of the gothic ledge. Stepping off, the pair vanished into the bright jewel of an April sky, black jacket flapping wildly behind them.

Precisely three hundred and thirty one feet below, somebody screamed.

Chapter One

April 30th 1999

" *I*n Wales, which was the stronghold of Druidism, the profession of the bard was held in high honour. The poems of Taliesin, Merlin and other bards of the sixth century, still remain…'" Evie read.

Picking the lid on an empty pill bottle, Evie considered the poet's lot when viewed through a curtain of Welsh mist circa 500 AD.

It would suck, she concluded. No puffy jackets, no fleecy boots, no cell phone. In fact, nothing to help trudging through the soggy Welsh countryside seem like a really great adventure. No wonder anyone with half a brain went to Spain or Disney for their holidays.

Turning the book over, she studied the broken spine, 'History of English Literature, W.F Collier L.L.D.' Published in 1881, one-hundred eighteen years ago.

"Long dead, mate." A reference to the dreadful name 'Peregrine', scrawled across the inside cover. Evie wondered if he had ever been beaten up for it at school.

But Taliesin, she'd never heard of that name before. Breathing it into voice, Evie let the strange name cross the threshold of her lips and into the quiet room. She quite liked it. Far better than poor Peregrine. In any case, Taliesin could not have existed. Every idiot knew Merlin to be a myth; therefore Taliesin fell into the same boat. Surely people in 1881 hadn't been that friggin' stupid.

The book couldn't be blamed. In fact Evie had been quite happy about purchasing the volume from the dusty little second hand shop in the center of Liverpool. She just felt like crap. No big surprise though considering. She picked at the label on the bottle, providing a sort of physical reminder to her anxious nerves.

Ultimately the book attracted her because of its survival and once home, she packed it onto her bookshelf along with an already swollen arsenal of literature from centuries lost to dust.

April 30th, the Eve of May, twelve years ago, she acquired the first volume. Her eighth birthday. Evie recalled sneaking past her mother and grandmother, Harriet-Rose at some Catholic jumble sale. Discovering a table positioned dead center to Jesus, Evie found it full of old books and hovered over the various contents. The click of her mother's heels on the wood block floor twenty feet away assured the child some temporary privacy. `

No time to waste, Evie examined a wobbly stack balanced precariously beneath the Lord's feet, crowned by a red bound history book. Standing on tiptoe, Evie lifted the scarlet cover, its age determined by a nearly faded stamp dating the book to 1907.

Lowering her eyes toward the empty pill bottle, Evie recalled her child's hands pressing the freckled paper. The noise invading her head from the verse her mother and horrible Harriet-Rose sang on their way to the church, impossible to ignore.

'Evil Evie, Evil Evie
Born on the Eve of May
Pagan Child, Satan's Bride
Tie her up and burn her.'

Human slaughter. Acres and acres of wasted flesh rising beside rivers of blood and rotting corpses. Armies of Britons, abandoned by the retreating Romans, hacking the Saxon invaders to pieces. Searing pain, blood, a sword, the deep plunge into flesh, and a dark rise of pure evil. An overwhelming smell of sulphor, then nothing.

Found wandering around the church car park by a woman wearing a pink hat with a plastic daisy, Evie was returned to her frantic mother, book still in hand.

"Where the hell were you?" Her mother gripped Evie's shoulders hard. "Ten minutes we've been looking for you! Ten bloody minutes of you showing me up in front of all these people, and all you can do is stand there with two glassy eyes and a bloody friggin' nose."

"My head hurts." Evie complained then.

Handing the child a crumpled tissue, Harriet-Rose chimed in, "Even on your birthday you have to go and be selfish. Thinking of yourself all the time, you should be ashamed to be alive, you should. God took your sister away; you on the other hand were kept here for the devil's mission."

"Destroy us all, you will." Swept into the car by her mother, a long ride of silence followed, punctuated by an occasional threat.

Even now, years later, Evie could recall a cave of emerald water and frozen crystals but at the time had kept that information to herself, knowing better than to say anything like that.

Evie got the book for free.

Afterwards, she scrubbed the kitchen floor for making an unholy show of her mother, followed by fifty lashes across her back. Harriet-Rose's son, uncle Colin, drunk, up for anything and very much his usual self didn't need asking twice.

Stripped to the waist and forced to lie face down across his bed, Evie counted each lash of the belt as it tore her bare skin. Defying tears she willed herself toward the pale waters of a quiet stream instead of the stale sheets heaving against her face.

Afterwards, when her mother and grandmother left the room a pair of sweaty hands lifted her slowly and glazed, drunk eyes lingered over the small bud of each developing breast. Defiant, Evie stared back, willing him into the pit of hell as he forced her to raise her arms. He reapplied her T-shirt then, pushing it over her head, greasy palms tracing the rise of goose bumps pricking her shoulders.

Watching him thread the hideous belt through the baggy loops around his denim hips, Evie wished him far from Eden Park. Away from the same house he shared with his older sister Maureen, Evie's mother. After the funeral of Elaine and her father he'd been given Elaine's old room, the one with the teddy bear wallpaper, his rent always spent on drink.

Shaking the familiar memories, Evie tossed the book aside. She had come upstairs to die not read or bloody well think. Flinging the empty pill bottle across the dresser, Evie looked toward the window.

The surprise of an April fog diverted her attention from the waiting. Face pressed hard against the glass, Evie observed the quiet mist's descent upon the road. Only the lamps were alert, struggling to light the silence while everything else fell into grey.

"Global warming," muttered Evie to the emptiness. If polar ice caps could turn into a vanilla shake, why not get fucking lost in fog on April 30th?

Not that she had anywhere to go for twentieth birthday, no, God forbid. On the anniversary of her fifteenth year as Hell's Child following the murder, suicide of Elaine and her father, chores must be completed. A detail that included scrubbing the kitchen floor, wiping out cupboards and polishing the brass fire surround. For reasons unknown every afternoon when she came home from that hideous job selling tacky shoes, she must immediately press into action.

Anyway, she had a riot of a headache. The sharp pain extended into her right temple, making it difficult for the girl to hold her head up.

The scent of lavender breathed forward.

It arrived around the same time as her headache, the curious fragrance from her favorite flower compensating for the bitter tang of bleach from the grey cleaning cloth wrapped around her hand. Passing the soggy fabric across the kitchen floor until the entire area shone with wet, Evie inhaled the lavender fragrance like a gift. Struggling to her feet, she took a step back and checked for dull areas that would indicate she missed a spot.

Head hurting to the point of tears, Evie chucked the dirty water down the stainless steel sink then rinsed the cloth before heading upstairs.

Now Evie closed her eyes and resting her head against the cold windowpane drew the fragrance into her center, letting its touch fall amongst her senses. An image rose, a vibrant cluster of lavender spilling out from the base of that oak tree in the four acre meadow behind the house. Remnants of the three thousand acre Orchard Farm and the Georgian Eden Hall a mile away.

Another image rose from the fog, a cathedral rooftop and an intricate lacework of tiny gothic arches. A feather spiraling lazily downwards and a child's curious eyes, bewildered, following the soft descent until at last she saw and understood the vanishing of Elaine and her father.

Opening her eyes Evie refused the disturbing scene and the memory of arms that embraced her sorrow, perfectly invisible, stalling her desire to follow.

Seven fifteen.

"Christ, I should be friggin' dead by now."

Shouldn't something be happening? Evie's hands fluttered against her chest. Nothing, she didn't even have a bloody heart palpitation. Twenty minutes since chucking five little white pills back with a glass of hideously warm tap water from the bathroom. So far though, she couldn't even force a yawn.

Nervously, Evie touched her throat and traced the thin edge of a silver chain circling her neck. Stopping at the tiny pendant with the ruby center, she tugged at it, letting the sharp tip from an apple leaf dig into the top of her thumb.

The silver fruit had been slipped into the palm of Evie's hand courtesy of her paternal grandmother Evangeline. Evie had been forced to observe her father and Elaine's funeral from the parking lot. The evil girl had caused all this, and under no circumstance should a devil's disciple be allowed into the House of God. Having been told to wind down the window by Grandma Eva, the simple gesture as it fell against the child's cold skin explained how she should not blame herself for the death of Evangeline's son. That it could not have been prevented by Evie or anyone else.

Even now the origin of the pendant remained a mystery to Evie and without a clue regarding where it came from before the chain fell around her neck, the child accepted the secret gift as an unspoken acknowledgment between them, that in the Evil Evie Campaign, the girl at least had one ally. She had always loved Evangeline.

Five years later when Evie's allergy to apples really became apparent by the ripping pains tearing through her stomach whenever she ate one, the ruby fruit became the object of macabre amusement between them both. The idea of keeping the very thing that could harm you, close to your throat, provided something of a private joke for the two.

Three months after that, Evie's champion companion caught pneumonia and died, making the necklace one of the most sacred things she possessed.

Evie never removed the pendant from her neck.

Now though, beneath the dark red jewel, her throat felt tight, made anxious by the fact that she was obviously not going to die, as hoped. Searching for some clue as to what she might have done wrong, Evie re-read the instructions squeezed onto a tiny piece of paper wrapped around the bottle. "Take two with water."

Yeah, well she'd done that with five, counting them carefully into the palm of her hand. "May cause drowsiness."

"No shit!" She spoke into the empty room, "they're friggin' sleeping pills."

She felt sick.

Waiting for hell, the anticipation alone should have killed her.

A ribbon of silver mist dipped beneath the window. Lazily Evie wondered whether or not the thing was closed properly. The fog might have been reaching in, breathing toward her, like that dream of fog and mist from the night before.

She'd been asleep, at peace. A jewel of a river shimmered at her feet and she stepped into it, invited. Loved beyond measure she heeded the calm instruction to retrieve something, with no idea what it might be.

Evie shook her head to banish the dream. God, her head still hurt.

Perhaps she should lie down.

Invite death in.

She would be discovered here, carried into sleep. Arms crossed against her chest, a float of dark hair fanned carefully across her pillow, transformed in death to the texture of silk instead of its usual frizzy mess.

Ophelia's drift downstream.

The print was tacked to the wall across from her bed, Millais' portrayal of the young girl's madness. Evie stared at it now. An ethereal pose amongst a drift of delicate flowers, leaving Hamlet to the drama of his tragedy. And, Ophelia to her peace.

Evie stared at the small collection of prints picked up from the Walker Art Gallery. They were trophies of a sort, obtained on a rare free Saturday afternoon spent in town, when the kitchen floor sparkled and she had been allowed out of the house.

Often, when the house lay in its final darkness, Evie would think herself into each picture, a life one hundred times better than this one. They'd been nirvana to her anxiety, wrapped in cellophane; they'd helped control her nail biting anxiety. The quiet presence of the pictures harnessed her breath away from the inevitable doom the end of 1999 and the commencement of a New Millennium was about to unleash.

Looking at them now, her nerves felt raw. The inexplicable panic of something unknown jumping into her throat.

Inhaling the lavender room, Evie turned to the mythical castle. It didn't matter about the stupid friggin' Millennium crap and the breakdown of all things electric. Better instead to think about the amber stone rising from the pink wallpaper and the shore of a misty sea. The maiden Psyche, in the foreground, thoughtful and minus anything electric, sitting among the grounds of her lover Cupid's *The Enchanted Castle,* the painting's namesake. Inspiration for one of her favorite poems, Ode to a Nightingale.

And finally, this one. She would stare at this as she died tonight. When the fog had cleared and the moonlight rose at last into the sky above her house, it would be the knight's turn. Emerging from within the trees, each stride transformed the rose pink wall into the clearing of a secret forest. A girl waited quietly, hand stretched forward, beckoning him toward the siren of her beautiful face. The seductive length of her hair pouring over her dress spilling onto the soft grass beneath.

In the silence, Evie imagined his voice, the soft, careful words and the exchange taking place between them. The gleam from his silver armor breaking the enchantment of darkness. It wouldn't take much to transport herself there, it never did. Drawn into this otherworld, beautiful, fragile, worthy of interest and protection.

"La Belle Dame Sans Merci." Slowly, Evie mouthed the title of the painting named after a poem of the same name by her beloved poet, John Keats.

"'And there I shut her wild, wild eyes, so kiss'd to sleep'"

Evie whispered a line from the verse, willing as she did, for herself to disappear, to dwell within the darkest depths of the hidden forest. To sleep eternal. She would do so, clutching the small volume of poetry snuck into the house the previous Sunday afternoon after its discovery in a box of junk at a church sale.

On the cover, and embossed against the worn surface; a single word read simply, Poem. Peering closer, Evie had traced the missing letter 'S' faded into the tattered cover, Poems. A wreckage from the past, tossed against time. It had been enough to qualify as a rescue book.

Keats, 1817. She hadn't known until arriving home. The tragic poet, his quest for the soaring mystery of the senses over flat logic, all hijacked by a death in Rome at the tender age of twenty four. Consumption, the dramatic curse of any artist worth their salt back then.

Laying it on top of her bed, Evie carefully pried open the delicate leather binding, its dry layers cracking beneath her hands. She had discovered the fluid penmanship then, each dark stroke marking a peculiar inscription across the center of the first page. In ebony ink, it read.

To Evelyn,
'Your Dreams Are My Survival'
The Storyteller. 1848

At the time she had been excited at the thought of someone else with her name, even if by now they were nothing more than a skinny box of maggots and bones.

Skipping to the back of the book Evie then attempted to locate another inscription or message. Unfortunately she found nothing.

Nevertheless, in the dull headache of a week that followed her find, better to imagine who this Storyteller might have been.

A poet, bearing gifts in narrative and rhyme before disappearing into a labyrinth of shadows. Soft echo of his voice treading the quiet dark.

Disappearing into darkness.

How perfect an idea.

She'd thought of the pills then and the beauty of a long sleep, eternal.

Now, clutching the little book of verse, Evie settled against her pillow.

Lavender floated across the quiet room, making her warm against the strange curl of mist crossing the surface of her skin.

Evie inhaled once, then again, obeying the urge to gather more of it into her senses. Taking the feeling deeper a single name drifted into her thoughts, possessing the image that came.

A solitary figure lifted each word from the page, drawing them gently toward her soul.

Behind the ruby apple, the name lifted into her throat.

"Storyteller".

Beneath the slow intoxication, beneath the image taking form calling her name to itself, Evie waited for the final sleep to fall.

Chapter Two

He slips from between shadows, charging the memory of a dream to my soul.

A boy beneath a tree, lying and still, like death while the rain fell in a veil of grey-white mist. He needed it I think because as the rain continued to fall his mouth opened slowly, as though wanting. I waited, curious and from a distance, quiet behind passive folds of sleep.

Then it came, gentle and unnoticeable at first. The edge of each white petal touched with a delicate pink blush. But it came all the same, turning pink into something darker, moving up and toward the heart of the flower then falling like perfect tears toward the open mouth, red and welcome.

And he drank and I grew so thirsty, and I despised him, this boy, this slip of a man who remained unaware of my private intrusion.

I wanted to drink, wanted this blood too. Needed its rush against the depth of my veins, filling every sinew with its scarlet path.

Stinging jealously at the peace of his sleep, and the dying of a burning thirst.

Then he turned, not his whole body, just his head, turning toward me in my green rage, staring without accusation, without judgment and I became aware of what felt like the inevitable pull of my soul toward his.

A name I wanted to understand but could not.

Stepping from darkness, his presence comes quite matter of fact and without surprise.

My thirst is unbearable and driven from sleep, I slip, quiet from the edge of my bed, each step rattling into my bones and I wonder if I might be catching the flu, such is the ache pressing my head.

Soundless, everything. The night drawing its breath away from my presence. It is so dark, so lovingly dark within this silence that I might be somewhere else, just drifting without the sting of direction.

Am I being watched in my secret walk? Perhaps my quiet tread upon this floor wants to be observed, to be claimed with neither touch nor knowledge of possession.

But let the darkness touch me still, its velvet wrap, a covering across my bare shoulders. Permit me to feel this night whisper against the brush of each eyelash as they fall against the dark air.

Let me love its touch without fear.

As I have before.

A single trail of blood flows beneath my nose, traveling toward my mouth. Vaguely I recall the one who would take this from me, his mouth claiming my last breath.

I recall also, the boy and the delicacy of the blood rain. Thirst, deep and cutting so that it might be dangerous.

He has come for me.

The swift beat of movement against the dark tells me so.

Then stillness.

At last.

My angel, immortal.

I cannot fear this.

He stands before me as one with the night yet separate from it, his features sharp, striking recognition against my eyes.

"Yes, I know you," I whisper. "Have known of you always."

I am no longer thirsty, the thought suddenly occurs to me.

Tall, taller than I, much taller. The breadth of his shoulders hidden beneath the expanse of his black coat. Cashmere, the finest. Instinctively I want to reach out, touch it, be inside somehow. To disappear. It has been so long.

I stare into the face of this being, this entity who understands me as no one else can. Dark curls tossed amongst each other as though he might have fought the raging path of a storm to get here. He stands, green eyes piercing the stillness of his face and I understand that it is he who watched my descent on the stairs, observer of my red thirst.

I wait, my face drawn toward him, wanting what must come next.

A sudden rush and I cannot breathe.

Murder, lies, death, so much of it flashing against my thoughts.

Images, so many, delivering blood from my eyes until they fall like crimson tears to my face. A house lost among the tangle of a forgotten garden, a secret death and a betrayal so old I feel the thrust of its ascent from within the hot stones of the earth and its release into my soul.

There is knowledge I must have and its hunger rips at every cell. I see a path and my tread upon its ancient dust, forbidden. I hear my name called forward, and want to follow.

His hands brace my head and I am against him, feeling the push into my soul, binding every cell to him so he might feel me there again, claiming me for himself.

His tongue floats against my skin, following the trace of blood from beneath my eyes into his throat

"Know me once again, my Evie. Know me in every breath, eternal."

A faint whisper stalks the side of my face, stroking the fragrant air.

I struggle beneath a sudden pressure against the side of my head, his eyes challenge the pain, making me take this, telling me I need to, that in order to understand, it must be so.

A final push inwards and another fast image comes; a river, a crystal emerald and its liquid release into a silver palm.

Peace now and the name of one whom I recognize but had long ago forgotten, falls against my breath, but I am permitted to say nothing about it.

The blood and the death have gone. I sigh at last, permitting breath into my throat in thin, exquisite strands.

"Evie, finally."

My skin trembles against his fingertips as they dance across my throat, making me thirsty, making my soul's journey rise toward him as he claims each slope of breast and hip with each impeccable touch.

He is within me and I want to cry for the sense of him beneath my skin, my breath coming sharp against the pale flesh of his neck as I am lifted toward the black forever of his coat.

"Come with me."

Outside it is raining and we move beyond this place, he and I, toward the forgotten orchard and the one who waits.

Chapter Three

Emerging from the gloom of the urine-soaked subway, Evie caught a taste of decadent spring air. Expelling the inside of her nose from the sharp smell of ammonia, she blinked hard against the death of an afternoon in May. Delicate pearls of apple blossom burst from the trees lining both sides of the street, their pale shimmer vibrating beneath a contrast of storm clouds threatening to steal the precocious little buds from their dance.

Rain or not, she'd better be home within the next five minutes or accusations would fly. Yeah, like she'd really snuck the fuck off to that maligned Orchard Park estate to shoot heroin or have raging sex against the perimeter wall. Even if she knew what to do, hell could have a friggin' blizzard before she'd let someone rip her knickers off against a backdrop of burned out cars crashed into the scarred concrete.

Checking her watch, Evie climbed the two flights of concrete steps, inhaling the sweet apple blossom fragrance. Once at the top she had the hill on Eden Park Avenue to descend and she would be home. Once there she would be told to clean the toilet. She always did on Saturday evenings.

Struggling with a plastic shopping bag housing a ten pound bag of potatoes and three loaves of bread, Evie watched as the first puff of apple blossom lifted toward their storm captors, each flurry chasing the other like tiny breaths of snow.

The music came next.

Behind her and on the other side of the road, it became an unmistakable sound. The hard, bellowing rush travelled in her direction, down the hill and towards her home. No one else was about, leaving Evie alone to hear the bagpipes.

At her side, the piper kept pace with the girl, and staring straight ahead, seemed oblivious to the peculiar disturbance he caused.

Facing the curious figure with the dark hair, Evie confronted him with a hard stare, willing the stranger to notice her. But he continued, marching toward the struggling sun falling behind the distant marshes, oblivious to his audience of one.

She had never encountered anything like it, this person dressed as though he might have walked all the way from the Scottish Highlands.

She couldn't believe his clothes. Evie observed his white Jacobite shirt worn full through the sleeves and body. She could see it was secured by a set of ties criss-crossing at the open neck, the sleeve cuffs fastened tight around each wrist by a set of ebony buttons. Over the shirt, he wore a black doublet.

The bagpipes fascinated Evie, their vast noise, resonating from both sides of the street, bullied the air in a hard blast as each finger pressed against one of the four black pipes, ornately trimmed in silver.

Still, he appeared oblivious to Evie's attention.

Near the bottom of the hill and close to the opening between two houses, the breach accommodated an overgrown footpath tangled with six foot high weeds, thorny brambles and ancient litter. Weaving across the backs of several houses it broke onto an unkempt part of the golf course where it yielded to the expanse of forgotten fields, remnants of what remained of Eden Hall.

Twice the year before, Evie challenged herself to cut through the place. Apprehension finally yielded to curiosity and the desire to face her fear before the overpowering reach of the path's green life trembled against her strangled nerves.

Both times she regretted her decision at the same place along the path; halfway through, too far to run back and too far to go forward.

But she had gone on anyway, running breathless, chased above and below by the sinister reaches of thick branches and angry nettles that did not forgive those who trespassed against them.

"Surely to God, he won't go down there!" Evie freaked.

Eyes screwed against the bright contradiction of sun and storm clouds, Evie squinted as the figure turned onto the path, an anonymous left shoulder first to disappear before his full body made a quick sacrifice to the darkness.

The music stopped.

Crossing the road, Evie hurried down the remaining hill and to the mouth of the footpath, bag of potatoes banging against her legs. The bread would be well crushed by the time she got home, but right now she couldn't care less.

No trace of the piper. Perhaps he had stopped playing, catching his breath while picking his way through all that undergrowth. He hadn't, realized Evie, taken a single pause during his entire descent down the hill. Perhaps that explained the silence.

Surely he wouldn't walk across those deserted fields with the marshland and hidden streams taking him dangerously close to the hideous Orchard Farm Estate. Segregated from Eden Park by that concrete wall, he would need balls of steel to walk through there dressed like Rent-a-Piper.

Jogging up the path after him, one of the handles on the plastic bag snapped causing a loaf of bread to tumble onto the ground, narrowly missing a pile of dog crap.

"Fucketty friggin' fuck." Evie muttered irritated. Grabbing the bread she flicked at the bits of dirt decorating the paper wrapping, knowing the kind of trouble she'd get into if she were caught here. Her grandmother was right, she really was good for nothing.

Fog? How? She had glanced at the bread wrapper for a split second to clean off the bits, so where had the stuff come from?

But it could be smoke, Evie decided. From the grey mist, an overpowering odor of charcoal and sulphur had emerged. The pungent mix stung her eyes. Blinking from the assault, tears ran onto the girl's face. Evie's throat hurt.

Slowly now, she approached the vast open space ahead of her with extreme caution, somewhere there might be a fire, and music man had walked right into it. He would head back this way, Evie reasoned. Whatever was going on down there, it wasn't the place play the bagpipes.

Tempted further into its grey presence, the silent air stroked the sides of Evie's face, beckoning the girl further into its domain.

"Evie." But that was the breeze, it had to be.

"Eeevviee." Her name drifted through the trees.

Shivering against the sudden chill, she cast a glance toward the canopy of oaks, leaves stretching toward spring. Through the mosey branches she could see the sky, a tumble of storm clouds pressing the remains of an afternoon, nothing more. But down here, down here was sulphor.

"Come and see Evie. Come and see it, Evelyn Edern, come listen."

There were the bagpipes again.

Amazing Grace.

They had sung it at church a couple of Sundays ago. Mrs Bellows, the ancient pianist, played the notes to a different tune as she always did. Nobody ever had the heart to tell her.

"Come on Evie, hurry. It's here Evie. For you it is here."

This couldn't be happening. It just wasn't possible, the familiar child like voice sewn into the breeze, clear against the strange music and the acrid smoke. Elaine.

She should be gone from here. Every part of her said that she must leave.

Yet she had to know. She would spend her life wondering otherwise.

Was any of this real?

Pressing further along the path Evie arrived at the opening to the expanse of fields and marshes. The smoke was thicker here, yellow.

She needed to be sick.

"Evie."

That voice again, playing through the bagpipes, Her name, harsh, tinged with brittle laughter.

"Come in Evie. You belong here, with us."

The shadow of a man walking forward, bearing the bagpipes with ease.

"Dad?"

Tears stung the corners of her eyes.

Her father was here? In this place, living here all along? She had seen him go, had watched his flight into nothing.

Her fifth birthday.

Hers and Elaine's.

How? Her father never even played the spoons. But it was him though. Dressed in the same dark suit he wore when walking off the cathedral tower; smiling, holding Elaine's hand as though the pair were simply strolling into thin air.

Which is essentially what they did.

"Dad?"

But it couldn't be, not like this. He was cremated, they both were, reduced to ashes and scattered across the Welsh hillsides where the family loved to walk.

He was coming straight for her. Amazing Grace resumed.

Turning swiftly, Evie spun around but already he stood ahead of her, pipes blasting her ears.

And then he transformed into a man in a mud splattered overcoat, its tattered reach trailing the damp earth. In the silence raging toward her, his mouth pulled back into a thin smile, mocking the girl's frozen presence. His neck too, lay at a strange angle and Evie noticed how it had been broken. Acknowledging the conclusion, he cracked it straight.

A thin blue veined arm withdrew from the frayed sleeve of the ruined coat, his purple hand, fleshy and swollen indicated a cluster of trees standing to her back. Hardly daring to take her eyes from the horrible spectacle, Evie turned stiffly around.

A flash of a noose, a dead tree, then nothing.

Gone. The sulphur had cleared and she stood alone, at the edge of the path. In spite of everything she had witnessed, she might never have walked onto it in the first place.

She could barely stand from the fear of it all. What she had seen, her father who wasn't; her sister's voice. Five year old Elaine, childish; fifteen years into the past.

Shaken to the root of her soul, Evie dragged herself back toward the street, legs barely able to carry each step. She wasn't a pothead but she could be one now. Evie wondered how many bags of weed it would take to get the last few minutes out of her deranged mind. Straining her ears toward the silent fields, she made futile attempts to make sense of the impossible, searching, listening for something, an audible glimpse of what had just been.

But only the breezes returned, falling around her ears, mocking, caressing, and daring her return.

Chapter Four

Hand shaking, Evie pushed her little bronze key into the lock on the front door. Hard to keep the thing steady, it took three fumbled attempts to align the tiny object into the lock before noticing how the usual twist to the left couldn't be twisted. Instead it pushed open, having been unlocked all the time.

Dragging her feet through the hallway, Evie recognized a familiar voice and made a face. Potentially this was far worse than the thing on the path.

Cell-Phone Pam.

Pamela with the orange lipstick and sleeveless Laura Ashley dresses in the freeze of winter and who dished out sandwiches and coffee to the straggle of women protesting the emergence of cell phone towers in remote little Welsh villages. Hence the three bashed-in loaves of bread Evie had been forced to carry home.

Yeah, it might be Pamela and Maureen taking the glory at the base of some skinny little tower but behind the scenes stood Evie, wielding a knife, butter, a block of yellow cheese and all the enthusiasm of a stale sandwich.

The floorboards creaked, she'd been caught.

"Is that our Evelyn?" Hovering outside the door leading to the living room, Evie hesitated before answering, still hauling the tattered shopping bag before opening the door.

Her mother seemed not to notice the hesitation, preoccupied with the task of listening to the other woman prattle on about chemical weapons; how most likely your eyes would be the first to burn before choking to death on what was left of one's lungs as they melted into a gurgling throat. "At least you wouldn't be able to see it!" Thrilled Pam, sounding as though she couldn't wait.

Evie hovered at the threshold of the living room.

"Come in and say 'hello' and make us a cup of tea."

The statement was made as though it might be possible to accomplish this task behind the sofa.

Biting the inside of her lip, Evie shifted the plastic bag cutting into her hand. Later there would be a deep crevice.

"Well what are you standing about for? She can be awful bloody slow, can our Evelyn." Chided Maureen to Cell-Phone Pamela, and waved her hand at the wall, behind which stood the kitchen.

"And don't forget to clean that toilet. I've never known anyone so friggn' lazy."

Slowly, Evie closed the door behind her, abandoning the sting of remarks aimed at her back.

Shivering, an icy sweat soaked her clothes.

Maybe she had gone crazy, certified fruit and nut crazy. Perhaps that's what the sleeping pills had done. Instead of catapulting the girl into a voluntary death, they'd somehow tripped a switch, making her see more of the things that quite simply did not exist.

Balancing a combination of fresh tea things onto the tea tray, Evie replayed the history of images against the side of the shiny milk jug. I mean how many times has shit like that happened? Biting hard onto her lower lip, Evie swallowed the inevitable trail of blood, following the drops that straggled onto her chin with the tip of her tongue. The figure on the path was just one of many.

For starters, what about the time when that rusty blade slipped through the wall at the side of her bed in the room drunk Uncle Colin had taken over after Elaine's death.

Waiting through the fifty odd lashes and lying face down on the bed after being caught wandering around the church car park on her eighth birthday. Evie had watched a little knife slice through the teddy bear wallpaper whose harmless characters until then were enthusiastically engaged in sports.

Now, the leading lemon colored bear in the egg and spoon race would suffer the consequence of losing the lower portion of his right leg to the determined slice of the blade. And then it had vanished, quickly restoring the unfortunate little bear to his victory and leaving the young Evie, despite the agony of welts breaking her skin, fascinated by the macabre episode.

Then there was the figure.

She had been too afraid to breathe then, fearing its reach to claim her soul. Bad enough to hear the frantic clickety-clack of typewriter keys banging into her head.

Opening her eyes, her childish breath staggered to short rasps as the sound continued. The moonlight, and how it drew her bug-eyed terror to where the sound grew louder. The wall by her bed. A fountain of pale light softly illuminating a pair of hands grasped desperately around several iron bars and framed into a dark window pressed against the wall. Bravely the child closed her eyes again, but when she opened them, he was still there, his blank silhouette of a face, staring forward.

She had stayed awake then, never moving from the still figure until the sound of the milkman clattering his usual three bottles onto the doorstep signaled the onset of a rosy dawn and the prospect of sleeping in safety.

Perhaps this was death now.

In the darkness Evie stared at the wall across from her bed.

The Enchanted Castle, its stonework returning as an amber jewel against the gold moonlight streaming through the branches of her favorite oak tree where it stood in the dark meadow behind the house. The open window of her bedroom carrying the magic light forward. If you believed in that kind of stuff.

Staring into the picture Evie willed herself inside the castle walls, exploring what she knew lay inside, the painting, the opulent furniture, vast rooms to hide and explore. What had been hers until some tragic misfortune enforced an absence she would someday reclaim.

Inside, the one who continued to wait, kept vigil. Patient always, searching for the light of her inevitable return so his spirit might rise to the restored surroundings of the castle, once again.

Her protector, eternal.

The one who drew her bitten nerves toward his possession.

But nothing would happen this night and closing the window Evie reached for the switch above her head and flicked it on, bathing the little room in a warm glow. She needed to think.

She couldn't be dead. Everything was too much the same. If she had pegged out on her twentieth birthday, things would either be a zillion times worse, a.k.a hell, or she would have somehow managed to carve a sort of strange heaven out of her imagination. Naturally, she would be halfway to eternity by now, drifting through the castle on her wall.

Instead she had poured tea, rammed her hand down the toilet to clean the friggin' thing then made dinner all against a backdrop of Y2K hysteria. Maureen had better build a nuclear shelter beneath the living room floor advised Pam, North Korea was replacing Russia in its nuclear arsenal, there were chemicals brewing in the desert, cell phones could be used as bombs; "there are recipes all over the internet!" Cell-Phone Pam freaked. It was only a matter of time before something happened.

Yeah, there was fantasy everywhere.

And Evie thought she was the crazy one.

Now alone in her room, she stared at her copy of Poems, open as usual to the Storyteller's inscription and snuck under her pillow before collapsing to bed. Next to it and across the pink cover lay several sheets of paper and she stared at the heading; *Among Other Edens* penned in bold letters across the top of page one.

Shaking, the words ran beneath her skin.

She wrote it after chucking back the useless sleeping pills, when, lain across her bed, she waited for a death that refused arrival. Observer instead to the reach of mist curling the edge of her windows.

The scent of lavender had been everywhere, invading her senses and Evie recalled how it made her feel cocooned, shut away from everything, safe.

The Eve of May.

In death she was protected.

The soft fragrance alerting her skin.

It was then the words came.

A boy lying beneath a tree, waiting, mouth open, ready to receive each drop of blood as it fell bleeding from the heart of those flowers.

And the figure stepping from darkness; drawing her toward his presence, understanding, pressing images to her thoughts so she might know the truth at last.

And the blood that came, falling onto her face, captured against his mouth, his tongue, the play of his hands, drawing her toward him.

Her life, her desires scrawled across the pages of *Among Other Edens*. It might have been she who took the gloved hand beckoning the girl toward the secret quiet of a hidden orchard. She who had wanted him. She again who begged the darkness to yield his shadow at last.

It made Evie want to touch the pages now; the memory rising into her breath. She inhaled the lavender air stroking her face, its scent curling against her skin. The sudden rush of breath, teasing her insides until they almost hurt.

She could see him now. His face, the dark length of coat and his hands, drawing her toward his inevitable return, making her ready, to need this; his presence pouring into her soul, between her legs, hot, delirious, wanted.

It was overwhelming, the sense of something existing beyond herself, reaching inwards, pushing until she could stand it no longer, her insides begging for his return.

His touch was taking everything, making her want more.

She could cry for this.

"Storyteller!"

Heat driving inwards.

Arms reaching for the invisible.

She knew who it was.

But he didn't exist!

She had to save herself.

Wrenching away from what could not possibly be there, Evie trembled away from the spell of lavender and the author of an inscription long since dead.

Her head was pounding.

But she didn't want to move. She wanted it again, the feeling. To imagine him there, against her like that, moving inwards slowly, gathering her senses toward him. It didn't matter that he didn't exist, or was no more than a story lifted from a message written long ago.

"Make me live again." Her voice traced the darkness as though it were his words she spoke.

Words claiming her thoughts.

Lying among the softness of lavender, his name floated against the edge of her tongue, claiming her last breath to itself as she knew it must.

"Storyteller." She could barely call it forward.

Her eyelids were heavy, her breathing slow, so that she was aware only of the rise and fall of her breath against the warmth of this strange invasion.

But she had to do it, she must suffer the terrible loss. She would lose her mind if she didn't. Between the thing on the path and now this, she had gone insane. There could be no other explanation.

Bathed in moonlight, the amber castle seemed to glow, lifting away from the wall so it might have stood there, independent, breathing. Should she be crazy enough to touch it, thought Evie, it might be possible to feel every rough little crevice against her hand.

But they locked people up for thinking shit like that.

She needed to get rid of it. She would destroy *Among Other Edens*, the dark little fairy tale, where rain fell like blood from the dark center of apple blossoms and each step haunted the embrace of shadows.

Gathering the loose pages, Evie crumpled them into a ball, then not convinced of their destruction, tore the whole lot into a dozen jagged pieces.

Next, slipping from the bed and standing over the small waste paper basket she dropped the torn prose, watching as each fragment drifted on the lavender breeze, downward.

She was deeply tired.

Her head ached.

A thin trail of blood fell from the edge of her nose.

Chapter Five

It is cold here, freezing. But the little gathering persists nonetheless, hanging onto themselves, despite the blows from a bitter, unforgiving wind. Above the scene, clouds tear through the black sky. If there has ever been any stars present this night they have been driven away by the fearless dark.

There are only three figures present, four if you count the smallest shape, a baby? It is difficult to tell from this distance. It would need a closer look, but not right now. Now it seems best to stand apart, quiet and just watch. Whatever the bundle is, it remains still, held in the arms of the form standing opposite what I assume is a tree.

It is difficult to adjust my focus at first, but if I concentrate hard enough and push my eyes through the blackness, then really it is not that bad.

Yes, it is definitely a tree that the slow, murmuring party stands beside. You can see the way its branches stretch out, even darker, if that is possible, against the deep night. It must be quite old this tree, because it is gnarled into a series of twists and notches bending into the trunk. Although it cannot be more than twenty feet high, it's full canopy of leaves, supported by thick, steady branches extend outward providing the perfect arbor for the small trio who press themselves further into the covering.

Huddled together, they whisper while the one in the middle punches a glance over his shoulder. Is he waiting for someone, or is he ensuring the trio remains intact, uninterrupted by intruders? It is impossible to tell except that as he looks over his shoulder, his head tilts upward as one might stare at an upper window and I wonder if there may be somebody observing these events here, whatever they are. Maybe that is why without a word, the huddle draws itself tighter together, defining further the secrecy of their covert purpose.

Any attempt on my part to glance in the same direction, back, away from the tree is pointless for it reveals nothing, save for a dark relief thrown against the torn sky. Presumably it is a house but no lights are present, so I cannot tell, only draw a loose conclusion.

Above the group and spread throughout the tree like tiny lights are delicate pink and white petals, shimmering and vulnerable in the quick breeze dancing across each bloom. They provide the only color in the darkness and you can't help but notice them, which is what the eye is drawn to now, across the grass to the tree and up into the blush of its foliage. I want to move forward and touch it but something tells me it is best not to try, better to keep my hands still for the time being.

My eyes are adjusted fully so I can see much better now, assisted by a small corner of the moon daring to defy its current status amongst the clouds. Are they aware of an intrusion beyond their small collective? If they are, it does not show itself and they continue amongst themselves with little regard for anything beyond.

The small bundle moves, generating further whispering from the others, a little more urgent this time. One, the man on the end, they are all men I think, throws his hands up and begins to walk away, before the one carrying the infant, I am sure, no positive this is a child, turns and grabs the man's shoulder, gathering a handful of his coat as he does so, preventing his leave and returning him roughly into the fold.

For a flash of a moment, I can see the man's face, the one with the infant, long, drawn and pale, very pale. His lips are thin, pursed is probably the right word, an involuntary curl inwards, forging a mean quality against the mouth. His hair, which even in this darkness I can tell is short, is maintained in a style difficult to recognize, long sideburns and a moustache. His body, now turned inwards is bent forward from the shoulders, initiating a stooped profile.

But there is something else there too and it lurks beneath the depth of each line etched below his eyes and the shot of blood which might have been finely drawn into each one. The effect suggests a level of emotional trauma so deep it tears at his conscience and into his soul. Yet they remain focused, intent upon their surroundings and

I believe he will not defer from what he considers to be right. I don't believe I have mentioned that the man who tried to leave wears some sort of band across his throat, a flash of white skimming the collars on his long overcoat.

From this, I assume a religious attachment, a Catholic, or an Anglican priest maybe, it is impossible to tell. Anyway, denomination seems of little consequence here.

The man on the far side of the trio has remained motionless throughout, leaning forward, head bent as though party to serious thought. Hands clasped before him, they rest on what can only be described as a stick or pole of some sort. His face is not visible, but he wears the same calf length overcoat as the others, the cut of the cloth as good a quality as that of his companions.

So there they are the three of them plus a quiet bundle, huddled, serious below the shimmering blossom of an apple tree, beneath the thin slip of a moon and discarded strands of temperamental clouds.

Speaking of this spring moon, unwilling to play second fiddle to the dirty weather, it has shifted now, taking center stage, so that weak as it is, it gives sufficient light to further illuminate the humble gathering. Whatever they are doing, this small addition of light is not welcome, prompting the men to walk further into the coverage provided by the canopy. Now, should the petals fall it would rain a soft pink shower upon their serious shoulders.

It is only fair to mention the infant again since I imagine its presence provides the focal point for the gathering. I wonder where the child's mother is, that she should be absent from here, and think maybe that accounts for the nervous glances earlier. Perhaps that is why they venture even further now beneath the tree, rather than enjoy the light this revealing moon has struggled to offer. Do they not want to be seen? Why do they not wish to be seen?

This tiny form, this little innocence shifts slightly, its head, nothing else, just its pale head trying to push itself upwards as though aware finally of its surroundings, the pink blossom and the night air. But oh, it is so weak, so dreadfully weak. It is pathetic, sad. The movement itself is not remarkable yet the significance lies within a struggle to coordinate the desires and limitations within an obviously weak body.

It shouldn't be out so late. It shouldn't be out in this cold. And it is cold, bitterly for spring, and I wrap my bare arms to my chest. Where is its mother? What is she doing? Is he the father, the one who holds this shivering child? You could die for this cold.

It is impossible to tell the sex, dressed or rather wrapped as it is in a sheet and strips of cloth. Each one torn roughly and wound around the child, covering the body and binding arms, legs and feet. But thankfully the head is visible. Thank God, its head is still visible, because it is still possible to breathe.

What are they doing, these curious figures, dressed as the night in long heavy coats? No, I cannot ask, cannot speak. Instinctively, I know it will make no difference. But wait, they are agitated and because the quick breeze has stopped, it is possible, barely, to make out what is being said. Strain the ears a little, the same way I pushed my eyes through the darkness in order to see.

What are they saying? It concerns the infant. They thought he had died? He was dead? So it is a he? Listen closely, listen very closely. Do not allow the words to disappear before you have taken them for yourself. Then the one who has been leaning on that stick speaks at last, his voice although deep resonating with uncertainty.

"All the signs informed me he was. I do not understand this at all. I checked his heart and it had stopped beating."

He must be a doctor, this one. And he continues, with the sort of restrained urgency reserved for addressing someone for whom you are compelled to respect.

"Sir, I cannot in good conscience continue in this manner, with this affair. In the light of what we three..." He breaks off and glances along the miniature line, "have just witnessed. It is bad enough that we...." Again, he hesitates, clears his throat then resumes, although with obvious difficulty. His voice is shaking. Why?

"Sir, we could be doing an awful lot more than committing his body to the ground in this manner. Indeed, we could be party to something which holds greater implications. Sir, you understand surely, we should wait and see what happens!"

Stopping at last, he turns to the religious presence facing the other two with his back to the tree. Under the luminous moon, he too looks pale, the corners of his mouth turned down, giving the effect of two straight lines running either side of his chin. Both hands clasped to the front emphasize his prayerful disposition. "This is unholy, sir."

The man with the child speaks. In earnest, in desperate anger even.

"You dare speak of what is unholy, clearly you know nothing of the religion clinging around your neck!"

His voice drops, pitching lower than the others. I wish to move forward, slowly, intrude upon their secret mission. Listen.

"This child is unholy." *Quiet, angry voice, but struggling all the same.* "My only son, this union between my wife and whatever it was." *He finishes without having really begun his point.*

"But, sir". *The priest interlopes but fails to the impatience of the child's father. That man must be the child's father.*

"Enough! Confine your lessons and preaching to young ladies on Sundays. Live by your religious convictions, or are you too weak when called away from the safety of your pulpit to confront evil beyond the clean pages of your King James Bible!

"And as for you." *He turns to the silent, anxious doctor,* "Wait until tomorrow? What if he lives, what then? What is to become of this family when that child thing walks among us, knowing our secrets and tonight's intentions, spawning generations who will bring us down!

"Its mother is mad. Sleeping for days at a time and when awake, she remains in a trance, talking to herself, laughing, crying even and pleading to no one, there is never anybody there. It is all I can do to have the servants deliver food to her room.

"But even that, I can assure you would not be enough to prejudice myself against this infant, but when you consider its condition, the contents of my wife's papers which you have seen with your own eyes. Such thoughts and acts can only be born of pure evil."

"But sir." *The doctor speaks.*

Keep trying, please speak, I am sure you are important in all of this. And I am crying. What has happened? What awful things could have taken place within this family?

"Your child is dying sir. He cannot possibly live for much longer. I wouldn't even give him until morning."

The priest moves forward, arms outstretched as though attempting to take charge of this tiny form himself. "I beg of you. Let me take

37

him, let me return this child to its mother where he can fall asleep in her arms. You need not see him again. I understand how difficult this has been for you, believe me, but you must let something good come from this evil you inform us of. If judgment must be done, leave it to God."

"God! You talk to me of God? Where is He tonight? If you can find Him within this house and within the walls of this garden, then I will immediately relinquish the child into your hands."

There is silence now. The garden draws its breath through the grass and through the ageing core of the apple tree. I am conscious of the dampness beneath my feet and am aware for the first time they are without shoes. I push my toes downwards and feel its cold.

Are we waiting for God, our strange and secret collective? Are we giving Him a chance to tread this garden and prove His presence? "Please be here, God. Please come". I breathe to myself. I want to fall onto my knees, feel the sharp blades against my skin and pray, pray for His presence, pray that He can stop this talk of evil and unholy alliances, and the condemning of a child that did not ask to be born.

"Give me the infant! Give me the child and I will love it for the moments he has left." I long to scream but no words come. Curiously, I am silent and the plea must remain in thought only. What is its condition the father speaks of? What sin could this infant have committed that his light must be extinguished before he dies by his own will?

Murder! They mean to murder this tiny child, I scream through my mind. No! They mustn't, "You mustn't!" I cannot call, there is no voice. Why am I without voice? The child's father, the priest and the doctor, this has been the purpose of their dark alliance. More voices, more continuing voices as their hidden intent becomes clear.

The father to the priest.

"You read the last rites and then you saw him die. Ten o'clock by my watch."

Father to the doctor.

"How do you explain this new breath within his body four hours later, if not for the purpose of evil? The devil has entered this house through my wife and into this child, and it must be removed tonight."

More heavy, pressing silence. The air is fragrant suddenly, carried forward above their conspiring heads and toward my unknown presence. Lavender and apple blossom, softly, I inhale the elixir, permitting its claim on my ragged senses.

The father again.

"You forget, I have provided service to both of you at different times, you," he says this to the priest, "I recommended you for the position of chaplain at the new Ladies College. And has that not been a suitable position? Given, I hasten to add, that your own humble background hardly lends itself to the occupation of a gentleman.

"And you." Turning to the doctor now, "Have I not provided some very rewarding recommendations concerning your services within these parts, good families too, some with considerable property even. Eden Hall for heaven's sake!" He adds this by way of exclamation.

Both bow their heads. Apparently, this is true. And importantly, it serves to remind the party that although they are all sewn together with the same merciless threads of dark desperation, equals they are not. Clearly the father has a much higher social standing.

"Quite simply, I feel this is an appropriate time for some return. You both understand my position; I absolutely cannot afford public scandal. And since you are both so obviously indebted to me, I believe I can depend upon the highest discretion."

More silence as they consider the limits of their options, but I think he has them, their futures, their careers, their souls. Both appear quite young. Perhaps they would marry and have children of their own some day. Walk away, you don't have to do this! My silent voice screams.

I see the child's head move again, just a little, very slowly, so pathetic and frail. "Scream. Scream and wake the household. Do what babies do best, let them know you are alive, even for five minutes." But my voice, this voice of mine does not exist here.

It seems as though they have chosen. The doctor, he withdraws from his prop, slowly lifting the object from the ground. He walks head down to the trunk of the tree, prompting the priest to move away and back to his original place at the side of this child's father.

I see now that this stick thing the doctor has been leaning against all this time is actually a shovel. I understand what they intend to do.

And the tears come, without invitation they fall freely down the sides of my face, beneath my chin and onto my neck. I couldn't wipe them away if I tried.

The soft earth, rich from an early summer rain is torn open and tossed aside where it collapses into a black pile beneath the dark green canopy and silken buds. And still the digging continues, deep, deeper, they have to be sure. No surprises, no loose ends. Still, my tears come and I want to fall but cannot do so.

Does he want to name this infant? Asks the priest of the father but the voices are becoming distant as though it might be something I'm overhearing, although the tattered sky, its struggling moon, the tree, the three figures and the large garden remain clear. I have a headache but understand there is nothing to be done about it.

It is finished now, this hole with the lovely black earth, soft, cool set to the side. Waiting. Still, they continue amongst themselves, unaware of my intrusive eyes and ears. How long have we been here? Harborers of this dreadful conclusion. It seems like forever, yet not, somehow. Is it destined to repeat itself and repeat, this one dreadful moment capsuled forever?

"The child is not moving." He looks skyward, this father. "This must be done at once, before it is too late." And reaching into the inside of his coat, withdraws a circular object, gold, its surface providing a small and temporary illumination in the darkness. A watch, it must be, and I observe the efficient manner with which he snaps open its heavy cover. Yes, it is a watch and after a brief glance, snaps it shut again, returning it immediately to his pocket. Time is of the essence.

Indeed there is a change in the light, a very subtle one. The clouds are tinged with a deep blue and somewhere, perhaps from within the tree, there is a quick rustle. A bird? We must have been here for some time then, playing as actors and audience of one. I feel the inevitable gather itself around me and its panic in every breath.

Adam. They have called the child Adam. First born, Adam. And he is handed to the doctor, and the father steps backward, removing himself from the dirty act. And the priest removes a little book from the inside of his coat and utters some words I don't want to understand, do not wish to hear.

The shovel is cradled against a low branch and the doctor receives the child, Adam. His face is blank, it reads nothing, only that his good conscience is no longer present and he will live out the rest of his life trying to forget this night, and that no good he ever does can make up for what he is about to do.

This single act.

Oh, my child is being placed into this hole. "Adam breathe. Let them know you're alive! Survive, survive despite them!" I call, I shout, I rage but it makes no difference, I am of no consequence. "In the name of God, how can you do this? He is alive". I can feel his life, his breath.

And I can. I can feel his tiny infant breath through me, drawing air from my lungs, taking from me. And I want him to take, want him to, if it means his life.

I watch the horror unfold. The priest is still talking at the head of this awful pit and I see myself lying within this place, feel its cold, see the torn sky and disappearing moon. But I know I am standing, can feel myself standing. The damp grass beneath my naked feet but I can feel him too, lying there. He is alive, they are burying him alive and he can see, feel!

And then the dirt. The terrible cold dirt, blinding my eyes, my face, bruising the delicate layer of my infant skin.

Simultaneously, I am watching and feeling. "They think I am unholy, I who have no choice concerning the circumstances of my birth. For this I am punished! Yet what they do is more evil than anything I was born to do.

"I can see the stars, I can breathe this earth. I cannot move, my legs and arms are bound in wicked strands of cloth. And yet I am not warm. I am cold and damp. But I no longer look for warmth; it is the cold I seek now, the cold that will embrace me this time."

I feel his thoughts, his pain and childish outrage at this injustice. To not be allowed to die properly, the denial of a proper burial alongside those who have gone before.

"The soil grinds my eyes, my nose. I cannot breathe, I really cannot breathe now. I struggle for survival but none comes. I want to move but it is impossible, the weight is too much. It crushes, it is crushing me now. The sky is smaller. I see nothing. Just blackness. I feel the cold creep inwards, seeping beneath my skin and into my

fragile bones and I know they are broken, crushed beneath this weight. Do not panic. There is no need to be afraid. Just wait and it will come soon, this death."

"Adam!" I am screaming. "Adam!" I hear no more. And my voice doesn't come. I feel him, have felt him but I am not part of this wicked drama. I am so weak. My legs buckle and I can hardly breathe. I am choking on tears. How can I cry and yet have no voice? I run forward, digging deep into what strength I have left, ready to claw back the earth and pull this child from his unholy grave.

I am getting nowhere though. But I am running. Believe me, I am. I am using all my strength and can see my legs move quickly, bare feet flying through the grass. Yet the scene is ever farther. The tree, as it shakes in the early morning breeze, the priest as he makes a sign of the cross and puts away his book, the doctor, coat dirty as he leans against his shovel at last. And the father, still motionless, standing, head bowed.

Silent, all three.

What a picture.

The single apple tree in the far corner of a vast walled garden, the dull little grave and the melancholy trio.

But on I run, to nowhere, fast, very fast. "Adam, I can change it, I swear." But I cannot. Even as I make my noiseless shout, I know the declaration is useless. My Adam. Dead, buried, murdered beneath the piles of earth thrown cruelly onto his face, filling his nose and crushing him finally.

It isn't over. Oh, God, what next? I am on my hands and knees, weak, sweating, cold beads of sweat and tears. Unable to do any more, I am in the grass, crawling and breathless.

The shovel is back in place, nestled into the crook of the low branch once again. The three move together, and this father, Adam's merciless father, withdraws something from his pocket. A small knife and in a single gesture, the three turn their left arms skyward, their inner wrists facing the dying moon. Joined together they form a closed pattern of arms, the three of them on three sides of the grave.

"An oath to write the secret of this night in blood." From the man with the knife, Adam's father.

Sobbing, I watch the silver knife flash against the sky in a series of quick incisions. And then the blood, dripping onto the soil above the small mound of earth, falling like scarlet rain where his innocent face would be.

Mercifully, they fade, these three. Their unbearable presence is receding. Their clothes, I hardly recognized save that they belonged to another time, another place. And still they fade. It really is over, finished, they are done.

But I cannot move. I want to crawl forward but can't, my exhaustion is too great. I feel as though something has been torn from me. Such a deep sense of loss this feeling. I want to lie in this grass forever, twisted into each blade, eternal.

The scene changes and the garden reveals a tiny hill, its secret green quiet behind ivy covered stone walls. And I am here now, within this dreadful enclosure and the people have gone. I don't move, do not want to, such an overwhelming sense of loss and despair, and weeping, so much weeping within this garden of sadness.

There is someone else here, a shadow perhaps. Through my tears anything is possible. But he is more solid now, emerging from the side of this tree, and I don't know when he got there, and why I did not notice him before.

I watch.

He moves forward, this figure, toward me, long quick strides and I realize he can see me when the others could not. In spite of my misery, I am amazed at the speed with which he travels.

I recognize him, vaguely. Some recollection and I am not afraid. Why should I be? I have seen worse this night to cause fear.

What does he want?

"You."

A wisp of a voice darts my thoughts, soothing, healing, trying to make me whole. I have read his mind. Can he read mine? I hadn't spoken. I know I should be amazed but I am not, it all seems natural. I tell him I want to get up but am too tired, too broken. It doesn't matter though because one final stride and he is beside me, understanding my sadness, lifting me upwards and toward him at last.

Chapter Six

S he stared at Rossetti.

Sneaking out of the house on a Sunday afternoon after the cannibal act of communion.

Hovering uselessly between her mother and Cell-Phone Pam in the construction of the nuclear shelter beneath the lily patterned carpet in the living room, she had slipped out, leaving them engaged in talk about supplies and speculating how long anyone would really last padding around an empty world.

Frankly Evie couldn't care less. She had wanted death a month ago and what had it got her? A nut job of a story about a boy drinking blood rain from the blossom of an apple tree and a figure whose truth ran beneath her skin until she could cry from the agony of knowledge.

That and the child.

Rossetti was better, sweeping her thoughts toward the past. It meant she didn't have to know pain. 'Dante's Dream, the largest Rossetti painting', Evie listened to the small cassette player tucked into the palm of her hand, headphones pressed against the sides of her head. "1872" the narration continued, "the culmination of Dante Gabriel Rossetti's life long interest in the Greek poet, Dante."

Sure, she knew all of this. She had only paid for the headphones on account of it blotting the sounds in her head. So far it seemed to be working. Rossetti, founder of the Pre-Raphaelite Movement in 1848, the use of color and imagery as a way to reach deep into the senses. He'd drawn from myth and poetry in the same way her favorite poet Keats had and whose own work helped inspire the Movement.

She thought of the Waterhouse print on her wall; the one inspired by Keats's poem; the dark forest and the image of a knight leaning toward the waiting girl drawing him forward. Reluctantly then she thought of the inscription in the little book of poems. 'Your Dreams Are My Survival.' A dream, like the painting she was staring at now; the nightmare of a dream she had been dragged through.

She tore the headphones from her ears.

Dante dreaming he visits the object of his unrequited passion, led by Love toward Beatrice lain upon her deathbed among spring blossoms, poppies and red doves. Red Doves for love, blossoms for the purity of innocence and the poppies for sleep and death.

Death and the infant. Adam murdered beneath a canopy of apple blossom.

The end of innocence lying beneath the soft blood rain baptizing his sleeping face.

In the week since the morning she stumbled out of bed then fell back into it again because she looked and felt like crap , she had done everything possible not to think about what she had seen and the sick, you're-not-right-in–the-head story she'd somehow written.

Until now where she had hoped for sanctuary in the cool quiet of the art gallery.

Evie studied the painting. Tonight there would be no lover drifting toward Evie in dreams, only Adam claiming one last pearl of blood against his mouth, breathing a riddle against her cold flesh that beyond death he lived, although in life he never existed.

She thought of the figure in the forgotten orchard, each stride reaching into her terrible sorrow and the knowledge of a death that would remain hidden.

Except it wasn't real.

None of it was.

Adam was not real, he had never been born. There was no orchard. None of it was anything more than a stupid story penned under the influence of some ridiculous delusion she did not understand.

The dream was one thing, but just how in the name of rubber room insanity was it possible for those torn up sheets of paper to reemerge into a half dozen pages, hosting the same pathetic little story she had sought to rid herself of? She could have sworn everything had been ripped up. Hadn't she observed as each ridiculous paragraph of *Among Other Edens* ended its imaginary drama at the bottom of the waste bin?

So why then, when she made her bed the following morning was it lying underneath her pillow? A smooth display of blue italic penmanship on white lined paper, exactly as before.

"I've lost my mind, I've lost my mind, I've lost my friggin' mind." Evie recalled chanting to the bedroom furniture as she peeked into the waste paper basket and discovered they were not there.

But then, she argued to the black plastic container and her departing sanity, "why the fuck would they? When during the night, at approximately the same time toy clowns with hideous red slash grins and cuddly lions with razor teeth come alive, my pages reattached themselves, discovered an iron, set it on cool and pressed out the creases".

Evie retraced several steps back toward the bed, muttering to herself and not caring a jot.

"Then, you bastards, not content with this achievement you marched right across the room, jumped onto my frigging bed and slipped beneath my pillowcase."

But then she hadn't torn those pages the night before had she? Cracking her knuckles, Evie argued with her thoughts. It was just another case of seeing something that wasn't there.

"No! I did see it. I am not crazy. They are not in the waste bin and I am not gripping a fist full of thin air".

Biting her lower lip, Evie began to look doubtful, as though unable to trust herself.

Reality versus imagination.

Perched on the edge of the plastic bench facing Dante's Dream, Evie recalled the unbearable pressure forcing through the side of her head. Touching her temple Evie remembered the impact driving into her skull, sweeping a sheet of darkness across her eyelids pulling her further into its depths. That had been the fastest part, the lightning snap of some strange invasion.

Closing her eyes, Evie relived the intense pushing that followed, as though in forcing the recollection, she might better understand.

"Like I was shot." Spoke Evie to the silent Dante and imagined what the muzzle of a gun might feel like. Then, the devastating impact, she recalled, invading her head, forcing its way through the flesh and bone of her skull.

No pain, just overbearing pressure, not on the outside now but inside, holding everything in. The grip, fast against her brain, and the breathing which stopped, trapped within her chest, paralyzed.

Everything paralyzed.

Except her brain.

Her mind, hyper alert, telling her in a smooth, clear way this was no bullet, that she should breathe again, that she must do so, she would be alright. Slowly then, carefully, the suspension in Evie's chest relaxed and breath came, folding into her body, sweeping through her mind and turning her back, once again, toward sleep.

The following morning, Evie would discover the magically restored pages and the new, horrific little story.

Retrieving several scrunched up pages of *Among Other Edens* from her jacket pocket, Evie spread the creased paper onto the bench, carefully studying the contents.

It was all there, right down to the figure in the long black coat, everything.

"Who the hell are you?"

Lifting her right hand, Evie struggled to wipe the tiny beads of cold damp already decorating her forehead, an all too familiar response in the last few days. She had literally fallen back into bed after making an initial read of the contents, such was the sickening headache that followed.

Now, slowly, Evie slid her hand against the pages, pressing each word against the palm of her hand. A hidden orchard, its dark stillness forging a backdrop against a quiet murder unfurling beneath a crown of emerald leaves, rose into her thoughts.

"Go away!"

Blinking hard, Evie fought the image, then stuffing the pages back into her pocket resolved to burn the things if necessary. Preparing to leave, Evie stared at the painting of Dante one last time and sighed. If she had hoped to reach some sort of understanding here she had failed.

But the image stayed.

"Leave me alone!"

Shouting at the painting Evie rubbed the image now burning into her eyes. "Damn it". Cursed Evie, this was not Dante and his lover Beatrice but the orchard, her hideous dream of an orchard living, breathing within the frame of what was a Rossetti painting.

"Damn you to hell!" Evie cursed the emerging figure, slipping from the shadow of the apple tree and the tremble of blossom yielding toward the deceit and the fall of a garden at the gate of spring.

Evil Evie

Evil Evie

Spawned on the Eve of May

Devil's Child

Satan's Bride

Marked with an X for a Hex.

Another verse of her birthday chorus echoed through her pounding head. A gift composed by her mother and grandmother for her sixth birthday the year after her father and Elaine walked off the top of the cathedral, it represented their tribute to her unwanted existence.

They were right though, they must be. What kind of person would have dreamt something like that? The live burial of a child? Again the verse mocked her, melding the image of the terrible orchard and Rossetti's Beatrice on her deathbed.

Emerged fully now within the painting as written by her hand, the secret evil pulsed within the frame.

"I didn't create you. I wrote none of this." Drawn forward Evie rose from the bench anyway and stepped toward the living painting, entranced.

In her handwriting, the words had appeared on paper, the morning after feeling as though she had been shot in the head, but other than the hard shunt into brain and the moment of paralysis, Evie recalled none of it.

Now, as written and half hidden within this darkness were three figures, one of whom clutched an infant.

It was the fate of the infant that most disturbed Evie. Buried alive, his bones crushed beneath the weight of earth so callously thrown upon it. A fate no being should have to endure.

"Adam", Evie whispered now. Strange, the intoxicating pull; drawing her beneath the quiet breath of his name, sliding her into the heart of the story making her dizzy for the fall.

She stopped then, breaking the spell of this dark enchanted garden. What secret thoughts had she harbored only to be revealed from beneath a canopy of sleep?

"Why me?" A single tear crested Evie's left eye before tumbling forward as the figure moved slowly across the damp grass, green eyes holding her face.

Could it be her, his hand reached for?

Panic rose beneath her skin and a line of blood ran from her nose, its scarlet descent feeding the dark earth that spilled over the frame and onto what had been shiny white tile.

She was terribly dizzy.

She should fall into this.

"Your dreams are my survival."

His voice, in every breath, making her part of something impossible to understand.

Rising from the page and into her soul, the dark edge of his cloak swept beyond the frame, claiming her senses for himself.

Impossible to breathe.

His presence tracing the edge of her neck.

Lavender air willing the girl to inhale this and be calm. To trust the longheld promise of a return to a place forgotten.

"No!" Screaming at the painting, Evie tore an escape, hurling the headphones to the floor.

It was raining out.

Running through the rose garden opposite the museum and the art gallery, Evie hurried toward the long line of bus stops, afraid should she slow down, she might be forced to see something she didn't want to.

She knew him.

That long black cashmere coat falling across his shoulders, following each stride like a soft cloud of darkness. The sweep of curls, the sharp green clarity of his eyes, missing nothing. His hands too, dressed in the finest leather stretched across his skin, emphasizing the long reach of his fingers.

Poems

The inscription in the little book of poetry.

Evelyn, Evie's namesake, written in a flourish by the Storyteller's hand.

Hadn't she tried to imagine him then, this figure, swooping down with the image and words you could die for...? She had been thinking about him that foggy night on April 30th, the Eve of May, her miserable birthday and the useless attempt at death. And then hadn't she penned the original Eden story hours after chucking back the useless little sleeping pills?

It was slotting together.

The Storyteller, her Storyteller. Unwittingly she had created an image of him as she wanted him to appear. Drawn into the realm of fantasy he had started to play, concluded Evie, head pressed against the dirty window on the bus.

Stupid not to have realized it sooner.

"But what happened in the art gallery was my imagination". Determined to reassure herself Evie refused to believe it could be anything more. She had always been like that, Evie continued to soothe her frantic nerves. Headaches, nose bleeds the lot.

Yet for a moment she had resurrected this figure from the pages of a book, breathing life into her creation of the Storyteller, and gracious as always, he accepted Evie's invitation, crossing the threshold to her soul's core.

Until she had torn it all to pieces, destroying the life briefly given. In sleep her anger split against itself, forging an image so disturbing it drew her into a sort of half sleep, creating another story so she might gain redemption through words, and punishment in the insanity that followed.

She had only thought those pieces of paper were torn to shreds.

All she had needed was the time to consider everything, reasoned Evie as she popped the key into the front door just as Cell-Phone Pam and her mother were leaving.

Dashing upstairs, Evie retrieved the book of poems tucked behind the wardrobe along with everything she had written so far. She needed to collapse onto her bed and think.

Her head had never been clearer; in fact it was wide open.

The scent of lavender was everywhere.

"Hello, Evie."

Swiftly, the door closed behind her.

Chapter Seven

That voice was unmistakable. Smooth, unhurried, it trickled through her mind like warm liquid. Struggling to stand, Evie grabbed the edge of the dressing table so she wouldn't go crashing through the floor and into the room below.

Cold, very cold, she sank onto the grey carpet, knees tucked to chest, clutching the little book. She would have to throw it away, destroy it even. An obsession had risen into her head and she needed to make it stop. She would take the prints off the wall and throw those away too.

She had lost her mind.

The verbal explosion continued.

"My Evie, there is no need for your fear," he soothed.

"Shut up, shut up, shut up!" Evie covered her ears with her hands.

"I should tell you, it is impossible to shut me out."

"You don't exist, you're in my head!" she screamed.

She became sad, a deep penetrating misery followed by a large spill of tears. Evie let them fall, her inability to explain what just happened hijacking the use of her hands so they hung loosely, fingers trailing the rough pile of the carpet.

Somehow the voice had reached in, churned her despair, manipulated her emotions. The misery belonged to someone else, making it that much harder to bear, to have another's sorrow inside you, suffocating everything of your own until there was nothing but that terrible invasion.

"You make me sad when you do not believe," he murmured.

From her position on the floor, Evie stared beyond the panes of her window toward the silent street. Refusing to acknowledge any part of the conversation, she attempted to block the voice.

"I love you, Evie. I have always loved you. Before, now and always."

Hauling herself up from the floor, Evie crossed the hall to the bathroom. Reaching for the little cabinet above the sink, its mirrored door transported her reflection sideways and against the wall as she sought the aspirin on the top shelf.

"You cannot work against me like that. You tried before and it did not work, remember?"

The voice, his beautifully textured voice, rolling around her head.

"I don't understand," Evie whispered.

The three words struggled forward, dry and caught against the back of her throat.

She had retrieved the aspirin and it lay in her left hand, while the other clung to the cabinet door as though it were the only thing standing between herself and the long dark fall into the pages of Alice in Wonderland. Only instead of a rabbit hole, she would tumble down the sink into the labyrinth of drains below.

"Do not make me sad, Evie please. Sad is not good for you."

Again, tears trickled down her face, their bitter salt stinging as they drenched the edges of her frozen mouth. Working hard on the inside, Evie struggled to reclaim fragments of herself.

She thought she'd had it all figured out, the analysis of the Storyteller's appearance. She had been through this already, her fruitcake imagination creating an image of who she wanted him to be. Yet instead of helping she had only made things worse.

"Put the pills away, Evie. Do not defile yourself like that. I have told you, they will not make any difference."

Such a horrible, patient, kind voice that shouldn't be there.

Obediently she replaced the bottle, wondering why she should listen to this entity, then pulled herself away from the sink and closed the mirrored cabinet door.

She doubted there would be enough to finish the job anyway. If five sleeping pills hadn't tossed her toward eternity, Evie stood a fat chance with a half empty bottle of supermarket brand aspirin.

But she would return to her room, sit on her bed and deal with this. You could control these things couldn't you?

When you really got down to it, that's pretty much all it amounted to, managing that side of your personality. She would instruct herself in everything, down to each detail of her day. She was disciplined enough and it would begin now.

Breathe, breathe through this, pretend everything is perfectly normal. Pretend enough and perhaps it would be.

It was getting dark, the light over the meadow and oak tree behind the house submitting at last to the stretch of shadows reaching across the clear sky. Before long she would need to close the curtains, but for now, Evie stared at the perfect space, watching the silhouettes of lavender stalks bow to the evening breeze.

Pressing her face against the window Evie imagined how it looked long before anybody thought of an Eden Road. Before its destiny fell beneath a hand whose intent lay with molding the perfect nature beneath its instruction.

Such beautiful sharp cold. Evie pushed the right side of her face closer against the glass. The coolness was welcome, keeping her present, anchoring her thoughts and delaying their final drift into nothing.

She could see it suddenly, all of its vast wildness. A green valley unspoiled, sweeping out toward thick forests and grasslands, uninterrupted except for the thread of a stream weaving its slow journey to the shore of an impatient sea, miles away.

Intact, lovely, a time apart from the ruptured earth and stamp of concrete. All of it, everything she walked upon were remnants of its history. Cast offs, unwanted by the present and annexed by time, willing to unfurl their secrets to those prepared to tread the forbidden paths and reach, without fear, into the centre, feeling the seductive pulse, the heart of Eden.

"Yes, so very beautiful Evie. The loss of it makes me weep."

Again misery ran beneath her skin.

"Ignore it, ignore the voice and it will go away, it has to," she said aloud.

"Evie, I want to cry."

At his words, deep, soul wrenching sobs, tore at her heart. Turning from the window, she brought both hands to her face, holding them there as tears ran between her fingers.

Never had she felt such sadness, not even when her father and sister had died. This sorrow consumed everything, taking her energy, leaving her with nothing but a misery that belonged elsewhere.

"Please, leave me alone. I don't want you here," she begged him.

Forcing herself into action, Evie resolved to go downstairs. For once she would be happy to clean the kitchen floor. She might even throw in an extra chore for free. She couldn't stay here in her room and hide forever. Sooner or later she must face people.

Hand trembling, Evie opened the bedroom door and taking the first step onto the top stair, grew aware of herself as one entering a world of pretence. A place where she looked perfectly fine on the outside, while inside her head, raised a slow death.

Evie heard a key strike the circular brass lock. Her mother had returned.

Inhaling the remains of sadness, Evelyn Edern descended toward the noise downstairs.

Chapter Eight

Funny really, how you could fool everyone, provided you swallowed every natural emotion as it threatened to make itself known within your heart.

Later that evening, Evie, despite the panic and sickness, could give herself credit for turning in a poised and polished performance.

Cell-Phone Pam had bought Evie's mother a computer. The pair of them, after hauling the various essential bits and pieces into the dining room decided it would be better off in the living room on the little table beneath the window. Together they huffed and puffed the thing in there.

Evie, not allowed to touch anything so 'valuable' had been instructed to play the part of observer save for whipping up a plate of pale cheese sandwiches and cups of sugary tea which the two devoured without thanks.

It was the Internet apparently, that Maureen needed, a prescription handed out by Pamela. Evie watched her mother's ever narrowing eyes absorb the various instructions and the distinction between a web address and an e-mail address. From here, encouraged Pam, they would know where all the "cell phone tower demos'" were taking place.

"Speaking of which, I need to call Ollie," cheered Pam. Removing her own cell phone from within the depths of a smart leather bag, she called her son on speed dial.

Rolling her eyes, Evie grabbed the empty plates and tossing them into the kitchen sink, listened to the buzz of activity in the next room. The reassurance that a Webmaster or Web mistress was not something questionable in the 'sex department.'

Evie, turning the tap on full blast banished images of rubber hoods and the like, and thought she couldn't listen to anymore.

Nevertheless, against the secret raging within her head, the conversation at least offered the glow of normalcy. Beneath the cozy activity, the dish water, warm against her skin, Evie felt the dread of its loss.

At eight thirty, Evie had permission to go to her room.

Except for the reflection of a street light on the opposite side of the road throwing an orange glow through the side window, the scene of trauma and misery was fully dark. Anxious for sixty-watt security, Evie switched on the main light, flooding the tiny space with a soft glow. Next, she drew the curtains, tugging them to a swift close. A final assurance that the inevitable breakdown would remain hidden from the world at large, or at the very least, Eden Road.

Silence.

Sitting on the bed and drawing both feet underneath her Evie anticipated the next act to the sad little charade.

The voice spoke into her head! That's what made the whole thing so bloody disturbing. And if that were not enough, it came exactly as she had imagined it when reading from the stupid little inscription.

The book's fault, it had to be. Evie wished she had never found it in the first place. *Up until then I was fine,* whined Evie. Except of course, the occasional sighting of things normal people couldn't see.

Had her desire for the Storyteller been so great she had drawn him into reality, even though she knew he didn't exist?

"Thank you for the invitation. I have been waiting for so long."

"You're nothing but imagination, ignore you and you'll go away, she hissed into the bright nothing.

"Then explain how I made you cry." Countered the patient voice.

"Caught by surprise, that's all." Evie thought back. "I hate you for making me think I'm mad. I never want to hear you again, you're disgusting."

"Evie."

Like notes from a harp, the voice trilled across her mind, clear, sweet and beautiful. In spite of herself Evie allowed the perfect melody to rest within her, before despising him again.

"Stop it!"

"You felt that, did you not? You felt what I gave you, the sense of peace, the connection." He wasn't giving in.

"It is impossible to feel what doesn't exist." Getting louder, Evie would have to be careful.

"Trust Evie, that is all I ask."

The voice, it covered all she had left. Evie loathed herself for wanting it, to love this sick invasion inside her head. Yet she had no other way to explain the longing that picked at her insides, moving deeper into the wound it had created. The image of him licking the blood from inside her, sweeping his tongue deeper so she might heal.

It was evil.

Everything about this must be wrong.

Accepting the touch inside her head was darkness, but the idea of him refused to leave, someone willing to take her without judgment.

Exclusive, her secret, if she chose it.

This powerful rush toward him could that be real also? This rising of her soul toward his non-existence, making her wish she could see him, alone and away from everything. The strange figure drifting through the pages of Among Other Edens. This man, her Storyteller, lifted from a Victorian inscription and resurrected into her soul, surrendering the deep paths of her imagination over to his private thoughts.

In accepting him into her he had become real, like the beings she saw who weren't there to anyone else, yet to Evie had form. An ethereal communion in flesh and blood offering themselves up to the light in her eyes, asking her to accept these gifts without question.

But there were other things, more than the Storyteller's thoughts touching her own.

The quick invasions of 'flash thoughts' invading her mind, so called because without warning they jumped in and out of her head before she could fully realize they had ever been there.

Trivial things mostly. Flashes of information like the quick message that she had missed a spot when dusting the living room, and for sure would suffer for it later. But there were more serious thoughts, the worst of which took place a few days after her eighth birthday.

Exercising an event forgotten until now, Evie recalled that her mother had purchased a new car a few days before the child turned eight. Evie also recalled now, how when drunk uncle Colin lingered his eyes across the child's small naked breasts following the beating he gave her, she had wished Colin dead.

Nothing had been said about the fifty lashes, recalled Evie. After their sharp delivery, the child limped downstairs, skin bleeding through her clothes.

The thought fell into Evie's head then. That Colin would die and that it would be soon. The message disappearing as quickly as it came, leaving Evie to wonder if it had ever been there at all.

Three weeks later some unfortunate jogger discovered the brand new car embedded in the trunk of an oak tree. The driver impaled through the chest by a leafy branch, having been flung through the windscreen first.

The news of Uncle Colin's death made Evie sick, and running upstairs shouted, "I killed him!" before throwing up in the bathroom sink.

She had made all that happen; therefore she made the Storyteller happen.

Leaning against her pillow, Evie let the house breathe around her, and keeping company with the night waited for the Storyteller's inevitable return.

Chapter Nine

In darkness, time lay quiet and unused. The silence pushed against Evie's head, a reminder of the space his voice no longer occupied.

Impatient, the waiting had become a threat to her eyelids willing themselves toward sleep.

Once she slipped out of bed, retrieved *Poems* and stared at the inscription done in his hand all that time ago.

Beneath the leather gloves she wondered what his hands looked like, stained perhaps in black ink from endless writing. His eyes she somehow knew were green, while the remainder of his face, yet to lift from shadow, further teased her desire. And his touch, running beneath her skin, tempting, drawing her closer into his world.

It would be better there, soft words, graceful gestures and always gentle, always. Slowly she leaned back, sinking her head into the soft folds of her pillow.

"My beloved Evie."

Words, tracing the edge of her thoughts, stopped her heart as the end of her name fell into silence. She still held the book, the palm of her right hand resting across the surface of the page. She must have fallen asleep because the texture of his voice whispering into her soul threw both eyes wide open, to search, to see.

Now, breathing into the darkness Evie wanted to touch him.

"I have been watching your wait for me."

Still though there remained a small measure of fear that these words embodied within her head should come again.

Swallowing hard, Evie pushed the fright aside, refusing to give it the ghost of a chance.

"Do not fear me, I have so much to tell you."

"I'm sorry", she whispered into nothing, ashamed at her lack of trust. "Let me see you, so I know none of this is me. I won't freak out, I promise."

"In writing you have seen me live and in dreams you have given me life."

"You speak in riddles, how do I know you're real? That this isn't just my imagination? Your voice made me believe I had lost my mind."

"I am sorry, truly I am, but I am real, this voice is real, everything you experience through me is real. But you cannot see me the way you want to."

"Why?"

"You do not need to see me to feel my presence, to know I am within you. I have been here always, I am here always."

She didn't understand. To have been with her since forever was impossible, yet she felt him, the inexplicable feeling of his existence inside, haunting her soul, running through her blood, possessing every sinew. Wanting her.

"Was it you? Did you give me those stories? Adam? Everything? Where did they come from?"

And then finally, the question she knew should have been asked first but had been too afraid to ask.

"Are you from the inscription? Are you the Storyteller?"

"Yes."

"But why me?"

It was a stupid, lame question and Evie regretted the watery choice of words before they became sound. He had just risen from the page of a nineteenth century inscription for God's sake and she could do no better than that?

She heard him sigh, the slow breath slipping through her head. A sign perhaps of impatience.

The echo of his abandonment rattled around her head and her thoughts fell quiet. If only she could have been brighter, smarter, funnier and prettier, perhaps he would have stayed. Sadly, breathed Evie, she possessed none of these qualities and never would.

"Stop this, pull yourself back up!"

A hard voice, so different to the Storyteller's gentle manner.

"Stop doing this to yourself."

Same voice, impatient, unwilling to stand any nonsense. It was her own, it had to be. He had gone and she had lost her mind, leaving nothing but a tired, split version of herself to drag into tomorrow.

But then soft, familiar tones returned.

"Such pain you invite into yourself, Evie. Were I here to destroy you, and believe me I could, I should sit back and watch as your soul bled dry. But I am getting tired of entertaining your paranoia, that is not what I am here for and besides it has become rather dull. I feel your misery and can understand your confusion, however I refuse to bathe in it any longer on your behalf.

"Nevertheless, if misery is your true desire, I am only too happy to oblige. I have trodden the path of pain and suffering, have stalked its presence and could tell you its many tales of grief and anger. Believe me, I could lay such images before you, forcing them into the deepest part of your imagination so that the cries of others never ceased.

"Words with neither sense nor meaning colliding with your thoughts, leaving nothing of yourself. I have made these things happen, have watched the effect of the images and words I deliver as geniuses, possessors of brilliant minds and exceptional creative gifts are reduced to painting distorted images, or writing realms of delirious verse and prose in a frenzied attempt to exorcise mankind's misery onto page or canvas.

"I have watched as nothing they did made sense, watched too as others thought them mad, pitying them at first, before turning away, ashamed at the mere sound of a particular name. But still the work must continue. Projects, half finished symphonies tossed aside in favor of something new, some other attempt to deliver the peace within that never comes as slowly the madness descends. My hands have reached into the dark side of genius, drawing more images forward, weaving and sliding toward sanity's fragile core, crushing it finally. I have done this and for the most part have felt no shame in doing so.

"With barely the breath from my voice I have given you my sadness, watched as you succumbed to my thoughts and feelings, my life running into you, through your veins. You have scarcely begun to feel and I, mindful of my strength have only caressed the fringes of your imagination, careful of pushing too deeply before I know you to be ready.

"But with you I am patient and can forgive your sojourn into self-hatred if only you withdraw from this and pull toward me instead. In this you have nothing to fear, I promise. I wish only that you take my gifts into you, allowing me to nurture the path to your imagination in ways impossible to others."

Through everything said so far, Evie held fast to each word, absorbing the cadence of every syllable as it layered the core of her mind. Her soul, rising to meet his voice accepted all of it and through shallow breaths she listened.

Her Storyteller, stalking genius before stealing sanity with every stroke of brush or pen; beautiful, vengeful, destroying his creation so that words ran like poison into the pristine valleys of an imagination in which he once so lovingly dwelt.

Closing her eyes Evie glimpsed the side of a figure dressed exclusively in black save for the loose folds of a white shirt. Familiar dark curls swept back were secured at the nape of his neck by a black ribbon. Then he disappeared, leaving the cobbled street to the company of night.

She had grown cold and considered slipping into bed. Closing her eyes she would find him in dreams. He would like that she suspected.

"Stay alert, there is much still that I have to tell you." A little pause, then, "and I need to feed, already too much time has been lost."

She didn't understand. It was very late now, the luminous hands on the green clock next to her bed teetering on three-thirty. She would eat in the morning, then he might feel better, but for now she needed rest. The voice, the surprise of his presence had left her tired. He could talk into her head while she slept. Already the closeness she felt toward this strange presence was complete.

But in the silence that followed, a new kind of fear erupted as the unspoken implication snapped together.

"Why?"

Terror detached Evie's voice from anything more except if she slammed her head against the wall it might be possible to get rid of him. What could this thing possibly feed on except her brain? Frantic, Evie searched for something with which to hurt herself. He would make her insane. That had been his plan, to drive her crazy. Quickly Evie calculated how many attempts it would take to slam her head against the wall before killing the man in her brain.

"Evie, take away the unspeakable horror you imagine and be calm again, accept me. You are afraid because you do not understand; there is nothing to fear in me, I have given you my promise."

"How can I believe you?" She breathed into the early dawn.

"I have hurt others, I will not lie, my feed driving them crazy. And sometimes I killed, causing the brain to hemorrhage for my indulgence. But you Evie, with you I have no argument, only love and I beg your forgiveness for the fear I caused. In my haste, I became impatient and began things the wrong way around. Of course, I do not expect you to understand what is meant by any of this, therefore since I was the author of your terror I shall begin where it would have been better to end; giving you the first of my lessons."

Chapter Ten

"*Breathe for me, inhale the long slow drink of warm air, open your lungs and relax deep into your center. Draw breath again, slowly and into your blood, pulling me toward you as every sinew, every cell fills with us. Then into your brain finally, pushing me deep into the core of who you are, your desires, your imagination, your essence. Now hold me there, breathe into me. Know me.*

"*Keep breathing like that, slowly, with trust, there is no harm here, nothing to fear between us. Relax in this space for a moment, breathe steady, feel my presence, be aware of how I slip further into you. I feel the way you rise to receive me and the joy that is felt in every muscle beneath your skin, within your blood.*

"*And I haven't even begun to feed yet. I can go deeper within you, if you permit it, if you trust enough to take me there. Deliberately, slowly, I can move into who you are, making you feel more, bringing your awareness further toward me. Already I have seen into your truth, your strength, you are more than who you think you are.*

"*But let us stay here, in this state for a moment. Listen, stay alongside me, do not fall away from who I am, my voice, my love, everything I wish to give you. Breathe me in, take these words, absorb me, absorb who I am and learn.*

"*Let me teach you how to take me in each night, where I want you and where I can feel you want me. Let me slip, unnoticed into your sleep, taking your senses, your breathing and hold them to me without fear. Let me teach you how to disappear into yourself, so you might drift amongst nothing, absorbing peace, absorbing my act within you.*

"Holding your breath steady, learn to breathe, Evie, learn to breathe without completing your ascent too quickly. Be aware now of how this feels as I slip deeper into your mind, so good as your soul rises at last to touch me. Feel me Evie, feel me go deeper toward who you are. Your mind is open, I can feel you draw me in, further, further still. Such trust, I can only love you even more for this.

"Keep breathing. I can feel your pleasure, can see it in your veins and I take it into me, your response giving me strength, driving me deeper still to that place where I have existed before.

"You will recall this feeling as I go here now, only better this time because accepting me has made you ready. The pressure against the side of your head, the same as before, know this and do not fear it. I feel you anticipate the final impact. And it comes, this impact, fast, deep into your center, delivering all of who I am into you. It is paralyzing this intensity but only for a moment, then you breathe again as before. Learn this Evie and fear none of it.

"It is safe for me here, this garden among your thoughts and I watch your drift toward sleep and the peace you seek, the gentle tugging inside your mind. My feeding, you will get used to this, even want it, I promise.

"Dreams are my survival, your dreams flow into me and I want more. I have done this to you at a time while you slept, unaware save for a strange invasion sliding behind the darkness and to you what felt like a bullet, piercing the shadows with its silver light tearing through bone and skin lying beneath.

"The first time in you that way. Afraid. Needing you to understand, hurt by your rejection and angry at your refusal to accept the story-gift I had given you, tearing it to shreds. How I wanted to cry for that!

"The boy lying within the grass, thirsting for the blood as it fell from the canopy of blossom above. And your first move toward me, wanting the journey toward my darkness. All of it torn. My anger because in the midst of your useless attempt at death I gave you this without feeding and without pushing deep into your core, absorbing your response to the words and images I carried into your senses. And later how I came to you in air as you read what I had given, drawing your desire for me forward, laying myself against you so you might feel at last, the realness of my presence.

"It left me weak all of that, giving so much and taking nothing. It left me empty, this sacrifice of myself into you. Understand my fear also. Your willingness to reject who you are, your truth, the power of your imagination and the strength of your creativity both of which are exceptional, weakened me further.

"So I had to make you listen, stealing your attention toward me so you might See what I needed to show you. And in my desperation I made those images and words come, calculating the effect of each disturbing vision as it tore your soul to shreds.

"The passion of your response, I loved. The way it made me feed, drawing energy from your panic and your fearless outrage at the horror of Adam's burial. And because I fed so well from you, I could give more in return, ensuring you would never forget who you truly are, inviting me in at last, legitimately, forever.

"So I gave you Adam's pain, the agony as each infant bone was crushed beneath the dark weight of the earth. And his last breath, drawn against the cold finally as his soul pulled toward its enforced destination.

"Your energy, perfect as you ran toward the small mound beneath the tree, wanting, needing to claw back the earth, to take everything back, I fed from that.

"The perfection of your sorrow lying among the damp grass, all of this I took without shame, growing stronger to give you more. Your inability to move pulled me closer, drawing me there to watch, taking your pain and its purity until I could bear your sorrow no longer and moved toward you as before. Your response to my presence pleasing me.

"And you have to admit, it worked. I waited, patient in the belief you would return to yourself at last and the part of me that has become you. I listened, interested as your thoughts struggled to make sense of it all, of me, the garden, Adam, so perfectly and without my influence. Then finally, the moment when you returned to the truth within yourself, I cannot describe the joy that brought me. How I could have wept when you opened your mind finally to accept the gift of my thoughts and the touch of my emotions to make you believe.

"And I am real, very real. I do not believe you doubt this any longer. And I feel you accept this without question, your trust sweet, even as I tell how I fed forcibly, caring not about your pleasure but *about delivering pain into your mind instead. I love you more for this and feel the want of answers to your questions, therefore I feed lightly now, slowly because there remains much that needs to be said, so you might understand.*

"I draw your acceptance inwards, the awakening of your desire. I feel its strength and it nourishes me. You do not want me to leave.

"The pleasure of us, as you enter my world where the more you take, the stronger I become as I push deeper, feeding from the image you create.

"Let me teach you, let me make you ready. You learn fast but tonight is a lesson in understanding my presence, and there is a danger too in going too far. I have killed in such a way, this you know, diving deeper until their brains bled from my strength.

"Already you know how I can manipulate your senses and how my emotions are bound with yours so that my sadness becomes your heartfelt grief. But my happiness with you will bring pure joy, and my love, intense pleasure. I do not need to feed in order to accomplish any of this, neither do I need to feed before speaking with you.

"So, I exist outside of you but within also, speaking into your mind, turning all of who you are over to me if I wish it. And my desire to move through you will be constant, and always, you will want this. Remember Evie, I know who you are and I am with you constantly, my voice as you heard it, lifted from the inscription.

"I am glad you discovered that book, waited for you to find it, and it is of no coincidence that you did, having long waited to lay it within your hands. It was time also for you to discover the inscription, knowing you were at least powerful enough to create an image, drawing me into your reality. Your ability to understand, irrelevant.

"But my time was long before then. A traveler, yes, but my existence as you thought it goes far beyond the imagination of Romantic art and literature. Although for a while I stayed, happy there, taking nourishment, feeding upon its ideas and creating more in return before I fell into revenge.

"And yes, I have killed for you. This is something you should know. Understand this, in my current state, which in time you will appreciate, I like to kill. Revenge is an act I relish. It is true what they say, life does indeed flash before a person's eyes, or thoughts,* *providing the most satisfying feed imaginable. All I take is strength for myself, returning nothing but death.*

"I observed the one who made your skin bleed, forcing your face against the stench of sheets, as the belt struck and kept striking. The Eve of May Evie, your eighth birthday, standing at the feet of Christ, and I recall the rise of history within your head and the blood as it fell from your nose at the images cast into memory. Thousands of wasted corpses and the rise of pure evil. The very rim of hell.

"Your punishment for this, fifty lashes and what came afterwards, the putrid want for you, his touch against your bare skin. Observer of your pain and bravery I delivered the knife through the wall, piercing the leg of the bear in an effort to distract and amuse. The macabre image driving your curiosity as I knew it should.

"It was only a matter of time, let him drink a little and borrow the doomed car, half drunk on an empty road, twisting into a bend he failed to see because I flashed the image of you pouring blood from your wounded skin.

"And it was wonderful, the fast invasion of his mind, and the shock of this as he sped around the corner, distracted by the sudden pop inside his head as he skipped the side of the road, plunging into the tree, his body jousting the windscreen and receiving the broken limb of that oak tree. Oh, Evie, the satisfaction, the feeding, it became my frenzy in his final crucial moments before the brain finally closed to my greed.

"So you see, your life is bound to my soul and I have known you forever, watching, nurturing your strength and understanding your powers until now, when I made myself known to you at last. The inscription, drawing me in as your mind traced each word, pondering its meaning.

"You are the first, more powerful than five generations previous. None of them listened, though I tried speaking to them the way I have you, if only to pull me from the darkness I exist in now. Until you, Evie, the first one since Adam to possess these extraordinary powers of sight and hearing. A seer, he had those too, strong, like his mother, had he lived, until his infant murder, a death I swore would be avenged. And still it is not finished. I have been waiting, but I am patient. I have seen in you what lies ahead.

"But that is all you need to know of me for now. Stay with me, I will make sense of who you are, your connection to Adam, the reason why you feel the past connect within your hands, the stories, the poems, the art, everything. I will bring it together for you. You will See it and I will make you write while I feed so such things will again exist in your hands, and you will never again fear the path you know to tread.

"I have waited Evie, stalking time until your twentieth birthday, April 30th, the Eve of May, a time when I am strongest, making it possible for me to craft at long last, the first of the stories through your hands. Adam, patient for the descent of blood rain against his waiting mouth and it was I also who delivered the mist and the lavender air into your senses, forcing you away from a death seducing the edge of your soul.

"You cannot die like that. You must not. To win, you can never do so, for the claim then will be complete and for the sake of all things Evie, this cannot happen. Time will pass before you understand why it is so, but for now, in the quiet hours when you feel the threads of its whisper stalk your desires, walk your thoughts from its temptation, for the sweetness of its touch will never last. It is a trick.

"Know also that you are different, accept it. Remove the guilt of things past, the loss of your father and of Elaine, you are not to blame as you will come to understand. Understand also, you are not the evil one, although one day you will know of its presence as certain as it wants your soul.

"I believe I have said enough and all of this has exhausted me. Never speak of my existence to anyone, acknowledge it only within yourself, to do otherwise is dangerous, bitter experience has taught me this and I should warn you, never, ever cross me.

"But there is one other thing I should draw to your awareness. You are right to fear your tread upon that path. To take your journey into that place is dangerous and indeed, your walk upon it is forbidden. Evil waits. Do not doubt what you saw there. It wants you.

"But I shall give you dreams now while I feed from the pleasure they bring. Sleep now, my Evie and rise toward me once more."

And she did.

Deep, engulfing breaths of sleep inhaling his pulse and welcoming the possession at last.

Chapter Eleven

They were getting a lodger.

An environmental student named Chris who spoke in algebra and, according to Evie's mother, hated art, literature, poetry, and anything that couldn't be reduced to an element or quadratic equation.

The whole idea was spawned by Cell-Phone Pam. She'd spent the entire morning relegating the final remnants of Elaine's abbreviated life into the dark space beneath the attic rafters.

A student. Evie couldn't understand the logic, except that Pam had persuaded Maureen to rent the spare room, for extra cash. As clever as he was, at twenty-three Chris apparently had nowhere to live, neither Maureen or Pam had thought to ask why, but had simply accepted his need as an opportunity for additional income, and so the deal had been struck.

Contact was first made in a chat room dedicated to wind turbines, then via e-mail and finally in person at the base of a cell phone tower opposite a village pub in Wales. Afterwards they'd all gone for a pint, Pamela standing at the bar ordering three pints of strong cider while Maureen wrote 126 Eden Road on a soggy beer mat floating in the center of the wet table.

That was a Sunday afternoon. By Tuesday, traces of Elaine and the remnants of Colin's existence had vanished to the purchase of a new bedspread, matching beige curtains and one of those prints with an illustration supposedly hidden behind a trillion multi-colored dots.

With Pamela and her mother engaged in conversation, Evie faced the task ahead of her.

So much had taken place since the Storyteller last spoke to her and given the present circumstances Evie felt glad that among his private whispers, he had told her to remain strong and unafraid of her destiny, *whatever may come*, Evie added as an afterthought.

She no longer feared his departure. He would return, she knew. There was no panic in the silence anymore. Respectfully perhaps, he was leaving her to find her place among the developments as they unfurled around her.

Now, she struggled with a new fury. A complete stranger sleeping in the next room to Evie when she was forbidden to have friends. And, she would have yet another person to clean up after!

"What's wrong with you?" Evie's mother had asked. "Don't worry, if I thought he'd be after you, I wouldn't have moved him in, but you're far too plain and bloody dumpy to interest him."

Evie wished her Storyteller would just show up and feed from her.

Restless, Evie needed a walk. After being stuck in the house all day preparing for Chris's arrival, she needed the fresh air. Maybe it would kill off the beginning of her headache. She could feel it now, pushing against the front of her head.

She wanted his feed too, could kill for it. Every cell in her being cried for the caress of his images and it was unthinkable that it shouldn't happen, she had waited long enough.

"Please."

She had to have it, the jolt to her brain, the intense pressure against the side of her head.

"Evelyn, just who do you think you're talking to?"

A brittle voice shattered the secret talk and without waiting for a response, her mother continued.

"Only idiots talk to themselves Evelyn and you're useless enough as it is, without carrying on like that."

Spy game over, she turned on the low rubber heels of her fuzzy pink slippers and waltzed out of Elaine's old room leaving Evie to the company of sheets and the brand new bed she was to make up.

She needed the feeling. Having turned her fears over to his invasion, his presence became addictive and she wanted her entity to stay, could have remained in his existence for eternity.

That first time he had given her his energy. All of it, the explanations and understanding, she had taken it all in, absorbing the flow of his voice. Taking in his lessons she learned to breathe, welcoming the push and tug inside her mind, had felt the rise toward him, the exquisite stab of burning pleasure against her soul.

That, and the impossible fingers pushing downward, holding her thoughts to his, and her quest for his knowledge, driven deeper by his encouragement.

She wanted everything, her mind alert, telling him to give more, that he could do so, that she needed him to do so, as this was not enough. She was capable of so much more. Instinctively, Evie knew this. Her mind would not bleed like the others had.

Slipping a pillow into its cotton case, she felt it then, the air across the side of her face, warm like a kiss. Transfixed, she inhaled deeply.

He was here, stroking her face, a careful reminder of his presence. Closing her eyes, Evie let the warm air drift across her skin, against her mouth.

Sneaking downstairs, she closed the front door behind her.

Her Storyteller was back and she needed to think.

Chapter Twelve

The top of the footpath stretched before her, Evie recalled the bagpiper and his disappearance into the green darkness, and the image of the man with the snapped neck trapping all thoughts of escape.

As usual the display of nettles and ancient brambles threatened the flesh of anyone with enough daring to draw near. Peering closer Evie watched, shadows stalked the edge of her feet, drawing her curiosity forward.

The dense blackberry shrubs with their delicate flowers and deadly thorns were moving, of this she was positive, their reach searching the edge of her feet, drawing her in, piercing skin and bone with their gift of thorns. She was bleeding, the dry earth below claiming each scarlet drop for its thirst.

Was he making this happen, her Storyteller, taking her eyes and making her See as he wished it, making her blood fall into the shifting dust?

The Forbidden Path.

The Storyteller's warning rang in her ears, how she should not go there. Should never tread among its evil.

A carpet of blossom and thorns stretched toward her, a contradiction of pain and exquisite softness.

Waiting in the still air, Evie listened for her Storyteller, finding nothing. Already, her shadow extended the length of the path making the taller version of Evie the one to enter the place first. She might have been tempting herself forward.

Sod it, thought the girl. She would take the bloody invitation despite the stupid warning. Where was the Storyteller anyway? He wasn't exactly hanging around filling her head with advice.

Anyway, hadn't he said something about her ability to See things beyond the sight of others? So why shouldn't she welcome this into her senses? Perhaps the Storyteller was wrong.

Fear made the path more terrible, nothing more. Every branch and twig tainted with the stuff, turning even the smallest whisper of a leaf into a conspiracy against her.

Staring at the thorns and ancient dust, dry from centuries of living with its own death, Evie fought a sudden urge to escape.

'Adam.' A flash thought and she caught it before the word disappeared, then, 'leave.'

So her Storyteller had bothered to show up after all. But it didn't make any sense, hadn't he told her to accept these things as part of understanding herself?

Driven deeper along the path, a twisted contradiction of dirt, thorns and blossom crawled alongside each quick step.

Stumbling among trees; the terrible pressure of each limb clawed the raw surface of her skin, mocking her fate in the dizzying loop and twist of evergreens.

Bewildered Evie wheeled around, determined to escape the sharp clutch of twigs.

"Evie, I do not like this fear." His voice, pleading. Too late, Evie was terrified and could only watch helplessly as the path crawled toward its frozen target. A long sweep of tangled green seeking its inevitable claim.

Forced by the breeze holding itself against her, Evie fell into the deep coppice, eliminating her escape. Now, if the trees didn't take her, the path would.

"Are you doing this?" Knowing the answer Evie screamed the question anyway, terrified as the tangle of foliage closed around her face and arms.

"Evil here."

His voice, hitting the side of her head, miserable for her plight.

"Then make it stop!" but she knew had anything to do with her Storyteller.

"A bad place Evie, you should not have come."

She must run now, breathless through the undergrowth, breaking the green sinews that begged her fall.

'Adam.' Another flash thought. Why? He was just a story, where did he fit into any of this? And then desperately now, "Run, Evie, break through the trees."

Her skin was broken, the torn flesh on her arms and legs bleeding into the shifting green, as though in offering, her life might be redeemed.

She could see the clearing, beyond several ponds and a shallow ribbon of a stream that lead to the heroin hell of Orchard Park estate.

'Evelyn Edern.' Another one of those thoughts, her name, why? And where the hell was her friggin' Storyteller? He possessed magic, so he could make this shit stop, but he had disappeared, abandoning her.

Behind a cluster of thick oaks, a clearing teased the horizon, tormenting the need for escape. Sweeping downward, they might have sensed her plan, each branch seeming to untie the ivy so it sprang to life, crossing each tendril and producing another, stronger version.

But she must get through, it was the only way out.

'Finding.' Ignoring the thought, Evie ran faster, determined to crash through the line of trees. But if the girl was fast, they were faster, each branch threading every twig and leaf into a punishing weave, banishing her escape.

She had nowhere else to go. On all sides, ivy slipped forward, certain of their claim. Blood, staining the insides of both wrists fell into the ground.

Pitching into the thick bracken, clods of earth gave way sending her head first into the thicket, several thorns narrowly missing an eye. Dragging herself upwards, Evie fought to breathe against the force of a sudden gale and the hard rain that accompanied it.

Blood traveling across the side of her face ran to the edge of her mouth and she drank it, refusing its descent onto the terrible earth.

Sprinting headlong into the storm Evie broke toward the threat of branches poised to strike her courage.

"Adam, find."

Then bursting through Evie's head in a torrent of words, "his name, it will stop. Adam, stop." Then finally, "Shout, it will stop! Adam, call, shout, Evie!"

Stupid, nonsense messages pushing into her head.

A story told in dreams of an infant whose last breath was stolen by the solid crush of wet earth. She had called his name then in desperate sorrow as the secret orchard escaped her and in desperation now, would call it again.

"Adam!"

Hurled around the trees, Evie braced for the impact of her head, slamming into the trunk of an oak and when nothing happened, fell onto the damp grass anyway. Unable to explain the soft presence of a pink tide washing the declining sun behind the line of trees, she lay still.

Unscathed with no trace of the blood ripped from her skin and into the earth, Evie made a cautious study of the bizarre transformation. Gone too was the ivy, returned to the trees, their tendrils permanent tenants of the soft bark beneath. And the thorns, they too had gone, retreating to the walls and ancient bracken, their creamy petals of blossom intact.

"You did this, why?" Furious, Evie screamed into the bucolic scene. He had made everything happen, playing with her mind, possessing her imagination and fears of this place.

He had warned her never to venture onto this path, he had tested her and she had failed. But so what, the stupid Storyteller was no different than her mother or drunk uncle Colin in his cruelty.

Angry with herself anyway for falling for his stupid entrapment, Evie chewed the inside of her mouth. Of course he wasn't afraid of anything that could happen, when you had the power to bleed thoughts, what could you possibly be afraid of?

Well thank God there was nobody about, she must have looked like the insane let loose flailing about like that. Self consciously Evie ran both hands down the length of her skirt. It should be wrecked, the long layers of diaphanous fabric torn to shreds, but there was nothing wrong with it, not even a crease. The white top with the scoop neckline was okay too, the tiny embroidered lavender stalks intact. Nothing made sense. She should be staring at a wreckage of herself. Even her hair lay perfectly straight, casting a dark shadow against her shoulders. She brushed it with her left hand, attempting to understand its present untangled state.

Her watch had gone.

Glancing at her empty wrist, Evie cursed her Storyteller. Her mother had given it to her a few Christmases ago, an act of generosity when she usually got nothing. Throat tight, Evie imagined the sorry little scenario if the woman discovered its loss. She would have to make something up, thought Evie, she had no choice.

Yeah, between the hallucinations and the lies, the Storyteller's presence was turning out to be really frigging useful. Searching through the thick grass, Evie kicked the blades apart, muttering in anger when nothing turned up and cursing her Storyteller back to the darkness he came from. Pressing through the dense thicket Evie entered the woods again.

A rabbit darted across the clearing, its white puff tail the last to disappear beneath the hedge. Somewhere a wood pigeon settled in for the evening, its gentle sound resonating across the trees. No, there was nothing to fear here unless you were the sort of person for whom a soft carpet of green and the pink wash of an evening sky filled you with screaming horror.

Scanning the history of each panicked footfall, Evie stared hard at the entire area but the search yielded nothing. Everything including the watch had disappeared.

She couldn't see any point in going any further, already an evening breeze possessed the sky and the sun had taken a final dip behind the deadly trees. She must admit defeat, go home and lie about the gift she had been given. Never one to give up that easily, Evie threw a final glance toward the tall grass and oak trees. She saw him then, a figure in the centre of the clearing.

He startled her, this man and the way he stared across the space toward her, watching. His shoes were muddy and the long black coat flapping in dirty folds from his body might have been dragged through the dirt for hours. More than that though, she recognized him, the man with the cracked neck. He had been on the path before.

Now would be a good time to throw up.

His eyes sought her fear, finding it against the grip fastened against Evie's silent throat.

His presence, a perfect encore to what had taken place just minutes earlier, a siren scratching the suspended air pressed against her ears.

Then he had gone. She hadn't even blinked. He had simply vanished faster than it was possible to see the disappearance.

Wanting nothing more of the place, Evie scurried along the narrow strip of black gravel separating the tangle of brambles and weeds on either side. Crossing the threshold bordering suburban pavement and dark earth, Evie stepped at last onto the safe relief of the street and prepared her return home.

Only once did she glimpse back toward the path, her thoughts binding to the further most corner of the now dark space, compelling her to hesitate in spite of urgency.

Positioned in the same place she stood just moments earlier, he stared through the early darkness, piercing her eyes.

Real or imaginary she felt it then, the purity of his intent as the silent communication passed between them. He despised her, this man and the knowledge impaled Evie's breath to her throat.

She ran then, turning away, needing to know no more.

Chapter Thirteen

"Find me. Seek my voice and take its life into your soul. Move forward, accepting the breath that touches this dark air and know me here. Trust your eyes, permit the adjustment to this darkness and they will See as before. Rise to my voice and let my feed take place within your mind so you can come to me again and forget this anger that makes you resist me now. Breathe slowly, the way I have shown you. It is necessary and I make you want this, absorbing your senses into mine.

"Understand, I had nothing to do with what happened among the fields, so breathe through the anger stalking its memory and the fear of what you saw. The figure in the clearing and at the edge of the path, watching, despising the curiosity that drew him out.

"The earth beneath that place wants your fear, and the poison scratch of each leaf as it touches your skin feeds you with the knowledge of its darkness. It longs for the nourishment of your panic and I wish I could walk alongside you then, but your fear is my intolerable pain and I must abandon you to yourself, sending quick thoughts, my only ability.

"Stay strong, courage is the enemy among fear. You have no choice but to follow and my words push you forward, one careful step at a time. And I am in you and see the way through your eyes, giving this place to you in my secret talk.

"Open your mind Evie, hear the stones shift beneath your feet, the only sound permitted into this silence. And feel these stones, hundreds, thousands of them, fighting against your skin. I can make their soles bleed and I do.

"Watch, cast your eyes down at the only color inviting itself into this place. Crimson. There is pain in this too, much discomfort, I know, because I give it to you. Its delicious response sustains me and I return more of the same, holding your wounds against the earth that seeks its claim. I could take this away but will not, could make this journey easier but choose not to.

"Instead I give you this, my suffering, my anger and the pain you delivered into my heart when you entered that Forbidden Place. Your accusations, that it was I who did those things, that I would harm you that way, after I had pulled your trust into me, taking your soul into mine forever.

"But it was you. Evie recall who you are, a Seer, drawing spirits to your eyes, both good and bad alike. Everything was you, I would not lower myself to such a display of trickery. And you understand now how that path knows your uncontrollable fear, playing its razor edge against your imagination and your ability to See beyond the veneer of things. You must never return there, ever, or until my voice calls you into its space, but never in the physical sense. Always you will go like this, and I will give you all you need to know.

"I could kill you for what you did. However, your fear and the journey toward its core was honest and you took the words I gave you, tearing Adam's name from your thoughts and into reality, so ending the terrible illusion you created for yourself. In dreams, in my feed and my desires, the figure you saw will not come here. I would not bring him to you.

"But he waits on that path, and always with your return in mind. He too knows your curiosity, understands your fear of that place and its effect on me, that I am driven from you then, that I cannot protect you. His hate for you is as pure as my love for you and as dangerous.

"Yes, rise to this knowledge and absorb its truth with neither challenge or question. Take this also. I will hurt you for your own protection if you fail to obey me. Better from he who loves you than the one who would slip from behind your shadow to cause you harm.

"Evie, these wounds are deep and in your pain, you wish to stop, but I push you forward, it is my will.

"And I want this pain, sweeter because it is yours, and it makes me stronger. I will go deep into your core and give you everything this night if you suffer me this, your walk upon these tiny knives. I want your blood to make history with this dark earth and for you to remember.

"You know this game, have waited for its dance inside your soul. I am real to you now and you know this, I can tell. Your breath pouring as I trace the edge of my fingers against the bare flesh of your shoulders. Lean into me further, know my form. Learn how I feel against you, solid now, as you wanted, as your desires said this must be.

"Walk with me, believe in what you See and hear, and do not fear this. Remember Evie, you must not be afraid of what takes place between us, the visions I place into your mind. But it is the taste of your pleasure I desire now.

"Take my hand, become aware of its pressure against your skin, and walk through here, beneath the crumbled arch and the shield of ivy, guardian to what lies beyond. Walk now; invade their quiet secret and the soft hush of grass beneath your feet.

"You are no stranger here; its life breathes toward you, pulsing with the blood of your history and the stretch of time reaching toward you, drawing you to a place you once dwelt. This garden of time, suspended, waiting for your return. It is safe here; it will always be safe in this place.

"Observe Evie, the mound of earth, fresh from Adam's betrayal, I give this to you. All of this is yours. Fall to your knees, thread the cold of each green blade between your fingers, push your hands into the fresh earth and understand. He waits.

"Watch as the scene transforms, unfolding above the canopy of white petals you lie beneath. Observe their gentle descent, falling like quiet snow to their death against the edge of your mouth. Accept the flow of this sweet drink; let it nourish the life that longs to exist again.

"Find me, Evie, find me in the depths of yourself, in the broken earth held between your fingers and in the blood that feeds your soul. Rise to my voice at last, I want to live in your existence. Slip behind the words and fall now into this changing space of life and death.

"Carefully, I lift you from this earth, away from the changing seasons and the rain that seeks your skin. Your transformation too, as you move toward me, not as you are now but in your becoming, the dark length of your hair, the pale slope of your shoulders, the shape of hips and thighs, formed now, untouched save for the hands that draw you toward me.

"Let the serious play you desire, begin."

Chapter Fourteen

*T*he scene changes rapidly, season after season of rainfall and petals. We don't get wet and I don't marvel at this either because it doesn't feel as though we should be touched by things such as these. It all seems beyond me, as I become aware of his hands on my shoulders and my eyes wanting his face, and I am reminded of a time when I was pulled into him this way. I think I wanted it then. I know I want it now.

His mind voice tells me to trust and to lean into him. And I do. Slowly I move inward and feel the full weight of his presence push against me, wrapping me within the length of his coat. I think we are moving now because I am surrounded by a light breeze but feel nothing of this motion, except a delicate cold against my face.

"Where are we going?"

The question breathes through me, although I don't care about the answer, and there is none anyway. Instead I am held close against the long black folds of his coat. I recognize the feel of this, the exquisite softness and recall we have been here before, he and I.

It is dark here, very dark, our destination. Our arrival into this thick black nowhere. Willing him not to move away, an overwhelming fear of falling further into this nowhere place, alone, discarded. But trust is needed, this I sense, without it there is nothing, and I am unsure if I think this through him, or if my own thoughts exist still.

Everything is mixed up, his thoughts and mine as I become less aware of myself as I was and more as I am now, surrounded.

And he is everywhere while remaining in place, holding, no, pushing against me as though fearing my escape. One gloved palm cradling the back of my head, the length of his fingers lost behind thick strands of my hair while the other lays across the center of my back in an upward sweep to the base of my shoulder blades.

And where would I run to in this darkness? Besides, I am enjoying this, this play of his fingers upon me, within me.

Yes, they could be within me, these fingers, his hands beneath my skin, into my core, pushing inexplicably into my soul.

I lean in, no, he is drawing me closer, impossibly closer, and I am breathless, but I breathe in the pure warmth of him. And my hands, my own trembling hands pull the fabric at the top of his coat, searching for the flesh beneath. His presence is larger than the void in which we exist and I am aware of his breath sliding in hot waves across the back of my neck. I become aware of his hands also, as they spread out and around to the thin edge of my collarbone, his fingers tracing the surface of my flesh when it is his I so badly want to taste.

This is so confusing. I am so confused. How can this be? His breath, his hands, the force of him weaving through every sinew, running with my blood, surrounding completely. And his fingers, the ends of his fingers, impossibly on both sides of me, beneath my flesh. I cannot describe how I want this endless pulse and surge through him, into and beneath my skin.

My hands pushing at his shoulders, dragging the heavy fabric backwards reveal the creamy flesh of his neck and shoulders as they extend from the low scoop of his shirt. White, impeccable against our darkness.

How I want this neck, at the side where it meets the shoulders, want my fingers to pull and twist through the length of his hair lying in careless waves along the back. Please allow me to sink my teeth into you, as you run your fingers beneath my skin, let me kiss and taste your flesh and be in you as you are in me.

I remember Adam, through this spinning confusion, I recall the child beneath the earth and the deliberate darkness of blood spilled onto the ground where he lay. I see a young man too, lying beneath the protection of the tree, and the rain turning each blossom red. His mouth open, smiling, accepting, loving every drop.

I want his blood.

Want to drink the blood from this being who has delivered me into darkness so I can remember the history of my path. And I want to understand, seeking knowledge through the flesh and blood of his body. I taste, taste the warmth of him upon my lips, searching with my mouth and tongue to discover the perfect place to make that final push inwards, to do something I have never thought of before but which my soul desperately needs now. To take him into me, the only way that makes sense.

I don't know if I am equipped for this endeavor but continue anyway, finding the critical artery to take this essence into me. I am not disgusted at myself for needing this, and feel its anticipation run with the electrical impulse of his touch, pushing down until I can no longer breathe.

So I push my mouth, hard into his neck and bite, and push further, not sure how to do this and not caring. Does he want this? I don't know. Does he want me to break into him in this way? I am aware suddenly that I haven't asked. Then with a sharp clarity which I believe is from him, my concern is countered. It doesn't matter. My manners, this time, have been forgiven.

His hand still rests against the back of my head, encouraging the thing I need to do, while the other pushes open the top of my gown, leaving two deep rose tinted ribbons torn apart, stranded at either side of the opening. My own hands are around his neck and the back of his head, finding, wanting.

And that gloved hand, that unbearably soft gloved hand of his that has dispatched the ribbons at the top of this gown now traces each full outline below, moving, touching until I could die. And I am aware of him watching me, green eyes stalking my face, watching as I work the creamy flesh against my tongue.

Words breathing through me, rising from the depths of my soul.

"Bend your blood to my mouth."

And he does, yielding toward my urge to take the blood that comes. I push further, his blood, warm, taking my mouth, my tongue, my chin and the flesh of my neck, and I am so thankful he gives himself to me like this. In flesh, in blood, in my mouth, into my throat and into my soul at last, flowing, streaming into me.

And I drink, I drink, and he pushes me closer to him, holding me captive to his release, the pressure of his stare urging me to take this vital fluid. And I do. God forgive me but I want this and tilt his head slightly, better access there. I swallow each essential drop as it leaves his body, entering mine in a long, slow drink.

Removing the hand from its position at the back of my head, he traces a pathway down the side of my neck, slow to my shoulders where it rests, grazing the surface of my skin and splintering white light through the blackness. The other hand lies against my breastbone, massaging that strip of flesh running between. He is reaching in and in, searching for, finding and finally touching my soul.

Searing hot, the heat from this pain comes quick, scorching my quest for pleasure, its flame lapping and feeding to fuel its gain. His blood is hot too, blazing the edge of my tongue as I attempt to clear the wounds I caused in my need.

Trying to step back, I tear myself away, yet he is there too, withholding my escape and I become aware for the first time of the danger living within him. As I struggle for each hot breath, I understand I have taken too much, straying from boundaries unseen.

This, I realize is his reminder, that he is capable of delivering more but chooses not to. Yet for my sake and perhaps his, he does not wish to destroy me.

Instead he chose me, inviting me into his loneliness, and long ago I accepted this invitation without question, loving his attention, the lavish turns of phrase and conversation, seeking him out in my mind, in my thoughts, wanting him there, always. It is possible to almost remember this, as I sting within the heat of his grip.

Is he waiting for some response, staring at me like that? Hard, clear eyes, capable of both kindness and alarming malevolence, the seductive bow of his red mouth sad, as he searches the contours of my face for an answer.

And I discover this in the blood he has given me. In the wound against the flesh of his neck and the scarlet strands that escaped my eager tongue and discovered the untouched line of his poet's shirt, destroying its purity.

I feel ashamed, despite the lick of flame within my lungs, I am ashamed of my selfish act, tearing into this being who can enter my skin, exist within me. My remorse is total, tearing my insides, I had thought only of myself and I am sorry for it.

His eyes change. Still bright, penetrating the darkness but without malice, and the mouth, brooding, is quiet. But his thoughts no longer exist within mine, instead we exist separately, he and I, and I feel the desertion, mourn the separation of his fingers running into my veins.

The furnace that invaded my soul disappears, his grip withdrawing from my chest in a final blaze of heat, as though pushing back through flesh and bone. For one moment of pain and grief, I fear he might hold my soul within his hands and search his face for hatred, a shred of evidence that he is in possession of what was mine.

I find none, he would not punish me that way.

Quiet descends upon us, greater than before, and I believe I should be still, waiting for his what must come next within this endless dark.

A faint smile.

Slowly the sulky play around the edges of his mouth disappears and his voice returns to the silence. I experience the reassuring circle of his presence hold me within this nothing.

Everything is slow. His hands, drawing me inwards, cradle the sides of my head and I am conscious of the familiar invasion delivering me to my knees in this alliance with my mind, my imagination, all of me.

It hurts this, but his eyes tell me I need it, that I must become stronger so I might some day understand. Unlike the near suffocation of my soul, there is no warning behind this gesture, only kindness and the concern that I should know.

Flashes, incomprehensible disconnected flashes of faces and rooms, occurring too quickly to withdraw any real sense, but always he is there. And then his voice, for the first time in this place, he speaks. The soft, clear tones reach forward as the sensuous curve of his mouth touches mine and his breath pours into me.

"Your dreams are my survival."

"I know this! I know where I have seen it, a long time ago. I know you!"

I know him. I am confused, how could I know of him for so long, yet not? I want to say as much but cannot as his mouth, his tongue searches mine, smothering the pain inside my head. But I understand some of what is there, "My Storyteller," I breathe into him and push myself against this figure whom I have waited so long to finally touch and see.

My secret entity, stealing darkness with his tapestry of stories and poems woven into the fabric of midnight and beyond. Soothing my nightmares with words and caresses so beautiful I would wish the morning away and pray for the darkness of sleep where we would keep company in the images I created of him. While others thought I had gone mad, no one understood me more than my beloved Storyteller.

My hands trace the sides of his neck. I want to touch the soft skin, feel its realness against my own. No trace remains of the wound I created and instead feel the pulse of his blood beneath my touch. And in the midst of wondering how this is possible, with his hands on the side of my head, I understand that it did not occur. That the blood rush into the back of my throat was an image, a powerful intercourse with his imaginings, my desires and his concerned willingness to manipulate the perception. He gave me what I wanted, despite how this extraction could leave him weak, giving him no choice but to trap me within the flame of his heat while he gained strength once more.

I no longer know what is real and tears press against my eyes. I had felt it, felt the dance of its warmth tease my throat.

In my confusion I rise toward him again and it is him I want to do the taking now. From me. Everything.

His breath, moving through my veins and into my heart. Then the breathtaking pierce of his entry into my soul, drawing me further inward, touching my shoulders, seeking the opening at the embroidery of my white gown.

Flowers, I recall, tiny silk rose buds wrapped in pink thread. Mouth on my shoulders, kissing the skin and it is his tongue this time that discovers my flesh. Moving with his free hand each of the lace shoulder straps, they fall to my arms, each abandoned to a crooked angle.

Before was play. When I drew his blood, he was playing, amused by my desperate act of need and want until impatient and a little sad, I suffered the return through my soul, a reminder of his strength.

A hand enters the opening and I understand his intention, want him there, to feel the tips of his fingers against me. He does and I am gasping, breathing the black air, taking it into my lungs forever.

It is so powerful this feeling, much better than the drink. I can hardly stand and want the fall into him. His lips, his mouth, his tongue, each one in turn, pulling, tugging, sucking, taking from me.

I am dizzy and I start to fall, his arms protecting me while his mouth still drinks.

That's what it is, the overwhelming, pleasurable extraction, a touch so powerful my breasts could fill for his need, and I hold his head there, willing him to take each nipple between his greedy lips and drink and drink. And I feel his tongue, caressing, encouraging more liquid to the surface, delivering breathtaking painful ecstasy within me. And his gloved hand, that soft leather bound gloved hand, with its long fingers, possessed of such sublime dexterity, pushes inwards, then squeezes, playing and scratching across the surface. From somewhere, I hear myself cry from the raw perfection of this pleasure and watch, dazed as the milk from each swollen breast is drawn into his mouth and between the ends of his fingers.

We are still falling and I no longer care. I am protected by the strength of him and the many layers of this ecstasy which supports my descent. His fingers work into my mouth, lying across my tongue so I might taste this sweetness bound within the delicious scent of leather.

I work at his fingers, my tongue pushing down between each one, tasting myself for the first time, while he takes my other hard, pink nipple between his lips and extracts, beautifully, painfully, taking me into his mouth, inviting me into his blood.

"Fall into him."

The words in my dazed head.

He knows, can feel them, understands and drinks harder, taking so much of me it might be everything.

My heart pounding, I feel this substance pour from me into him. I am in him. I run with him, race through him, I am in every sinew, every bone. In him, his body, on the inside, staring at my passion through his eyes. My gown lost to the waist, soft against my stomach, watching the lines of milk down each breast, feeling the edge of his tongue stroke the pale skin, wasting nothing, tasting the hot pinkness as I am received against his throat.

Warm, wanted.

His mouth on mine, this beautiful mouth.

Heat rushing into me, hurling me back into myself. I want to cry. Cry for the overwhelming confusion of him in me and I in him.

I am lifted, arms around my waist, held against the black air he stares deep through my eyes, into my head, as if to say, 'wasn't that better, my way?' Amused by the seriousness of his game, a smile plays against the corners of his mouth.

I realize the coat has gone, when? And for the first time discover the length of his legs pressed against my thighs. I am aware too of his hands against my skin, moving, pushing beyond the useless fabric at my waist, to the wetness that lies between, waiting.

Returning the favor, my nails push into his back and again the light in his eyes dance. He likes this, my coming to him, breathless save for the occasional cry to push further, deeper.

We are lying now and he, the observer of my rolling pleasure stares downwards, curling damp strands of hair behind my ears with his free hand, pressing his lips against each closed eye, for this is too much.

The pressure in my thighs drifts into my throat and I am wet from the sex he has given me, moving deeper, feeling for and touching my pulse.

Sit up, lean into him, lean far back gripping, tugging at the buttery leather wrapping his legs. One arm reaching across me, hand inside, the other around my waist, holding me still.

Making me ready.

I am ready.

Feel the deep shudder from within that tells me this and want to lie back, to take this through my whole body. But he won't let me just yet. He is still building the final rush and I struggle to believe the effect it has within me.

Breathe with his breath, with the rise and fall of his chest. Take deep, pleasure seeking breaths, pushing into my core, slowly. Hand against my heart, he regulates each beat. Not too fast, but slowly, let the feeling rise.

His tongue sliding inwards, hard, claiming the tip of mine, and my heart accelerating, the strange sensation of him pushing it slower while the edges of his fingers slip between our mouths, yet still they move within me.

Sex against our tongues, warm, ready.

He knows this. Understands it is the final straw.

"Evie."

My name breathed into existence, the sound slipping from his tongue into me. My pleasure screams against his lips, biting the skin as my climax tears into our souls. My pulse against him, as skillfully he pushes back, just enough to sustain this soul wrenching ecstasy.

Horizontal.

My fingers tearing into his flesh.

Wetness, and the sweat mixing with the heat of his tongue circling the pale flesh of my stomach.

Rolling backward, the final wave falls away. One final arch of my back, my hips and it is gone and I am aware of a quick thrust of pain afterwards.

His hands touching my face, both of them sweet, sticky.

He lies with me, this lover, he and I, a vague throbbing between my legs.

The cotton gown is pulled upwards, hands replacing the wayward straps at each shoulder. Carefully he reties the little pink bow as I lie still, loving him for this, breathing, recovering. Never can I recall feeling this cared for, this safe.

Leaning in as before, arms possessing me, aware of a slow breathing against my neck, warm. I am told to look and I do.

Silk. Beautiful, shimmering ivory colored silk, heavy, expensive, the finest. How?

Don't ask. Does it really matter, after all that has happened, in this strange place of nowhere? It graces the middle of my thighs, this luxury and I notice a small split on one side, a purpose for which I am aware so long as I remain in his company, and I feel the trace of a smile play across my mouth. Taking my hand, he slips it down the length of this fabric and I feel each contour slowly rise and fall beneath my touch and his.

I don't want to leave this place of darkness. Want to stay where I am safe, away from everything. Where the hurt does not exist, where the bruises slammed into my mind are healed, taking with it, sorrow, anger, pain, and above all, betrayal.

My sorrows, my uncontrollable sorrows, speak through my eyes, falling like quiet rain onto my face. Already I feel a longing brought by an absence yet to occur. So close this contact, drifting within him, calm breaths rising and falling inside. His thoughts in mine, forging me to him.

My Storyteller, my enigma, my eternal lover, feeding me with stories and images, charming my desires, crafting my reality.

Safe, lulled, within folds of dark cashmere, arms sustaining my presence against him, the edge of his fingers reaching into the core of my mind.

Sleep, I feel its power, fight against its strength, afraid to collapse into myself that way. The warmth of him pushing me down, telling me not to fight. I can give into this, it is safe here.

Wonderful, this tranquility, his presence drowning my fears as slowly his hands rest against my eyes, slipping his fingers across each one, closing them and delivering peace, welcome and deep.

So charismatic.

Such stories and visions, slipping between shadows. Forever careful with his small temptations, beckoning my sleep toward dreams. Willingly I rise toward him, await the jolt and slam of his thoughts into mine.

Familiar this feeling, paralyzed before my breath comes again, opening the path to my imagination where he feeds respectfully so I don't completely lose my mind in this sleep. Bearing the pull inside my head and the subtle persuasions, I am carried closer and inevitably toward him.'

Chapter Fifteen

". . . .the body of Christ, who died for you. . . " Called to the Cross with Maureen and the new additions of Cell Phone Pam and Creepy Chris, Evie accepted the warm offering into the back of her throat, the taking of His blood. She pictured her entity, willing the dark liquid to be more than fruit juice most likely purchased from the soft drinks aisle at Safeway.

This Sunday she hadn't been paying much attention to anything, her mind in other places as Evie thought of her Storyteller, his frequent word-gifts and the power of his presence. He was real, she knew it, his feed and existence unquestionable. He had taken away her fear of madness, replacing it with the wonderful depth of needing him. He was alive within her soul, treading among thoughts, shaping her desires.

A perfect distraction.

Her entity, a secret breathing within her head.

The memory, branding the history of his presence against her core caused Evie to literally forget where she was. Shoved to the back in the limp scuffle choreographed mostly by pensioners clutching beige and off white, square shaped handbags with brass clasps, and those still clinging to plastic raincoats despite the presence of an adequate roof keeping the September drizzle on the outside, Evie prepared to meet her fate.

Craning her neck up and down the line, Evie counted heads. A half dozen waited to be served before her, all squashed together in a similar fashion.

Shifting from one knee to the other, she fell against a man with three strands of hair placed carefully across the top of his shiny head. Arrangement disturbed, a stray piece dangled across the top of his thick brown glasses, blocking his communion view.

"Sorry." Muttered Evie.

Gazing at the plain wooden cross, she considered the deep pain in both knees. Perhaps, this was how communion was supposed to feel. An absorption of Christ's suffering. But then, she counter argued more likely she was being punished, right here, in church and before God, given everything she had written lately.

That and her continued alliance with her Storyteller.

True, so far she hadn't been overwhelmed with head spinning revulsion on entering the building like you saw in horror movies. Usually those reactions lent themselves to substantial gothic structures, topped off by a couple of bug eyed gargoyles and a seriously tall spire, not crisp, modern churches with clean lines and glass door fronts like this one.

Still, it didn't mean she was off the hook and in some ways this was more personal, less dramatic, requiring none other than Evie in its involvement. Nevertheless, at least she was still capable of entering the place, for now anyway. So perhaps she was in line for some sort of redemption after all, provided she took the Body and the Blood and the two inch dent in her knees without complaint.

Evie wondered what the Storyteller would make of all this. He never did come to church, in the five months since giving her his haunt he never followed her inside, making it the one place where he was quiet. Where, reflected Evie, she could bury herself in prayer, find peace and ultimately beg for forgiveness on a weekly basis.

"Our Father who art in heaven," the Lord's Prayer, "hallowed be thy name. . ." Evie swallowed each word as she did every week and waited, as she did each time, for her soul to ascend just like the angels suspended against the stained glass windows. Were she to die now, would she go to heaven? And she closed her eyes tighter attempting to forge a glimpse, but no, she didn't think so.

". . . lead us not into temptation . . ." the prayer continued, rising above the collection of bowed heads.

"… and deliver us from all evil. … "

"Lead us not into temptation..." She was struck by that line, pondering its meaning. Hadn't she been there already, into temptation? And didn't she court it still?

She was considering the implication of this courtship during the announcement of the final hymn and felt herself dragged to her feet by Chris, his sudden touch burrowing beneath her sweater and into her skin.

"God, Evie, you're so slow!"

"Deliver us from all evil." The other bit stuck in her head forged the same analysis every time she heard it. A lot could be riding on this. The prayer specifically stated, "all evil," meaning everything, not just select bits, or the things you wouldn't want to do anyway, like kill someone, or bury someone alive. She thought of Adam, lying cold beneath the black earth, knowing.

"All evil."

The phrase pressed against her mind. Was it wrong to take the gift of his blood? Drawing the flesh at the side of his neck to her mouth and accepting the welcome release against her tongue, wanting more. But if her Storyteller was evil, did she want deliverance? Did she want to be deprived of his delicious seduction and the talks they held in confidence?

He was the only one who understood her now, the only one she talked to and in return he let her See things, providing visions and glimpses while he fed, her response nourishing his needs. The more he took, the stronger he became and the more she wanted, driving his desires even further. And so the cycle continued, except in church, a confirmation perhaps that he was evil.

Still, Evie concluded, as she had for several months, she wanted him to remain, vampire to her reality, driving him deeper inside, binding her soul to his. Yes, she would pray each week for forgiveness, seeking solace in prayer for the rest of her life if necessary, but no, she could never live without him, her eternal Storyteller.

They were making small talk and shaking hands with the minister at the entrance to the dim foyer. Evie, one foot pushed over the threshold hoped to signal her Storyteller that church was finished and she was his to do with as he saw fit for the rest of the day.

"How are you?" The question, of course aimed at Chris, the opinion of Evie not mattering a jot.

"Oh, I'm fine." He smiled, lips dividing his thin face so that it might have been hacked part way through with a sword, dark red tongue floating against the edge of his yellow teeth. Dear God, Evie hated him.

Evie stared at the Reverend Shrapton, who at a little over six feet placed her mother in plump miniature. Peasant stock, her grandmother, she had forgotten on whose side, told Evie once. Predispositioned to work the fields or crawl beneath oily machines come the Industrial Revolution.

Looking at the minister, Evie tried placing his frame into some sort of historical context, noting how it resembled an endless river flowing beneath the length of blue robes trailing across the tile floor. And his hair was the sort where it was difficult to tell if it was blonde or a very light shade of red.

"So everything's working out swimmingly then?" Furrowing his brow, Shrapton appeared to care. "Gossip at dinner, that's all" thought Evie to herself. She was unimpressed.

"And Christopher, I do believe you're very good with numbers, perhaps your presence here might manage to perform some small miracle with the budget. We might get our new roof after all."

Shrapton and Evie's mother giggled, Chris joining in, keen to insert himself into the expanding Edern clan. Pamela, arm against Maureen threw an obligatory laugh. She had only started going to church recently and was already the life and soul of the Ladies

Circle, collecting magazines for the various protest groups and serving fruit cake after the Family Service every second Sunday of the month.

Oh here we go. Thought Evie.

"A welcome addition to the fold."

Oh yeah, she thought again, *Chris with a criminal amount of body odor and who smoked with his greasy head hanging out of Elaine's old bedroom window. Very religious.*

On balance, the whole affair, at least from Evie's perspective had been a certified flop. To all appearances he had been weaned onto quadratic equations at around six months and had been ingesting numbers ever since. Each evening after class, he doodled mathematical phrases onto scraps of paper then casually left them lying around so everyone thought him thoroughly clever. The net effect meant sudden amnesia when it came to asking him to ferry his plate to the sink or make sure his room stayed clean. Of course, this meant Evie picked up the slack, emptying Chris's ash tray and sorting through his stale laundry. It made her sick just thinking about it.

"It must be lovely to be that clever." Evie's mother laughed with Shrapton, obviously discussing Chris and his mental prowess.

"Yes, it all sounds rather jolly actually and such a wonderful impression for Evie."

Again Evie pictured Chris with his head sticking out of Elaine's old bedroom window, smoking, dark, greasy hair flapping in the evening breeze. Oh yeah, he made an impression alright, representing the pinnacle of her aspirations.

Turning his back to the family and locking the foyer doors, it appeared as though the conversation was over. Relieved, Evie prepared to get the heck back home and to her Storyteller.

"And how's your job at the boutique or whatever it is, Evie?"

He seemed determined not to let them go.

"Fine."

Forcing a thin smile, Evie jabbed the toe of her right shoe into the black tarmac, feeling its impact shimmer into the offended ankle. Catching the girl's attitude, Maureen flashed a look of reproach, the woman swooping in for damage control.

"Oh, she loves it. L-ov-e-s it! Don't you Evelyn?" Laughed Maureen a little too high. "I can never get our Evelyn to look up. Look up when you're being spoken to Evelyn. The only time she takes her eyes off the floor is when she's either puttin' them in a book or to stare at a picture. You should have seen the face on her when she realized I wasn't gettin' an art student to live in the house. I never heard the last of it."

They left then, Evie practically dragged out of the building by both Cell-Phone Pam and Evie's mother.

"Well, Evie, you've done it again, made me look like a friggin' idiot. Honest to God, why you couldn't have walked off the top of that cathedral on your fifth birthday I'll never bloody know. If Elaine was alive she'd at least appreciate Chris. She was good at math. At five, she could count to ten."

Turning toward the hideous student, Maureen shrugged her shoulders as though apologizing for the death of one daughter and the life of another.

"Our Evelyn, she's so stupid. We always knew there was something wrong with her, talking into thin air at the age of nine months. There was never anybody there, but my mother always said the child was a living sin. I mean anybody born with black and blonde hair has to be born evil and it certainly showed itself the day her father dragged her sister off that roof. And do you think Evie stopped it? No, she was too busy chasing after a friggin' feather to be bothered.

They were walking down Eden Park Avenue, the four of them, Chris having moved to the front, Maureen and Pamela side by side with Evie trailing between the two of them.

"Are you listening Evelyn?"

The girl's stomach flipped dangerously and she felt sick. It was going to be one of those afternoons, she could tell.

She was selfish, very selfish for always thinking of herself and would burn in hell to be sure. But then she was evil to the core, born with coal black eyes and black and blonde hair, what normal child of God was born looking like that? Maureen restated. No bloody wonder the girl would never amount to anything. "Sell shoes, it's all you're friggin' well fit for."

Beneath it all, behind the terrible pressure, Evie screamed for her Storyteller, tearing his name through her head, begging his presence to come forward. She felt dark inside and was losing herself fast, sinking into a blackness different from the gentle depths to which he took her.

"Where are you?" She muttered aloud finally.

"What?" Maureen interrupted.

"Nothing." Replied the stricken girl. Sick from everything, she wanted to lie down, to accept the gentle pull inside her head.

"Do not worry, Evie, I am here."

His voice at last, piercing the despair. She could stop sinking now and re-emerge without fear. The lavender came next and slowly she took it into her senses, drowning everything.

"Who are you talking to?" Taking the front door key from her handbag, Maureen slipped it into the circular brass lock.

"You've been muttering to yourself a lot lately, are you on drugs? Because if I find out that you are..." The rest was lost to the hallway's interior as the front door swung open, revealing the dim center of the hallway.

They ate the usual for a Sunday lunch, boiled ham and cheese sandwiches. Under instruction, Evie took the remainder of the cheese, made sure everyone got their sandwich first and ended up with two slices of doughy bread, a scraping of margarine and a little white cheese for herself. But it hadn't mattered because lavender traced the edge of her senses, overtaking the smell of cold meats and withdrawing her slowly from the domestic scene.

After plunging her hands in and out of the hot water, Evie stacked the lunch plates and cups onto the dish strainer before making excuses to go upstairs. Pamela, Chris and Evie's mother were making plans to go out and by the sounds of it they didn't want Evie tagging along.

Left alone, thought Evie she might sit in quiet solitude to read and listen to the Storyteller without fear of anyone overhearing her replies.

Now, climbing to the top of the corner unit in her room, Evie set about retrieving Poems from the top shelf. Without notice, a hand clasped suddenly around the girl's extended free leg.

"You could do yourself an injury climbing about like that. You should be more careful. Lucky I happened to be walking by."

The light tones of his London accent, floated across the side of Evie's face, tossing words around in a freefall of inflection.

"Here, let me help you."

Reaching for the book, he retrieved the object from Evie's grasp, running his left hand up the length of her leg as he did so. Resting it in the centre of her thigh he swirled his fingers against the fabric of her jeans.

Midway between shelf and air, Evie had no idea what to do, this was an entirely new situation and it left her confused. If she jumped down, would he think her ill mannered? Actually, you could even argue that he was being nice.

In a foggy outpost of her mind, the Storyteller ranted. She had a headache.

Thanking him, Evie took Chris's weight against her back as he helped get her down. Now his hands pressed against her hips. Landing with her back against the bookcase Evie faced him, his right arm positioned casually against the book case frame. In his left hand Chris held the little book toward the girl. She went to take it.

"Wait a minute, you didn't say 'please'."

"Oh, sorry, please." Feeling stupid, Evie just wanted the book.

"May I."

"May I what?" Reaching forward she missed its edges as the volume snatched into retreat.

"Repeat after me, 'may I'."

"May I." Feeling ridiculed, Evie's face was hot.

"Have my."

She swallowed hard, "have my."

"Stupid fucking book back."

"What?" Flying his invisible rage, the Storyteller thundered against her head.

With each feed his strength increased so by day his voice was never far away. Now his fury leapt in a jumble of threats and curses, and for the first time, from the outside, beyond her mind.

Turning the book over in his hand, Chris studied the worn cover.

"Literature, eh? I didn't know you could read. Until now, I assumed you were just an uneducated little slapper. You must think you've really come up in the world. Keats, well I never would have guessed."

He might just as well have been fucking with fire, the Storyteller hurling invisible rage around them both while Chris told her 'Keats was a low class gay bastard who could only write if he wanked himself off first.'

"Give it to me, please."

Leaning further in, the length of his inside leg pushed hard against Evie's hips. Tossing the book onto the carpet he placed both arms to the sides of the girl's head, resting them against the bookcase.

"I shall kill him Evie, I promise." The entity's voice fell low against her ear.

Dizzy, her head throbbed, the Storyteller's rage punching the still air. If Chris only knew would he be like this now? Staring into the grey float of color washing his narrow eyes, Evie attempted to pierce his gaze.

"Give it to you? What is it that you want, the book, or something else?" Slowly, with his right hand he pushed against the space between her legs.

Struggling to control the tremble in her voice, Evie held her gaze. "The book."

The edge of his left hand followed the length of her neck. Speaking slowly, he breathed into her face, twirling the precious apple pendant between the tip of his thumb and index finger. "I'd rather it was something else, but you won't be alone long enough, if you catch my drift."

Kicking the little book into the centre of the room, he tore himself away.

"I'll just have to find another low class bitch to do it with. Pity really, I quite fancied 'aving a go, but one night, trust me, I'll make you feel really lucky. Oh, and by the way, I wouldn't say anything Evie, as bad as they are, we've all heard your stupid fucking stories, and as everybody knows I'm only interested in numbers. You don't want people to start calling you a liar, or fucking mentally ill. After all, you do make up some bizarre shit."

He left then, bouncing brightly down the stairs, slamming the front door behind him.

It took everything for Evie to persuade her Storyteller not to kill Chris. Furious, there was no gentle voice this time, the enraged power crashing around the pink room where Evie crouched against the bookcase, deprived of strength.

Head against a set of bunched up knees, she listened to the dangerous rantings, convinced an object would fall or something might crash. He reminded the girl of a verbal poltergeist, if such a thing existed.

"Stop it!" Unable to stand any more, she screamed into the busy, empty room.

"I will kill him Evie. I shall turn his thoughts into chaos."

"Didn't you hear me? I said stop it. I'm ordering you to stop this or go away!"

Silence. The sudden quiet pounding against the sides of her head. Perhaps he had returned to the peace of his darkness to brood and sulk before emerging again.

"No, I am still here."

Close, he might have been beside her, kneeling, staring into her worried face. Evie turned toward the direction of his voice.

"So you would have me banish myself into darkness for the purpose of sulking? I am not a child, temperamental perhaps, but not a child."

"I thought I made you angry because I asked you to stop shouting."

"I was selfish in my response, please forgive my behavior. I am not angry with you, and no, you did not order me to stop Evie, you cannot order me to do anything. I do as I please. I am with you now because it pleases me, less so because I must."

"You scare me when you talk like that."

"Why?" His voice moved closer.

"Because it means you're uncontrollable, you can do exactly as you wish, including the kill if you want it."

"I want only to protect you."

"From what?"

He sighed then, a deep, soul wrenching sigh of despair that she didn't get it, that after everything he had done and said, he had failed to reach her understanding.

"I'm sorry." Tears spilled onto her face. His, she knew and she let them fall, waiting for the moment when he would speak again.

"I must be patient, you could not possibly know everything yet and I do not expect you to. Each feed makes me stronger and you have given me so much, sustaining me now so that I may exist, as you have already noticed, for short periods beyond your thoughts.

"But with each feed, you too are changing, faster even than I anticipated. It is how you hear me, my presence for the moment beside you. My voice touching each particle of air you breathe so you can draw me in."

She felt it then, his unseen presence braced softly against her shoulder, a wisp of pressure, barely noticeable had she not known of his existence. Was he kneeling beside her? Slowly she turned toward the careful weight, and found herself shocked by the vacant space beside her.

"But I am here, right beside you. Do not imagine I have gone. For now, I will leave this Chris whose life you seem to cherish. But believe me, if again he dishonors you, I shall kill him and enjoy my small journey into his thoughts. Driving him insane with my images and hallucinations will be a pleasure, the panic of his response, a delicacy."

He seemed a little disappointed that he must postpone setting the idea in motion. Perhaps he would sooner have Chris return and idly brush her shoulder so he might taste the fear in his thoughts.

"Evie my love, remove your concerns, of me there is no fear, I have sworn myself to protect you. But the deaths I have pleasure in delivering and I wish to taste his death. Although you cannot will me to your wishes, I seek your approval, it nourishes my strength also.

"Remember, at my choosing I can turn all of you over to me. Sadness, Evie, take the sadness I have for you and pour it into your soul."

"But I don't want to cry."

Heavy sobs threatened her throat, his sadness for what must come and the slow appreciation that Chris meant harm.

Shivering, she scarcely believed the sound tumbling into her throat, rising from the pit of her stomach and the place Chris had sought.

"Kill him. If he touches me again do whatever you wish, you have the pleasure of my approval."

"My innocent accomplice."

Unbelievable. The breath from his kisses sweeping across the surface of tears, touching her face, her eyes and mouth.

"Why wait? You sensed my impatience correctly, my desire for this act. A feed from his insanity would entertain me."

"No, you must wait. You have my blessing if he does it again, I'll know then he truly deserves everything you describe and I won't be angry with you, I promise."

"Evie, I have touched the shape of his thoughts, taken the poison of his desires into my throat. Beyond the willful greed of my revenge, I plead for your innocence and the light which remains in your soul. Why would you hate me for doing this now?"

Oh God, her headache had grown to the size of China. She must be evil, terribly evil, agreeing to something like this. Biting her lip, pushing until the flesh bled and falling beyond redemption, Evie sank into the strength of his presence, lifting her face to the mouth seeking the warm blood.

"My Evie. In so many ways you return life into me."

His words gliding gently across her lips. How could she hate him, her Storyteller, when all he ever gave was the simple purity of his truth?

Pulled upwards, the lightness of his touch drew the girl toward where he must be.

"I could prevent what is to come, yet with courage you sacrifice yourself for the sake of his meager rent helping your mother."

Warmth against the back of her neck and she shivered no more but the headache remained, spinning her thoughts. Blood rushed toward her nose and her heart raced furiously. The fallout became unbearable noise and she wanted to faint away from everything.

Something about his hunger and then the fall.

Chapter Sixteen

This time there was no story, no secret walk through the garden to Adam's inevitable death, no cold earth tumbling between her fingers and the hot tears that went with it. Instead the soft fall from each foot descended onto earth unfamiliar and she walked without words alongside him, following the length of each stride.

She could live here in this place of quiet, with none of the soul piercing misery and confusion of the other place.

"We cannot stay long." Already he read her thoughts.

"I want to remain here forever." She clung to the dark edge of his coat as though in grasping the soft fabric the image might hold together. "Where are we anyway?"

"A place familiar to me."

"You existed here?" She felt a rise of excitement, questions and statements running together. "What did you do, who were you? Tell me what happened, so you don't have to go into it alone. Let me See things as they were."

"That is not possible Evie, its depth will kill you. One day you will See and understand my betrayal, but for now we move in darkness here and it seems not to bother you which is good. I am sad for you and what you choose to endure for others' sake, and angry because I know of things to come, therefore the gentle pace of our walk and the warm night suits me. Nevertheless, if you insist upon it, I will help you understand a little of what lies here."

Drawn inwards, his tears melted against her mouth and his fingers moving beneath her skin traced the path to her soul. The breath pouring in took shape then, a sound stroking the edge of her throat, giving force to a simple chain of letters, "E-d-e-r-n". At first she didn't understand but his hands lay against the sides of her head, thumbs pushing into the temple.

The first bolt threw Evie to her knees, the tremendous pressure inside her head and the brightness behind her eyes. But still he held on, shaping her thoughts, delivering the shock of more jolts, sending her into the grass finally.

"Breathe with me."

Impossible, she had fallen too far away, ripped from his grasp and pulled beneath the ground, the descent tearing her from the safety of his presence. But her heart was racing, could feel its rush and the breath that wouldn't come. Panic as she fell from the voice begging her to breathe, to take his breath and return with him to the place with her name.

Other names too, one, more significant than the rest, its accidental discovery hurling into her thoughts.

Struggling, Evie reached for it as though it were a lifeline. She must remember, she must give this back to him, her Storyteller, for which the deep knowledge of his name and who he had been she almost had, buried now in the core of her understanding.

"Return to me." Each desperate syllable clung to her senses, undercutting the fall, drawing her to his presence again. She needed to speak, the door to her mind was flung wide open.

"You lived in this place with my name, Edern, a long time ago." She fought for the words; this was too important, far more important even than her having the same name as where he lived. "I almost knew who you were."

"No!" Furious and withdrawing from Evie, he stared into her face, challenging the unexpected revelation. "You went too far and I almost killed you, it should not have happened."

"I couldn't help it! You came to me as you were. I saw you in a place called Edern. You are more than from the inscription, you're from a time before that and you lived here, you had a name. I don't care if it makes you angry. All I have to do is sleep to find you, whether you want to feed or not. You should be pleased!"

"No! When I want you in this place, I will be the one to pull you into sleep. You walk on dangerous grounds Evie, I can leave you in nothing should I wish it, removing this place from your thoughts and leaving you with no more than the memory of the death I almost gave you. Do not think that you know me, believe me, arrogance would be your serious mistake. I give you what I want, that is all."

"Look, if you don't want me to know anything, why did you invite me here? What's the point?"

Struggling to her feet, Evie wrestled to free herself from the length of his coat. "I'm leaving now, wake me up."

"It is too soon, I cannot allow your return."

"What the hell are you talking about?" Screaming, she stared into his darkening eyes. "I'm not ready to know, not ready to leave? What do you want from me if everything is too soon, why bother with me at all?"

She pulled away. Leaving his silhouette behind her she moved toward the shadow of a dark forest. He stood ahead of her.

"There is no escape, Evie. I am where you are long before you arrive."

"Liar! Let me go! This is my memory now and I can do what I like with it. I bet I could kill you if I wanted to." Shoving him out of her way, Evie pushed past the tall figure but he was there again.

Breathless, she turned on him, angry sobs choking the words struggling to break free. "Is this making you stronger, my anger and suffering? Are you making this happen so you can feed from me?"

She had never known such anger and drawing back her arm delivered a respectable blow to his ribs. He didn't move.

"You cannot harm me."

"I made you bleed before."

"That was my will, my seduction. You wanted my blood in your veins and I gave it to you but at a price, remember? I could make you relive it now if you wish, but my patience is wearing thin, the drink this time will be heavier and the price greater."

"I will be the one to make you suffer!" Drawing her hand back again, Evie prepared a second strike instead she caught a shattering pain to her arm, freezing it in place, his right hand grasping the wrist.

"I delivered you into the precious seclusion of my world yet you repay me with screams and tantrums, destroying the peace I built here. With patience and the love of one who understands your desire to know, I bore tolerance to your childish behavior, yet you would make me suffer? That amuses me, my darling. I could crush the breath within your body should that be my choice."

Challenging her Storyteller's darkening eyes, Evie spoke.

"Then why the hell do you continue this haunt if I am not ready for anything? For your feed and strength, is that all? I feel you, I need to take all your existence into me as you have taken mine, yet you hate that for one moment I knew who you were! You are more than the Storyteller, I knew you completely and I hate that now I can remember little of it."

Exhausted, Evie kicked listlessly at the silent figure. "I knew you." His name, floating against the edge of her tongue, remained invisible to the breath waiting to form it. "I know more than you want me to know. I knew you then, but I don't understand. It was more than a flash thought."

His arms she remembered, folded gently across her back, telling her that he understood, that everything would be alright. That she was a Seer after all and the knowledge she had taken was separate from his intentions. He should have been more careful, it was his mistake.

She lay in the soft warmth of the grass but couldn't remember how, his face, staring at the fallen Evie.

"Show me." She breathed into the dark air.

Chapter Seventeen

Plunging through eternity, the Storyteller, one hand against each side of her head, pushed inwards, depressing his thumbs into her temples, reaching in. But she had wanted this and despite the pain allowed him in, following his existence with each breath as she sank further into memory.

And all of this from him. His name dropping into her head then out again. And such suffering at the hands of others, betrayal, by those who would swear to protect. This time she would See and remember.

His name.

Something about a lie.

Pulling it in, Evie absorbed the word before his touch dissolved the thought.

Always his voice remained present, cautioning her to resist the seduction to See beyond what he chose to give, that it was dangerous. But his name she couldn't help and felt a sigh of resignation set into her soul. He would agree to that at least.

Pulling the flash of his betrayal into her head, Evie took his images deeper. Understanding this, he pressed further into her head, capturing what remained of her thoughts.

This time she had no panic in the fall, a confusing dropping away from, yet toward the figure whose hands remained steady against the sides of her head. Always there was his voice, telling her to breathe through the descent and into the journey, that he would be there when the consequences came.

*****

"Evie." Then, "Christ Evie, what the bloody hell have you been up to in here?"

The voice she recognized, but she didn't understand, she expected someone else.

"Evie."

Beneath her feet tufts of carpet and a set of windows stared onto a late afternoon, substitute to the green clearing in the dark forest at Edern. In her hand lay several sheets of paper balled up tight, their scrawl distorted through the many creases.

Forcing her eyes open, Evie struggled to her feet pushing the hand away in a violent swipe.

"Hey, I was only tryin' to help!"

"You shouldn't have woken me."

"It's a wonder you didn't wake the bloody dead, the way you were carryin' on. I could hear you shoutin' as I put my key in the front door. I thought you 'ad somebody up here."

"I wanted to stay. You pulled me away from him!"

"What the hell are you talkin' about? You're a weird bitch, you are. If it weren't for the fact your nose 'ad started to bleed and you didn't look so fucked up, I'd give you a hard one against that stupid bookcase. The shelves would dig in a bit but judging by the look of this room, you'd like it rough anyway."

Evie's senses quickened, her Storyteller was present. He had followed her out of memory, watching, leaving Edern to kill.

"No! You promised to wait." She yelled at the ceiling, but he was everywhere.

"Jesus Christ, you're insane. You're really fucking mental!"

For a moment Chris cast his eyes toward Evie's throat. Her nose was bleeding she could feel, the blood running into the ruby apple nestled against the soft flesh behind it.

He continued, stepping closer toward the girl, grabbing a handful of her dark hair as he did so, pulling it and making her head dip slightly toward her assailant.

"Don't think I haven't heard you talkin' to yourself, all hours of the day. I watch you when you think no-one's watching, muttering to your invisible friend."

"Let me go. You have no idea who you are messing with." Evie begged.

"Oh, fuck no."

Ignoring the girl Chris continued.

"Let me see, what's his name? I heard it once."

"No!" Gasping, Evie brought both hands to her mouth, chasing the blood across her face. Surely Chris would be dead soon.

"Oh yeah, Storyteller. Now who the fuck's that?"

"Let go of me!"

Sending her foot forward, Evie delivered a blow against Chris's left shin. He released Evie's tangled hair immediately.

"You bitch!"

Stepping closer, he clasped Evie's hands in his, a dead calm cast suddenly against his face. Slowly Chris circled the tip of his tongue against her forehead.

"So you like it a little bit violent. Well that can be arranged, but take my advice, give in, you'll be a lot better for it. We could even do it now, a quickie. No-one will be any the wiser. I won't tell." And he turned toward the bed sheets, dragged partway toward the floor.

"Touch me again and he will kill you, I swear. I've already told him he can do it."

"Fair enough then. Stupid bitch, you're insane anyway, talkin' into thin air like that. You've made your choice, so I'll bide my time. Oh, by the way, tell your Storyteller that when it happens, he can watch, he might even learn a thing or two."

He left then, disappearing into Elaine's old bedroom, the door slamming behind him. Chopin followed, a soft nocturne, the melody making Evie sick. With Chris in the next room and no one else in the house, Evie didn't know what to do. Technically, with Chris still around Evie should leave the house, but she needed her entity. Had to find him, the pounding in her head meant she had to have him. In sleep, he could feed, giving him the deepest part of her thoughts until her responses died in the final pleasure of his extraction.

She lay on the bed.

Against her skin the pillow felt smooth. Pushing her face into it further, Evie sought its cool relief. Closing her eyes slowly, she formed the small sound that would become his name, while in blackness she stared into nothing, eyes grasping for the tiniest hint of movement or silhouette of a figure lost among the dark.

Twice, she called into her thoughts, shouting into the silence until her mind hurt. It was no good though, she couldn't concentrate. What if Chris came back, bursting into her room?

Evie's heart freaked.

"Sleep, you are protected."

The voice, a quiet breath against her ear tumbled across the curve of her neck, pushing Evie toward sleep, leaving her with nothing to do but rest. Inhaling the lavender presence, she sent it into her soul.

"My memory harmed you."

Touching the edge of her lips, he took what remained of the blood into himself. The pressure of his body as slowly he moved in alongside, pushed further, hands across her eyes, holding her to sleep, thumb and forefinger pressing gently against each temple.

Rising to meet the pain and holding her breath against him, Evie pushed his hands harder against her head before the paralyzing jolt inwards.

"Dream and make me live."

Afterwards he stayed, in the calm that followed, nurturing her to sleep with careful words and tales lost to myth and legend, and that one day she would know and See. There were those who waited, wishing for her return.

Awakened by the sound of a car pulling into the drive, Evie bolted upright, startled that she had slept so deeply. It felt like an hour and yet it was still daylight.

Checking the clock at the side of the bed, Evie was amazed to notice that just one hour had elapsed since entering her room then dealing with Chris.

But there was something else, something stretched across the window sill. Shiny, it reflected the afternoon light streaming through the window from the meadow beyond.

It couldn't be. How was this possible?

Reaching toward the gold object, Evie picked up her watch. The same one lost months ago among the fields on the Forbidden Path.

"But how?"

Studying it carefully, Evie checked the timepiece for scratches, dents, anything to detract from the impossible miracle of its return. Four thirty. Evie compared the hour to the one currently illustrating the face of the clock beside her bed. Exactly the same. In all that time, the watch hadn't lost a minute.

Turning it over Evie lay the prized object in the palm of her hand so that in studying the little silver disc securing the hidden mechanism, she might somehow understand the phenomena. Engraved into the back lay a small stamp and Evie wondered why she hadn't seen it before.

But then, realized Evie, it wasn't a stamp at all. Casting her eyes across the room, Evie searched for his energy.

The inscription, small but delicately clear held itself to her eyes.

'Eve.'

"Taliesin?"

Sliding the gift around her wrist, Evie slipped off the bed, leaving the last breath from his name suspended quietly in the quiet room.

Chapter Eighteen

Evie wore the watch when she stepped onto the number seventy-nine bus on her way to work. Later she would pick up some lunch from the dim interior of the shopping center and the fresh fish her mother wanted for dinner as a special treat for Chris the Creep.

Taliesin admitted returning the watch to Evie, inscribing her name across its tiny back after she caught his name within the flashes of Edern. He said he must write 'Eve' now she had found his true self. Now three weeks later, he continued to call her Evie, while she, although acknowledging his occupation as a Storyteller, called him Taliesin anyway which by and large, he no longer seemed to mind, provided his host didn't push for more information.

"Taliesin."

She loved how his name rose against the back of her tongue, sliding gently to its tip before transforming into breath. Often during the day, despite swearing him to silence, she called him forward anyway so his name might kiss the lavender air in front of her face. And always he would oblige, interrupting the ridiculousness of each hour with the cool wisp of a touch or the sweep of her new name, 'Eve' before disappearing to his place of darkness, or Waiting Place as he preferred calling it. She could continue with her work then, disturbed only by the continued longing for his presence, nurtured by the knowledge he was never far away.

The bus rides though were another story, with Taliesin talking nonstop, sometimes feared the girl, loud enough for others to hear.

"It is impossible," he reassured Evie earlier that morning while she dressed for work, "there are none strong enough, and even if they were, I can hide myself, remember?"

"As long as you don't expect me to talk back, people will think I'm crazy and I shall tell you to leave."

"But you don't want me to leave." His voice, heavy with the kind of patience reserved for temperamental children folded gently into her thoughts, resting the fury.

"At night you call my name, when you think I have returned to my Waiting Place. In thoughts you cry for the pull of my words and images, and the feed that goes with it, and you beg for the memory of Edern. But I see everything and have known you, always."

"Sod it Taliesin, why do you always sound like a friggin' poem?"

She felt dizzy, falling against the white plastic chair to the front of the dressing table. He had touched her, in reality; in the real world of things seen she could feel him, solid. But it didn't seem possible, this was more than the barely there touch against her skin, more certain than that, all he lacked was visible form.

He laughed, amused at her surprise. "I am stronger yes, but your own ability now makes this happen."

Struggling against the dizzy tide, Evie reached for her watch, the inscription, 'Eve' facing upward. She had left it with the name face down, could swear to it. Turning the watch over, Evie fastened the timepiece to her wrist.

"Question nothing, this is real, I am real. Your developing powers draw me out, making it easier for me to touch you, I am in you now, completely and you accept me. That is good and in return it is easier for me to cross further into your reality. Your watch, for example, I could have returned it before, had wanted to but you had to be ready to accept what I gave just as you accept my touch now.

"I have many gifts you will see. My powers are vast, I took lessons from the best on my journeys. There were those willing to exchange magic for stories and one in particular with whom I would sit often. I really learned then, taking what I had and making it more."

His hands swept through her hair, running down its length and releasing the ponytail she struggled to contain earlier.

"Eve." Her name taken into voice. It stroked the air in front of her face, moving toward the slope of her neck.

The silver necklace with the little apple pendant slowly lifted.

"Let me see you." She could scarcely breathe at this new phenomenon.

She didn't want to leave her room. That she must exist beyond his world and walk among her own brought her to sickness.

"My eternal Eve. Always impatient, always wanting to know, curiosity your disease. I will teach you to See better, to make sense of the thoughts that come, those things I will help you learn again. I will leave you in nothing and teach you to See. The magic given to me I shall pass to you as part of your becoming.

"Trust and fall into me, such things begin now. This time there will be no feed, you will find me without it. Learn this, it is necessary. In dreams also, you must learn to find me. I am gone, seek Evie, See through the sleep I give you now and find me again.

"Accept my invitation, enter this Waiting Place of quiet dark, you have my permission, I have delivered you here before, now I want you here again. Walk forward, have faith in my voice. Someday you must find me here, uninvited, without words, I will need it then. Believe, do not hesitate, it is possible to walk on nothing, it is within you. One day, in your escape, you will change this place, you will be strong enough. Learn to draw me out, to See, you can find me here, I am watching.

"Breathe my name if you must, if it helps draw me from within darkness. See me here, enter this Waiting Place and take its shadows, claim them, sense each shape as they move forward.

"Sense my existence and walk fearless, the eyes inside your core have seen me, have drawn me at last from darkness and toward the pleasure of our connection. Let me put my mouth to yours so you know I am here and that I am pleased, I breathe warmth into you and sense your hunger, your thirst.

"Come, take this blood reward from my throat, I give it to you freely. Drink, your hunger delights me. Take this magic into your soul, taste its essence, drink deep, absorb its energy. Lie with me here, I want the taste of my blood upon your lips. Come to me, breathe against me while I touch your skin in other ways. Yes, let the shadows watch and know you are mine, eternal."

"I don't like it back here." Grumpy, Taliesin vaporized the memory of Evie's morning lesson.

This was another phenomenon, Taliesin's moods, making him seem more human than spirit to Evie.

"Well, it's just too bad." She thought back. "Be grateful there's somewhere to sit after you made me late this morning."

"Will we go past that old building?"

She might have been listening to a four year old. "Of course we will, you know we do, we go everyday."

Indeed, everyday, twice a day, the bus took them past the old Round House situated in the center of what had been the tiny Wavertree village in the days before an encroaching city gathered the rows of cottages and the village green into itself.

Now, set among other modern buildings and opposite a supermarket the black and grey structure viewed activities through a series of rusty bars.

"I don't know what you find so fascinating about that place, it's a dump." Grumbled Evie settling into her seat.

"I hold memories of you there, as a child, dashing across the circle of cobbled stones, close to the cholera death the Round House held once. You were unaware of the eyes that watched, peering between narrow bars, longing for the light in your soul and your ability to See them. But you couldn't See everything as a child, sometimes you were just at play."

"You really give me the creeps, the way you talk sometimes." Evie thought into him, adding, "are they still there?" despite herself.

"Of course, those who wait, who do not understand their death."

"Did many die?" He had peaked her curiosity, probably his intention, she thought.

"Many of the poor," he slowly lectured, setting the scene with the measured tone of his voice, "and in 1832, faster than could be buried, the Round House played host to the diseased corpses."

"Christ, Taliesin, do you have to be so graphic? Did you ever feed from them?"

"It was never my true desire. I stood, watching, Death's quiet partner, enduring its lingering visit with my impatience for the suffering of pain in the limbs and stomach to be over. Sometimes though, unable to stand it any longer, when their skin transformed to marbled grey, I jumped into the mind of the wretched victim, sending my thoughts and images with such depth and speed, their end came in minutes, hemorrhaging finally. But not without beauty before their half conscious eyes, and the soft lull of some quiet verse taking their dying thoughts. My purpose always to ease their suffering, relieve them from the stench and misery of their bleak surroundings. For them, I was Death but with more mercy than they would have known. You are quiet Evie, why?"

"Because one day you will end my life."

"Evie."

"I know it, suddenly."

Her voice fell against the dirty window and his hand brushed gently across the side of her face. In a far flung corner of her mind, Evie wondered how it could be possible for him to fit between herself and the woman with the purple anorak and matching headscarf sitting next to her.

"But I don't know why I know."

The sound escaped her lips, breathing forward and against the dirty window splashed with muddy brown spots. She watched a circle of breath make a damp cloud in front of her face, burying the city beneath its shroud.

"When?"

"Evie, do not speak."

He was in her head, the familiar jolt and pull back into his thoughts. Evie, staring ahead losing the damp window and the street beyond to his images and words.

"Sshh." His voice floated toward her.

Inside, she drifted toward him so that nothing mattered except he was there, the full weight of Taliesin pushing against her head.

Beyond the filth before her eyes, rose slowly the amber walls of a castle, its vast circular turrets reaching toward the pale sky stretching above an emerald sea gently lapping against the dark rocks yielding to the support of the magnificent structure. Trees, black-green and lifting from the curve of the cliff's edge down to the shadows of soft grass lying across the meadow below reached gently along the slope of the lush green hill.

The scene from the print on her bedroom wall, The Enchanted Castle. Inside her head Evie forgot about dying and instead began laughing, unable to contain her amazement. He had given her this and she wanted to run up the slope and along the cliff's edge, staring across the endless sea.

Beneath her, Evie felt the bus move, aware of its stop and start along the busy road, jostling for position among traffic, but the scene never changed. The castle, glistening beneath the cool mist of an early morning, remained steady.

"Thou was't not born for death, immortal Bird!"

Ode to a Nightingale, it was the painting of the castle that inspired Keats' poem. Taliesin's voice pouring into her head, framing the honey colored scene. But something was missing and it took her a moment before realizing the absence of the figure in the foreground, Psyche.

"Look beyond what you See, train your eyes, search Evie, remember who you are."

Lifting the fog from her mind, he held the girl within the grip of his thoughts. "Hold what you See to your eyes and look beyond this."

No. Impossible.

"Try. This you must learn to do at will."

She hadn't been expecting another lesson but pushed her struggling mind against the scene anyway, trying harder.

"Learn to control the gift you have. Manipulate the veil you See through at times and call it to your will. Breathe, take everything in, absorb its secret life."

"But I don't know what I'm supposed to be looking for!"

Frustrated by her failed efforts, Evie whispered aloud, staring into the unchanged scene, never taking her eyes from the scattering of trees and the dark castle windows behind which she wished she could See.

Asked to do the impossible Evie broke concentration. For a moment the grey street and narrow rows of houses crushed side by side buried the green delight of the hill. But Taliesin wanted none of it.

"Snap back! You hold this now, I gave you the scene, it is for you to sustain and to find what I ask you to find. Move your thoughts forward, See."

"Help me." She thought back to him.

She couldn't sustain the image, let alone find something she had to create. A frustrated sigh returned, breezed into her head.

"When will you learn to trust the abilities you possess? Stare forward, lean into my words and make them part of who you are. Believe you can do this, you are a Seer, now See."

Again Evie pushed against her eyes, willing them to See the impossible, reminding herself that if she was capable of similar things when she didn't even try, she must be capable of this now.

"Relax Evie, breathe the image into your core, absorb the sense of it. Use the knowledge I have given you. Let all other thoughts sleep."

Rising from the litter and dull houses, the castle glistened like an amber jewel within the dawn mist.

"Now push your thoughts forward and hold the image there, do not break concentration, it is all you." Instructed Taliesin.

Leaving her mind with a strange tug, his presence remained near. Now, against the side of Evie's head Taliesin's voice whispered, providing further instruction as every particle of her mind forced the glassy sea, the cliff top and the green hillside to remain.

A flash-thought and grasping the word before it fled, Evie slowed it down.

"See into the image beyond where you know Psyche to be."

She saw him then and as her eyes grew accustomed to this new focus, the single form drew itself further into being, so that within moments the new presence on the plateau of the cliff was undeniable.

Sitting on a small mound of earth and apparently lost among thoughts, the boy stared toward a small gathering of trees as though they might hold the answers to his unspoken questions.

One leg bent at the knee he faced sideways, foot pressed firmly against the top of the earth mound, while the other leg, the one closest to Evie stretched to the side. The heel of his boot dug into the grass and she imagined that should this person stand up and walk away, a deep impression would remain long afterward.

Slowly, he moved his head. Something struck Evie in the manner with which he did this, slow, so that barely a strand of his dark hair moved. The boy's face, a translucent oval, punctuated the depths of his near black eyes, the only other color besides his deep crimson bow shaped mouth.

He looked at the girl, unblinking, a faint smile pushing the edges of his mouth upward as if possessing knowledge of something as yet unwilling to share. No more than twenty, Evie studied the handsome face, drawn by the fascination of a strange familiarity.

And still, he didn't move, drawing her gaze toward him as though waiting for a response.

That crimson mouth, why must her eyes focus there? And then she knew, the quiet realization pitching her further into understanding as she watched him reach into his pocket.

It was the boy from the story she wrote on her birthday, the first one, the one Taliesin had given her. The tale of a boy, lying beneath a tree, heavy with blossom, waiting, mouth open for the rain to turn each petal into a delicate fountain of blood. And later, as an infant, his murderous burial beneath the same tree, the blood oath pouring onto his covered face where his mouth would lie. Adam, the name glanced a soft blow to her head, nudging the link between the two boys. They were the same therefore the name belonged to each of them.

The object retrieved from his pocket, he tossed it casually into the air, catching it with the same hand, the one farthest from the girl. A perfect green sphere, rotating quickly as it fell toward the outstretched hand. An apple.

Throwing the fruit away from himself suddenly, he tossed it toward Evie, who, leaning forward to catch the offering before it rolled down the hill beyond reach, struck her outstretched hand hard against the window, banishing the fragile scene to the reality of dirt and rain.

Arriving some thirty minutes late for work and with the air of one aware of a much greater destiny, albeit one lacking in name, Evie breezed through the shop doorway. Slipping past the customers rummaging between rows of discount footwear and assorted handbags, she smiled brightly at the furious supervisor.

The woman sported neon pink lipstick today and already at nine thirty, it feathered into the hair above her top lip. Evie watched the color balance precariously as the mouth articulated and distorted, that one more day like this and she'd be out on her 'arse faster than you could say shoe shine'.

The exchange to her back, Evie emerged from the crowded stock room, the smell of dust and old boxes already stuffed into both nostrils. Facing the endless displays of shoes, Evie saw it for all its sad reality. Sad, tacky displays dressed up in fancy names like, the 'Estelle Line' and the 'Ophelia collection' to justify rip off prices.

Picking up one such item in lime green with a pink polka dot bow Evie sauntered toward an interested customer, twirling the object by its three inch heel.

Against the memory of Keats and the boy from *Among Other Edens* everything seemed brash without the possibility of redemption. Nothing could make this good and

she wished for the fluorescent lighting to go away, plunging everything into the mercy of darkness.

But it was Monday and the flash-thought falling into her head told her, two weeks.

Somewhere, Taliesin smiled.

Chapter Nineteen

The television rained hard, on the inside at least.

Caught in a downpour, the dancers apparently thought being soaking wet was the best thing ever if the running up and down wet fire escapes was anything to go by. The guys in the scene, thrilled with the display, lived as though it were sunny, and despite the rain turned tight pirouettes, catching tanned leggy girls poured into tiny shorts.

All because of diet cola.

Disgusted, Evie pressed the 'off' button at the bottom of the remote.

Chris, in an effort to install a combination of the latest technology and general phony goodwill had made a present of a new television and DVD player to the Edern household. Maureen, the flushed recipient upon walking into the living room and finding the thing installed had shrieked a single cry of joy before demanding why Evie hadn't done the same thing. Evie, hovering between living room and hallway feeling useless with a box of Thornton's truffles purchased as a treat for her mother had remained silent. In the light of his behavior toward her, Chris's gesture made Evie want to hurl.

Now, two weeks later, she still hated the flat screened silver box stuck in the corner of the room. The ancient clunky T.V which they'd had since before the death of her father had been carted off to Chris's room where he watched the thing until four in the morning, the sound pushing through to Evie's room, driving her to fits of silent screaming.

Besides, everybody in the cola commercial was having way too much of a good time. She had just finished the last drop of a diet cola and was having none of the fun everybody on television was having.

Unless she'd just been subjected to a quick lobotomy, Evie's recollection of the previous sixty minutes reflected none of this. Friday night being 'Nuclear Drill Night', instead of dancing and living it up at the weekend beneath sparkling drops of rain, she had spent the best part of an hour beneath the floorboards with her mother and the near permanent Pam, lying like three sad corpses minus the funeral and a couple of stone angels.

Afterwards, she had climbed out with the others and went straight to the fridge for the diet cola, then sprawled out on the sofa attempted to offer some sort of reprieve to her stiff neck.

Alone in the house, Evie thought of Chris who, thank God had disappeared for the evening, most likely trying to get himself laid with some poor unsuspecting girl. The image of him, ass in action made her cringe.

At church, mother and Cell-Phone Pam wouldn't be back for several hours. Both engaged in a meeting involving something floral followed by another meeting about the role of women in the 21st century. Probably the same as now, Evie mused at the time, housewives still coming over all excited by dirty dishes or a spotty shirt collar if the state of advertising was anything to go by.

Switching off the T.V finally, Evie played out the set of instructions she had been given for the evening and pulled back a corner of the lily carpet in the living room. She hated doing this but the task always fell to her and she hauled the heavy textile into the center of the room, suffering the sharp fibers as they dug into her skin. Then pulling back the latch on a little trap door Cell-Phone Pam had fashioned from several pieces of floorboard, Evie slipped into the musty darkness.

It was only three feet high so you had to move very quickly onto your hands and knees, crawling around until you found a space comfortable enough to lie during the drill. The drill being that at the alarm, an old clock set to go off at seven every Friday evening, everyone present had to drop whatever they were doing, throw back the living room carpet, up the hatch door then jump inside.

There were just two minutes to accomplish this; finding a spot, dropping the trap door and waiting for the all clear, another alarm clock positioned beneath the floorboards and set to go off some twenty minutes after the ordeal began.

Dropping to her knees, Evie prepared to crawl inside the small space, her job to make sure enough Ritz crackers and granola bars were available to last during a nuclear war, a chemical attack and the subsequent fall out depending which of the two it happened to be.

She couldn't stand this part, she could ignore the dead spiders lying flat on their backs with tucked in legs, she wasn't that bloody squeamish, but it was just the gnawing concern that it might be possible for the trap door to slam shut leaving her unable to push it open again from the inside. Once inside though, you could pretty much crawl beneath the entire house if you didn't mind the surprise of what you might put your hand in next as you fumbled about.

Time spent beneath the floor made Evie feel a bit like a vampire. This Friday night being no exception, she had risen, pale and dusty toward the late September evening. Now here she crawled again, reduced to her hands and knees, winding up the little clock with the luminous hands and picking up a crumpled copy of the 'Liverpool Echo' which Pam always managed to read by the light from the same dazzling clock.

She needed to change the water in the thermos flasks. Four altogether, including one for Chris if ever he decided to participate, and so far he hadn't. Thank God breathed Evie through a spray of gloomy dust. Lifting each one through the hole and into the living room, Evie hauled herself out after them. She'd run to the kitchen, tip out the old, pour in the new, shove them back in the hole and be done.

Lying in the pitch dark with her mother's heels digging into the top of her head, Evie tried recapturing the castle and the boy with the apple as seen that morning from the gritty bus window. It turned out to be an impossible task however, with Evie failing to manipulate the image into anything beyond memory.

Yes, she saw the castle and *yes*, Adam was there also but she couldn't turn it into something beyond the frame of her mind, and so the darkness remained.

It didn't matter anyway because in a few hours she'd be in bed. Now that the weekend had rolled around, Taliesin could feed as deep as he liked. He might even show her the castle again if she asked nicely enough.

Screwing the top on the last flask, Evie wondered where he might be, enclosed within his Waiting Place or lost among the forest of Edern. Jealous, she wished her presence in either place instead of jumping back into a black hole for the benefit of returning four supplies of water to their makeshift nuclear bunker.

A key grinding the lock on the front door, footsteps, then, "So that's what it looks like down there, I've never bothered looking before."

Chris.

"Shit."

Swearing under her breath, Evie pretended not to hear. She had just popped back into the hole and was shoving the flasks into a corner.

"Hey, Evie, I said, I've never been down there, fancy givin' us a tour?"

"There's nothing to see, just supplies and a load of dust. You wouldn't like it." Keeping her back to him, she thought he might go away, discouraged by her lack of conversation.

"I might like it. As I always say, you can't knock a thing 'till you've tried it. Aren't you going to invite me in then?"

"Really, there's nothing to see." Her throat was cold.

"I wondered about that space beneath the floor, your mother told me I could use it. I don't know how the fuck you expect to survive though you'll fry like all the rest. It's all bullshit anyway everybody knows nothing's ever going to happen, chemical weapons, terrorism, it's all a pile of fuckin' crap."

"I thought you were with some girl."

Changing the subject, Evie stared at the figure dressed in jeans and a dark green sweater underneath which he wore a white shirt and a red and black striped tie. A circular brass belt buckle shone beneath the ensemble. He seemed to have grown taller over the summer and more muscular but perhaps that was because right now, she might just as well be buried in a hole.

"I came back for you, why else would I bother with this fuckin' dump?"

Smiling then pulling up the sleeves on his sweater, he added, "looks cozy down there, I'll 'ave a look round for m'self if you don't mind."

Swinging both legs into the hole, Chris hopped down and stood, or rather knelt facing the girl who unable to get out wondered what she should do next.

"We've got dried fruit and boxes of crackers." Tilting her head in the direction of the rations, she kept the conversation meaningless, all the while controlling the rising fear in her voice.

"I don't give a shit about that, like I said, it's you I came here for."

Slowly he removed his tie then leaned in closer. Placing both hands on her shoulders he drew the rigid girl to his chest.

"How's your friend? What's his name? Oh yeah, the invisible fucking Storyteller."

His tongue completed the sentence against her earlobe, before pushing inside while his other hand pushed against the side of her head, stalling the girl from an attempt to pull away.

"Remember what I said, it will be so much easier if you want it."

"Chris, no, stop!"

Pressing his mouth against her lips, the rest of the words, 'he will kill you' remained in thought as the inevitable journey of his hand traveled down the pink front of her sweatshirt, pausing to stroke each breast before resting finally between her thighs.

She could hear his belt buckle lifting.

"There'll be no marks I promise."

Evie didn't care, her mouth was free from his and it presented an opportunity. Taking it she bit hard into his shoulder, biting through the scratchy green sweater and the shirt beneath. Momentarily she hung on, tearing into the wounded flesh as though all along this had been a game, that she lured him into the space beneath the floor where he was now her prey.

"Fuckin' wolf! I always knew you were a fucking freak!" His protests blasted the hollow darkness. Seizing her opportunity, Evie pushed past him, scrambling over his legs and reached for the opening into the living room. Once out, she would close the trap door, lock it and hold him there until the return of her mother or even Pam.

"Not so fast." Hands grabbing both legs, Chris pulled the girl from the merciful opening and she felt the burn from the carpet above as her hands dragged backwards.

"So you like to play rough do you? I thought I 'ad you typed right. I know your sort, face like an angel but when it comes down to it, you're a slut like all the rest."

Struck across the face and pushed to the ground, Evie lay in the dust, winded by the force of his hand. Her head hurt also, he hadn't only cracked his hand across her cheek but glanced a closed fist to the side of her skull.

The brass belt buckle fell hard against her face.

"It could have been easy, I could have made it nicer than it's going to be now."

The little trap door knocked together from several planks of wood one innocent Sunday afternoon a far off time ago fell shut, plunging the space into thick blackness.

Bringing both knees up, Evie tried kicking him in the stomach, preventing him from lying on top of her, but he was too fast. Even in the darkness he knew where her legs were, forcing them apart and pushing his other hand into the space.

Tears rolled onto her face.

"Chris, no I have never."

With Taliesin it was different, his kind seduction bringing Evie to him in ways impossible to understand in reality. The tease of each image, each word pouring into her head, surrendering her soul so that she knew of herself in the single form no longer. She longed for him now, begged for the hands that tore at her clothes to be his, wished this to be the shadow of Taliesin and not Chris shifting before her eyes.

"So I'm your first then?" He breathed into the stale air between them. "I'd better make this last then hadn't I? I'd better make this really fuckin' special."

With both Evie's hands held above her head, Chris's free hand dragged the sweatshirt upward, covering the girl's face. Now the sweatshirt fit like a mask, ensuring as she inhaled through nose or mouth that the fabric went in with it, making shallow breaths the only thing possible.

She was suffocating.

The other hand, moving from between her legs, traveled to her back, tearing open the bra strap and pushing his nails into her flesh as he did so. Again, she struggled to free. Pushed back against the floor, a knee this time forced the space between her legs.

"Try that again little girl and I'll send you through the fucking floor."

His mouth pressed on hers, Evie felt the moist surface of his lips claiming her body while his free hand moved to the top of her jeans, releasing the metal button. The zipper was next, creating enough space for his fingers to slip through.

Inside, Evie felt the light in her soul die and begged for Taliesin, sobbing his name into the dust and the fabric, taught now against her face.

"I am here Evie, within this evil, I am with you. Breathe as I have taught you and do not struggle now, it is too dangerous."

"Taliesin?' She sobbed the name into the black air, her jeans were being discarded.

"Sshh, my love, do not say my name. Think back to me only. I am here, lying beside you and I love you."

Releasing the hand pinning the sweatshirt against the girl's face, Evie swore she wouldn't struggle as he found it "so fucking irritating".

Anyway, she couldn't do anything now. Chris's weight pressed upon her as the rough surface of his hands moved against her thighs, making them ready.

"Didn't think I'd be taking a tight little virgin."

"No, please!"

"Relax, you'll want this believe me."

Slowly, he moved into the place he wanted, forcing his control, body hard.

"See, you want this."

"No, I don't!"

Determined to have the last word, Evie reached out, searching for Taliesin's hand and felt the gentle wisp of his touch in response.

Snapping her wrist in two, Chris told the girl not to 'fucking move again.'

"Help me!"

Screaming inside, the girl thought into her entity, taking the breath of Taliesin's kiss against her mouth and swallowing it like cool water for the hot pain, as Chris entered her for the first time.

Chapter Twenty

"Take my hand, where it is safe."

Never having let go, Evie slipped away following the smooth path to his voice. Soft here, the way an easy darkness stroked the surface of her eyes, and the cool thread of air, touching without menace, the edge of her neck, bringing her forward.

There was something deeply familiar, the way the earth pressed against the soles of her feet and the thick blades curled around the ends of her toes. But long ago the girl made a promise not to See and Evie closed her eyes against what the visions might deliver in this quiet place of safety.

She wanted to touch the grass, be in the earth, she knew it so well. The urge to understand and to know stealing the words from her throat, there were so many, making it impossible to form a single one.

"Because our purpose here is not for that."

He read her thoughts.

They stopped in the clearing of a large forest, Evie inhaling the scent of earth and crystal water. But she felt so weak, the long journey into him taking everything she had.

Her body ached deep into the fibers of each muscle and she felt dizzy. Pain ripped through her stomach, stealing the breath from her lungs. Inside, Evie began to fall.

Descending into this cool softness was nice it meant never having to get up again, until something stopped her descent. There was pain, but she didn't understand why.

"My love."

A soft, familiar sound.

Keeping her from the fall, the voice held her weight, making it his. She knew his name, knew of herself here also, but it took too much effort to think. She needed to slip away, it would have been nice. She had no fear of this place.

"Take this strength for your survival, Evie, stay with my voice."

"I know here." Again, the urge to See confused both pain and sickness. A bright flash skated across the surface of each eye and quickly Evie fell into its white relief, but the voice would not let her go, gentle, careful, holding the girl within its cradle, refusing the descent.

"You exist here for purposes other than to See. I return you to Edern for healing, so light may return to your soul. Descend into yourself if you must, but you will never reach the end of this fall, instead you shall rise to meet the life I give back to you."

"Yes, you know here and among your confusion, you know me but that is all, there shall be no feed this time. A touch from me that way will kill you and I have reserved my taste for death to the one who forced my need to deliver you here once more. For my part I have brought you into this place of safety where you will always be protected."

The voice, lifting, urging her departure from the sleep begged its claim against her tired eyes and the body that longed to give in.

Dark shapes floated against a night sky. Trees, she realized vaguely through half closed lids, and more vaguely still recalled the name of the one who carried her forward with the touch of his hand.

She wanted to talk but it required a strength she no longer had and he knew this, thinking into the stricken girl that she should not bother trying, that she need do nothing.

It felt good, having him think into her, permitting his possession of her mind, much better than the muddle of confused words she struggled to produce. Bursting through every muscle and sinew, pain tore through her soul, taking what remained of Evie's breath. Yet, even in this state, it only drew her closer to the sanctuary he provided, continuing to drift beyond the thing he sought to take her from.

Safe this place, she wanted to stay forever, always did when possessed by this strange voice whom she knew of but lacked the ability to fully recall.

Exhausted, and glad for the deep sense of connection, Evie could have cried for it all. For the softness of grass, the dark shadow of trees, the failure to understand herself here and the presence of love out of hate.

Lying here like this, you could see into forever, lose yourself among other edens. Yellow stars flung against the deep sky made for a bright, haphazard pattern, and the night, folding around the trees, squeezed every branch, gently tracing the surface of the earth with its dark embrace before sweeping upward, circling the golden moon in its play.

And this being who talked to her, dressed as a knight, his pristine armor capturing so perfectly the silver reflection from the ribbon of water threading the river bank.

Slowly he leaned toward her still form, the reach of his words haunting every moment, he gave her lessons, this being, visions and the words to write down. Teaching always, giving more than she deserved. "Taliesin." She was able to say at last before her eyelids won and sleep came.

Chapter Twenty-One

Larger than any room she had ever visited, the expanse stretched far beyond where Evie lay. Constructed entirely from slabs of honey stone, a huge fireplace hollowed from the same amber material stood at the far end of the chamber. Thick orange flames danced inside, leaping upon the kindling in pursuit of their hunger, the roar and crackle, snapping the silent air.

Stranger though, the way she saw into her eyes, flung open and seeing nothing of this new version of herself standing apart, disembodied from the original.

Pain and an escape from something, but nothing like that could come here, she was sure of it. Standing to the side of herself and looking on, Evie felt safe. A tandem partner to the motionless version and aware that in this strange sleep the girl remained observer of everything.

Curious, she stared at the still version dressed in a white gown, dark hair wrapping her face and neck, green eyes, challenging the decision to go or return.

But she liked this mysterious room, its firelight drawing her curiosity, urging her away from the pallid face, luminous in its death and speaking of a pain the girl no longer wished to be associated with.

She wanted to know who delivered her here, making her this way, a guest among shadows, observer to a dying she could not recall. A name she knew in the final moment and a name tracing her thoughts now as she saw how with great care she lay within the deep bed. Each flicker of amber light withdrew from darkness, the steady weight of a cover bearing protection to the stillness below and suggesting that in an effort to preserve what was left, all steps must be taken.

Trimmed in gold, silk strands dipped and lifted along the scalloped edge of dark green velvet draped above four vertical posts. Each carefully crafted beam shaped into wide twists travelled toward the green canopy draped across the top.

Planted firmly upon the stone, an oversize chair upholstered in the same rich fabric squatted alongside the bed. Possibly drawn up to observe the girl's motionless figure, the nameless occupant for the moment had gone.

Who would care to wait here all night? Nestled among the glow of a hundred flames, half listening to the crackle of the miniature inferno and for breath held within the silence of the still form to come again. And where, long fingers, marking a careful outline against the deep carvings etched into the chair's broad sides touched an aerial display of birds. Nightingales.

Her attention pulled toward the wall by the rapid jump of flames, Evie scanned the quick reflection captured against the sides of a dark gold frame. Against the lower portion of the gilded frame, a small gilded plaque dropped below. Ducking behind the chair, Evie leaned in closer to read its contents. Already, even as she whispered the name into the quiet shadows Evie knew every stroke lapping its surface.

The Enchanted Castle 1664.

All those times she spent lying awake, patient for the moon to sweep its yellow light across the dark sky beyond her open window. And how many times had she anticipated the press of this moonlight against the image of an amber castle rising from her bedroom wall and the shores of an emerald sea? How hard she had tried to be in it, to explore the rooms, begged every breath for her existence there, forcing her thoughts forward until her head hurt with longing. This was more than she dared believe; to dwell here at last, within a place loved so much.

Beyond the walls, beyond the roar of the fire, if she listened, Evie heard the sea collapse against ancient rocks, each wave cresting the night air before dying against her ears. Followed by the next wave then the next hypnotic crash.

Pure contentment lay here. A quiet eternity spent exploring every room and corridor embraced within the walls of her Enchanted Castle. Safe, always. And always, the whispers of ancient stories, legends told by the one who brought her here, of a time before her time and of a time long before that.

And outside, beyond the amber walls, the fall of snow might brush the whitest of winters. A watercolor where every step left footprints so light they vanished before each tiny shoe lifted, as though she had never been.

And blossom too, in spring. Leaning against the apple bark, her face warm from the sun, she would catch its innocent scent, gathering the delicate pink and cream flowers as each petal, plucked by the fingers of a fragile breeze, rained softly into her outstretched hands.

Everywhere, gentle opulence, it traveled through the warmth of everything, the sumptuous fabrics and the peaceful way with which she lay, protected. The rich comfort of knowing no pain.

Again she studied the white gown, resting neatly across the top of each foot. Her throat, pale and barely moving seemed to flood the small opening at the neck. Wrapped softly in the same fabric, the subtle slope of shoulder to arms lay captured at the wrist. An embroidery of tiny roses, each luminous thread drawn into a scattering of pink buds.

Cradled within the warm light and against the deep green fabric upon which she lay, the figure appeared wraithlike, as though she might rise from sleep before fading into a wisp of fragile mist.

Turning at last from her motionless form, Evie wished to see beyond here and delighted in the discovery of a large window cut into the opposite wall. Situated beneath, a little window seat jutted from the rocky support, the top hosting a rectangular needlepoint cushion; a nightingale arching toward a setting sun.

Favoring a view from the window, Evie abandoned her other self to sleep, moving without effort and realizing how it didn't take much more than thought to transport herself between destinations. Within seconds she stared through the window pane divided into small squares by strips of soft lead presenting a somewhat checked interpretation of the outside.

Above everything, a full yellow moon stood charge, ordering an assortment of stars into their assigned positions. Held in suspense, the little hill and small collection of trees lay still, waiting for morning's quiet breath and the presence of dawn's inevitable ascent.

Below, each small hill folded into the next, pausing at the stream in the foreground before leaping forward then running in a green tumble toward the distance.

Familiar, all of it and she searched for the figure boy, a connection to something seen before. Nose pressed against a panel of glass, she grew cold.

Bitterly cold.

Another presence flooded the room.

Emerging from shadow, the figure, sliding from folds of darkness, slid quietly toward her awareness.

Waiting for the sweep of his dark approach, Evie drew each painful breath, struggling against the sudden chill. The figure made her feel this cold, thought Evie, had waited long for the girl's gaze to break from the window and return to the silent death taking place within the chamber. He might steal forward then, stalking her response.

He neither noticed or cared she knew this, looking instead toward the motionless figure set in miniature against the expanse of four poster bed and the soft luxury of accommodating bedclothes.

He touched the shoulders first, tracing their outline with the tips of each gloved finger. From the edge of the hearth Evie watched, eyes haunting the edge of this darkness made narrow by a moon claiming the night and their private theater to its yellow light.

Taliesin, she recalled his name, hadn't she fought about it? Something about being too strong for her own good. Now as the sleeping version of herself lay there and he touched her eyes, lightly running each thumb against their closed lids, Evie felt drawn toward him. Envious inside the pale light and abandoning the window for good, she watched.

Beyond where she lay, Evie heard him sigh and hoped desperately that in his sadness, the figure might turn and realize the new version of herself waiting. Instead, a flood of tears ran into her soul forcing the girl toward despair.

"Taliesin!"

If she could just talk to him, perhaps the sadness would go, but his name refused to call forward, She had no voice, why?

Intending to shake the wooden beam, Evie snatched the nearest post at the foot of the bed, wrestling for the attention of this sad figure. It had no texture. Instead of deep twists carved into the dark mahogany, there was no sensation beneath the cold flesh of her hands. Instead she absorbed the material! Horrified, Evie drew her hand away, resting it uselessly against her side.

Again, she tried shouting, and again, despite the siren rising into her head, the effect was soundless.

"But I'm right beside you!"

Pulling frantically against the long black mantel he wore, she couldn't even touch the fine cloth.

"No!"

Furious, Evie kicked the deep fold at the top of his leather boot. How dare he ignore her? He could see the future and the past, so why couldn't he see her? Sickened, Evie watched as her foot absorbed the leather making her toes disappear. Staring in dismay at the ghost of her hands, she clenched both fists in desperate rage.

Determined now, Evie rushed to the front of him, pushing between the bed and the heavy chair. She would make him see. Turning away, his face remained hidden beneath the wide brim circling the dark circumference of his hat.

"My Eve."

The breath from his kiss against her stone face ripped through her soul.

"Taliesin, no!"

Pulling back his chair he appeared to be giving up. It was unthinkable.

"Don't leave me here, how can you leave me alone in this darkness? Find me!"

Without voice, Evie screamed and pounded on the bed, dragging the top sheets and making a miserable failure as her hands vanished into the cool linen.

Smoothing his gloves and adjusting the tilt on his hat, the figure continued his retreat. Again Evie screamed his name, feeling her soul tear for the want of attention. She could forget about the stupid castle and return to her body and the pain if only to hold his presence once again.

In her panic Evie recalled Adam and his infant burial alive, inhaling the crushing weight of his death, and again but older, wanting the descent of blood pouring from each blossom. His appearance too, from the window of the bus, chasing the dirty streets with the rise of the castle grounds, teasing her with the apple, hurling it toward the muddy window.

So much she still needed to understand.

She recalled Chris and her desperate call to Taliesin. He had taken possession of her thoughts, giving all he could to ease her pain, and in the sanctuary of his voice, she had fallen away and now stood beyond herself, desperate.

How could he give up this easily? Taliesin with all his magic and powers!

"No! Stay!"

Frantically she watched as the figure, drawn to full height pushed the beautiful chair behind him, its scrape along the stone floor echoing the cavernous room. Head bowed, he began a return to the quiet shadows and Evie felt the sense of his loss rain tears against her face.

"But I'm here!"

Again, she made the noiseless scream, he couldn't leave her. This could not be the end. Leaping forward she grabbed at the mantel, wanting to pull it back from his shoulders but the touch fell to nothing.

Alright then, she would follow him. Scrambling across the bed and jumping over her still form, Evie prepared to cut him off.

"Taliesin!"

Catching his shoulder, Evie shoved it violently, appalled by the sight of her hand disappearing into the ghost of this human being. Unaffected, he continued his journey toward the shadows.

"Help me! For God's sake, don't abandon me to this death."

"Concentrate your thoughts on the action, not the panic."

Guiding Evie's foot toward his shins, the quick instruction fell into her head, delivering her intention into the middle of his right leg. Turned up at the corners, the crimson mouth smiled toward her.

"You will have to work harder than that, little spirit".

His mouth and eyes smiling in their game evaporated all trace of sadness.

"The misery of your despair became unbearable and for your sake, I told you what you must do. It is a lesson that takes time. Nevertheless, I admire your efforts and take pleasure in the speed with which you learn.

"But it is too dangerous for you to exist in this way and although un-intentioned, I understand your desire to move beyond yourself. Do not think however, that I will forget this when the time comes for my alliance with the one who caused you harm. Now calm the panic in your thoughts and take my hand."

Afraid the effort might come to nothing Evie reached her hands forward with deliberate slowness.

"Courage, you are strong and cannot fail."

The ends of her fingers met his, throwing her back into herself and the trauma that went with it, then catapulted forward again, she stumbled. But he had her and it was into and not through him as she initially feared.

Breathing against the fabric at long last, Evie relished the finely woven fibers upon her skin. She needed stillness, to feel the solid weight of his presence, and he seemed content for the moment to let the girl remain steady against him. But she had to ask, the question claiming all other thoughts.

Hands traveling to her shoulders, gently he turned the girl toward the motionless form. Knowing what she wanted to say, he was telling her to do so.

"Have I died?"

The terrible, uncomplicated question hung in the dark air and seemed to contradict the light amusement playing across his voice.

"Evie, such worries, will the drama of your fears ever rest? But to answer your question, some would say so and therein lies the danger. You have the ability to project, to dwell beyond your skin and it is this infant ability that facilitates your elevation into me during my feed. Now however, without understanding how to return, you have taken the next step, to move beyond yourself completely. What you managed to achieve here was accidental and in your innocence, I cannot find anger. One day you will move in and out of yourself at will and without the panic of your return, but not for some time."

Absorbing the panic of loneliness and shadows Taliesin's voice tumbled into her head.

Yes, he watched from inside the darkness as she shifted beyond herself studying the room, discovering the castle and then the view beyond the window. She became cold there because he made it so, forcing the return of her attentions toward him, her desire to return into herself.

"Seeing you perfectly, I ignored your presence and it worked, you wanted my sadness to end, your panic ensuring the will to return into who you are. Your determined efforts were of great amusement and I wanted to smile but dared not, keeping up the charade until I could bear your sadness no longer. Now though, I must assist your return and beg your trust in me once more. Walk with me here."

Grasping the ends of his fingers, Evie walked to where she lay, waiting for life.

"Move into yourself."

"How? I don't understand."

"Empty everything from your mind and think only of where you lie. Now be there, step into your core, go to where you belong. In this, trust me Evie, I will not fail you."

Taking the girl's left hand, Taliesin pulled it forward, reaching as he did, for the right hand on the motionless version of Evie. Tired, Evie watched as the length of his fingers carefully clasped both her palms, then she fell.

Panicked, Evie grasped for Taliesin. Nothing, no Taliesin, not even her other self. Petrified, she spun around, hands outstretched. He had been wrong. She had died and in his mistake let her go. Choking in despair, Evie fought the darkness.

"There is no need for fighting here."

Her hands stopped grasping at nothing. In the far corner the dancing fire jumped and leapt. Above lay the heavy canopy, its deep green staining the flickering light.

"Welcome to your return. You should heal now."

The voice said again.

Chapter Twenty-Two

Battling the dark air, Evie dragged herself up, grasping at Taliesin's arm. Urging her against the soft collection of pillows, she obliged, permitting her head to rest. Sitting in the chair he studied her closely.

Removing the black gloves, Taliesin's lack of announcement only indicated the seriousness of the gesture, his eyes never leaving her face as he placed the discarded item, palms together at the side of her on the bed.

Without daring to speak, Evie observed the emergence of each long, pale hand seeming to mark a critical turn in their relationship. It made her sad, that he must do this because of her, of the terrible thing taking place.

Studying for the first time, the nails; pink, well trimmed and healthy, Evie wanted to touch the length of each beautifully shaped finger as the broad surface of each hand reached carefully toward her.

Pains creeping into her body stole her breath and she could only gasp that he didn't have to do this, that he should not affect himself by it.

He spoke at last, the serious tones breaking each delirious thought.

"Do nothing, heed everything I tell you now and trust me. To heal you must remain within yourself, leaving again will be fatal. Follow my voice, do not fear what you See and remember always, I am with you."

Rubbing both palms together he maintained the same, steady glance, studying the girl's responses, aware of her desire to touch the smooth skin unveiled by the removal of each glove.

"Stunt your curiosity and drink this, from now on there are no questions."

Cupped within his hands was a large silver Chalice, the sides of which depicted ebony nightingales soaring toward a sapphire sky, a scatter of diamond white stars lifted the dark blue.

Examining the object's seamless arrival, Evie stared into the tiny emerald eyes pressed into each bird, the bright surface drawing her toward their activity.

She was soaring, at least she felt like it, moving fast and airborne but lying down all the same. A hand too, reached forward, brushing against her throat.

Deep thirst and a spinning fall.

She felt sick.

"Drink, Evie."

Her hands barely lifted toward the shining object and they struggled forward, but not before her eyes caught the shadow of another movement; the shadow of a man, his reflection captured above the wing of a bird. A gnarled stick went before him, tapping against the stone floor, the length of his silver hair returning into the flickering dark before disappearing.

"Say nothing," returned Taliesin's reminder, staying the question forming its first word.

Clutching the silver stem, Evie saw then the transformation of his hands, a pattern of dark veins rising to the surface of pale skin above. It reminded her of the blood rain and its fall from the scatter of fairytale blossom in an orchard far away. A place she wished it were possible to recall

"Drink."

She couldn't lift her head. With the cup's smooth edge pressed against her mouth it might have been turning each muscle to stone. The more she touched the silver Chalice, the heavier Evie felt. She couldn't move, it felt like a living death.

Again the patient voice rolled forward, balancing on the air between them. He would sooner fall into hell than fail her, however she must continue to trust.

The first crystal drops of water captured the edge of Evie's tongue while Taliesin's right hand made a careful gesture toward the center of her back so that he bore the girl's weight until she felt almost as air.

His touch drew a veil across her eyes making everything fade. Frantically Evie struggled to hold onto the light within the fireplace, afraid that if she lost that, she lost everything.

Hands gripping Evie's neck crushed the air struggling into her throat. Choking, the girl fought desperately, digging her hands into the flesh of the one doing this to her.

Thrust into a place of nowhere, Evie saw and felt too much of everything. Catching the swollen bruises adorning face and neck, Evie screamed. A necktie, digging into her flesh strangled all sounds from the girl forcing the terrified sounds of begging to remain within her head. Blood from her nose had long since spread onto the floor but not before marking crimson stains against her throat. A dark crust of blood cased the socket of Evie's left eye.

"Fear none of it. Fall into my voice and breathe as you know how. Let me take this from you."

Tracing the path to her pain, carefully, slowly, the pattern of his hands floated across Evie's stricken face down toward length of her neck claiming the bruises and the blood.

Power flowed from his touch, shuddering through her lungs and into every cell, delivering vital breath, making her breathe.

His invasion, pure, wanted.

The fall came again.

Receiving the blood against her throat, his tongue drew the scarlet liquid into his body. Heat from his hands pushed into her veins, delivering life among the spinning tumble of death and the terrible sense of falling.

A cold explosion against the back of her tongue. More water came next, healing the thirst and dry pain.

At last, the fireplace returned and Taliesin also. Gasping into the lavender air, Evie cried for what she had seen. She wanted never to leave the safety of the castle, resisting as gently, Taliesin pushed her away.

Looking at his hands, Evie noticed their transformation. Once perfect, the skin now replicated the swelling and bruises he sought to remove. Instinctively she reached toward him, wanting to take everything back, to save him from this. He had taken everything to himself, her pain, her injuries and the near death. She could have cried that for her, he had done this, suffering on her account.

"Your hands!" Sobbed Evie, tears raining against the wounded flesh now stretched thinly across the backs of each one.

"Remove your concerns, sadness cannot help this, think only of yourself and become whole again."

Such a selfless act and it ripped her heart to pieces.

The Chalice reemerged but she wanted none of it. In fact its very presence made the girl shiver. She didn't want this drink again and resisted the cold silver forced against her lips. The last of the drink froze her insides and horribly Evie felt her final breath die as a hand, invisible to her vacant eyes lay the girl back against the pillows.

Something touched her arms, floating against the flayed skin and she fought it. She didn't want this, never did want it and wished for the strength to kill him, to stop this sickening movement beneath her flesh.

"Evie, it is me in this, I am here, do not fight against me."

His voice brushed against her face and she felt it then, the full embodiment of him within her core and the sickening sensation of falling away from herself and toward his voice.

He told her to look but she didn't want to. However, the patient voice insisted that Evie must See this to remember her time here, so there would be no doubt when the consequence came.

"Take everything in, everything."

She could see everything from above, dizzy from the confusion of how it was possible.

Her arms, dear God! Purple and dark blue branded her ruined skin. The rise of angry welts protesting her bare shoulders after being forced down by the one who did this, and after being struck, and struck, then struck again by the brass belt buckle long after leaving with Taliesin.

The sight of her left wrist made her sick. Turned inwards, three of her middle fingers lay twisted into the hand, broken.

Horribly too, the skin on the top of her right breast flapped open, lazy, a pattern of teeth marking their assault and telling the final story of how afterwards he continued to hurt anyway, even when she no longer moved.

Seeing into the pit of her attacker's thoughts, Evie found nothing but flaring rage. Raising the ruined wrist slightly, she screamed from the pain, recoiling as Taliesin placed it gently onto the bed.

Inside herself now, the pain flared everywhere, blood running between her legs soaked the white gown and the linens beneath. Forgetting her wrist, Evie screamed again, tearing the sound through her body and into her head.

"Taliesin!"

Sobbing into the grass, Evie rolled onto her side, curling her knees inwards. She could hear that stream again, oblivious to the horror taking place upon its banks.

What happened to her castle and the fireplace? Confused, Evie wanted the bed and the comfort of Taliesin, to be free of the blood and the pain. Eyes closed and wishing for nothing but sleep eternal, she was instead lifted then carried without a word from the one in whose arms she lay, useless.

She lay on the ground again among soft earth, a battered body covered in a bloodied gown captured within a floating reflection rippling sideways.

She felt beyond anything good.

"My eternal Evie, be without pain."

He pushed her then, out into the cool channel of water where she could drift, untouched, forever.

"Sink beneath the surface where it is warm, and let my hands hold you so the peace of these depths may surround you. Watch as the light breaks the golden surface and rise toward it, drifting there, reclaim what was taken from your soul and heal. Know yourself as you were and return, taking my voice and my presence within you."

Floating toward the pale light, Evie caught her image, captured from above. Already the blood and the bruises had vanished, her skin, unbroken, restored. For a moment she observed her drift upstream, dark hair cast about the sides of her face, pale arms placed across her chest, and the long, soft dress, embroidered with delicate silver threads escorting her arrival.

Sleep came next.

In dreams, she remembered everything, her escort into a place beyond herself. Depleted now, Taliesin would recover within the Waiting Place, gathering strength, watching, still.

To kill Chris.

The stream resisted and Evie accepted its falter as something inevitable. Holding onto the memory of Taliesin's presence, she recalled the castle, the roar from the sea beyond and Edern's stream where she longed forever to remain. Already Evie wished to return.

Opening her eyes carefully, Evie held them in narrow slits, just enough to peer below her eyelashes to be really sure, to know Chris had gone. He had of course, abandoning the girl to her swollen face, the blood and the death he ran from. Coward that he was.

Crawling to her hands and knees, Evie half expected to be overcome by searing pain, reaching as she did, for the discarded clothes. However, the action was mere reflex she was already dressed, her clothing without so much as a crease.

Amazingly too, as her eyes adjusted to the shaft of light filtering through the open hatch door from the living room above, Evie noticed the provisions gathered earlier. Cell-Phone Pam's newspaper, folded and in the corner, the ration of dried fruit standing next to it.

Only the small thermos of water, lying on its side suggested an incident. That and the silver chain supporting the apple pendant around her neck, sliding down her front as she stood up. Reaching beneath her sweatshirt, Evie withdrew the object, upset that it snapped in two, the dark ruby center representing the heart of the fruit, gone.

Fighting the wall of tears standing at the ready, Evie slipped the broken gift into her pocket and hauling herself through the floor climbed into the bright living room.

Chris would pay; it was simply a matter of the wait. Meanwhile she would lock the little trap door, return the carpet to its rightful place on the living room floor and since no-one would believe her anyway, act as though nothing had happened. Besides, there were dishes to wash, they must be done or she would be punished.

Entering the kitchen, Evie fell upon an unwelcome display of pots, pans and the cold remains of unwanted food. Scraping them into a plastic bag hung on a hook at the side of the sink, the scratch of metal fork against pan, grated into a sudden headache.

Trying her best to ignore the pain and rolling up her sleeves, Evie filled the bowl with hot soapy water, plunged both hands into the scorching liquid and accepted the aerial rain of kisses descending against the back of her neck.

Chapter Twenty-Three

One frustrating hour of tossing and turning was all Evie needed before realizing staying asleep was a tall order. Dead tired when her head hit the pillow all she did now was swear at the scratchy cotton sheets pricking her skin with a million tiny needles.

Exasperated, she sat up, then disgusted she must sit up in the first place, flung herself back onto the uncomfortable bed and wished instead she were sleeping at the Enchanted Castle.

Just one night, just one perfect, peaceful night, that was all she needed to feel those rich, smooth fabrics float against her skin once more, instead of feeling hot and itchy like now.

Evie hated nights like these because it meant exhaustion the next day with her mother accusing the girl of smoking weed or scrounging for a pre-filled syringe over at Orchard Park. Tomorrow was Saturday and she should be washing the living room curtains, if she put them in the machine at the wrong temperature, there would be hell to pay.

It wasn't necessary for any curtains at the window in her castle chamber given there was no-one for miles. Any way you chose you could stare into forever, down the slope of meadow or out across the sparkle of emerald sea, wherever the slant of moon fell, the eye could receive it all.

No moon here, lamented Evie, slanted or otherwise, its absence plunging the room into the sort of darkness reserved for her journeys with Taliesin. Longing for the scent of lavender, Evie knew calling him was useless. He was hunting and despite the fact she knew it was well deserved, Evie wondered about his prey, what it would feel like. Staring through the gloom of pitch darkness, she trembled slightly for the inevitable, recalling Cell-Phone Pam and her mother's return to the house shortly after Chris's attack.

Evie hadn't been expecting company and having just put the last cup in the cupboard, reluctantly lifted it out again, reaching for another as simultaneously she filled the kettle. Tea would be expected so she'd better pony up a couple of tea bags. Several chocolate biscuits followed, Evie tumbling the little pile onto a plate with pink rosebuds.

"Hurry up," Pam's orders barked from the living room.

"Sorry." Scurrying back to the living room, Evie trod across the Lilly carpet, trying to ignore the rise of nausea threatening her stomach as she did so.

Handing a cup of tea each to her mother and Pam, Evie waited for permission to leave, perhaps they might want something. Indeed, reaching into a plastic Safeway bag, Pamela withdrew a pair of hiking boots, dried mud from some miserable hillside caking the sides. A pair of soggy red shoelaces limped toward the floor.

"Clean these for me will you? I've got a demo' tomorrow."

Sending the cracked leather boots in the general direction of Evie, Pam leaned toward her smart leather tote bag and reaching in withdrew a cell phone.

"I'll call the team and find out what time the cell phone tower demo' starts."

Without giving Evie another glance or word, Cell-Phone Pam breathed a barely audible conversation into the little black phone, a tone obviously not meant for Evie's ears.

Saying nothing and armed with Pam's hideous boots, Evie returned to the kitchen feeling her feet sink into the pit of hell with every little step.

Casting her thoughts toward Edern, Evie chaffed the mud from each shoe. Of course he wasn't there. Then in the reflection on the tin of shoe polish, she attempted to recreate the Enchanted Castle. First, as seen through the window on the bus, and more recently, the small miracle of its existence within her soul. She got nothing but criticism when her mother walked into the kitchen and caught her staring at the little round tin.

"You're bloody stupid you are, that's your trouble. I rue the day you didn't walk off that roof with your friggin' father but then you probably pushed him and your sister off anyway. I knew you was born evil, knew as soon as I looked at you with a pair of jet black eyes staring back at me. If I'd have had you at home I would've drowned you in the sink."

Too far gone, Evie didn't care. He had sent it to her at last, the lavender fragrance elevating her soul above anything words were capable of doing. Smiling at her mother, Evie walked past the woman and handed the immaculate boots to Pam. She had washed the laces, informed Evie, they were drying over the sink in the kitchen.

"Were you listening to me?" Undeterred, Maureen followed Evie into the living room, feet all over the earlier crime scene.

"I mean, just what were you doing in there staring at a bloody tin of polish. You're in another world you are, that's half your trouble. The other half's that you should have been dead a long time ago, either that or never been born."

Slipping past her mother, Evie returned to the kitchen. Chris was being chased, she could feel the rise of his panic in her throat and it made her smile. Taliesin, her beloved was sending a message. True to his promise. Her protector eternal.

"What are you laughing at?" Following Evie, Maureen re-entered the kitchen. "Anyway. I've got some news for you. Pamela's moving in."

Pouring a glass of cold water for herself, Evie listened to the rest. Cell-Phone Pam was going to live at 126 Eden Road. There was no point in two women living alone. This apparently being the logic suggested by Pam and shared over a cup of milky tea post floral arranging. The two would share a room, Maureen and Pamela sleeping in the same bed.

"I mean we're both girls." Argued Maureen to Evie's back.

Rinsing the cup then drying the inside, Evie popped it back into the cupboard.

"Good".

Against her ears, Chris's neck snapped.

Now though propped upright, Evie slammed an impatient thump into her pillow in the vain hope it might make the synthetic filling more malleable than the lump of concrete it felt like now.

One eye drifting to the hands on the luminous clock revealed it was two-thirty. "Why aren't I tired?" Evie fired the angry question into the dark room.

Kicking furiously at the quilt, Evie forced it to the foot of the bed. Her skin felt like fire and she had begun to sweat, soaking through her night gown. Eyes firing into the darkness, the girl wondered what she should do next.

She'd had enough.

Swinging both legs to the side of the bed, Evie sank her feet into the carpet, the soft impact igniting thoughts of Edern's long emerald grass. What if she went out? It was an outrageous idea but she didn't care, compared to recent events, walking alone on a dark street in the middle of the night was nothing.

Reaching for the clothing heaped into the corner of her room, Evie imagined turning the hideous jeans and the pink sweatshirt into a perfect fire, each flame transforming the nightmare of Chris into dark ash.

Instead, picking each item she lay them against her hot skin, feeling the rise of aversion stretch the pit of her stomach. Her head ached and the nausea was coming again.

Being the only pair of jeans and sweatshirt she had, she would never escape the memory behind these clothes.

Dressed and doing her best to bury the hideous association connecting her with Chris and the rape, Evie rounded off the ugly ensemble with a pair of white socks and the flat black shoes she wore for work, catching as she leant forward, his stale scent drifting against the soft pink shirt, sailing into her nose.

The final assault.

Walking with Chris, each step and tiny gesture molded the fabric until it formed a second skin, his. Withdrawing every sinew from the ghost of his touch, Evie retracted as far from the clothing as she could, hatred burning into the back of her throat, mixing with the rise of nausea.

Compared with that, sneaking downstairs was a country picnic, even though at night each stair creaked and you never knew which one would go first. After that she would prize open the wooden front door and face the embracing dark.

But the stairs were quiet and an amazed Evie descended all fourteen without drama.

Already she could see the key, a silver glint hanging from the little brass hook next to the weather barometer that worked in opposites. Dry if the dial read rainy, cloudy when sunny, and so on.

Lifting the key from its perch, Evie quietly turned the series of locks running the length of the door, a silent breath of relief rising into her throat as she encountered the deserted street at last.

Pulling the front door closed and snapping its lock, Evie crossed the path to the yellow front gate then hand against the cold latch lifted the little handle. Swinging open the metal frame she turned quickly onto the empty pavement with neither hesitation nor a backward glance. Inhaling the dark silence, Evie extinguished at last, the remaining heat scorching her raw nerves.

Chapter Twenty-Four

It felt like mere seconds before reaching the top of Eden Road. A scatter of tiny stars illuminated the night.

Hundreds, more than she'd ever seen; and the moon, a perfect circle surveyed the Forbidden Path, dropping darkness onto the fields beyond and where Taliesin once warned Evie never to tread.

All of it, reminiscent of a place once visited.

Taliesin, he had re-created it, an invitation signed among shadows calling her presence forward. It would be alright to go, taking the path against her feet, Seeing into his memory and finding him. She would not be afraid, he would be waiting, giving this to her, the edge of Edern.

This was not the Forbidden Place.

Within moments Evie reached the soft entrance to the path beyond which lay the dark sweep of fields and hidden marshes.

"Find him."

Yes, he waited, she understood this as the words tumbled into her head. She must find him in the reversal of reality, the Between-World existing beyond what others saw.

Already, the cruel path and the fields she hated were transformed into the deep softness of Edern and now, with the gathering of her own powers, she held it to herself. So long as she did this, he could offer protection from the reality of the place, reasoned the girl.

She would exist for a time here, safe.

Picking her way through the path was easy. Illuminated by the moon, its golden circle floated above the tree line, a yellow ball, mused Evie, which once thrown into the air, had forgotten it should fall back down to earth.

Carefully, she moved along the path, following long fingers of moonlight as though it were his hand she held. No trickery this time, no trail of brambles threatening to claim her ankles, no reach of ivy holding her to the earth. Reaching the edge of the fields at last, Evie stepped into Taliesin's Edern.

Soundless here, not even a blade of grass whispered among the warm breeze touching their surface. Her feet too, despite the length of each strand wrapping her ankles failed to carry the tug and snap as each dark ribbon broke. Fearing for a moment that perhaps this wasn't Edern and she had been tricked onto the path again, Evie pulled for courage, wishing for Taliesin.

But she must be patient; her lesson was to move through this image, keeping it intact. She shouldn't be concerned with sound effects, one day she could manipulate whatever she wanted but for now, Evie must learn through baby steps, she reminded herself.

Rain, silent and deliciously cold stroked her face. Taliesin's doing, so at least she had that, the sensation of water. He must be watching and she jogged toward a small cluster of oak trees breaking the moonlit horizon, pausing for breath as she reached the first canopy.

Watching the rain Evie thought of Adam and wondered if each drop were to become blood like in the first story given to her, should she let the edge of her mouth invite each crimson pearl against her tongue? Curious, she wondered what his blood might taste like, warm, flowing against her throat and into her veins. Feeding, nourishing her desire to understand everything shown to her so far.

Wishing for the secret canopy of apple blossom instead of the gnarled trunk leaning into her back, Evie observed a sudden shift in the moon's course. No longer hanging over her head, it had drifted further into the trees.

"Find him."

Heeding the request Evie headed inward, stealing forward and creeping deeper into the wooded maze, invited by the thread of moonlight, it stopped suddenly, leaving the girl in the middle of a dark somewhere.

It felt different here. Studying its effect against her senses, Evie inhaled the transformation. It wasn't that the rain made a soft landing on the damp branches and wet earth, she could hear that. No there was something else, a very specific sound directly above; a sort of twisting creak with a bit of a swing, slow then quick depending on the breeze circulating the trees.

Slowly, Evie faced the broad tree standing to her back.

And then it became obvious why she had been drawn here in the first place.

The figure, swinging, legs idle against the slow circle, red and black tie forming a neat circle around his swollen neck, its polyester end making a careful knot on the third branch.

Chris.

Taliesin's offering to Evie, fulfilling his promise to protect her, always.

Chapter Twenty-Five

Strange watching the figure swing like that, while some part of Evie thought she should fear this, alone in the woods with nothing more than the moon and Chris's dangling corpse for company. Instead she stood, fascinated, feet deep rooted into the black earth, a quiet audience to the silent marionette.

He was bleeding and again she searched for the horror in this. Finding none Evie discovered this to be the strangest thing of all. That she would not run from here, darting between trees, arms flailing against every leaf and branch until, breathless, she reached the clearing and the path beyond.

Yet she should fear this offering, Taliesin's demonstration that he was indeed powerful, and yes, he could do as he pleased, had done so beyond her time and deeper into the time before that.

But still she watched. A light breeze twirling the body lent a carefree quality to the scene, and for a moment she half expected Chris to begin laughing, calling her a stupid whore for thinking she could get away that easily, and she had better start running for there would be no head start and hell to pay once he got down from there.

Again a soft breeze pushed against the figure, sending it back the other way and rounding off the awful display with an aerial pirouette before returning to face a transfixed Evie once again. He smiled, Evie could swear to it, two purple lips stretched to capacity.

Taliesin's work, all of it, the moon, the breeze, everything. Evie wondered if he was there now, toying with his kill, observing her reaction from his place within the trees. The sick choreography stilled, switched off suddenly, making Chris appear to rest on an invisible mid-air platform.

Staring at the figure Evie reached for sympathy, this had been a life, but hadn't this finished human being just hours earlier left her for dead beneath the floor of their home? She shrugged off her remorse.

Nevertheless, he could not escape Taliesin's anger. After taking Evie's wounds into himself, her entity had returned her, whole, from the Enchanted Castle and his mercy of Edern and left her in the hunt for Chris. Driving him mad, Taliesin made Chris hang while feeding from the merciless images slamming into the thoughts of his prey.

A thin blood line extended from each eye, and in the remaining moonlight Evie saw how they were flung wide open, receiving whatever horrors he had been given. Blood also ran from his nose, all of it mixing with the stuff from his eyes, pooling at the base of his neck and soaking into the top of his scratchy green sweater.

Yes, Taliesin had fed deeply, taking everything from the terror of each response, gaining more strength then driving deeper into his brain until under pressure, it had given up, hemorrhaging as her entity withdrew from the wasteland he created.

Seeing this, she understood the Storyteller's warning, her frequent nosebleeds as he fed on the responses to the stories and images he created inside her thoughts. How she begged for the knowledge of his past, of Edern, and his patient refusal because the feed would be too deep, killing her for the effort. Now though, this was the power and the magic played out in vengeful storytelling and staring at the wounded corpse, Evie could only imagine the visions Chris had been forced to endure.

Taliesin sent her here for this, so she might see his work, his art. The flash-thought had been to find Chris, not to seek her entity as first thought. The lesson instead, to look and to understand.

Stepping closer, Evie approached the hanging figure, cautiously staring into the bleeding face, still half afraid he might say something in his death. But, Evie rationalized, that would be Taliesin's magic if he did and he would never scare her like that.

She wanted to touch his hand, harmless now in its dreadful sleep. Carefully Evie stretched her fingers forward, searching for what earlier had been the cause of such pain.

She had never touched death before and her breath refused to come forward, strangling the back of her throat as she felt now for the first time, the permanent frost buried beneath his skin rise against the tips of her fingers. He moved then, slightly, as another breeze shifted the branches, partially rotating the swaying body.

Catching the fast scream, Evie fought its ascent. Courage would be had here. She would not be afraid of this and refused the natural urge to recoil as a single, shoe-less foot bearing a dirty white sock kicked against her legs. The head fell forward revealing a bloody mass at the top of his skull.

Taliesin's point of entry?

Perhaps, but what really mattered was how the fingers on this ruined body gripped hers. In death he refused to let go, as though he wanted a partner in this terrible sleep.

Staring at the slash for a grin, Evie wouldn't let him. He would not take the satisfaction, and with her left hand prized his fingers away from her right. She hated him and could only be happy that Taliesin fulfilled the promise made to her months earlier.

An image, sharp, flashing into her head and she tipped forward, inhaling the sweet death within his clothes. Someone running, impossible to tell who, but the effect was exhausting. In fact, she might be moving too, fast, incredibly fast.

Traces of fear jolted her heart, vibrating her throat. Still the panic continued, pouring into her veins and making her terrified of something unseen.

But this fear had no place within her, it did not originate from anything she had done, yet the flow continued, flooding every nerve until nothing remained except cold, shaking terror.

She was running now too, impossible though because she still held onto his dead grasp. Clutching the fingers of her left hand, his aerial corpse floated against her body. In spite of Taliesin's revenge, Chris might have been coming to her again.

But this was the least of her troubles as she became less aware of the dead weight hitting the side of her leg and the slow blood falling from his nose and eyes onto her reluctant grip below, and more present in the panic screaming through her thoughts.

The voice she recognized.

Chris.

Another image came.

Chapter Twenty-Six

"*I'm removing the tie from my neck because it seems the most logical way to do this, the last thing that makes any sense when certainty has fallen away. He, or whatever it is that chased me here, inside my head, insists I carry it out, that it is the only thing left for me to do. I am dead anyway.*

"*My hands tremble at the tight knot nestled between both shirt collars. I have always worn my tie small, no reason, I just preferred it that way. It was the same at school when everybody wore their knots big, but that was a long time ago. Anyway, it seems stupid I should think about that now, irrelevant. When all is said and done what does it matter?*

"*As I do this my head doesn't hurt as much, just like the voice said. It has kept its promise, the one I laughed at, the Storyteller. It's in my brain now, feeding, I feel its tug, pulling from my thoughts. But for now the images too have gone, but only enough for me to release this knot from my neck and slip the smooth strip of red and black fabric forward while I still can. While it lets me do this without agony. It will come again though, soon, that much I have been told.*

"*It must be the third branch; the first two are no good. I am informed that it is not as strong as the other and I must do as I am instructed. Besides, even I agree, there wouldn't be enough clearance between my feet and the earth I stand on and it is imperative I do not touch the floor for this to work. It would defeat the purpose, there is, after all, a point to all this.*

"*The only drawback to the plan is that I must climb while wearing my black shoes, the expensive ones with the leather soles. They had* been purchased in the men's department at Evie's shop just two weeks ago. She didn't know I watched her, purchasing the shoes so I might remain longer, to stare, listen to the one sided conversations, observer as she slipped seamlessly between two worlds. So they remind me of her, these shoes, and I'm aware they will scuff very badly against the rough fragments of bark. I don't suppose that really matters though; it won't be the shoes they look at when they find me.

"Pain in my head and I am reminded I must get this over with, that although the end will be the same, it could be much worse if I don't obey and so I climb.

"Actually, it is surprisingly easy considering there is no particular foothold, so long as I dig my fingers into the damp bark. I feel each piece dig beneath my nails, sharp, and know they must bleed now and know too that if it wasn't for this impenetrable blackness, I would see the gathering of this blood color each finger. But I cannot care about that either.

"It watches inside my head, this thing, marking time and movement toward the third tier. If I take too long the pain will return, reminding me of its intentions. Slipping once, my face strikes the trunk, a dreadful pain in my left eye follows, but not from the thing inside my head, no, I believe something stabbed its surface. Yes, this is excruciating and it moves now, my eye, as though it were cold jelly.

"If I were to survive this night, I would not want to survive this night.

"The climb continues and I reach where I believe the third branch extends from the tree and its wait for my terrible presence upon it. I think I am being told what to do because it all seems fairly easy from here. I straddle the invisible branch, take the length of this tie wrapped around my hand and prepare to secure it around the damp width.

"Everything is dark here, even the moon remains hidden and not a single star can be found, but my hands work anyway and despite their raw pain, manage to fix the practical knot. My eye hurts still. Such a sick throb this, and I want it to be over. I cannot think straight but I continue anyway.

"Another image, I see without sight. A girl, her, Evie, lying on a dirt floor, posed, bruised, vacant eyes, staring, blood, so much of the stuff. The quick flash eats into my brain, pushing in, punishing and I *almost fall from the impact. It is beginning again, it grows impatient, this thing.*

"*Grasping the other end of the fabric, I secure the knot around my neck, feeling how cold the flesh is here. Indeed, there is a wicked chill in the air, impossible to ignore. Its effect settles into my bones and I wonder for how long I will feel this cold after my departure from this height.*

"*'Evie'. Her name, that girl, thundering into my head. It won't leave and I must remember why I am here. Indeed, it demands I know that she, his love, is the reason.*

"*If I jump now, how long will it take, two seconds, maybe three? Vaguely I ponder their worth, given that's all I have left.*

"*Go now.*" *There is no kindness to this voice, its ordered tone slamming cold against my head, claiming my last action to itself.*

Death, I must find it.

"*The fall comes, its descent rising into me, the length tightening. It is pleased, this thing, I can tell because his grip releases, leaving me for the dying that must be next. And still I continue the fall beyond the length of makeshift rope. Meeting the earth, I inhale the buried damp of worms and rotten leaves. It is not pleased.*

"*A quick image, then it is gone but long enough for me to know of its presence. A figure standing at my head.*

"*Boots, long, dark, turned over at the knee and the muddied hem of a mantle, black. Instinctively I know not to touch it, it would make things much worse. I sense I am a failure and it tells me I am. There is anger that I did not do this right, that I was given the mercy of a chance to do it by independent means but failed in my endeavor.*

"*All of this I know as I am pulled from the ground and slammed face first into the tree, breaking my nose. This is brutal and I want death to come. The night wraps itself around me and I cannot breathe, something pushes against my lungs and a rib cracks, the thin sound fracturing an otherwise still night.*

"*It is outside of me, but in my head also, as before when I ran through Eden Park to escape the thing that forced me into this dead wood. Escape is impossible, it is enraged. It is him, it was him who I saw, Evie's Storyteller and I want to scream his name, beg for forgiveness but that takes breath and very little comes now.*

"Fury surrounds me. I should be dead by my own hand but he will kill me now for sure as again I am slammed into the tree, and again, losing more ribs to its impact.

"Climbing is crystal agony, each step tearing into my throat. But I must do this, I must be discovered in this way and I will do it right this time, I promise.

"I am assisted, pulled upward, my face dragging along the rough trunk, and on the outskirts of everything I want to know what sort of tree I am scaling. It is important suddenly.

"The third branch again, Evie's ruined image in my head, the pleasure in taking her, exquisite. A castle, Evie at the window, face pale and staring. A painting, I have seen this somewhere, then blood comes, flowing across its dark surface. In the short time remaining, I shall never understand any of this.

"I scream for the pain, but it remains inside, all breath has lifted from my body, leaving the terror of this and the terrible push and tug inside my brain. Was I pushed, when my hands had barely re-tied the knot? I believe this is true, I don't believe I jumped. I was never given the opportunity. But I am glad for the darkness that comes and the small explosion as my brain releases its blood from my staring eyes and nose at last. A large moon shifts the sky."

* * * * *

"Close your eyes my love and rest, you have written this night as your powers know how. Remove your touch from the useless corpse, take his poison no longer. You have seen my vengeance and I have kept my promise, swearing to your protection.

"Let me deliver you from this dark place and return you once again to the depths of your sleep. I brought you here, to the Forbidden Place, now permit my guidance again and follow me. Slip from among the trees, beyond the fields and the path that despises your presence.

"In dreams you were safe to tread there and See but in reality still, you must not return until the time for that comes. Take my words into you and the rest your soul needs, and although you want the pull from reality I shall not feed but will remain near, watching.

"I cry for your exhaustion and I am beside you always. Sleep deep, my hands press soft against your eyes. Breathe against me, draw me in and know me in your reality. The boy's death served me well, I have strength enough for this.

"No longer as you were, move now into who you are. Your fledgling powers, take them into every cell and understand their existence. Your changing at last has come. In every sleep, a little death, rest and be ready, there is no more play."

Chapter Twenty-Seven

Friday, Chris's funeral. Evie, staring at an image of Adam and Eve arranged in luminous slivers of stained glass. Eve, golden hair trailing her hips, turning toward Adam, crimson apple in hand, and the hopeful snake coiled around the edge of a long thick branch, poised, knowing. From this point, all things would change.

Except in search of distraction, the boy Evie once wrote about made something of a cameo appearance, interrupting Eden and placing himself at the foot of the tree where he lay capturing drops of blood rain into his eager mouth. Evie meanwhile stood at the side of the trunk, minus the biblical Adam, waiting, she had no idea what for but her hands reached into the deep canopy of leaves and creamy flowers where Taliesin perched comfortably on the highest limb.

He wore a white shirt secured loosely at the front by a pattern of cross laced ties, the sleeves flouncing slightly before gathering at the wrist. The fabric ruffled suggesting a light breeze. One leg bent casually at the knee emphasized the fold at the top of his knee high boot, the dark leather forging a shadow against the tree. Hanging loosely on the opposite side of the accommodating branch his other leg swung several feet above Evie, tantalizing her shoulder with the thrust of each swing.

Ungloved, his hands revealed the texture of clear, un-bruised skin. One hand balanced a copy of *Poems* against his palm while the other held onto a dark red apple. It was this, assumed Evie, that she reached for. The faint smile playing across Taliesin's mouth suggested he might be enjoying himself.

Unblinking, he stared at her, not at the Evie squashed between her mother and Cell-Phone Pam accommodated along the hard wooden pew of the chapel, rather Evie up in the window, dressed in the same golden dress, flowered with tiny silver threads that she wore when cast into the waters of Edern. Its length swept her ankles while a strand of red blossom collected the slender waist, emphasizing the subtle curve of her hips.

Perhaps, considered Evie, given her present situation, it might be just as well she placed herself into the window where she could view the proceedings below with those she trusted, Taliesin and Adam. Here, within the sanctuary of stained glass she felt protected, extracted from the morbid events without having to be physically absent, which of course had been her first choice.

And so, miserable on the pews and lonely for Taliesin, Evie thought it might be fun to at least position the chief characters from Among Other Edens onto the stained glass biblical version of Eden. Taliesin, once you included the Adam she knew and herself as Eve, remained something of a spare character in the scene, but he came in useful anyway playing substitute for the snake. A position he seemed to take without complaint, occupying the top branch, his volume of Keats, a quiet companion.

And so there they were, a glass tableau featuring the story given to her; the tree sustaining the life of the boy lying beneath, and Taliesin delivering Evie to herself with truth and knowledge, the depths of which she barely understood.

Indeed, during the last seven days she spent almost every waking moment alongside her immortal companion. Finding herself in the twilight of the castle grounds at noon on a Tuesday, or lying on the grassy slope of the slow river in Edern, doing nothing except understand she had much to learn and there was more to know. For now though, healing must be done, there must be quiet in her head, peace within her thoughts and the reconciliation between what was lost and who she would become.

And during the times she must dwell in reality, he remained present, talking to her, easing her passage through the terrible hours that hallmarked each day.

During these moments Evie discovered she could exist in two places, living both in her Storyteller's world and her own. Such were her new abilities. Only her outer shell dwelt in reality now, just enough to let people think she was there, while the rest belonged to Taliesin. And it was just as well.

Stealth-like the coffin gathered its presence within the little Methodist chapel. Brass handles punctuated the dark cherry wood, one at the front, one at the back while two others flapped noiselessly on either side of the wooden box. Gathered around the funeral hub marched the somber procession made up of several grieving relatives, including Chris's father who stood at the head of the sad pageant, each resonating footfall playing to the finality of what was to come.

Evie continued to distract herself while Taliesin, still sitting in the tree, continued to read, thoroughly disinterested in the proceedings unfurling below. Perhaps now would be a good time to manipulate the scene so all three, Taliesin, herself and Adam might sit around the base of the trunk and watch.

Sniffing miserably into a ragged ball of tissues, Evie's mother crushed the damp mess. Having taken Chris's death hard Maureen believed herself in some way responsible for the boy's suicide, even though his parents, dropping everything at once and arriving with matching red eyes and an overnight bag, willfully denied that she was. Nevertheless, a stricken Maureen, in the presence of adults at least, seemed determined to retain sole culpability.

She'd had "no idea", the distraught woman exclaimed, that "the poor lad had been in such a state to do a thing like that!" 'That', being suicide, a word very much underemployed whenever Evie was suspected of being within ear shot, as though it might offer protection from a storm already passed.

Publicly.

Altogether another matter in private, Evie dreaded each raw moment, running through the forest at Edern for protection. Taliesin in pursuit.

That she caused the suicide of another.

"That's three now, not bad for a certified demon. You should be well satisfied with yourself. And then there was your poor uncle Colin, God only knows what he did to deserve being impaled through the chest by a bushy branch."

Recalling Colin's touch against her childish skin after delivering the fifty bloody lashes to her back, Evie blinked the memory away.

"If you were as good at everything else as you were at sending people off roofs or having them dangle twelve feet in the air by their friggin' tie, we'd be millionaires by now."

The aftermath; the police, the description of how a teenager engaged on a drugged up quest for magic mushrooms discovered Chris's body hanging from the third branch of a dead tree just yards from Orchard Park Estate became a fast legend in the living room, destined to be told then re-told on dark rainy nights somewhere around the end of October.

The blows to his head and body, discussed at length by efficient types in white coats suggested a severe beating attributed to a bewildering struggle to climb the tree in order for him to carry out the "self asphyxiation". That there were no other footprints in the muddy earth supported the absence of another presence and other than those belonging to Chris, neither were there any fingerprints on the tie.

When all was said and done, by Wednesday, in a musty little room at the top of a tall Rococo building housing a desk, a companion of yellowed papers and a crusty old ink well, Chris's departure had been ruled as "death by hanging, accompanied by a cerebral hemorrhage".

"Presumably," explained the soft spoken coroner in a mud brown suit with matching tie and a white shirt, "from the head trauma". Leaning forward, he cracked his knuckles then making everyone jump.

Evie hadn't felt in the least bit sorry for Chris, but for Taliesin's magic, he had all but killed her. Nevertheless, even through her self-imposed exile from reality, she pitied poor Albert and Dottie. After all, they hadn't caused any of it and both seemed nice enough.

Arriving on the Edern doorstep, Saturday afternoon, clutching a photo album, they looked stricken, sitting awkwardly with the guilt ridden Maureen who, having ordered another cup of sugary tea from Evie, declared she would never "forgive herself for not seeing it coming".

That the Edern household already knew two suicides, remained in the family lock box. God forbid anyone should have the impression that bumping yourself off was an occupational hazard once you crossed the threshold of 126 Eden Road.

It was during this time Evie discovered her ability to divorce herself from reality in favor of conversations and journeys with Taliesin. She could disappear inside herself for hours with no one any the wiser. So it didn't matter if she got shouted at for being too slow, or she missed a speck of dust on Chris's nightstand, because she wasn't there. The yelling and screaming that she was evil, and everybody always died because of Evie, quite literally flying over the top of her head.

Mercifully, Evie would lay on the dark grassy bank next to the river in Edern Taliesin's hands pressed gently against her head, easing the pressure, absorbing the blame. None of this was her fault, she was not evil, born gifted she should lie her thoughts with his now and rest.

Now, staring at the funeral party from her position on the window, Evie surveyed the gathering of one hundred or so mourners huddled into the small Welsh chapel. A large black and white photograph of Chris aged six stood to the side of the cross. Holding what appeared to be a pet rabbit, Evie wondered if he killed it afterwards,

It turned out Chris was not from London after all, in fact, Evie now doubted he had ever set foot in the City. It had all been for show, the accent and everything. His parents, both accountants, spoke with the soft, sing song lilt known to Welsh voices. That he faked his origins caught even Maureen by surprise and although she did her best to hide her shock, saying things like, "I thought I heard him say something in Welsh," the Jones-Davies' clearly saw their son had lied and departed for their hotel shortly after their arrival at the Edern household.

To Evie, on hearing this small revelation while wading through Edern's clear waters, she thought Chris even more pathetic. Falling backwards, arms outstretched, she broke the river's glassy surface, washing him from her thoughts.

Still sitting at the foot of the tree with Taliesin and Adam, Evie observed poor Dottie and Albert at the front of the little chapel, dressed in black, pale faces drawn tight from grief. They looked older, the sudden events of the past week aging the couple some fifty-years between them.

Caught between pre and post burial, the coffin had come to rest at the bottom of the aisle. Meanwhile, the pallbearers, momentarily seated in the front pews coughed and fidgeted in a sort of preamble to the next stage of the proceedings.

From the back of the church, a thin, slightly graying minister, positioned himself behind the casket. Promptly cut in half, a pair of black shoes and trouser cuffs peeked out from behind the trestle supporting Chris's body.

The service began, a sensitive prayer followed by a nice, familiar hymn. Above her head, Taliesin hummed 'Onward Christian Soldiers' rather casually. Slung carelessly over the branch, the Storyteller's left leg swung merrily, as one amused by the entire affair.

From her lofty position Evie observed her mother, Cell-Phone Pam and herself, singing and praying like everyone else, all dressed for the occasion in black outfits purchased the previous day during a last minute trip into town. Evie's maligned green work jacket lay flung over the back of the pew, Maureen flat out refusing to spring for a black funeral coat on the grounds that it was bad enough they had the hotel bill to fork out.

Between the two rows of functionally hard seating lay a grey stone floor, its surface worn shiny and dipped in places from years of foot traffic. Biblical passages etched the surface of several stones, Evie scanning the inscriptions until the center stone caught her attention.

Larger than the rest and a paler shade of grey, beneath lay two skeletons, side by side, girls, she knew. Dated 1646, the stone told how they died by drowning, and while technically true, they had in fact been pushed into the water. It wasn't an accident at all but for almost four hundred years, the carved inscription declared the 'tragic loss of two beloved daughters' by the same hand that sent both girls below the surface begging and struggling until their release at last, into death.

Saddened by the discovery, Evie sought a fast diversion, finding it in the formation of the chapel ceiling. Substantial oak beams stained dark by time crossed above the bowed heads of the mourners below. Further beams, pressed deep into the walls ran between each stained glass window of which there were six on either side depicting various biblical scenes. The one illustrating Adam and Eve and which Evie presently occupied being one of them.

Another prayer, hushed and reminiscent of a secret murmur, hovered midway between chapel floor and the white painted ceiling. An account of the deceased from a family member followed, voice wobbling from grief, watery eyes making constant reference to the carefully constructed message on a piece of creased, lined paper.

Reciting the Lord's Prayer, Evie lost sight of herself, Taliesin and the boy. Moments later, Adam, Eve and the inevitable serpent returned to their original positions at the window. She thought about trying to re-create the scene then reconsidered, there wasn't time.

Lifted by the solemn pallbearers, the coffin made its way to the damp graveyard. Awkward and stiff after a lengthy service the rest of the congregation rose silently from their pews and forced to exit through the same narrow doorway, politely squashed each other as they shuffled out.

With a small sense of the macabre Evie fastened the dark green coat she wore for work, dragged herself through the door and inhaled the late September air.

Straggling at the rear of the group, Evie thought about dead Chris. It seemed to smack of hypocrisy, to stand there shivering in the wet cold along with everyone else, while inside she applauded Taliesin's act.

Sneaking a peek at the bucolic scenery, Evie's head tilted forward anyway in order to sufficiently fake the prayer foisted upon her, while keeping both eyes at full circle.

Yeah, she could love it here. This place had the lot! Tripped out scenery, decked out with sheep and rolling hills, air like champagne and a tiny yard of stone angels leaning toward graves long forgotten. *How could someone born among this lot grow up to be a bastard?* Queried Evie about the nearly-buried Chris.

Lifting toward the horizon, a kestrel slipped across the darkening sky distracting Evie from resurrecting hell beneath the Edern living room floor, and while the intense silence broken only by the respectful murmur of a religious message meant Chris was never far away, Evie searched further afield for distraction.

The little scene was framed, observed Evie, by a low stone wall, the uneven top suggesting the significant loss of many slabs and facilitating its craggy charm. Wondering whether or not anyone ever bothered to fix the missing stones, Evie thought perhaps whoever it was changed their mind at the last minute fearing perfection might ruin the sort of rustic presence critical to tourists.

Beyond the stone wall, the rolling hills and the line of trees, a small village reduced by distance to a tight cluster of houses balanced on the upper edge of a sloping meadow. Smoke from one or two chimneys curled slowly toward the soft clouds, and behind the low rooftops a church spire reached into the cool autumn sky. Specks of orange and yellow lights already flickered in the early darkness and quietly Evie imagined what it might be like to dwell in peace among fairy lights and majestic steeples.

She would have loved the endless walks here and saw herself gone for hours with Taliesin's voice as her guide, telling her the story of every slope and stone set into the rambling walls. The graveyard too, a tumble of forgotten headstones enchanted her curiosity and instinctively Evie wanted to touch every stone and angel, tracing the outline of date and history to discover the forgotten stories lying beneath, quiet, patient.

"But is it not enough that you know ours already?" Taliesin, interrupting her thoughts with an impatient stamp.

Having been relegated to the sidelines in this place of death for long enough, he wanted a little fun and Evie felt the secret brush from his hand against hers.

"Taliesin, I haven't the faintest idea what you're talking about."

"I do not wish to discuss it now."

"Then why are you here?" Evie thought back.

Was he sulking? Other than sitting in the Tree of Life inside the chapel, he showed no interest in attending either the service or speaking with her.

"My desire to see everything through. And I never sulk." Speaking close to her ear, he whispered softly, teasing. After all the seriousness of recent days, her Storyteller wanted to play, finding the funeral of the one whom he killed an appropriate time. Taliesin continued.

"I must admit, I admired your translation of the stained glass window and quite enjoyed my time spent sitting in that tree reading Keats. Although it must be said, I am not very happy you chose to substitute me for the snake."

"You could have moved if you wanted to, you're the one with all the powers, not me!"

Ceremony forgotten, Evie yelled at the oak casket making a solemn descent into the vacant earth. For a moment everything stopped, the coffin pausing mid way between this life and the next. The minister ceased to speak and even the quiet backdrop of steady grief pausing momentarily before politely resuming as though nothing had happened. Having never anticipated Evie's comment in the first place, no one knew what to do with it.

"You'll make a show of me, you will!" Maureen, standing alongside her daughter pulled at the sleeve on the girl's viscose jacket. Even Pamela shot a reproachful look. There would be trouble once they piled into Pam's bright yellow Volkswagen on the three-hour journey home. Quickly, Evie dreamed up ways of disappearing into her head.

Undeterred, Taliesin continued, "You called me there in the first place."

"Well I thought it was just an image, I didn't think you were really there. Anyway, you've never gone to church before, I always assumed you couldn't go in." Carefully, Evie thought toward his voice.

"Evie, I am not the Devil, of course, I can enter. Until now, I have simply chosen not to, that is all. I have my reasons and before you ask, that is not an invitation to question why. Besides, I became bored inside my own space with little to entertain me and when you called me forward, I thought it would be fun to join your small distraction."

It wasn't the breeze brushing the length of hair from the sides of her face, it was his hands Evie felt sure of it. Lifting each strand her entity claimed the girl's neck with the breath from each airborne kiss. Oh God, she needed to be left alone, to collapse into his long awaited feed.

"Feed from me." Whispered Evie aloud. She wanted the push against her head and to take his blood into her veins again. Yes, she would drink, while he took from her.

Tossed onto the coffin, the black dirt landed with a sort of slow, scattered thud, reminding Evie of the funeral taking place.

"Adam." The name dropped suddenly into her head. "Adam?" She repeated but he didn't reply. "Adam?" Evie spoke a little louder, interrupting the opening line of, "ashes to ashes…", so that it came off as, "ashes to Adam" before gathering back to its proper form.

"You're determined to show me up here today in front of all these people." Maureen shot at Evie, "just you wait 'till we get home, I'll make sure you're too busy to say anything for the next twenty-years, now go and wait inside that church."

Expelled from the gathering and thankful for it, Evie slipped into the chapel, her muttered conversation with Taliesin uninterrupted.

"Why won't you answer me? Why did you give me his name? What does Adam have to do with anything? Taliesin, c'mon, just tell me!"

Frustrated, Evie kicked at one of the pews then pulled at the ends of her hair. She hated it when he behaved like this, turning everything into a bloody mystery.

"Temper, Evie." He sounded amused, the smile dancing across the edge of his mouth, leapt into voice. "Please refrain from collapsing into a bad humor, you sound like a spoiled child."

"Why don't you just tell me, I promise I'll wait for the rest. Are you talking about the child buried beneath the tree? That was just a story, you gave me the scene in my sleep and to make your point, you made me write it down. Other than that, it doesn't mean anything."

The swish from the black mantle Evie always imagined Taliesin wore, brushed past her. Its effect startled her. Never had Taliesin seemed more real. The measured tap of invisible boot heels on stone followed then he paused, taking the space before her. Her entity's breath swept the air cold, was he angry?

"No, but at times a little frustrated. I have told you so many times Evie, Adam existed."

Slowly, Taliesin's hands moved to the sides of the girls' head, his fingers moving through her hair, pushing painlessly inward. Reaching into her thoughts, the strange sensation continued. Leaning toward where she knew he must be, Evie accepted his presence inside with just the slightest scrape inside her head. She wanted to say something but found she could not.

"See instead." He breathed.

Already an image lay before the girl. Carefully he directed Evie's thoughts toward the window where earlier they sat around the tree.

Like before, both Adam and Eve had vanished, replaced now by Taliesin standing at the base of the broad trunk.

Dressed in the familiar mantle, hat and boots, he stared toward the girl from his position on the window while pushing into her head from the chapel floor. His eyes, brilliant green illuminated the scene, throwing the scattering of apple blossom into relief.

"See," they instructed her.

Dizzy, he pushed into her head and the strength of his eyes forced the need to lie down. All around the scent of apple blossom rose against her senses and vaguely Evie wondered if she fell into it, would the landing be soft, already she might be lying on a cloud.

She fell inside. Fast. The aroma of beeswax and the dust of ancient masonry crashing into her senses. The headache unbearable.

"Taliesin!"

Breathless, Evie surveyed the chapel, his hand moving into her hair brushed the back of her neck. In need of support, she leaned into it.

Quiet now, the calm silence contrasted with the calamity inside Evie's head as she attempted to slot everything together. He was telling her to breathe, she was with him and was safe.

"You will learn to bear this better, eventually."

Such patience behind those words and she began to cry; for the dreadful image on the window of Adam's infant murder, suffocated beneath the tree. Then the boy again, older this time, standing alongside Taliesin, as part of him, belonging. Bright sea green eyes fixed toward her. Only his lips moved, dark red against the porcelain skin of one who has yet to look upon the sun.

"You."

He whispered, delivering the single word slowly, carrying its importance into her head. She understood then, the purpose of the two stories given to her, what Taliesin tirelessly tried to convey.

More than a story and image, Adam was indeed real. Like her he remained under Taliesin's guardianship.

"But how?" Evie whispered into the empty building.

"You show me now that you are ready, your rest and the time spent in my presence has made you stronger. I knew this when I touched you without gloves, absorbing your wounds into my soul. Magic moved into you then, as I knew it must. Your time in the Waiting Place, fashioned for you as The Enchanted Castle so you would not be afraid, and the one also who brought the great Chalice forward, filling it with waters from deep within the earth. The Chalice too, your lips touching its ancient surface, taking the powers and the life returned into your soul. All of it Evie, has delivered you to who you are now. Soon you will fall into me where I shall feed again and you shall know finally, that which you seek, your truth at last."

Vanishing, he left the girl to the hollow chapel and the memories of the boy and the silent history beneath her feet. As usual, his departure left a void in the space around her, but ready now, Evie rose from the uncomfortable pew and stepping toward the curved doorway surveyed the dying sun.

Hovering at the miniature white gate separating the chapel from the fields beyond, Maureen Edern made small talk with several of Chris's relatives, the funeral having just ended. They were in the middle of an invitation to a post-funeral tea at a grandmother's house, on whose side, Evie wasn't sure.

"Oh, God, no." Evie bit her lip, a trip to grandmother's house in a sweet, rose covered cottage with photographs of Chris at five, ten and beyond was more than she could stand. Pushing every particle of mental energy to the front of her head, Evie willed a decline from her mother.

"Thank you but no."

Denying Maureen a chance to speak, Pamela spoke first, citing the need to "get on the road before dark."

They left then, waving good-byes and empty promises to stay in touch. As Pamela navigated the narrow country lane, looping and twisting away from the sad crowd, Evie, for the first time felt genuinely happy for the woman's enforced existence in the Edern household.

Rising from the edge of the road, a tall bramble hedge had already begun shedding its leaves, brown and gold from summer's decline. On the other side, vast fields swept down to a pale river, its faint blue shimmering against a low sunset.

"Ooh, look at the sun on that river, isn't that lovely?" declared Maureen, it was a question but they were expected to agree, and a prompt chorus of "yes," followed.

"It must be lovely to live in a place like this, you couldn't go wrong," added Cell-Phone Pam. Then considering the purpose to their afternoon, countered, "Well you wouldn't think so."

Her mother was right, it really was lovely here. Gradually, Evie enjoyed the display of sloping fields and whimsical scattering of sheep grazing along the grassy banks. Apparently Maureen seemed to have forgotten Evie's earlier display at Chris's graveside and nose pressed against the passenger window the girl relaxed a little.

They came to a fork in the road and through half closed eyes, Evie read the signs. To the right lay the town of Groesfford, they would head out that way to take the major road toward North Wales and ultimately home. And to the left, Evie saw as the car pulled in the opposite direction, lay Edern.

Chapter Twenty-Eight

Having dodged into a shop doorway in the middle of Clayton Square, Evie decided it best to wait until the rain let up a bit. An hour ago when she left for work, the weather was fine but by the time the bus had driven past the Round House where Taliesin's cholera victims were packed like rotting sardines back in 1832, the sky opened.

Shifting, so that most of her weight rested on the other leg, Evie leaned into the cold wall. Noticing a splash of dog pee she stepped away again. Considering her options Evie wondered what to do. Either she could make a run for it, arriving at work even more soaked, or she could wait it out. She was late anyway, and judging by the number of people fighting a losing battle with umbrellas tossed inside out, she wouldn't be the only one. Decision made, Evie thought she might just as well stay put and delay the misery of another day for a bit longer.

Jabbing the toe on her right shoe into the concrete step, Evie smeared a stray leaf blown into the doorway during the morning storm, transforming the grey into a greenish brown. The colors reminded her of autumn in Edern and the sign at the end of the road telling her the one, indisputable fact; the place was real, existing beyond Taliesin's storytelling and the parameters of her imagination.

In fact, the discovery that Edern was a real village in Wales and not just a place created by her entity after her own name had thrown Evie's mind wide open and it had taken everything she had not to shout, "Taliesin, you were right, it does exist!" in front of everyone in the car.

Pushing into the space on the back seat he whispered, "yes, that is the place, however, at present I can return only in memory, not in reality as I am elsewhere."

"Why?"

Inside, her thoughts became cloudy, Taliesin's work. He told her she asked too many questions and did not wish to impart any further information. Wasn't it enough she had found the place? Nevertheless, Evie continued to think back while still capable.

"Evie, I do not wish for this conversation, it is irrelevant for now."

"Just tell me and I promise not to ask again." Evie persisted but her eyes began to close. Soon there would be nothing but sleep. The sigh of one bearing much tolerance filtered slowly into her thoughts.

"I am cursed Evie and your questions are endless."

A week later, standing in a doorway waiting out the rain, Evie pondered her Storyteller's curse.

True to her promise, she hadn't questioned him further, but it didn't make a redundancy out of curiosity. And so at odd moments since that afternoon the previous week Evie caught herself thinking about the nature of his curse. Like now, until a pigeon, blown sideways by a quick breeze made nonsense of Taliesin's problems with its comic dance among wet litter.

Bored and in dire need of a little entertainment, Evie wished for her Storyteller. She couldn't find him and it wasn't good enough. He was supposed to protect her from shit like this, said as much himself. Sullen, Evie fiddled with the damp hem on her her coat before glancing at the street again. She stared rather stupidly at the sun pouring dry light onto the cracked road. What happened to the rain? Something else too, and it took several moments before she grasped it fully.

The real road had gone.

Cobbled in some places then broken in others, what was once black tarmac now gave over to a rough dirt track. A flower seller shouted, "violets!" to her right while to her left came the unbelievable surprise of hoof beats striking stone, rapid and busy for their journey ahead.

She saw the figure then, casual, leaning against a tall building, its corner the gateway to a narrow street.

Dressed impeccably, it seemed he shouldn't be there at all, not leaning into the filth of pollution cast against what was once white stone. A boy, barefoot, trousers torn to the shins ran past the immaculate form, basket of green and red apples in hand. Black double breasted frock coat, matching tall bowler hat, black breeches and green silk waistcoat.

Taliesin.

Stepping from beneath the arched doorway, Evie slipped into the busy square, entering the scene with the purpose and familiarity of one who having been away for a short time must now re-emerge upon the theater she had been forced to leave.

She would miss nothing.

Chapter Twenty-Nine

"Eh out! Watch where you're goin'!"

An excruciating screech as sixteen hooves scraped to an unwilling standstill.

"You could 'ave been killed there." The voice came again, obviously an answer was required and Evie managed to gather a strangled word.

"Sorry." She waved at the driver who shook his head and muttered something about the girl having "cloth ears." Flicking both reins the hunched little man signaled the quartet of horses to resume their journey.

Hovering along the edge of the cobbled street, Evie considered this new phenomenon. She hadn't expected to be seen by anyone and on reflection, the carriage driver hadn't even noticed Evie's modern clothing, let alone the stringy ponytail limping down the back of her neck. Switching gears for a moment, Evie recalled Taliesin's appearance and the 1848 inscription. So, could she actually be slap bang in the middle of the mid-nineteenth century? Convinced, Evie's heart leapt forward.

Never had she heard or seen anything like it, dozens of busy hooves clattering against her cars, impatient and preceding the steady roll of metal wheels. Some wobbled along, barely able to convey the rough wooden carts they dragged, while others, better equipped for the journey, bounced against the peaks and troughs along the cobbled road.

Directly above the flower seller attempting to make the most of her sale of violets by aggressively shoving a half dozen at anyone naïve enough to walk past, a sash window flew open. Unconcerned by the activity below, the occupant of the upstairs room hung out a small area rug and hitting it ferociously with a carpet beater delivered a plume of thick grey dust onto the unsuspecting woman beneath. Snatching a wet rag from a bucket of dirty water, the injured party tossed the soggy cloth in a perfect arc toward the still open window, determined not to be outdone. Aim satisfied, a string of abuse between the two women followed.

Transfixed, Evie observed the busy display. Smoke dusting the city air, breathed through stone chimneys then exhaled into a soft blue sky. Everything, Evie marveled played against her eyes as though never having stopped at all. As though their history remained locked into a constant present; the action of each person wandering about, the horses plodding along the street, some poorly fed, tired, while others still, tossed their heads against the bit.

Everything assured all taking part, that tomorrow the same would be the same as today, that nothing would change, everything would remain forever.

Milliners, shoemakers, sellers of cloaks and mantels, similar Evie imagined, to the one her entity wore. With all the time in the world, Evie could explore them all.

Inhaling the rich aroma of bread which teased her nose from the open door of a bakery, Evie pondered the history of her own family and wondered what they might be doing right now.

Probably breaking their backs scrubbing some ungrateful bastard's floor if the state of affairs in the present day Edern household was anything to go by. Evie thought to herself with some disappointment.

But that wasn't her lot now. Pressing her nose against the window, Evie pondered the many loaves on offer, hot, crusty, their tops bursting over the stoneware containers.

Perhaps she would go in later. Right now though Evie wanted to know what that stupid boutique she worked in might look like some one hundred plus years into the past. If she was on the right street, the place should be in the middle of this row.

What would her supervisor have looked like a century earlier?

An assortment of ladies ankle boots; brown, black and beige decorated the spacious window. Marching up the center of each piece of footwear, a smart row of pearl buttons reflected the clear sky making each little piece shine as though it were an iridescent jewel. Lying in the center of the display, a cream dress whose delicate lace ribbons emphasized its soft elegance drew Evie's curiosity.

Perfect. Evie imagined herself wearing it, a gathering of soft edges trailing the ends of her shoes, ruby red sash mimicking the contours of her waist, high neck circling her small throat.

Beautiful, for once.

Biting her lip, Evie peeked through the open door, hovering at the threshold, uncertain whether or not to enter the busy store. What would Taliesin say?

Briefly, she recalled the figure standing at the narrow edge slicing into the back street, the still, singular presence drawn apart from the flow of movement threatening to engulf him. For a moment, she looked away, enticed by the scene at large, and when she looked back, he had gone.

Tucked behind these streets a labyrinth of dark overcrowded alleys and courtyards ran sick with the decay of waste and festering disease. Of these things Evie knew. Raised as a child on a diet of inverted fairy tales narrating family sickness, absent sanitation, six to a bed, and walls from which a dubious mix of green and black slime ran in summer and froze in winter, Evie might have lived the horror herself.

But more importantly, that figure? Could it have been Taliesin? Absent from his familiar black mantle and knee high boots, Evie no longer felt sure. Surely if his intentions were for her to follow him into the maze of dark streets, he would not have disappeared. A quick glance over her shoulder confirmed the figure hadn't followed her.

The shop looked warm, interesting. Evie walked in.

Immediately she hated it.

She was met with intense, hostile stares, not just odd little glances. Returning the same glance, Evie observed a woman step toward her. Wearing a long dark green dress sporting a series of pin tucks from neck to waist, the woman approached Evie with the familiarity of one who might know the girl. Standing her ground, Evie refused to be cowed.

For once, delighted Evie, she could do as she pleased. Magic ran through her veins so she might sustain this image just as Taliesin taught her. Moreover, moving through a time before her existence elevated the girl above consequence. At last, she could do as she liked, getting away with anything, possibly making this the single most important benefit to her special "gifts".

Dressed in the same plain dark green dress, another figure joined her companion, the two muttering something inaudible. Finished talking, they faced Evie.

She couldn't care less.

Evie ignored the stern women, and switched her attention to a replica of the dress she had seen in the window. Evie decided she must have it. The garment was wasted on this lot.

Holding the dress to the pale light filtering through the shop window, Evie touched the scattering of diminutive rosebuds thrown randomly against the creamy background. Unnoticed before, four ivory buttons adorned the high neckline and tumbled to a series of small gathers before resting at a waistline trimmed carefully in ruby silk. Below the waist, loose pleats made a soft descent toward the hem finished with the same ivory lace encircling the delicate wristband.

"I will try this on," Evie stated, since she could do as she liked., she could at least look the part.

"What?" the stunned women inquired in unison. "You will do no such thing. You will put that back and leave the store this moment. You are in quite enough trouble as it is."

Surging forward, the sudden force in Evie's voice pushed the assistants backward, their shock licensing the girl's bold fury. The dress was in her hands and she would do as she liked.

"Taliesin's magic might have brought me into your world, but my powers sustain you now, breathing life into your pathetic souls so you might live for a while."

She had even begun to sound like him! Evie admired the speed with which she grafted Taliesin's tone into her voice. The dress lay slung over one arm while the other rested, hand to hip.

"You can't stop me from wearing this; in fact I can do exactly as I choose. So go on, touch me, I dare you and I'll laugh while I watch as your hand disappears through my flesh."

Aware of the commotion, shoppers stopped in their tracks and the store fell quiet. Undaunted, Evie fired into the silence.

"You're not real, all of you are dead you just don't know it. If I chose, I can make everything vanish in an instant and return every last one of you into darkness. Don't think Taliesin isn't somewhere observing this. One snap of my fingers and he will kill anyone who dares raise their hand against me. Believe me, I am protected."

The dressing room was right where Evie knew it would be, to the back and to the left, behind the collection of corsets and the latest covers, as well as boots and button-up shoes which she hadn't even bothered looking at.

Retreating into the private space, Evie closed the door behind her, locking it. She needed to move fast. Tearing at her clothes, Evie threw her jacket to the floor, ripping at the zip, before doing the same with her dull green skirt. Next Evie dragged the horrible green sweater over her head, then recalling the screwed up plastic bag stuffed into her jacket pocket brought with the intention of some afternoon shopping, Evie shoved the lot in there. The dress was next and kicking off her shoes Evie placed them against the wall, while simultaneously stepping into the ivory dress.

"Yeah okay, it fits big deal", Evie muttered. There was no time to admire her handy work; she had to get the heck out of here.

Emerging from the cramped quarters of the dressing room and shoving past the small army of speechless Victorian shop assistants Evie emerged at last into the sunshine of 1848.

Evie held the scene against her thoughts, determined to float the smallest detail across her eyes with the magic she had been taught to use.

With a swell of pride, the girl congratulated herself on such skilled use of magic, sustaining the scene unassisted. Contented, she inhaled deeply. Without paying any attention to exactly where she might be going she drifted down a series of back streets and narrow alleyways before the overpowering dark stench sank all self congratulatory thoughts.

Nothing more than a thin slip of a street, the bony cluster of houses pinned together on either side pressed against the threatening gloom, suggesting that among such poverty, sunlight was considered a trivial luxury and should be denied entry.

How could she have been so stupid to end up here? Whined Evie and despaired at the dismal surroundings.

Beneath her bare feet a cobble stone road fell to large patches of thick mud making every step an awkward risk.

In the rush to leave the store, she had left her shoes in the dressing room, most likely pressed against the wall, neat, useless. Framing a look of sick disbelief, the girl stared at her toes, each one making a scarlet protest, scratched, bruised and completely bare.

"Why didn't I realize?" Evie bemoaned to no one and leaning forward, cupped one hand around the top of each damp foot, noting with disgust the treacle like substance embedded into each toe nail.

Already the muddy effluence flowing through the open drains on both sides of the miserable little courtyard settled between Evie's toes. Reluctantly she moved them only to be immediately sickened as the greenish liquid squelched upward, rushing across her skin like an infected river, dead to all but disease.

Moving her hands, Evie touched the dress instead, its hem clinging against the top of her feet. Slowly she traced the delicate lace trim. It was ruined of course, defiled by the stinking filth draining into the street.

"Stupid, stupid!"

Evie chastised herself. Taliesin would never make the girl walk through something like this. Journeys with him ended up in nice places like her Enchanted Castle or Edern. Neither would he make her ruin a dress for the sake of an afternoon together.

But thinking about her entity was pointless, he wasn't following her around, and he hadn't bothered showing up for her to follow him. Again, Evie thought of the figure standing on the opposite side of the street. She thought it was Taliesin, but chose instead to do things on her own terms and have some fun. Now, a pair of bruised feet and one destroyed dress later, Evie wondered if she had made the right choice and stared again at the destitution looking back at her.

Debating her predicament, the unexpected sound of men, shouting, spurred a decision to action.

With no idea who these men might be, Evie had no intention of hanging around. If she could be seen, worried Evie, she could be harmed and ducking beneath the archway entered as feared into another dim little courtyard on the other side.

So much for Taliesin, her protector and so called friend.

The voices grew closer. Gathering the ends of the ruined dress Evie began to run, exiting through another archway and onto a hilly street. Against the steep incline, Evie ached and puffed along.

She had to get away. One could be locked up forever or even hung for lesser crimes than the theft of a stupid dress, puffed Evie and then realized with a shriek of horror that yes, they thought she had stolen the friggin' dress! Where was Taliesin? She would kill him if he finally showed up.

On the other side of the road, the hill leveled to a gentle curve and taking advantage Evie crossed the street, breaking into a full sprint.

From the uppermost edge, a dark phoenix emerged from the soot of industry, its leviathan mass stretching wing like from the bloated body of the main building whose blackish presence cursed everything around it to shadow and soot.

Throwing herself into the darkness, Evie thought about projecting her thoughts toward Taliesin. He would have no choice but to get her out of this hell hole.

Standing at the entrance, a set of iron gates caged the vast structure locked within. Her hand felt small against the giant bolt and as Evie struggled to draw it back, she cringed as the heavy scrape resonated around the courtyard. She held her breath as the sound echoed a slow death. No one came out.

Latch drawn back, Evie relaxed a little, then pushing open the gate placed one bare foot across the threshold. Carefully, her eyes swept the imposing courtyard.

In every direction, black hexagonal walls broke from the ground, stealing any light daring invasion. Shadows cast by the dark walls loomed over her presence like a burst malignancy.

Giving the gate one last shove, Evie swung it open and stepping inside, noticed a wooden panel fastened to the blackened stone wall. In sharp white letters, it read;

'Brownlow Hill Workhouse- Established 1792'

The hideous nature of the place became clearer, the cheerless courtyard, the heavy presence of unseen suffering, lives lived among the shadow of sadness. Workhouses were the last resort for destitute families, some preferring starvation and death rather than face punishment for their poverty.

It seemed impossible that it should get darker, yet clouds fastened against the lowering sky made it a reality. Fog lifting from the River Mersey at the foot of the city arrived cat-like, silent, and curling softly around her ankles made a cunning companion.

Rain followed, sudden and explosive it arrived in solid sheets, slicing through the fog that persisted despite the wet. Within moments, Evie shivered behind a hard curtain of wet grey whiteness.

 Pushed back against the wall, Evie trembled in the useless dress. Pushing her thoughts forward she tried transporting herself into Edern or her castle but with no luck.

Frustrated, Evie thought of Taliesin. He must be somewhere the girl fretted. He seemed to spend his entire time framed in darkness, so why the hell wasn't he in this dump?

A sound like thunder rumbled and for a wild moment Evie thought perhaps Taliesin had at last come for her, striding through the mists of time to whisk her away to somewhere warm. The huge fireplace at the castle and the soft landing of the bed would make a good start.

But the splash of dirty water shaken from the murky depths of several deep potholes dashed her fragile hope.

It wasn't Taliesin at all, but carriage wheels bouncing along the potted road. As the sound drew nearer, it became less of a carriage and more of a rolling threat as the vibration from the enormous iron wheels ran beneath the ground to her feet.

Gathering her shattered thoughts, Evie held every breath. They had to be coming for her. Sick, Evie listened as the carriage drew closer, each hoof beat turning the conveyance in a small practiced arc toward the gate until the wheels stopped and the visiting horse, snorting its arrival gave one final stamp of its thick, dark hoof.

Pressed into the stones until her back hurt, Evie psyched herself up for a quick hanging from one of the dark spires cresting the workhouse roof. Maybe her neck would break quickly and she wouldn't feel a thing. If they tied the rope tight enough, perhaps she could choke before she was even hung.

"*Really, if you stop and think about it*", her thoughts freaked, "*it's actually quite simple and not that bad at all.*" It would be over before she knew it.

Forced against the damp air, the heavy gate yawned. Searching for a place to hide and coming up with a miserable nothing, Evie cursed the stupidity of the simpering rose bud dress in all this foggy gloom.

Against the wet cobbles, boots struck a hard path around the side of the closed carriage, followed by the sound of a door slamming shut. Obviously, somebody had got out of the carriage but it was too dark to see who it might be. A voice came next, nailing the darkness with its serious tone and informing whomever provided company on this quest, that, "it must be done properly."

So they had come for her.

"Taliesin." Begging the foggy night, Evie gave a muffled cry. "For the love of God, help me."

Slowly, as though parting the wet fog, a long black overcoat bearing a tall, lean man entered the dark courtyard.

Drops of crystal rain clinging to his shoulders threw tiny prisms of light capturing the contents of a torn sky and the promise of an advancing silver moon. Evie thought how bizarre it was that she should notice such a thing at a time like this.

Lungs fit to burst for the want of breathing, Evie observed the stranger, walked right past the girl making an efficient line toward a set of stone steps at the top of which stood a large wooden door.

But it was the bundle in his arms that now forced Evie's eyes through the pounding rain. Wrapped tightly, the man held the object away from his body as though fearing contamination from its contact.

Breath still harnessed to the tightness in her throat Evie held her silent watch as the man deposited the package on the lower step. Purpose completed, he retreated sharply and without looking back, returned to the still open gate. Within moments, the carriage door opened, then with a soft click closed again, the ensemble of horse, carriage and driver fading into the river mist as though their arrival never happened.

Danger over Evie retained a low profile, sneaking across the courtyard to the steps facing her. Fair enough it wasn't the police but who the hell was it? Stepping closer Evie suppressed a small scream of surprise as the small package shifted.

It moved again. In the foggy dark she hadn't imagined it. Uncoordinated and clumsy, the thing made a small protest struggling until a gap opened at the top of the cloth wrapping revealing the tiny face.

"Well, this is a workhouse" Evie spoke to the infant. Perhaps the mother was dead and with no one to take care of the child, it had been dropped off here. Disease, these times were full of it, recalled Evie, like Taliesin's Cholera victims.

Shivering, Evie took a closer look.

Pinned to the curve of the infant's tightly wrapped shoulder lay a note, its torn edge catching the tip of Evie's finger. A drop of blood rising to the surface baptized the infant's forehead with a tiny scarlet pearl.

Straining to read the blue scrawl, Evie squinted at the damp paper, yielding nothing more than remnants of a blurred date, the ink running from exposure to fog and rain.

A voice broke her attempt to understand.

"Miss, if you could come with us please."

This didn't make any sense.

Pulled up and away from the entrance, Evie tried resisting the touch on the underside of both arms however was too confused to present much of an effort. Nevertheless, she would keep arguing anyway, about the baby, and how it shouldn't be left in this cold. Only then did one of the officers ask, "What baby?"

She screamed then, kicking and resisting the hands that dragged her toward a present forcing her understanding from a deep pit.

She wasn't standing in the courtyard at Brownlow Hill Workhouse, instead she was huddled in the rear entrance to the Catholic Cathedral. Even worse, this was not April 30th 1848 but September 30th 1999.

Dizzy, Evie reserved her voice for the name she must call forward in absolute panic.

"Taliesin!" And again, "Taliesin!" Her voice resonated against the cathedral perimeter before disappearing into the blinding daylight.

Evie still screamed his name as she was dragged, fighting and cursing toward the waiting car.

Chapter Thirty

Her head hurt. Between her ears, the constant pounding made it impossible to stay upright. Needing to lie down Evie faced the bed-like structure, a feature that in reality was no more than a slab of hard grey plastic stained with graffiti and God only knew what else.

There were no sheets.

By way of distraction she stared at the graffiti stains for comfort. Blue and faint, you could tell numerous attempts at removing phrases such as, 'I'm going on a fuckin' hunger strike' and, 'All Pigs Are Gay' was met without success. The 'Pigs' part, Evie assumed must be a referral to the police and an unwelcome word association followed, Pigs to Police, Police to Parents, all beginning with the letter, 'P'.

Of course her mother would know by now. The thought made Evie retch and she wished she were one of the stains on the plastic bed to which no harm could come. Evie pushed her mind toward the faint blue ink. She wouldn't mind being a word just now, it didn't matter what it said, or how poorly spelled.

With the nail on her index finger, Evie scratched the letter 'T' into the plastic over the part that said, 'Pig', and withdrew her left hand, studying the faint letter. Given his glaring absence, 'T' for Taliesin above 'Pig' seemed appropriate.

Calling to Taliesin in between sobs and screams while being shoved onto the back seat of the police car had proved fruitless. Now, sitting on the hard grey bed, Evie cursed her entity, muttering epitaphs with what little voice she had left.

Two police officers had been sent to deal with Evie. The older of the two sported greasy black hair parted at the side and combed over to hide an intrusive bald spot. He had read the girl her rights in a bewildering volley of words.

The other, attached her to a set of handcuffs, giving Evie a chance to take a proper look at the junior of the duo. He looked no more than about nineteen, of medium height and soft olive skin. He behaved, Evie noted sarcastically, as one on a desperate mission to impress the more senior of the two. He double checked the handcuffs; carefully tucked her resistant head as she got into the car then triple checked the back door before getting into his own seat. Finally his seat belt snapped shut with an efficient click.

Onlookers, attracted to the drama and with nothing better to do gathered on the perimeter of the cathedral grounds. From the back seat, the wild-eyed Evie gave everyone the finger, in the same unfortunate moment as the greasy officer turned toward the car after ordering everyone else to move on.

"Make a gesture like that to me again, young lady and you'll know about it." He slammed the car door then, shifting in his seat started the engine.

She hated them both.

Several times during the journey to the police station, the infant officer fired a volley of questions concerning Taliesin; was he Evie's boyfriend? Was he hiding somewhere? Why would he want to kill anybody? And finally, was he Irish? The name was unusual enough, he could be. Was he a sympathizer with the Irish Republican Army and was he planning to blow something up, like a shopping center?

"Are you bloody stupid?" she screamed. "Taliesin can't be seen by normal people. Oh my God! You have no idea what you are dealing with."

She had even kicked the back of his seat then, pitching the officer forward. Furious she kicked again and then again delivering her foot deep into the black vinyl, leaving a cavernous impression.

"You fucking bastards, you pulled me away from 1848, you don't understand what you've done. She'll die from the cold!" She screamed again, pitching her voice in the confined space. She would make them regret what they had done; they would have to let her go.

"Taliesin! Taliesin!"

Sobbing, Evie pitched her voice higher, dragging the sound into her throat, making it raw. "Take my mind out of here now, I command you to!" Swinging both legs around, Evie kicked the passenger door. "I will get out of here!"

"We've got a right one 'ere Dave." The baby officer eyed the outraged girl through the rear view mirror. Sharply Evie fastened her gaze onto the back of his head. Yes, she would make him feel the full weight of her anger.

"Have you any idea who I am? I'm a Seer, you fucking idiot. You're cursed now. Taliesin will kill you both. I'll make sure of it!"

"Alright, I've 'ad enough of this."

Pulled up at the side of the road, the police car pitched forward, catapulting Evie into the back of the driver's seat.

"Ow, you made me hit my nose, you shithead."

Turned toward his aggressive passenger, the driver's eyes punched hard into the girl's face.

"Quiet! Now if I hear another peep out of you unless I ask a question, you'll be charged with assaulting a police officer, destruction of police property and if I feel like it, you'll be held under the Prevention of Terrorism Act. You'll be lucky if you speak to anyone except yourself for at least five days then, do I make myself clear?"

Could they do that, keep her for that long without seeing anyone? What if right now, they were combing the town looking for a bomb in a shop somewhere? And by crap coincidence, they find one and blamed it on herself and Taliesin, who not of this world meant she'd eat full blame. Moaning, Evie threw her head against the seat, while above, the siren, activated after their exchange wailed through the streets, settling painfully inside her throbbing head.

Their arrival at the police station a short time later, incorporated a series of blurry events in which she was whisked through a square foyer comprising of a desk, several plastic chairs and a number of public safety notices, toward a series of back rooms. An automatic lock on the thick metal door clicked shut, sealing the girl's separation from the involuntary hell she had entered into.

Refusing to appear as one recently arrested, Evie set her mouth in a straight line. Bad enough to be caught wearing a wet nightdress which clung to her hips and breasts like a desperate boyfriend, but without shoes, her feet were filthy. Glancing at them, she could hardly differentiate between the bruises and the dirt. And her hair, after an afternoon of rain, was a frizzy failure. She attempted to fix it, curling the wayward strands behind her ears.

From this point she was handled with very little said. Shoved from one personality deficient individual to the next, each one ordered the girl through a series of activities wrapped around bewildering instructions.

Even having her mug shot taken was an ordeal. Busy considering harrowing thoughts such as, this will follow me for the rest of my life and I wonder how long they take to get developed, and if they give you a copy, Evie became confused. Did she need to face her right or theirs?

Thrust into further activity, Evie was then ushered into a small square room with a one way mirror at the top end and a grey table with three plastic chairs in the middle. Next to the wooden door, a red alarm button marked, 'push' protruded from the whitewashed wall and Evie wondered vaguely if it meant her emergency, should she think she was having one, or if it was on account of somebody else.

Wet and dizzy, she shivered through what turned out to be an interview, her head ached and she felt in danger of collapsing inside. Searching for Taliesin, Evie found nothing and collapsed a bit further. Scarcely capable of keeping her eyes open, the brightness of the room made everything unbearable. Nevertheless, the two women sitting across the table seemed not to mind and where Evie could only squint, their eyes remained bright and at full circle.

Along the ceiling, fluorescent lighting alternated with polystyrene squares of ceiling tiles, producing a two tone checked effect in plain white and vivid white. Evie felt she might have been staring down the barrel of a flashlight.

Staring in the general direction of the brown door for relief, Evie was told in no uncertain terms to look at the women again. She did, eyes struggling against the dazzling bright. Both faces bobbed and swayed ahead of her, their voices floating toward the electric buzz from the lights, or sinking toward the murky depths of a shoe tapping hard against the floor.

From the pitch of this racket, it emerged that one person would be interviewing while the other would represent the girl's interests and did she understand? Bewildered, Evie nodded "yes" even though she didn't.

Already, the volley of questions had begun. Taking aim and well within striking distance of her head, they hit their intended target full force and she winced as the first one, "Who is Taliesin?" spun forward. The second question, "Where is Taliesin now?" set the overall pace of the sport playing before her, with Evie feeling too ill from the entire experience to make any sort of decent return.

Truthfully, she could answer in the negative to both questions. "No." She didn't know where Taliesin might be and perhaps more fundamentally, she really had no idea who he was ghost, spirit, entity or even in his day, what he had been, the mystery of his existence still veiled. When pressed again, that of course, she knew this person and that she was just "being silly" and "playing a dangerous game with her freedom," Evie faintly offered up "ghost". To which both women stared at each other in utter disbelief before making urgent notes.

Convinced in the futility of further questioning, a hand shoved a sheet of paper across the table. Through strained eyes, Evie stared at the words floating toward her face and attempted to make a conscientious effort to study their meaning. Somebody was telling her, in flat, patronizing terms that she was in "quite a bit of trouble" and should read "very carefully" what lay in front of her. And indeed some clever person had managed to consolidate the entire sordid affair into three sentences on a pristine white charge sheet.

1. Public Disturbance
2. Verbal Assaults, threats to kill
3. Theft, item, less than fifty pounds.

Did she have any questions? One of the detached voices asked.

"Yes, where is the bathroom? I need to throw up."

Chapter Thirty One

It hadn't stopped raining. Through the window, which divided into narrow thirds by three black bars, Evie observed a blurry display of raindrops crash and disperse toward the narrow window sill recessed into the wall.

How long she'd been sitting there, Evie had no idea. After the fiasco of an interview, she was stripped of both nightgown and dignity in general, before being given her original clothing, having been allowed to retrieve it from the plastic bag she'd dragged around all afternoon.

Shuffled into her old clothes, Evie was again passed along; this time to a burly, red faced duty officer charged with the responsibility of making sure the girl didn't "attempt anything that might make the papers". The last thing they needed was a hanging. Moments later, hands tucked into the baggy sleeves of her green sweater, Evie faced a dull grey door.

It seemed that everywhere, seeping from the concrete and metal pores of the corridor oozed the odor of cigarettes and stale lives. Barely able to draw breath, Evie stared in bewilderment at the dull surface of the metal door. Standing next to her, the man moved the underside of his arms, damp.

She needed to deny what stood in front of her. It was only a stupid door. In a minute, it would open onto another corridor. There were enough of them to go on forever. There was no end to being passed around. No way that this was the final place. Next, she would meet someone wearing perfume.

But a set of keys pulled from the underside of the sergeant's sensible navy blue V-necked police sweater provided the unwanted clue. Wafting body odor, he opened the entrance, the lock yielding with a metallic clang. Pushed forward Evie was told to go in then, the pressure of his broad hand to her back.

Barely had the heels of both feet crossed the threshold when the door slammed shut, its final throb resonating across the hollow little room. Unsure what to do, Evie turned in two circles, clockwise, then counter-clockwise, noting a small metal sink and a toilet next to it, both of which she would sooner die by fire, than use.

With nothing else to do, Evie dragged herself toward a strange slab of plastic attached to four metal brackets and sticking out from the corner of the back wall. Pushing her hands against its rough surface she hopped aboard and hoped it wouldn't unattach itself, flinging her to the floor, three-feet below.

Silence and the unmoving presence of the metal door. "Never" and "leave" crashed into her skull and breath rasping through her lungs in desperate spurts, stuck to the back of her throat. She wanted to die but only after throwing up first. This was her reality, this time she could not make it go away. Nobody would tell her what was happening.

Frustrated Evie slammed her head against the wall.

Striking her head again, she willed herself toward the nothing she wished for and when the grey light remained, rolled onto the tiled floor in the hope of making the darkness happen there. It didn't.

Headache worse, Evie cursed her stupid entity. She had achieved nothing and dragged herself back onto the bed. Leaning into the cold wall knees to chest, Evie admitted defeat.

She wanted to be sick again, she wanted to get out, she had to get out. Panic was coming. There was nothing in her head, not a word from a single poem or the vision of any of the paintings she liked looking at. "I want The Enchanted Castle!" Kicking the wall, Evie screamed into the empty, hollow cell.

What if she could just turn into Ophelia and drift toward a peaceful nowhere like in that Milais print on her wall? Closing her eyes, she pulled the thought into her core, cursing when nothing came. Angry, she threw another kick at the wall, then as a last ditch effort tried to imagine the pink innocence floating against the walls in her bedroom but thought only of her mother instead.

Bad enough she had killed Chris, or had him killed. Reasons aside, he had offered a reliable source of income. Now, after Chris, her mother's other source of ready cash had gone also, Evie's stupid shoe shop job, which, of course, by now had been lost to her life of crime. Now, having landed arse first in prison the girl would be lucky to clean toilets for a living, presuming they ever let her out.

Of course, freaked Evie, weakened by humiliation and disgust from having a criminal for a child, her mother was duty bound for a nervous breakdown and unable to recover would likely end her days in a rubber room somewhere.

She had to make the future stop!

Screaming Evie flew across the cell and hurling herself against the metal door, crashed painfully to the cold floor, her shoulder hurt.

"Taliesin! Why won't you come back?"

Bringing both legs up, Evie kicked at the door and screamed, the sharp noise resonating around the hollow square. She would make them send her home, she would drive everybody mad.

Instead a little hatch door opened, revealing the man with the blotchy face and the sweaty arm pits. In ten seconds or less, she was called a "spoilt brat", instructed to "sit back down" and if she didn't stop "behavin' like a nutter", they'd get a shrink in there to certify her.

She was a handed a cup of tea then with a two finger Kit-Kat balanced on the side of a blue ceramic cup and saucer.

"I was on my way to give you this before you started carryin' on." The red face grunted, "I don't want to hear another word out of you, do I make myself clear?"

Struggling to her feet, Evie reached for the offering and watched as the swollen hand retracted from the hatch door slamming it shut again. She was thirsty and the drink, albeit lukewarm was welcome.

Trembling from her efforts Evie drifted back to the stupid, ugly bed and shivering, tucked both legs beneath her. She wanted to cry for the pain in her head. Touching her scalp, Evie felt its pulse rise into the tips of her fingers.

After finishing her tea, decided Evie, she would lie down and rest among the graffiti and questionable stains. It was better than nothing.

"It will not help." I am angry and my fury invades your thoughts, hence the pain."

"Taliesin?" Evie called into the empty space, "thank God."

"Indeed Evie that I have not killed you yet, perhaps you should thank God."

The pain in her head intensified, she could hardly sit up.

"You're dong this why?"

"A question you are better able to answer yourself."

Footsteps, slow, striking the tile floor with immaculate purpose, on the inside or outside of the metal door? She couldn't tell.

"Inside."

Immediately he answered the question.

"I told you never to cross me and you have."

"What the hell are you talking about? I've done nothing to you."

Furious, Evie sprang to her feet. After abandoning her to all this, he had a raw nerve. Now she didn't give a fuck about the pain in her head. Unblinking she stared into the space where she thought he must be. Rage burning through her eyes, the cacophony of words scrambled into her throat.

"You bastard, after all I've been through, you have the nerve to be pissed off, when it was you who left me here. Where were you when I was dragged into the police car, you piece of shit? Or were you watching from a distance?"

Emphasizing 'from a distance', Evie mocked the poetry in his voice, dangerous, terribly she knew, but it didn't matter. Moving closer, she stood at his shoulder, felt the breadth of his upper body surrounding her space. She continued, defying him to stop her.

"What about Edern and The Enchanted fucking Castle? Any time during my distress you could have sent me there. But no, instead you let them haul me out of 1848, dragging me away from a workhouse that wasn't there and a child that didn't exist.

"And who was that child? Why do you torture me with visions of things that never existed, why do you do that? Is it fun for you, do you laugh when I run after things that aren't real? Why do you show me things that are not real? None of it is. My mother was right, I do live in a fantasy world. I even tried to recall where I've seen your name. I read it in a book once, something about Wales, Merlin and poetry.

"Taliesin, The Enchanted Castle is a painting, the clearing in the forest at Edern was inspired by a copy of that Waterhouse painting, La Belle Dame Sans Merci. Both prints are on my wall. And as for Adam, he was a dream and a terrible story but no more than that. Maybe I wasn't raped either and Chris, with no help from you, just killed himself."

Tears sprang into her eyes, unplanned. Forcing them back down Evie continued walking in circles as he, she felt sure circled her.

"Maybe I am mad and you're not real and this entire conversation is going on in my head. I hear you but you're not there, you're everywhere and nowhere, I hear the noise from your boots but I don't see them, they don't leave a mark. And look at what I did, I believed it was 1848. I watched the street change and believed that dress to be real when all along I was in the reality of now while moving through my own imagination.

"There's a name for that sort of thing. Delusional. You're not real, you don't exist and you never did. When I opened that book of poetry and saw the inscription, I imagined what the Storyteller might have looked like and that was when all this started. Discovering the sign pointing to Edern was just a coincidence. But I am immune to you now, you're nothing to me. My name ends with Edern and that's it, there is no connection to anything."

She finished, a residue of silence stinging the air between them, then even that seemed to retract leaving nothing but a vacuum, the atmosphere in the room sucked dry. He would speak, Evie knew and she waited, staring his presence down.

"After all I have done, you dare question my existence?" The tornado struck.

Thrown against the wall by the force of his response, Evie's head slammed into one of the bars running the length of the window. Falling to the ground, she kicked the empty air as though to strike him.

"We have been through this before Evie, you cannot hurt me."

Closer, his fury filled the small cell, colliding with her thoughts, pulling sharply against her mind.

"I will prove to you that I exist!"

Taliesin's voice thundered around the room, his anger exploding the air above her head.

Placing both hands to her ears, Evie felt the crack against her skull as his physical presence flashed against her eyes. Long black cashmere coat, boots; modern dress. The way he appeared on the first page of Among Other Edens. His eyes green, full off rage, burned through the dull little cell and then he was gone, leaving her with the terrible sense of him.

"Where are you?"

"Why ask, if I am not real?"

"I want to know where you are."

"I am everywhere."

Pulled up, Evie felt his hands supporting the underside of her arms.

"Get away from me, you bastard, you've just cracked my head."

Already a lump had emerged at the back of her skull, its throb pulsing her scalp.

Undaunted however, Evie struck the air, punching where she thought he should be. In return she was flung onto the hard bed, hurting her shoulder in the same place as it struck the cell door earlier.

"Am I real enough now?"

Fury raging forward, he was on her, his weight pushing her arms into the unyielding plastic as she fought again to kick the air. Arching her back, Evie aimed for the groin. But fast, a free hand pushed her leg back down, and then the other as she fought to kick with that. Now every muscle, every sinew lay against her, pressing inward, moving into her veins, taking her breath.

"I said, am I real enough now?"

"I won't succumb."

Arching again she fought his presence, only to be met by the same resistance, hand against her hips, pushing back down. Her skirt was higher, mid thigh, her shirt untucked.

He would rape her. It was Chris all over again.

"That would be ridiculous, Evie."

"I refuse to fear you."

"But you fear that one thing I would never do, that I have killed for. I could manipulate your thoughts right now for the want of sex should I wish it, but I will not do such a thing and never will, that would be base and I am offended you should consider me so."

Pushing against him anyway, she found it even more difficult to move, his hands lay against her head and for the first time since Taliesin's return, Evie felt real fear. His push inwards came slow making her breath tight.

"I could kill you now."

"Return to the hell of your curse, Taliesin, I will never give you the satisfaction of my fear."

"Nevertheless, I feel it rise into my touch and I haven't even begun. You are afraid because I let you inside my secret, my darkness. You know at least, a little of my truth. How I could steal your life."

Lifting an arm, Evie sent a weary blow to his stomach, her limbs felt heavy, everything suddenly was heavy.

"Your courage against the one who is not your enemy and who is sworn to your protection is admirable, if not a little easy." He was being sarcastic, adding, "your fighting skills however, impress me even less so. I could snap your brain with merely a whisper should I wish it."

"Go ahead, I don't give a shit anymore anyway, my life's over."

"Such self pity and dramatics Evie, what is it about artists that they must do this?" He withdrew, permitting her to inhale deeply.

Slowly, the scent of lavender filled the miserable little space, replacing the remarkable contradiction of stale sweat and fresh bleach water.

"Is that better?" Beside her, his voice returned to the familiar, gentle rhythm.

"I still hate you."

Closing her eyes, she could be in the meadow behind the house, beneath the beloved oak tree, gathering arms full of the delicate blue lavender to take into the house as she had done every spring.

Gently a sweet aroma filled the room, floating against the edge of her senses like a faint kiss. His hands brushing against the side of her head, swept through her hair, reducing the girl's headache to a trace of its former self.

"Look Evie, open your eyes."

Wearily she did so and could have cried with wonder. In place of chipped, grey and white floor tile, a carpet of lavender lay upon the floor, their bright green stems rising in proud determination toward the perfect sky ceiling. Now a stream of sunlight smuggling through the wire covered window poured through the dirty glass, scooping the perfect radiance from each petal before pressing the delicate color against the wall, creating a transparency of blue in place of the subdued white wash.

"How?"

His hands pushed softly against the front of her throat, removing the pain from screaming earlier. Her shoulder was next, his fingers tracing the outline of bruise and swollen flesh, kissing it softly until she grew aware more of its absence and less of Taliesin. Moving toward her feet, the pressure of his hands drew every cut and bruise into himself. She could cry for the lack of deserving this, for fighting this presence she claimed to hate.

Shivering from the wet and the cold, Evie needed to lie down. It was important to do so, she thought as her entire body began to shake violently. She would curl into a ball and stay warm.

Soft, fragrant flowers rising from the hideous plastic met Evie's descent and inhaling the bouquet, she sank beneath its scent. The coat was next, dark, familiar, needed, its gentle weight pushing against her frozen bones, claiming the cold, making her safe.

"Breathe and fight no more. You are tired, that is my wish so you will listen without argument. Rest while I tell you of the things you did that caused my rage. But you shall do so here, without Edern or the castle you love so much. My fury is quiet but my anger is real. I have made you comfortable but no more than that shall you have until I have spoken myself out.

"Through half sleep you shall listen with neither the ability to speak or move, but you will have perfect recollection of my words, appreciating at last the powers that lie within you. Rest deep, fall into my voice and listen carefully."

His voice rolled forward.

"My request when I introduced myself was that you should never cross me. To my disappointment you have done this.

"Of course, I observed your entry into 1848, I created it, watched your first step as I led you forward, emerging from the arched doorway of that shop as though onto a stage. Before your eyes I gave the image to you, my intent to guide you toward an understanding of the answers you seek.

"And I was there, standing at the corner yet you so readily dismissed my presence as though it were nothing to you.

"If you believe the brief time spent within your fairytale castle has equipped you with the ability to manipulate time, you are both mistaken and a dangerous fool. You are a Seer yes, and there are truths you must know, but you are learning, therefore you are no match for me.

"There will come a time for fighting against others, yet you choose to make me your enemy, I who have so carefully taught you. Believe me Evie, for what one day will come, you need me on your side. I am your ally and have proven myself so. Yet you would make me responsible for your current predicament, throwing rage and curses as though it were I that told you to take the nightgown which you foolishly believed to be a dress.

"I gave you an image so you may use your abilities to See and to follow, but it was real only to you, to others, not so. Everything you touched remained in the present, while you, with your own ability aided by myself saw what had once been, but it did not make it real. I did not take you out of one time and place you in another and you certainly did not do it!

"And then you threatened others in my name. Real or spirit, they had done you no harm but you did as you liked while I held onto the image for you, deploying all my strength so you could witness what went before, despite ignoring the path I held open for you. But inevitably your actions in the dress shop led others to your past, to a child, and a place that for others did not exist.

"I warned you also not to speak of me in public but your incessant calling of my name led others to think of me as your accomplice in a scheme to bring great harm to those with whom I have no fight. You could have gone quietly about your journey as I have taught you but you chose otherwise, going about in a manner with which attention would come, the consequence of which I can do nothing to prevent. I can only say, Evie that in your foolish arrogance you have made things more difficult for the path that lies ahead.

"And your language expressed in such vile anger, betraying your intelligence and dignity. I wish no more to hear words such as those, you are more than that and should strive always to meet that expectation, not fall below it. Among other things, you are an artist, a writer, it is in your blood, in every drop of sweat that has left your body, and you will learn to express yourself better, it is my will.

"Do not think I judge you too harshly. There are others to come who will judge you even more so and for that you must be prepared. I have tested your skills, and your courage, even when facing my wrath is commendable. However, you must learn to direct the fight that lies within you in the proper manner. In time this will come.

"But I am weak now and can no more fight than argue, you have taken what remains of my strength and I have not fed since Chris. You wished before for me to take from you and now I shall, and with the last of my strength I push into your head, where I sink deep into your core, taking.

"Do not seek pleasure from this for there is none to be had. I wish neither to deliver you into Edern or your castle, and neither shall you visit the quiet garden where Adam lies deep.

"Instead I need more, for this is not enough. In dreams, you have fed from me, now feel as I cross into your reality, my need this time for your blood, my desire at last to take you into my veins. Your actions made me weaker than I can stand to be. I shall have this."

The tea cup was as it had been left, empty at the side of the bed and on the floor. Quiet and knowing what to do, Evie pulled herself upwards, withdrawing from the lavender darkness and into the dim room.

Taliesin was there, nestled, patient within her core, vulnerable, needing as she had needed him countless times before. She would be there for him now, making him see how she regretted her behavior and would take the consequences with courage and the responsibility of one who knew both the extent and the limitations of their developing powers.

Never again would she call upon him to threaten others or to meet her own selfish ends.

Reaching for the tea cup Evie lifted it slowly to eye level, studied it for a second then threw it hard against the floor. She watched, satisfied as several blue pieces shattered against the grey tile. Selecting the sharpest piece, Evie tested its jagged surface against her thumb, shuddering with pleasure as its edge tore the soft flesh open.

Her entity was hungry and this would definitely do. In her head, he watched and he was pleased.

Quickly, Evie pulled her sleeve back. Taliesin was restless, needing, begging the girl to be quick. She must not let him down.

"Drink, my Taliesin."

Drawing a straight line across the inside of her wrist, Evie watched eagerly as the warm red flow poured from the open wound, running slow then fast along the underside of her arm. Thirsty, Evie placed her mouth against the opening, and falling into her bed of soft lavender fed his deepest hunger, taking the warm liquid toward his final pleasure.

Sleep returned, serene, gentle, Taliesin's reward. The last movement before her eyes closed finally being the little green sliding door pushed back suddenly, somebody shouting and the sound of many feet, distant but running.

Chapter Thirty-Two

With Taliesin gone and his blood feed satisfied, Evie's now existed within the depths of her own twilight. Patiently Evie waited for the withdrawal of the sleep he had pulled her into.

But she could not come back. Instead, the opposite happened, as she descended further into sleep, spiraling downward. There were voices too but she could neither respond to nor recognize any of them.

Fighting back, Evie resisted the rush of this descent, gathering her strength into the center of her thoughts as Taliesin once taught her to do, pushing outward. Still nothing happened.

She didn't like this, the presence of these unfamiliar voices threatening her ability to wake up. But among the urgent racket, Evie heard herself, the echo of a willful protest to leave her alone.

"Fight this Evie."

Her own words or Taliesin's? Too confused to be sure, but she would obey anyway, fight with everything she had. If Evie threw all her energy into one movement, it might be possible to beat this. She would bring herself back.

Gathering everything into her core, Evie forced herself upward and was met with nothing but a lightning pain burning into her veins with a determined force. Efforts impaled to the sharp stab, Evie tumbled into nothing.

The second time, Evie prepared herself for the struggle, only to be met with surprise when her eyes opened, with none of the former pressure against her lids.

How long had she slept? Her head felt fuzzy and she couldn't remember going to bed. There had been something with Taliesin, blood he took from her but she wasn't sure, everything was blurry. Something else had happened too, but the more Evie attempted to recall, the more out of focus the answers got. Presently, Evie would go downstairs and ask her mother, the woman knew everything. Evie just needed to give her head a chance to clear first. Why hurry? She would only be shouted at and told to mop the living room, or vacuum the kitchen floor, or was it the other way around?

Stumbling over every observation, slowly Evie questioned the presence of a narrow light, its fuzzy glow penetrating the thick darkness. Odd how it illuminated the small window especially considering her bedroom windows were large and weren't there two of them? Then Evie wondered why it should be so far out of reach and why there were a series of straight lines extending from one end of the window to the other.

Bars.

Heart crucified, Evie descended rapidly into a hot unholy hell.

Taliesin.

She recalled nurturing his hunger, the scent of lavender beforehand, the lecture, how she crossed him, abusing his name and her powers in public, and the long sleep afterwards, her desire to wake up and inability to do so.

Hyper aware, Evie gathered what remained of her wits. Something else was different, the room. There was something about the room, it felt less cramped. Where the hell was she?

Fast, Evie calculated the sum total of changes. She lay on something softer, but it was narrower without the same range of movement as before. Her arms felt cold too. Lifting her head Evie noticed two further critical pieces of information.

Instead of her work clothes, she wore a white gown. But even more frightening was her inability to sit up. In fact, she could barely lift her shoulders before the disturbing sensation of being pushed and sliced through the middle forced girl back down again. Stay like that a second too long and you wouldn't be able to breathe gasped Evie.

She was in the nuthouse.

She had to get out!

Pushing frantically against the restraints Evie forced both arms flat against the bed, her wrist was stitched, and she felt the outside edge of the metal buckle rub the surgical threads beneath the thin bandage. But Evie didn't care about the pain bursting through her skin, she had to get away. Someone had put her into restraints, and made a dreadful mistake. They thought she had gone insane.

Evie breathed into the dark, calming the sudden rush threatening to burst her heart. Taliesin possessed her blood, she had drank and poured herself into his soul, returning the strength of his powers. He would return and help her out of this, tell her what to do. More importantly, Evie would listen this time, she promised the cold silence.

But there was no sense of him anywhere. No sudden caress of warm lavender scented air and the light breeze touching her face with the mercy of his kiss. Evie needed him now, he must return,

"Taliesin", she gasped, "I'm not mad!" She choked on a bottleneck of words refusing to give voice. They didn't understand, she had not tried to kill herself, she wasn't in any danger. She had fed Taliesin, no big deal. She didn't need to be here.

Terror.

Evie pushed against the thick restraints.

If she had just followed Taliesin! Evie begged time to return itself to that critical moment, stepping from beneath the arch above the shop doorway. She promised to follow this time, to go wherever he took her, erasing the consequence of her own selfish desires.

"Taliesin."

Desperate, Evie hissed his name across an otherwise empty room.

"Taliesin."

Evie called louder, struggling again to lift her body upward, coughing as her breath, trapped against the restraints, caught her lungs.

"Taliesin!"

She must find him, he had taught her to do that, to find him in darkness. She would do it now, seek him out.

Closing her eyes, Evie thought herself into Edern. He would be on the river bank waiting for her to walk into his creation. Nothing came. Switching to the Waiting Place instead, Evie concentrated harder, scavenging the darkness. Again, nothing returned, not even the rough little whispers flirting with her courage and nerve to remain.

The Enchanted Castle, it was the last place she could think of, she would go there, beginning with the roar of the emerald sea in the background. When that failed Evie imagined the figure of Psyche in the foreground, perhaps, she could change it into Taliesin, or maybe Adam. But none of it worked, she could not go any further than the flat one dimensional image of the print on her bedroom wall.

Sobbing Taliesin's name into the darkness, it occurred to her, the connection between where she was and her current state of mind. A new, deeper terror drove from the tips of her toes and into her throat.

He had abandoned her to this.

Chapter Thirty-Three

She must have fallen back to sleep. Now, instead of darkness, thin light claimed the space around her. As far as the night before was concerned, observed Evie, this was definitely tomorrow, albeit a miserable, watery one.

Still, poor as the light was, it afforded a better study of her surroundings and Evie saw for the first time the metal gurney on which she lay and the thick leather straps holding her there, beige when all the time she had imagined them grey or black.

Three in all, not two as she thought. The one across her chest and the other across her middle, she knew of, but the one binding her legs together, she hadn't known about and it made for a disturbing sight to see herself like that, feet bare, mottled from the cold, peeking out below the hospital gown.

The rest of the room was at best spare, accommodating a narrow metal locker directly beneath the small window, and a blue plastic chair set to the side of that. Abbreviating the space between the top of the door and the ceiling trim a white plastic clock protruded from the wall, both hands heading south toward six thirty.

Far too early for her mother to visit thought Evie and wondered if the woman even slept last night, throwing her worries at Cell-Phone Pam. When she got home, worried Evie, she would definitely be in for it. These thoughts, despite lying down, made the girl dizzy and she looked away from the clock, the thing gave her vertigo.

Evie stared at the floor instead, noting sarcastically that the tile sported the same grey and white marble effect she saw the previous day in jail. She wondered if the city had bought a job lot of the stuff, dividing it equally between the police station, her psych' ward and God only knew where else.

Evie scanned the walls. They were different to how she always imagined they might be, not that she spent countless afternoons contemplating nut house colors. But she was surprised to see they were not white as expected but a light shade of pink. The shade reminded the girl of her bedroom back home, and with a wry smile considered that if color was anything to go by, she might have spent the last ten years preparing for this place. But of course, in the room with the sloping roof and the cherished meadow beyond, there would be Taliesin and at half past six in the morning, he should be lying alongside her.

Taliesin, he had been on her mind before succumbing to sleep and again the cold recollection dealt a single blow to the heart. In the beginning he warned her not to cross him, that he could drive artists mad. Hadn't he sent genius to the asylum where he planted chaos into their ideas, abandoning them to insanity?

So he had disappeared. After everything, he abandoned her now to this hell. All she needed was a fireball and a couple of sweaty demons and the initiation could begin.

Opening an old wound, Evie bit the inside of her mouth. Without Taliesin she could not escape, she was unable to create a vision of herself beyond all this.

And that was the other thing, more terrifying than her present location, Evie had nothing in her head, no thought, no pictures, no imagination. The harder she tried to See either Edern or Taliesin, the more everything fell from focus. He had taken the lot, the blood from her veins, her creativity and her abilities as a Seer leaving the girl with nothing inside.

Self pity? She could have none of that. Survival must kick in and she had to do the impossible, think a way out of this mess.

She would deny all knowledge of her entity, and as for cutting herself and drinking her blood, she would chalk that up to panic. Nothing more than sheer terror after sitting all those hours in that police cell without knowing what was going on. It was enough to make anyone go crazy, she would argue.

But the man sitting across from her wasn't buying any of it. Having drawn up the blue plastic chair he sat, legs crossed, nodding quietly. Soft grey eyes, tailor made to match the floor peered from behind a pair of round steel- rimmed glasses.

Dr Mariott Ambrose had arrived at around eight thirty. Exactly one hour earlier, a woman dressed exclusively in white emerged, whom Evie concluded was a psychiatric nurse.

Nurse Flipp, who didn't look as though she could flip if her life depended on it, was a short, stubby little woman. What she lacked in height she more than made up for in speed.

Bursting into Evie's solitary confinement at an athletes pace at seven thirty, her flat black shoes soundlessly covered the grey tile. Dividing waist from hip, a blue belt with a silver clasp hosted a double roll of fat that pushed against the white knee length nurse's dress, each stride generating an unselfconscious jiggle.

White on nurse Flipp was an unfortunate color because not only did it prove difficult for her to keep clean, as evidenced by the black ink stain on the breast pocket, but it forged a death pallor onto the woman's skin. Now the broad neck emerging from the open collar, trimmed in navy to match the belt, appeared in the poor light coming through the inadequate window, to be almost grey.

Her face too, an equal objection to the white uniform sported the same grey pallor and was framed by a misplaced halo of bleached yellow hair drawn into a poor impersonation of a bun at the top of her head. The ends frayed wildly about the crown, while a thicker strand, having escaped captivity hung loose behind her ear. Her face a map of make-up free days, oily skin and a wounded spot, smiled broadly.

"I wasn't supposed to do yer but they said, I 'ad to get yer ready so's Dr Mariott can see ye'."

The words ran at Evie sixty to the dozen. "So I 'ope yer don't go an' do sumpthin' stupid like last time. It's all over this floor that y'drank nearly a pint of yer own blood, that's nearly a whole bottle of milk! I don't know how yer did it without throwin' up. I'd 'ave pucked all over the place. I've gorra' baby at 'ome 'an even 'e can't drink that much. Milk, I mean, not blood."

That perhaps explained the expanded middle and tired complexion. Evie didn't say anything, being far too busy making a study of the woman's appearance to speak. She decided that despite the entirely unprofessional manner with which the woman behaved, Evie quite liked her. At least she was friendly.

"Reckon you'll wanna' see yer mum soon, won't yer?" She continued, pausing not for reply but for breath.

"Well, yer can if yer behave yerself, and after you've seen Dr Mariott. God, 'aven't yer got lovely eyes, eh? They're dead unusual, they are. When I first saw yer', I thought to me'self, wow, they're really green. Now though, they look like, oh, yer know."

Evie didn't.

Tapping her bitten finger nails against the strap around Evie's legs, Flipp searched for the right description, eyes scanning the white ceiling as though it might be written up there.

"What's the best way to describe it? Oh, I know, like the sea on a sunny day. What color's that?'

"Blue?" Evie felt it was a bit of a long shot given the level of thought involved.

"No, not blue. No, that's too plain. No, yours are aqua-green and almost transparent, you're really lucky to 'ave eyes like that, people would kill for those."

"I never really thought about it before." Replied the strapped down Evie.

"Well, you should, you should go in for eye modelin' or sumpthin'."

Evie didn't think so.

"Anyway, I'm gonna undo these restraint thingies now so I can escort yer to the bathroom and yer can get washed an' everythin'. You'd better not do anythin' to hurt yerself though. I'd lose me job if yer did, and you wouldn't want that would yer? Not with my new baby an' everythin'. I've only just come back off me maternity leave."

Evie agreed not to, she didn't want Nurse Flipp to lose her job. Besides she'd never wanted to kill herself, only feed Taliesin. Flipp continued.

"Yer should be alright anyway. Yer should still 'ave enough of them sedatives in yer system. You were in a terrible state when yer came in yesterday afternoon, you were, screamin' and carryin' on, it took three of us to pin yer down. I'd only been on me shift ten minutes, but it felt like ten hours by the time I'd finished with you. There was blood everywhere and you kept shoutin' that we was wastin' it."

As Evie journeyed between the corridor and the bathroom, both soft lilac, sporting illustrations of sunflowers and daisies, Nurse Flipp revealed that her mother, escorted by Pam, had already been here, signed some papers authorizing treatment then left with a promise to "be back tomorrow", meaning today.

Through all this, Evie trailed behind Flipp, whose navy ribbed tights bunched around her ankles. She was beginning to wish the chatty woman would shut up. She needed quiet, even their feet pacing the corridor was more than she could stand.

Overall, Evie was reluctant to leave her quiet room which, given her eagerness to escape this place, came as a bit of a surprise. But beyond the door everything was a threat. Terrified, Evie traveled the long distance passage, protesting that the orange plastic chair just outside her door was orange when it should have been blue like the one in her room.

In her head, saying she wasn't nuts seemed so easy, but when faced with the actual situation, it was impossible to speak. Instead Evie wanted to hide.

The time until her meeting with Dr Mariott was memorable only for it being a blur. The indignity of undressing and bathing without privacy, having to borrow a comb for her hair and the unrelenting chatter pouring from Flipp, assaulting the top of Evie's head.

And now, having just pulled together every fiber in her thoughts to convince this soft spoken man she should get the bus home, he just sat there and said nothing.

Folding her arms across the hospital issue dressing gown minus the matching grey belt, Evie stared back, waiting for an agreement. Perhaps he might reach into his pocket and pull out the bus fare, she could hope.

Since losing the restraints Evie hadn't been left alone and when Flipp departed with a cheery wave and a "see yer after," the girl discovered she had company.

Against the wall stood a single bed, its metal frame visible without covers. A grey mattress covering the springs matched the dismal floor, and the window, although still beyond reach was larger, allowing more light to flood through. Dropped off at the door Evie hesitated before venturing inside.

The man at the far side of the room had pulled up a blue plastic chair and sat at the side of the bed observing her approach. When the girl continued to hover within the apparent safety of the door frame, he beckoned her forward with a slight nod and a sort of half smile that it was okay, there was nothing threatening here, and that she should come in.

But even though the chair was the same, this was a different room nonetheless and it made her thoughts scatter. She would have turned and run then except the corridor was far too wide with too many doors leading to unknown places. And she still had the problem with that orange chair placed on its own against the wall.

Everything considered, the doorway seemed the safest place and recognizing this, the stranger turned his chair toward Evie, dragging its legs across the hollow floor. She winced, a reaction to the sound scraping through her head. He spoke very softly then, stating she could remain at the door if she preferred, it would be all right.

Without knowing what to do, Evie folded her arms, pulling the belt-less robe tighter around her middle and waited for the man to speak.

He was probably thirtyish, Evie reckoned, wearing the calm-in-chaos expression that comes only with experience. His hair, cropped short and teased into miniature spikes was deep black and she wondered if it really was that dark or an early attempt at hunting down the odd grey bit. Three earrings ran alongside his left ear; one silver ring and two matching studs.

The rest could be described as an attempt at normal, hovering around the fringes of conformity in jeans and a black crew neck sweater beneath which lay a white shirt, the ends of which were on display beneath the slightly baggy hem. His legs were crossed, the top leg swinging slightly, pushing the hem of his jeans upward so the top edge of his black Doc Martin boots with bright yellow laces were revealed, one of which had become undone.

If this was a shrink, then he was the antithesis. Instead, he looked more like an off-duty rock star, and privately the girl wondered if he might have a tattoo with the names of his last three girlfriends imprinted somewhere.

"Am I different than what you expected to see, Evelyn?" He asked softly.

Again she didn't reply, not that she didn't want to, but her voice had stuck to her throat.

"Which do you prefer, Evie, or Evelyn?"

Again, she could not answer, the soft echo of his voice dying against the light pink walls, he went on.

"Well, until you, Miss Edern, tell me otherwise, I'll call you by your full name."

"Speak Evie, or he will make things worse."

Taliesin! Quickly, her eyes darted to the space above her head. He had come back! Now she could get out. He would tell her what to do. Overjoyed, Evie fixed her eyes to the top of the door frame.

"Evelyn, what do you see?"

Dr Mariott, nice but very stupid. He doesn't have a clue. Evie thought.

Taliesin continued. "I never left your side, but the drugs Evie, I could not get through them, they take you away from me. But enough of that, do as you planned, deny my existence."

His voice, so clear and beautiful against the side of her head, cold across her face, welcome, needed.

"Taliesin." She wanted to breathe his name forward, trace it into reality but didn't dare. Even in this state, she knew better than to do that here.

Uncrossing his legs, Mariott clasped his hands and leaning forward, glanced toward the floor. Now each carefully controlled spike stood like a series of miniature exclamation points at the top of his head.

"Tell me Evelyn, is Taliesin here?"

"Who?" Perhaps if she sounded vague she could put him off the scent.

"Your companion, you fed him with your blood, remember?"

Talk about straight to the point! She watched his focus shift to the white bandage spanning the lower portion of her right arm beneath which lay an unknown quantity of stitches. Maybe if she threw the conversation into reverse, distracting him.

"Call me Evie."

"What does Taliesin call you?"

No, he was keeping up. The man was relentless.

"Eve, sometimes." Shit! She was an idiot, he had caught her out, Taliesin would go spare.

"Evie, be careful!" Irritated, he thought into her head.

Sorry. She thought back, *God, how much can one person screw up?*

"Walk forward Evie. Do not panic, stay calm."

Emerging from the doorway, but only because Taliesin said so, Evie moved toward Mariott Ambrose. Leaning into his chair he gave a slight tilt of his head to the left, indicating she should sit on the sad, grey mattress with white piping for contrast. Sitting down, Evie felt the metal frame push into the back of her knees. It was cold.

Closer now, she noticed a blue name tag pinned to the front of his sweater, the white engraved letters across the surface informing the girl that this was indeed Dr Mariott Ambrose, Clinical Psychiatrist. *"Yeah"* concluded Evie, she was at the Farm, and without another thought informed the man they had made a terrible mistake.

"Mmm."

Reaching forward he retrieved a blue folder lying on the tiled floor and sat, head bowed, reading its contents.

About me presumably, she thought, irritated that her suggestion elicited no more than a cursory murmur.

"Are you all right?" Closing the file, Ambrose re-crossed his legs, balancing the folder on the top of his thigh. It hung there precariously and she half expected it to fall. Fearing she might make it do so, Evie pushed the thought from her mind. She didn't want to be responsible for scattering his papers all over the place.

"Are you all right?" He asked again.

"Of course," lied Evie.

"You seem concerned with this folder, are you afraid of what's inside?" Was this a trick question? Would a "yes", mean she was paranoid, or, "no", an inability to connect with anything about herself?

"Just answer the question, my love. I swept through his thoughts Evie and whatever he thinks, he is honest. There are no tricks, otherwise I would have killed him."

She thought she could feel Taliesin move in alongside her, pushing with his hands against her neck. She wanted him there, asked him to stay so she would not be afraid of any of this.

Vaguely Evie smiled at Mariott while brushing her hair back, wishing she looked better than she did. Meanwhile she listened to Taliesin drift softly against her ear, reassuring her thoughts.

"They put the drug poison into you because that is all they know to do, but I had taken my fill from your blood while it was pure and so re-took the strength I lost while sustaining the image you misused for your purposes. And now, while the drugs wear thin and this man talks to you and observes you, you will become aware of me again, feel my presence, my words and the touch against you."

He began to kiss the curve of her neck, flaunting his ability to touch her in ways a mortal never could. Tilting her head a little to the side, Evie let the robe drop slightly from her shoulder, feeling the edge of Taliesin's tongue float across her skin. Staring at Mariott, she smiled. He knew none of this.

"No." She spoke finally, "I'm not afraid of what's in the file."

"There's nothing in it really, just the details of what happened."

Taliesin was biting the back of her neck.

"It seems to me," Mariott went on, "that you're distracted, I need for you to look at me Evie, to focus on me."

She was doing her best, but Taliesin was making up for lost time.

"Tell me, is your friend with you?"

Why ask such a stupid question, of course he was. Couldn't he smell the lavender breeze? It filled the entire room, she wanted to close her eyes right now and fall into it.

"Deny me, I will not be angry."

"Then stop touching me and I might be able to convince him." Evie thought back to the carefree voice dancing against her ear.

Ceasing his game, Taliesin left Evie alone but remained beside her. She could feel him, close and pushing slightly, persistent. It was then Evie thought he might be jealous of Mariott's attentions, trying in every way to possess her in public.

"I am not jealous!"

He jumped off the bed, his boots striking the tiled floor, pausing only when he reached the door. Was he leaving? It couldn't be that he was leaving, it was too much.

"I didn't mean what I said!"

She couldn't help it, her mind splintered at the thought. He could not leave when it was he who held everything together. Springing from the bed, Evie ran toward the door.

"Are you talking to your friend? Where are you going?" Firing questions, Mariott was on his feet. Now Evie stood between the invisible Taliesin and the psychiatrist.

"I want you to come away from the door Evie right now, I don't want to call for assistance but I will."

Already the palm of his hand hovered against a red button against the side of the bed. She hadn't noticed it before.

Both figures, visible and otherwise fell silent, leaving the girl to decide what she might do. Presently Mariott spoke again.

"He doesn't like this does he Evie?"

"Who?" She played it vague. Taliesin took a step closer, unseen, slow, his heels striking the hollow tile, resonating into her head.

"Taliesin."

"No"

"So he exists then?"

"No, he's not real."

"What was it that you said you didn't mean when you ran over there?" He gestured to the door where Evie remained.

"Nothing."

"I believe Evie that I'm making him go away and it scares you."

Tantrum over, Taliesin stood by her side, supporting her thoughts. He didn't need to speak, she knew what to say.

"I made it up, all of it." She would act as though everything was fine, which of course, it was.

Calmly, Evie walked back toward Mariott and resumed her perch on the edge of the bed, Mariott seated on the plastic chair once again, Taliesin standing behind him. Without looking away, Evie continued.

"I hate my job." She stated freely, "so I felt like doing what people don't expect quiet little Evie to do, rebel. You have no idea what it's like to be me."

"Good, Evie, keep going, you can do this." Taliesin breathed against her ear. Taking his hand, her fingers shifted to curl around his.

"Can you tell me what this person looks like to you?"

"No, because I told you he doesn't exist. How can I possibly describe someone who is not there? That would be insane."

In her mind's eye she saw the sweep of his black cloak and the long dark hair set in a low ponytail. Taliesin's grip growing stronger, urged strength of her own.

"I see." Mariott wrote something then stared back at Evie again. He might have kind eyes thought the girl, but he's no fool, he wasn't buying any of it. Leaning into Taliesin's hand resting against the back of her head, Evie sought reassurance. She waited for the shrink to speak.

He stared at her and Evie stared back, challenging him, trying hard to plant her own wishes into his thoughts, to go home. It was the only thing she wanted to hear.

"The charges have been dropped"

"What? Is that it?" Evie yelled into the hollow room.

"No." Patiently Mariott continued. You are to remain here until well enough to leave."

"But I'm fine now!" Evie spiraled into rapid chaos. The scent of lavender drifted everywhere and Taliesin was telling her to breathe, to take it all in, that she would be alright and she should not fear any of this.

"When can I go?" Evie pretended that she hadn't heard she was to remain at the Funny Farm.

It didn't matter that the stupid charges had been dropped. In the throes of panic she couldn't remember why they had been there in the first place.

"I have to leave."

Decision made, she tried to stand, yet it was impossible, she couldn't even lurch forward. Taliesin, he was holding her back, she could feel the tight pressure of his arms closing around her middle.

"No!" She had descended into hell again, "No! I thought you liked me, I thought I could trust you!"

"Taliesin, kill him!" She screamed out loud. Mariott Ambrose had betrayed her. He had seemed so nice, so decent. She couldn't trust anyone.

"No, Evie, you will make things more difficult, stop this." Taliesin's arms encircled Evie's middle, holding her there.

"Evelyn." He was unflappable, this man, still patient and his eyes so kind, despite her giving the order to kill.

"Trust him Evie." Taliesin's hands ran through the back of her hair.

Mariott continued, "I don't believe your friend wants to kill me, I think he understands I'm here to help."

"By locking me here forever?" Her voice fell to a choked whisper.

"Not forever."

Pushing away from the chair, Mariott began to stand, taking the offending folder with him. "Why don't we make a deal Evelyn? You keep your companion and I get to help you. Does that sound like something we can work with?"

"You can't make him go away, we won't let you."

"That would be unethical." Gathering his papers, Mariott rose to leave.

"You can't keep me here for the rest of my life." Too exhausted to argue any further, Evie wanted to collapse.

Evie, watching until the shrink's absence was complete turned toward her Storyteller, curling her knees onto the mattress. She was still enclosed within his arms and leaned into their protection.

"Taliesin, I'm not mad."

He kissed her then, softly, like cool air against the edge of her mouth.

"No, but you can write here, in fact, he will want it."

Taliesin's hands floated against her skin, making her breathless against his desires.

"Believe me, where you are now, in here, it is the best place for what must come."

Chapter Thirty-Four

Given the choice between a duet with Taliesin versus the full family choir, the former gig would be the one to book. So it was with a stab to the heart and a sick knot to the stomach that Evie watched as Maureen, Cell-Phone Pam and Evie's grandmother, the dreadful Harriet-Rose walked onto the stage for the first time in nearly two days. The song, 'I always said you had the devil for a daughter' led by Maureen's mother, with Pam on that old acoustic guitar she'd dragged into the Edern household along with the rest of her belongings.

Not that Evie spent much time rehearsing by herself. Since Mariott's departure an hour ago she had hardly been left alone.

First, someone came into the room and ordered her to stand up so they might equip the narrow metal bed with a set of crisp white sheets. "All for show," muttered the girl bitterly. Then she had been given a toothbrush, a small tube of toothpaste and a little black comb of the sort her dad used to carry in the back pocket of his jeans. The three items were promptly placed on top of the steel cabinet at the side of the bed, the impromptu display fielding the appearance she was one family photo away from paying rent.

Told to wait by a patronizing voice, Evie was instructed that if the girl didn't 'cause any trouble,' she might have a few visitors. Taliesin laughed softly into her head then. That nurse thought she was on to a big secret but Mariott had already said her family might be coming.

Still, knowing in advance did nothing for that special stomach churning sickness reserved exclusively for contact with her mother. In fact, it just made things worse, advance notice giving power to an already overworked imagination in which terrible scenes were pressed into reality once the small band arrived.

Nevertheless, Taliesin promised to remain in attendance and should things get really bad would guide the girl out of herself and toward Edern. From there they would cut through the dark forest toward the clearing at the foot of the castle. She wouldn't even have to See it for herself, he would do it all for her, assured the private whisperer.

"Just make sure you follow this time," cautioned Taliesin. "Don't defy me. Really Evie, I have no desire to take the blood life from you again so soon."

She wouldn't, Evie was certain. Besides, that entire episode was the reason for being thrown into the nut house in the first place. Slashing her wrist, and as far as everyone was concerned, drinking her blood for an imaginary friend living inside her head.

"Mariott knows about you." Whispered Evie in the few moments they were alone.

"He will try and make me not real, but trust me, he is your ally in this place so do not threaten him with me again."

Evie fell silent then, inhaling the calm of lavender floating everywhere, masking so beautifully the scent of bleach and antiseptic.

When you got down to it though, thought Evie, there were some advantages to being here. If nothing else, time spent on the psych' ward meant she didn't have to slave all day in that stupid shoe department and neither would she be forced to clean the house from top to bottom as she did every night now when she came home from work.

"Exactly,' whispered Taliesin and pressed his voice against her ear. "Someone's coming."

Footsteps preceded a tall, reed-like woman. Pressed into a stiff white uniform, the edges of which refused motion of any kind, she resembled one of those cardboard dolls with cut out clothes Evie had as a kid and which you simply folded around the figure with little white tabs.

Breezing through the open doorway the woman held a square metal tray at arms length. A blue name tag hovering against her flat chest fell into its shiny patina. The reflection inverted the woman's name so that it came off rather unbelievably as 'sM madD', versus her real name, 'Ms Ddam'. Or was it really Madd? Surely you wouldn't have a name like Ddam. Either one was so bizarrely suited to the present situation that it gave Evie a headache trying to figure it out and she finally gave up puzzling over the strange arrangement of letters.

Pensive, Evie made a quick study of the tray contents; a blood pressure cuff, dressing and scissors. The latter, when placed upon the nightstand were kept well away from the girl. Hardly a mirror image to the crumpled, friendly Flipp, grumbled Evie to Taliesin. Other than brief instructions, there were few words exchanged between Ms Ddam-Madd and Evie. Blood pressure was checked, normal, followed by a dressing to replace the old one.

For the first time Evie had a chance to observe what she did to herself. Staring at the severe line running along the inside of her right wrist held together by a pattern of dark stitches, Evie viewed it as something alien. Taliesin's fingers synchronized with those belonging to the cardboard nurse darting in between each touch, lingering for a moment across the ruptured skin.

"Well, that is odd."

Unimpressed, the woman stared at the bright pink flesh peeking out from below the stitching, defying its earlier status as a deep wound requiring at least two weeks worth of attention.

Taliesin, you've just healed it right in front of her! Evie shrieked silently to her ghost, hardly able to believe what she'd just seen.

Laughing softly he kissed her neck, while the nurse determined to go about her job regardless of the small miracle played out before her, journeyed a thin bandage around the girl's wrist. Without another word she made her exit, leaving the girl and her unseen companion to their secret attentions.

Evie knew her mother was in the building minutes before actually seeing the blue hem from the woman's skirt peeping around the corner. Her stomach flipped and the slam of pain bursting to the front of her head told Evie to be ready. Taliesin was there, but the girl didn't think she could wait.

The black toe supporting the end of her mother's shoe followed, and with a breath and a quick squeeze from her Storyteller's hand, Evie gathered whatever strength she could find.

Paper drifted everywhere. Hand written notes crunched into a bizarre origami were shoved into her face. And there were so many noises, shouting and ranting that she was crazy, that what she had "put this family through" was a "lifetime of shame." Harriet-Rose screaming the girl could be Satan himself.

Words slamming forward, hurting the inside of her head.

Evie was "criminally insane." They would never "live it down." She wanted to "meet this Taliesin, whoever he is," raged Maureen, "I want to wring his neck for the crap he's put into your head".

More of the stuff flying. Large printed moths, angry, coming at her. And they were talking. But that was impossible, how can moths read what is printed on their wings? Do they even have words on their wings? And then the hurry of footsteps; everyone trying to catch these insects, to stop the wings from striking.

Evie fought hard, but the words stung, permeating the safety of the castle walls and she was thrown suddenly to the floor, screaming until her throat grew raw and blood ran against the back of her tongue.

Panicked Evie had fled into Edern, leaving her entity's grip. Heading toward the roar of the sea in the distance, she crashed through the tangled woods. But the voices chased after her, hunting her thoughts.

She was the "Devil's Child, spawn from Hell" to have written such things and that the best place for her was the asylum. They'd known all along she should be in there.

Swept along by Taliesin, her friend, her eternal lover, the pair covered the distance toward the clearing and the silent castle. Waiting, as it had for centuries for her arrival into its walls.

Evie was there, watching from the little arched window, feeling the heat from the huge fireplace behind her. To her right stood the four poster bed where she once lay while dying from Chris. To the left stood the door through which that old man with the Chalice had appeared, the waters from which poured strength and powers into her soul.

Now Taliesin stood behind Evie, surrounding her, forging his protection as though it were a shield made to deflect the assaults hurled toward the castle. Beyond the window, clouds of white paper continued their fall out, descending onto the moonlit meadow where they lay, torching the innocent grass, burying its purity forever.

Enraged, Evie screamed at the flurry. They could destroy what she had written but they could never take her thoughts. Her Storyteller would bring the words back. No-one could ever stop them from coming.

Tears and rage as she pulled away from Taliesin, leaping onto the window seat, Evie beat her fists against the glass, willing it to break so she might catch each fragment torn from *Among Other Edens*. She would put it all back together, Adam, the secret orchard, everything. Somehow every precious word would be saved.

But she was thrown back, hard against the stone wall. Taliesin swooping in kicked at something she couldn't see. But from the receding vision at the window, Evie glanced at an image of herself dragged from a ledge, beneath which lay a rose garden, thorns reaching toward the grey agony of an October sky.

Burning in her veins, intense. Something sharp leaping into her arm and she was falling inside. It came again, deeper, this time, lingering. Fighting back, Evie refused to give in. She was stronger than this.

"I was raped in your stupid nuclear shelter! I put Chris's death on paper, I saw his suicide. In dreams Taliesin gave it to me. He killed him!"

Lying on the castle floor, Evie's legs remained free and she could kick back. Nothing they did to her worked. Nothing ever would work.

Taliesin, where was Taliesin? They had sent him away, she wanted to scream for him but couldn't. With Evie's voice stuck against her throat it was no longer possible to move. They had got to her after all.

Lifted then and carried onto something soft before the fall of darkness.

Chapter Thirty-Five

Inside her head Evie remained awake, so they hadn't fully got to her thought the girl, happy she still possessed the ability to think. It felt good to be safe, sheltered beneath the familiar canopy of the four poster bed, the protection against all that threatened to disturb her. Lying still Evie grew aware of an unwillingness to disrupt the fragile peace by lifting so much as a finger.

It didn't matter that the fire had expired, the room felt warm anyway so there was no need for its comfort. Slowly, Evie's eyes drifted to the paneled window, watching as a sliver of moon drifted into view, drawing her further into the quiet sanctuary.

She couldn't lie here forever though, she must move. Tentatively Evie shifted each arm, recalling the pressure experienced there just moments ago. Surprisingly, they moved with ease.

Sitting up and swinging both legs over the side of the bed, Evie made a study of the thin moon pinned between two immovable clouds.

Silence in everything, within the vast room and in the dark world beyond. Nowhere could Taliesin's presence be felt, the sense of him gone to the tide of drugs polluting Evie's blood.

He had prepared the girl for this, in her early lessons he taught Evie to seek him in darkness, to draw his presence from between shadows so she might see him. Surely he was there now, waiting save for the fact his presence was blocked.

The familiarity of this place gave Evie an advantage. Even in this poor light, the girl knew the curve of every wall as it swept around the bed and the fireplace beyond. Had haunted it. Smiling a little at the memory, Evie recalled kicking Taliesin until he took notice and returned the panicked girl to herself.

Fearless, Evie placed both feet onto the stone floor, flinching as the first shock of cold struck her heels.

"Taliesin." Expecting an answer she called into the darkness. Calling again, his hollow name threw back across the room, making poor company.

"Taliesin, I know you can hear me!"

Eyes forcing the darkness, Evie followed the path forged by her voice, circling the stone chamber until drawn by a peculiar glow. Her gaze rested at the crest of a little arched doorway.

A stream of honey colored light swam beneath the door.

The light moved in a soft thread beneath the door. Leaving the floor, it reached upward expanding toward the door's outer edge and pushed with enough of a defiant force to make Evie afraid the entrance might burst open.

Stepping forward, Evie reached for the handle. The lower edge hung loose against the door displayed a showcase of skilled metalwork wrought into a circular twist and weave design that resembled a rope. Touching it with the tips of her fingers, Evie let it settle there, its weight resting against her skin.

There was heat in this object, a soft warmth. Maintaining her grip, Evie welcomed the sensation into the length of her arm, then throughout her body, so she no longer felt cold but was instead relaxed into a sense of protection reserved for someone much loved.

There could be no fear here.

Slowly, Evie lifted the handle and laying her other hand against the smooth door forced it to swing open.

Met only by darkness, for a moment her feet caught upon the cusp of moonlight and a dark fairyland of unseen eyes and curious whispers, hesitated. Stepping inside anyway, Evie refused the possibility of choice. The door, slamming behind her, sealed Evie's destination.

Deep silence.

Reaching for the handle, Evie sought comfort in its presence. Might she choose to leave, she could. Yet despite not moving an inch, she couldn't locate it. Impossibly, it had gone.

"Hey!" Evie challenged the offending silence. "Taliesin, you can't trap me."

But hadn't he taught her better than to fear darkness? Her Storyeller's lessons, teaching Evie to withdraw his shadow from nothing. All that had been arranged to prepare her for a time such as now. Always he instructed the girl to walk forward, trusting as she entered his place of nowhere.

Cautious, Evie managed another step forward. There was nothing there, nothing at all beneath her feet.

"Taliesin!"

She refused to budge another inch.

Neither was there anything to either side of her. Stretching both arms to the side, Evie watched as her fingers disappeared into the nothing she had volunteered herself into. Nothing was visible here because she was in nothing.

And yet a strange familiararity about the nothingness made it less disturbing than perhaps it could have.

Inhaling the black silence Evie recalled drinking the life blood from her entity's throat, warm against her mouth, and her tongue reaching in, taking. And later, his own play within her, claiming her soul at last.

Taliesin's Waiting Place.

There could be no danger here, there would be no fall. Not in a place where she had been delivered to, invited.

Somewhere there was Taliesin and she was a Seer and he had given her the means with which to find him.

Punctuating the dark air with each stride, Evie dared herself forward before her foot struck something, the sound of scrunched paper fracturing the stillness.

A large piece torn roughly across the top.

Curious, Evie knelt toward the slant of writing. Carefully laying it against the palm of her hand, Evie feared its drift into nothing, vaporizing into mist as unexpected as its arrival.

The penmanship, thrown in a hurry across the page she recognized. The story of Adam's father and the collective blood oath following his son's burial, each terrible drop descending toward the silent earth.

Among Other Edens.

Taking another step forward, Evie clutched the ethereal page. Scanning the darkness for more wrecked survivors, she located three other fragments several feet ahead.

No longer concerned with their frailty, hurrying toward them Evie scooped all three, each telling of Adam and her watch from the secret distance, tucked deep into the swollen garden.

She was being given these. A gift.

The path, paved with everything she had written!

Her journey with Taliesin into darkness that first time, and the intimate trust that followed. Chris swinging from the dead tree on the Forbidden Path, his ruined image floating against her eyes. And the young boy beneath the tree, anticipating the blood rain to fall, slow and welcome toward the waiting mouth.

All of it now lay within her hands and Evie gathered the final story toward herself, her first encounter with Adam and the stranger who she knew now as Taliesin, drawing her toward him with words and his careful seduction of strange magic.

She was no longer alone, Evie realized.

Several feet ahead, watching, the tall frame offered nothing but a steady gaze cast sharp toward the girl.

Clutching the collection of stories, Evie studied the spare figure standing quietly in the middle of this dark nowhere. She would protect them and if necessary, fight for their survival.

Clothed entirely in white, she recognized him as the visitor who entered through the little arched door in the castle while she lay dying. But he had been much smaller then, stooped, delivering the Chalice to her entity, the base of his knotted cane, tapping the stone floor.

Now, drawn to full height he was hardly recognizable and studying the girl remained motionless, waiting for her decision to come toward him.

Luminous, his hair was the same as she remembered, white, worn long past the shoulders and straggly at the ends. It needed a trim, she thought. His beard, the same color and worn long also, might have suffered the same fate along the ends had it not been teased to a fine point at the tip.

Save for several deep furrows across his forehead and a series of small lines fanning out from the outer edge of each eye, the man's face, neither young nor old could only be described as ageless. His plump, translucent skin captured this contradiction of youth and age. From beneath a set of unkempt eyebrows, as white as his hair, peered sharp, crystal blue eyes, as striking in color as his hair was white.

From within the bell-like sleeves on his robe, both hands emerged, beneath which he supported the familiar tall wooden cane. Across the top, long pale fingers overlaid each other, supporting the object held in a tight clasp at waist height. His nails, pink and well formed drew testament to his health, while his skin, although pale across the backs of his hands and lower arms, lacked the bluish tint attributed to the very old.

Slowly and without speaking, the figure lifted the long cane toward her, jabbing the air directly above her head. Not quite sure what to do, Evie did nothing, but she was thirsty suddenly and it burned against the back of her throat, irritating the girl considerably. Could the timing be anymore off?

Again, the stranger tapped the air and Evie felt a hard shove to the back of her head. Spinning around Evie prepared to confront the intruder, hands scrunched around the precious paper, clenched into a ready fist.

A large rectangular table hewn from amber stone met her defense. Standing at about eight feet long, it was supported by two side pieces cut from the same rough material shaped by simple tools. Its amber presence possessed the girl who felt compelled to touch its surface, to feel the significance and power within the stones cast against her hands.

But she was drawn to the Chalice also; the silver cup balanced in the center of the horizontal stone. It pulled her attention making Evie long for the cool texture against her skin. She knew of this drink and needed it again.

He stood, quiet behind the stones and Evie, unable to recall at which point he had moved, stared toward his crystal eyes, understanding then his permission, that she could take what was offered inside and that she must do so quickly. There was no time to consider its significance.

Cupping both hands around the object's curved edge Evie lifted the silver goblet, delivering it carefully against her mouth. Already its mass pressed into her skin and Evie recalled its surprising weight.

Watching the girl, the stranger's clear gaze seemed to push the cup's outer edge, urging it upward, tilting it backward. Evie's thirst became worse, she must drink.

Throwing her head back Evie prepared to swallow the contents and as she did so caught her disturbing reflection shimmer in the cold liquid. Unmoving, she lay, eyes fixed open, staring. Then the fast tide broke her lips, banishing the image.

Pain struck the inside of her left arm, a flash of heat followed by a destructive path northward, all of it forcing the girl into darkness. But the waters, instead of moving into her throat made a rapid sweep into her veins, chasing the hot poison that threatened her existence in the Waiting Place.

So this was why she had been brought here. The man with the stick knew what was to come, providing once again the power of these pure waters. Bringing the cup to her lips again, Evie glimpsed the watery figure of Mariott Ambrose, walking forward, caring more perhaps than he should. She was safe, for now.

But it was no longer water pouring from the precious silver Chalice into her veins. Rolling it onto her tongue, Evie felt its texture. Warm, slightly metallic and heavy. Blood

A name struck her thoughts, quick, precise, singular.

Adam.

And it was no longer the old man who stood in the darkness.

Wearing a black frock coat, white breeches and knee high boots, he appeared dressed as Taliesin at the start of her disastrous journey into 1848. His hair, a dark mass of unruly curls was tied low to the nape of his neck. For the first time also, Evie noticed something else, a flash of white curls tossed carelessly among the dark, as her own had once been. His eyes too were black, as in infancy she once possessed before transforming to their present confusion of sea blue and deep green. Unmoving, Adam's coal black eyes carried their gaze toward her.

Quiet amusement played across the edge of his mouth, compelling the girl to drink again and she did, taking the blood into herself, pushing it down, willing its familiarity into her veins where it belonged.

Her mind had never been clearer. Adam, she knew of him and the knowing was deep.

Chapter Thirty-Six

Taking the hand that is offered is easy for I am beginning to understand the truth within this touch. The Chalice, drained of its water and Adam's blood has gone, as has the stone table upon which it sat so that nothing punctuates this darkness now except his presence and mine.

I follow, to where? I do not ask. It is enough for now that this being whom I watched first from within dreams has met me here. The rest I know will come.

Paper, like before, but untouched this time stretches ahead of us, then is lost to the distance. It is vast, this place. I gather each one and he does not protest at any delay this imposes upon our journey. Soon I have a collection of some forty pages and counting.

We move onward.

How long we walk is irrelevant, here time is of no consequence, I am no more tired now than I was when I set upon this journey. Besides, strength moves through me. No longer does it matter what poison they poured into my veins. There is magic here, stronger than anything they have. In this place, their efforts are meaningless.

There is something more I should know, more than this strange connection between us. Again I am aware of the width of my hand, spanning the thick collection of untouched pages and the curious knowledge between us.

I understand; I am aware at last that all this must be spoken onto paper and I recall too, Taliesin's purpose within my existence.

Pure truth.

Taliesin, hear my thoughts, deliver your knowledge and the power of this truth into me. I am here, ready. I will write again, for myself and the stories that lie within.

*****

Withdrawn from her chaos Evie had observed Dr Mariott Ambrose, his hands piecing together the torn pages she fought to collect. They had stuck her with something and Taliesin had gone, but the remaining fragment of herself knew enough to understand Adam, the Chalice and her quest now in this Waiting Place.

They had tried to dope her up some more, anything to put a stop to her thoughts and to prevent her trouble over the sad remnants of her stories. Too late though, already the nameless figure with the long white beard had administered the miraculous water, diluting the poison and allowing Evie to keep both thought and presence in that place of gentle darkness.

Even here, in the so called reality, Adam's touch came through, brushing softly against her hand, making the misery of the restraints somewhat milder. She lay without protest, watching the ceiling, absent.

Now, after pulling up a chair, Mariott sat quietly beside the girl, carefully withdrawing the crumpled papers from her hand before laying them across the top of the only bed sheet covering her still form.

Having arrived at the point where yet another syringe was taking aim toward her veins, Mariott tore the injection from the hand of a surprised Nurse Flipp, and told everyone to "get the hell out." Coast clear, Mariott withdrew a roll of clear sticky tape from his jacket pocket.

Without a word he proceeded to reunite one piece of writing with another, continuing until everything was taped back together. Shuffling the pages into some sort of order, he snapped open his briefcase, withdrew a quantity of white loose leaf paper and lay them on the bed in a neat little pile.

Feigning disinterest, Evie continued to observe her walk with Adam, stopping to gather each page as it lined the dark path.

But even as Mariott slipped the pen between the fingers of her right hand, a clear plastic one with a tube of blue ink running up the middle, Evie understood the risk this man took. Given her supposed state of mind, the use of a pen, even under supervision was the last thing the girl should be in possession of.

Yet within the darkness of Taliesin's Waiting Place, it was Adam who slipped the pen into Evie's hand. Between both worlds she understood what must come next, and grasping the object fully, indicated that she knew, that in both places she wanted this.

But she could not write lying down. Knowing this Mariott took another risk, removing each restraint and enabling Evie to pull herself upright. Slipping the stack of paper beneath her hands, Mariott leaned into the back of his chair and waited.

Beyond the desire to write however, came something more pressing. Thirst. Reaching for the plastic beaker at the side of the bed Evie drank its contents, realizing her mistake as the scent lifted toward her nose.

Already the juice clutched her throat.

Apple.

She hadn't known.

Chapter Thirty-Seven

*I*t is daylight here and I know this place, how did we get here? The two of us, Adam and I toward the tree. I am hungry, it might have been days since I last ate. Pains tear into my stomach.

It is no longer spring in this garden, the bloom of May blossoms as they appeared to me before has disappeared, replaced now by the presence of apples, perfect in their fullness with skin the color of autumn. The intensity of each red shape, bursting through their golden host of dying leaves.

A ribbon of mist enters this silent garden and begins its journey toward the tree, relaxed, unhurried. We follow the path laid before us. The long grass sweeping aside allows our passage until we are inside this mist, its sheer veil separating our presence from the rest of the garden. I am aware of its damp reach through the length of my hair, against my skin.

He stands against the tree, Adam, knowing my hunger and the reason I should not take anything from within these leaves. He reaches anyway, his right hand disappearing into the dark foliage, while his other presses against my right hand as though preventing my departure. But even if he thought I would, I could not leave this place and want the fruit he places into my left hand, untouched except by him.

The mist strokes my face and neck and I am aware of water running down the length of my throat, tormenting an unknown thirst.

He stands before me. Ebony eyes striking against the contours of his pale face, and his lips red, as when in our first meeting he gathered the slow drops of blood in their descent from the apple blossom into his crimson mouth.

I stand here now facing him in the autumn of all this. How jealous I had been, driven from sleep in my thirst, envious he should lie beneath a canopy of soft petals taking the drink as it fell toward him, his infant murder unknown to me then.

My Storyteller.

I want him, want the three of us here within this garden. Want Taliesin with his stories, haunting the core of my existence, transforming my reality into Eden.

Hunger, it could bring me to my knees and I need to eat. Gently my hand is pushed upward and it is no longer Adam but Taliesin as I first saw him, drawing me toward his presence and the dark folds of his black cashmere coat.

Without gloves, his touch is in my veins and I have no choice but to move my hand also, upward, toward my mouth.

"Take this."

His voice, kind, insistent, threads into my thoughts and I have no choice but to do as I am asked.

The first bite and I feel its descent into my throat, Taliesin holding my hand steady, drawing me toward him. I feel the pressure of his hand against my head and know what is to come.

The second bite and the pain comes, tearing across my stomach. The third and I am in the grass, unable to move against the pain exploding into my head. My throat burns, I might have taken acid into myself.

Knowledge from this tree, the truth rips through me. I am aware of too much, too quickly. It is impossible to breathe.

I am choking.

Images, words, almost two hundred years' worth slam into my head. There are noises and none of it makes sense.

I am poisoned.

There are terrible things to know.

Chapter Thirty-Eight

"Rise to my thoughts as you know how, as I have taught you. Our times together have led you to this and you are strong enough now. There are things you must understand.

"Your response to the fruit lies in the knowledge of the deceit of others and it is these deeds I will give to you. You are a Seer, it is no longer necessary for me to remind you of this but you must know the truth to your existence. Such things lie within you already, I am merely the messenger, your Storyteller.

"I love you therefore trust me as you fall toward my voice and breathe me in. The pressure against the side of your head, you are familiar with and you want this, have wished for its intensity.

"And like a bullet to the brain, I am in you and feel you rise to meet me at last and know you need me here. We are in your blood, Adam, myself, we rush into your history. Know us there, accept our presence Evie.

We know you.

Mark this, mark everything down."

*****

I cannot be afraid. The apple, its poison and the knowledge within me, the good and the bad, I take it all, absorbing every image and word, as you taught me to do.

Move into me Taliesin, and I will rise to meet you, I will take your soul into my blood and hold you there against my core.

The pull and tug inside my brain. Already his feed begins, taking the responses to the images he gives. And they come so fast it is difficult to know where I am. For a moment I fear I may lose the sense of him and panic, falling from his reach and the orchard where we stood. But as always his hand reaches forward, pulling me toward him and the image he places before me.

The feed is deep and the pressure becomes unbearable. I understand the method to his kill and wish for a moment, for the speed of death, for this to be gone from me. It is as relentless as he said it would be, I cannot breathe and I fight his presence, no longer wanting this. There is too much to know.

Blood comes, pouring from my nose and eyes, and there is nothing I can do. "Help me, Taliesin, for this is too much." My thoughts scream toward him, before these too are taken for his hunger.

"Stop this!" I cry out.

But the fall continues. Red washes across my eyes so I see nothing but this scarlet rain, then images striking the inside of my head with such speed they are hardly there.

But they come.

A villa.

A garden pulling toward a tangle of branches withdrawing into an impassable copse of trees, apple. May blossoms falling, and there is such sadness here. The creamy petals, they might be the fall of tears, and they must stop. I have to stop their descent.

'Orchard House,' the name scratches my brain, digging in, unearthing a memory.

I dive again and Taliesin is nowhere but I feel the reach of his essence in every sinew and it pushes me deeper when I think there are no depths left to fall.

More digging, is this how he kills? Is this what death with him is like?

"Yes" The voice returns and I cannot breathe again.

I taste the blood as it runs into my mouth and toward the back of my throat. I am choking, drowning among the depths of my own bitter fluid and the excavation of images from within my core.

I wish for Edern and the solitude of the Castle, the silver Chalice and its cold waters. I wish for strength.

The voice comes, Taliesin, holding me against the gentle rhythm of words. "Through everything I have made you ready for this and you will not die. This pain and the blood will not kill you, but you must trust it to be so."

Within me for a moment, he rests, easing the shudder of each breath, and I am aware once again of the cool grass against my skin and the soft drift of mist as it kisses the surface of each eye. The red has disappeared and I am no longer choking.

There is no blood, for now.

He breathes for me, this being, so I might return to the sense of him as he moves through my core and I understand this is merely a reprieve.

"Hold your soul to mine, inhale slowly and take the last fall, there is room yet for this descent."

It begins, the red tide across my eyes. And I, conscious of his movement among memories, feel the scratch against my brain as each deep recollection is breathed into life then hauled to the surface.

It stops, there is nothing.

"Come into this."

A road stretches before me, uneven and laid mostly to dirt, and I follow the sweep of Taliesin's cloak as each stride takes possession of this place. It is possible to walk and the sickening tug inside my head no longer threatens the breath within my life.

Screens of thick ivy displaying their dark emerald foliage burst from crumbling stone walls, framing the curve of the road in flow of green and amber.

He waits at the corner, pausing where the wall leans away from our quiet presence and I feel his hand in mine. It is without gloves.

I know there is work to be done, understanding to be had, I feel this in his skin, its brisk jolt lighting my core. Treading carefully in this place, I cast a curious glance at the dress I wear now, identical to the one I believed I took from the shop. It trails through dry dust, this dress, but doesn't get so much as a lick of dirt and I marvel at that.

For the first time I see Taliesin in daylight, notice the length of his cloak and its many dark folds sweeping across the top of his boots, both deepest black. His hat too, leather, almost luminous in the dying sun is pulled low but tilts upward slightly, lending further to his familiar possession of self assuredness.

242

And for the first time too, I see his face proper, smooth, pale skin, high cheekbones and the dark arch of each brow, his profile caught between the rim of his hat and the wide, upturned collar on his cloak, lined in a luxuriant wash of dark green silk.

He turns to face me and the blossom continues to fall, layering my skin. It doesn't touch him, I notice.

Green eyes, deep set, dark, holding the secret of long held truths, and his mouth, serious. Everything about him is serious, and as he stands there, quiet, staring into me, he might wear his cloak as though it were a burden. His face is troubled, I have not seen this before and I am worried.

His hands against my head reaching in, going deeper than before and I feel the final push of him there.

A white pain splits my soul.

Chapter Thirty-Nine

*A*lone here, I stand before a tall wrought iron gate. The apple and cherry orchard have gone. Instinctively I reach toward the entrance, my hand seeking the cold metal latch, green, heavy, against my skin.

On the other side of this gate, a gravel path stretches toward an imposing villa, an immense dark structure; it might have grown from the dense garden it stands amongst.

At the farthest end of the gravel drive stands the main house, embraced on both sides by the same ivy clad walls that marked my journey with Taliesin. Six chimneys stretching from their bed of red roof tiles weave threads of smoke between an assembly of clouds in the afternoon sky.

I stare at the massive house whose windows are trimmed in the same force of green as every leaf and grassy blade. Despite their size I imagine they must lack capacity for light, cast as they are against the tangled lawn. A white lace panel covering each pane makes it impossible to see inside.

Standing here, I know this house. Know this is a bleak residence. I want to run but know I cannot.

My eyes rest against a plaque fastened onto the center of the gatepost. Curious, I follow the inscription drawn in a careful series of gold letters against an ebony background.

'Orchard House'.

Slowly, my hand lifts the cold latch.

Somehow, I know I have returned.

I think of how you flashed the name into me when this feed began, after I retrieved the apple from your hands. Everything you need for me to know lies within these walls. Taliesin feed deeper if you must. Show me. I would die for the knowledge of this.

You urge me forward. Courage is the enemy among fear and I will not fear my intrusion here. I am not alone. You will not bring me harm.

Silence as my feet press against the gravel, crushing it deeper into the soft earth. Soundless, I might not be here at all, ghost as I am to another's past and slipping between the two posts framing the porch, slide my hand across the front door. It gives. I knew it should.

I could be sightless for no light comes here. Slamming shut behind me, my presence here is entombed. I am cold, this dress is not enough.

Nevertheless, I know I must go toward the stairs.

Something terrible is happening, I tread the first step and feel its rush into my blood. I am not wanted here.

Gaslights flicker as I journey upward taking the sweeping curve of this staircase underfoot. Shadow guests reach and climb along the wall beside me, a gallery of portraits whose faces might curse my sleep should I steal my eyes toward their watch.

Crying. A woman's cry, deep sobs and a terrible sense of loss. I could suffocate for its power among my thoughts. Possessed as I am by this, I cannot draw breath, for somehow this is my loss too. I must know why.

Driven, I push myself to the final stair. A wide hallway from which a labyrinth of corridors present themselves. Although Taliesin instructs my path it is unnecessary. I remember here and know I must gather myself for what lies ahead.

To the left, fourth door, the room where the window faces the garden. In every cell this I know. With the assurance of one who has lived here forever, I navigate the dark hallway until I reach my destination.

Illuminated by the fullness of a spring moon, a woman sits by the French window. There are shadows here too, and I observe their reach toward the single figure emerging from the depths of her wing back chair. Bent forward, head buried into the palm of her hands, pale against the crimson upholstery.

But to be dressed in this manner is careless, and although I understand how sorrow pours through her soul, there are those who might claim her appearance to madness. A woman such as this, attached to such a tight Victorian household.

Creased, the long white petticoat stretching from her waist toward the floor rests in a series of untidy folds at her naked feet. The camisole, white also, slips past her shoulder and caught at the intersection between both halves of her left arm, rests against the underside of her elbow. Four buttons descend the front of the camisole, the uppermost one thrown open. The decorative frill, scooping the low neckline has dropped forward, partially covering the trembling hands, pulling slowly at the skin, taught against her ashen face.

Danger exists here and I wish again she did not appear this way, with her long tangle of dark hair falling forward, reminding me a little of myself.

The comparison disturbs me.

But what stands behind this woman startles me more than the near living reflection of myself. It is the figure of Taliesin who looks at her also, gloved hands pressed against the carved outer edge of the chair.

Leaning back, she inclines into him. I know she is aware of his presence here, wants it and I challenge the jealously that comes next, that I should share him with one who came before me.

"My Storyteller."

She is addressing him! And lovingly he pushes the stray ends of damp hair away from the sides of her face.

"No! My Storyteller!" I shout into the room, but inside my head, he tells me to be quiet. This is the past, what I see now is what once was.

"Remember Evie." Floats his lovely voice, "long have I walked the path to your existence".

But I cannot help but be bothered by the sight of him there, still and collected.

At the eight o'clock chime, he might be invited downstairs to dine with guests.

If he were visible.

If he was of this time only.

If he were alive.

Here, in this room, he is nothing of the Taliesin I know, dressed in a tight frock coat and woolen trousers, yet familiar to this woman leaning into his hands. She is cold and says as much.

Removing his coat, Taliesin places it gently the woman's shoulders. She is cold no more and tells him so. Like myself, this figure knows him in reality and it matters I know who she is.

"Taliesin of my past and of my future, tell me," I plead.

Movement from the chair. She holds something in her hands and it is very important I should see what it is. Through the shadows and accompanying gloom, I do my best.

A book, clutched tight, making the small gold letters barely visible. All five characters are present, the breath stalling in my throat at the sight of the final letter, 'S' I know of this, I own it.

Evelyn, she is Evelyn. The one for whom the inscription was penned in 1848. The one with whom I share the same name.

"Poems."

That it should have fallen into my hands at all is unbelievable and I struggle to understand how. But hadn't Taliesin orchestrated my obtaining the volume even before I knew of his presence? Everything I have ever done, seen or read has delivered me to this moment. From the time I was born it was orchestrated.

"Literature, art, history, it was never a choice, was it Taliesin?" I ask.

"Your Dreams Are My Survival."

The words roll across my thoughts. This is so much larger than my existence both here and among my reality. I think there must be some mistake, that whatever I am supposed to do, or understand, the wrong life was chosen. I am not good enough for this.

Yet I know these rooms, the marble hallways and proliferation of Oriental rugs lining the pristine floors. The dining room with its solid presence of oak paneling and rich emerald green curtains. Velvet, drawn back and chosen because they overlook the garden so their color, even on gloomy days carries something of the outside into the house.

And that garden! With its sunny tangle of buttercups, oxeye daisies and foxgloves brimming to the base of the forgotten apple orchard, whose fruit come autumn will nourish the dark earth, and where stone angels keep their watch beside a trail of red and pink rosebuds unfurling to the sudden call of an English summer.

I might have lived here before and it is curious that we have the same name. For me, the book with the inscription was the beginning of everything I see now. Adam, the stories from Among Other Edens and Taliesin's presence within me.

"So is this 1848?" I think inwardly, crashing into his reply. The recognition comes fast, rising to my soul, and I fall deeper into the truth of this place. That this is Evelyn of the inscription, and this was the life he chose to haunt all that time ago.

Sadness again, a half sigh drifting forward, its reach turning my head. Two small cribs are barely visible through half darkness and I chastise myself for being so caught up in everything I missed them before, situated as they are a mere glance away.

I understand then, this place is a nursery, the quietly sobbing figure, the mother of the occupants within each crib. Twins? I had expected one, the tragic figure of Adam, but the other, I am unsure of. I wait for an answer, some clarity, but none returns and I move there, to see from above each wooden crib, drawing the memory through my core.

No longer does Evelyn weep and before staring into the cribs, I glance once more to the space behind me. Leaning into the chair, her eyes are closed, Taliesin's frock coat draped fully across the length of her frail body for warmth. A thin line of blood extending from her nose to the edge of her mouth tells me he is feeding. Taliesin, resting his hands across the sides of her head, has taken her away from this place of suffering.

Suddenly, her eyes are thrown open and she looks at me, head slowly turning toward the place where I stand with one hand pressed against the wooden crib. She is staring, this woman for whom Taliesin penned the inscription, fixes her eyes upon my face. I have been caught among things past, her present. I want to know, am I visible here, can I be seen?

"Yes." The simple answer returns.

How is this possible? I don't understand, I thought I did not exist here.

"In her state, I am helping her See."

I am not satisfied. "But if in things past, you gave her my presence here, then I have been here before, like this!" I think into him, I want to know how this is possible, that I was here, haunting the past to my existence before I was created. But he laughs, a low, secret chuckle and I am told to look again at the two cribs. This night at least, I am not to understand what has just taken place.

And so, taking precious light from the moon I stare into the first crib, knowing already what my eyes must see.

His head turns toward me, staring, knowing, studying the connection between us. My God, has this child seen me too? Is he aware of my presence also, aware of what must come soon? I could cry that he knows and for the unspeakable thing that cannot be changed.

This is Adam. Unnamed as yet but he will be this night, beneath the apple tree at the forgotten end of the garden and before dirt is thrown into his face, burying the tiny breath within his infant body.

Large black eyes make a careful study of my face, reading every shape and contour. Intent lies behind his gaze as does wisdom and a depth reaching far beyond his brief moments in this place. Ages are masked behind his stare, he too was born knowing. Ebony hair, interrupted by flat blond curls crown his translucent face and I feel the connection. I feel sick also as I begin to comprehend.

"Lean closer and see." Taliesin's voice.

I do as instructed. He is covered by a thin sheet on top of which rest his infant hands, pale, very pale actually and I notice that the ends of his fingers are almost blue. There is no effort to keep this child warm. In fact it might be they wish for him to die from the cold.

He is freezing I know this, feel it as I felt the earth once crush the breath from his lungs. Shivering, I continue my vigil of this child and the room in which he dwells.

Reaching over the sides, I attempt to place both his hands beneath the plain covering. It is then I notice how the skin between the fingers on both hands is webbed so the lower portion of each finger is scarcely separated at all. Slowly, I trace my index finger across the skin, shivering from the unexpected cold passing between his touch and mine.

I wish to make him warmer so I pull back the covering to place his hands beneath. I see it then as I knew it would be. How could I have dared hope different?

The small chest, so tiny in its infant form is perfect except for the sight of his heart beating, fully visible, a scarlet contrast against the surface of his skin. For this, Evelyn must be crying and I note how the flesh is a confusion of open cavity through which valves and veins are visible, the skin, poorly fused against the base of his trembling heart.

I want to cry out, scream at Taliesin for not doing something to prevent this, but I fight the urge. Nothing here can be changed and so I do what I can, replacing the cover instead, remembering my original intent to secure the hands below the single sheet. His eyes have closed and I wonder if he does sleep, waiting as he must, for death to come.

I could weep for my inability to change this scene, and for a moment would hate the one who delivered me into this, that I should know such sadness.

He ignores my reaction as insignificant, and I am pressed forward, instructed instead to take in the other child, the twin. So, I was right then, there is another child. Reluctantly I do so, leaving Adam and his patient wait for murder.

Identical in every way, I am a study before her black eyes and know I am seen, that where I am invisible to others, both children are gifted with the power to See. I am told I must be still, to inhale what I see and the truth that exists before me.

Oh this doesn't make sense! Taliesin tell me I am wrong in my understanding. I feel sick, the impossibility of the possible, it does not add up. But I know this journey and I know his purpose also, and he would never lie. The weight of this crushes my soul and I am dizzy, I can barely stand.

I turn to the image of you as you were in 1848, feeding from Evelyn's response to the poems and stories you poured into her thoughts. I see the book in her hand fall to the floor, my book, Keats, the one you sent to me over one hundred years later. Dizzy, I am dizzy from this.

"Why do I like those things now?" I scream at your image. "Why did I look the same as those babies? Tell me, why do I look like a younger version of Evelyn?"

And it is true. The similarities are striking, long dark hair, the same small build and fair skin. But you don't answer, this is for me to understand, your task is to show me, to deliver my story.

I hear footsteps and it is my instinct to seek cover but to where I am not sure and frantically, I scan the room for somewhere to hide. But I am told not to be concerned, that I cannot be seen, that those who come now are not gifted with special sight. Nevertheless, I stand awkwardly as the door swings open.

"I am positive she will not know we are here."

It is the voice that arrives first, followed by a black shoe and matching lower portion of a trouser leg. In spite of Taliesin's reassurance, I am frozen anyway.

He enters and immediately I know this is the father, can recall observing his blood oath raining onto the fresh dirt in the garden below.

Several paces behind, two other men follow, younger than the first and I recognize them also. The one with the straight black hair, I recall as the doctor, carrying in his hand a small black leather bag, presumably to accommodate his medical supplies. I run cold at the idea. The other hand, I notice with contemptuous interest is drawn to a fist, flexing open and clenching shut.

Yes there is tension here, reflected in his face, serious. His mouth half hidden by a dark, heavy moustache, the ends of which fall toward his narrow chin, further projecting the grim detail pressed against his mouth. With his long black coat, he may well be the bringer of death.

The vicar too, blond hair, bible clutched in both hands, I recognize. He too is clothed only in black, his white collar a bold line marking the circumference of his pudgy neck and giving me the sense that he must dine at houses such as these with frequency.

Oh, Taliesin, please do not let them see me. Don't let these people know I am here. Wanting to detract whatever energy I have, I think of something different and wonder rather insignificantly if the vicar is able to breathe under that collar and whether it digs into his throat.

The three gather themselves into a small half circle, very like the one they will form in the garden later. I think about this, about how I know of what deed is to come before they have spoken of it, and how the decision these men arrive at will change the course of things. And

251

as I stand, observer to the past, I see the future come from this and understand my present.

I am part of these infants, from their mother who exists for now in her grief with Taliesin, and from the father also, in his heartless evil. I am the good and the bad, and hate that from within these walls, one must die, while the other, banished from this place of comfort and all its future will know the pain of survival, and struggle always to understand the reach for things beyond herself.

I belong within this opulent villa, with its books, art and gentle culture. The past should never have left, it should never have been forced to go.

I stare at Adam's father, my grandfather four times past and wish for Taliesin to kill him now. But this is foolish for I know things cannot be changed, although I wish it anyway, on behalf of everyone's history.

The fire is re-lit, I feel its warmth drift toward me long before I notice its soft glow, a small act of mercy in this freezing nursery and I am thankful at least for that.

A sharp knock on the door and a maid enters wearing the long grey dress of her station. On her head, she wears a white cap, its soft frills flopping casually around the parameter of her head. Her face is flushed, suggesting she might have run through the entire house lighting lamps and fires. Her hand resting against the door handle is too small, and standing against the frame, reaches only mid way. She can be no more than about ten.

I note the surprise fall across the faces of the men, this little servant was not expected and she is dismissed without words.

They will not make the same mistake of leaving the door ajar again, and it is the father, deferred to as 'sir' who sets about lighting the room, but only one or two lamps are lit, just enough to discuss their affairs.

Out of shadow I observe the colors on the walls properly now. A scatter of pink and yellow rose buds floating against a cream background broken only by a large French window, beyond which a black wrought iron balcony stands above the early spring garden beyond.

I imagine these doors flung open on clear, honest days. I imagine also, a breeze gently brushing against the cream lace curtains, carrying the bloom of rose petals, lavender and apple blossom on fingers of light air. I want to stand on that balcony, want to drink in the soft air, the rich scent of earth and the green of every new bud of leaf.

I turn though from the vision beyond the closed doors and the daylight that came with it, and observe instead the twins' father in his discussion.

The boy, it is decided, when declared dead, they will bury in the garden beneath the apple tree. He must never leave this house, there must be no record of his birth.

"He never lived, do you understand?" The father's voice insists. "His evil presence will not be interred with those who have gone before. There will be no funeral, no mourning, you cannot mourn the passing of a demon.

"And the girl?" Asks the doctor, to the muttered agreement of the vicar. But I already know the reply.

"Well, of course, she is not to remain in the family that is out of the question. She will be taken this night to the steps of the workhouse where she will either thrive or die under the care of the Poor Law. Should she perish by morning, then humanity has been spared the evil of her witchcraft and I am vindicated in my belief she is born from the devil with whom my wife speaks. On the other hand, should she survive, then naturally, the child is innocent, spared the curse of her origins, although it is unlikely that should be so, spring has yet to fully arrive and the air this night is damp.

"Should she live however, I am taking every precaution that this girl shall never know her true parentage or the life she was born into. Were she to arrive here as a servant she will be thoroughly unaware of any entitlement to this family. No scandal shall come from this, for anyone here, I can assure you."

He walks toward the silent figure of Evelyn, dangerously close to Taliesin, and reaching forward touches his wife's shoulder. I gasp silently as his hand travels through the entity's protective arm and the invisible frock coat draped over her still body for warmth. And I see also, his face turning sharp toward the offending person, the heat from his eyes torching the air with hate.

There is more to come and I listen, sick from the words infecting the air between us.

"As for her, she exists with the devil and sleeps with his demons. They come here each night and she speaks with them, lying still for hours at a time.

"I believe in what I can see; iron, coal, ships filled with tobacco and cotton, we haven't made colonies out of things invisible to the eye. No, I will not entertain ghosts.

When you die, you go either to heaven or to hell and that's the end of it. As far as I'm concerned you don't hang around."

Withdrawing his hand from his wife's shoulder, he straightened the hem of his dinner jacket as though for effect, then continues.

"But then I consider my wife's present state and perhaps her feeble mindedness comes of its own accord but one look at those infants, I can see God's punishment and know they are not of me, for what have I done wrong? It is she who has attached herself to this evil, she who is punished for aligning herself with what I will continue to publicly state does not exist in this world. Yet privately, where only science existed before, I must now consider what I see before me.

"At first light, their mother also will be sent away. I know of a suitable institution dedicated to the healing of tortured minds and on her return, she will neither recall her children or her evil visitors. Rest assured her presence in this house will not be the same."

"No! You are a liar and it is you who is evil!" I scream, unheard toward the cruel husband and father to these helpless children.

"They are of you, but you would send one away to die and kill the other. Well I came back, I am here tonight in this room over one hundred years later and you would despise me now that I understand the truth to my existence. You cannot keep me away!"

I am angry too that he should call Taliesin the devil, say that he is evil when his presence brings nothing but honesty and kindness. I say as much both to the Taliesin whom I know and the one I hardly recognize but who stands with my namesake in the nineteenth century.

I was present as the child they wish to throw away lay abandoned to the pursuit of damp and fog, my great, great, great grandmother. Oh she survives, grandfather to my secret past and her future paces the room before you now, haunting the air you breathe. So go on, inhale, take me in, I dare my breath against your veins. I have returned at last to the truth you took from me and I am everything you would hate about your decision this night.

Bolder now, I step into the middle of the scheming trio, noting with pleasure how the fire flickers briefly as I do so. The doctor, chilled slightly, steps closer to the flame.

My ancestor speaks. "There is evil here, I can feel it."

I want to punch him in the face, let him feel that.

"His presence is here now, the Storyteller, note how she stares into the distance, she has been like that since the birth of her children this morning."

The doctor adds, "To all appearances, she is unaware she even has children, I would endeavor to say her mind has indeed gone."

Oh how wrong you are, how truly wrong you are.

The father has noticed the fallen book of poetry and I observe his face flush with anger.

"I told you he is here, whenever she communicates with this thing, she holds onto that damn book."

Snatching it from its fallen position, he lifts the cover, reading the inscription. "'Your Dreams Are my Survival'" Disgusted, he slams it closed then continues.

"When I first came upon this volume, I believed she was having an affair, that the inscription was from a lover, one of those damned artists in London, well that was bad enough. But hang it! When I questioned her about the volume, she simply stared into space, smiling, so I might not have been there at all.

"Well, I soon put a stop to her visits with that Bohemian bunch of painters, the Pre-Raphaelites she says they are called. Have you seen what they do? A lot of nonsense drawn from myth, legend, and the work of other writers, a complete waste of time if you ask me.

"While I'm out there financing railroads and ship-building, she is discussing art and goodness knows what else, and giving my money to these people most probably.

Tapping the book of poems against the back of the chair and through Taliesin, the cover with the inscription dangles away from the rest of the volume.

"Of course, preventing her travel to London failed to help matters. Instead she locks herself away for hours at a time, writing and experiencing some sort of delirium. Well, you know."

He looks to the doctor; presumably, he has been called to attend matters on a number of occasions, but the doctor turns toward the flickering gas light as one ashamed of events here and the ramblings of an angry tyrant.

The father continues.

"Then the servants began to talk, one or two flatly refused to attend her needs. I could not even get someone here to light a simple fire if it meant my wife was alone with them. I dismissed a scullery maid and the footman, both for creating rumors, claiming separately they heard her speak with a Storyteller when there was nobody there. Then I heard her myself, thanking this being for the gift of this volume." He taps it with his fingers for effect. "I cannot keep a proper staff and for that I am no longer able to entertain, which in my position is absolutely necessary.

"And that is not all. As I approached the bedroom, I heard her imploring this being to feed from her, that she wished to feel him inside her again! It was disgraceful to listen to. I can scarcely bring myself to speak of it now, but I burst into the room determined to discover whom she had invited into this house. Well, I cannot say what I was angrier at, that no-one was there when reason suggested otherwise, or the defiant smile across her face and the manner with which she positioned herself across the bed. I felt cheated, made a fool of despite her being the only one in the room.

"I hit her then, wanting to wipe the smile from her face, and again when it remained, untouched by my actions. 'Storyteller,' she called his name, the same as the inscription, as my hands tore at her clothing and at the flesh that appeared. I wanted to show her, reclaim her to me. I am her husband! For God's sake, she should know me as that!"

The vicar, face drawn, hangs onto the edges of his bible, as though to protect him from the demonic forces here tonight. But I have seen what lies ahead vicar, your part in the murder of this child and the inevitable hell your soul will surely fall into. I glance at the sleeping Adam, all efforts to drown out the voice of Adam's father failing, as curious I must listen, need to understand how events have come to this.

"But she has not spoken since, other than into thin air. And when I discovered her writings soon after the knowledge she was with child,

I knew then, even as a man of science and industry, she was possessed and had been driven mad because of it."

He stares at the book again, his own eyes are empty now, and I wonder at the content of her writings and where they might lie.

"I want it gone." He tosses it at the fire but it misses.

I smile slightly, "It is okay Evelyn", I think to her, "the future will deliver this book into my possession and I will know the one from whom it came. It will never be destroyed."

I stare at the figure of Taliesin, the evil Storyteller they would condemn. I watch as anger and disgust press into his face, making his playful mouth harden to a straight line. And his eyes, those wonderful jewel green eyes have turned black almost as something set apart from the rest of his face. A malevolent force drawing strength from the evil sustained within these walls and I wonder how it is possible for him to resist unleashing death upon these three.

Their attentions turn toward the crib and it is the girl they discuss first, lost now to the mercy of sleep. I am thankful for that, thankful she can enjoy what little warmth is to be had in this miserable room.

"What are you to call her? She must leave here with a Christian name at least." The vicar, pressing for one decent thing, his voice low and serious.

Silence drops into the space around us as the father considers his options, then he speaks. "It is April 30th the Eve of May, I shall call her Eve."

Waving his hand at the sleeping child, naming her is of little consequence. She is the devil's child and will not survive beyond morning.

I ask myself if later on, they will consider how ironic they should name her brother Adam, and that he should meet his death beneath the apple tree. Surely the vicar, in his complicity will consider the dreadful parallel from his pulpit on Sunday morning.

Let him begin at Genesis.

Again my senses are overcome, I am dizzy. Falling forward, I grip the sides of Eve's crib for support, finding none as my hands slip through the wood. Touching her face, I withdraw immediately, fearing I might cause harm. But it is not harm that I cause, instead, I See into her. I know this child is aware of everything, knows of her ill-fated brother and the disease and deformity he took from her. Knows he will be buried alive beneath the apple tree in the same spot their mother read to the Storyteller once, during a warm, clear August afternoon.

Things move quickly. Decisions now made must be acted upon. Having decided Eve should be sent away, she is wrapped tightly in two more sheets, her head covered, resembling a living parcel. Indeed a note is pinned to the outer layer bearing both first name and date of birth, April 30th 1848.

I read the dreadful message scrawled in black ink across the torn page.

'The child named Eve is the unfortunate child born to an Irish street prostitute, who died for her sins in childbirth. May God have mercy upon her soul and the soul of this infant.'

This, I realize is my legacy. I feel the fictional truth roll forward. It comes like acrid smoke, extinguishing the breath within the room, smothering the past. I cannot breathe.

Taliesin, my angel, help me, truly, I am no longer able to draw breath.

Darkness comes, blinding the life within me.

Chapter Forty

*F*lung *open, the French doors stand behind me and I lean into the
night, aware of its dark kiss against my face.*

*From the elevation of this balcony I observe the silent theatre. A
defiant moon, struggling against an assault of tattered clouds
provides the only light but it is enough to see, enough to fulfill my
part, one third of an unwilling audience. Evelyn stands also, my
grandmother times four. And Taliesin, my beloved Taliesin remains
here, guardian of her response to events as they unfurl below. But she
hesitates at the threshold, a strip of floor between balcony and
nursery, a self imposed limbo.*

*I do understand this, fearful of being seen, she remains
withdrawn, a secret spy. While I on the other hand have no such
concerns and position myself center, so I may watch and condemn.*

*Every gaslight has been extinguished; the room now is completely
without light. From the garden, the party of three will not know how
the doors stand wide and how from above, we take the steady drift of
secret words as they lift and rise toward us. How they thought the boy
was dead and hadn't the doctor signed the Certificate of Death,
stating as much?*

Shovels slice the damp air.

*All of this I know. All of this I have seen before from the wet grass
below, except now I understand the link that our blood runs together.*

My soul cries for the loss of this connection.

My bloodline.

It is enough that I hear, I do not need to see and turn instead to the tragic figure of Adam and Eve's mother, Evelyn, my namesake and her sworn protector Taliesin, his eyes black from rage. He does not acknowledge me but stares outward only.

We could lie upon a canvas. Three figures against a backdrop of darkness, illuminated courtesy of a partial moon, eyes fixed on something unseen yet inevitable as we relive this, eternally.

Evelyn, harnessed to the innocence within the nursery, lambent in her white petticoats. Face pale, framed by dark unkempt hair so she might appear slightly deranged. And myself standing before her on the balcony proper, to the left, dressed in beige, the lesser of innocence, tainted by the darkness and the knowledge of things taken into myself.

And Taliesin, invisible to Evelyn, visible to me only because of my present state, both of us ghosts here. Myself to a time before my time. Taliesin possessing time.

Yet our presence, our simple trio is grounded by the story breathing below, our senses pressed against the cold evening. The touch of breeze against skin, the slow noise of the terrible shovel packing the wet dirt, the sight of the moon restored, whole, unwilling to eclipse the miserable deeds below. Everywhere is the smell of earth, the aroma of it, damp, rich, swelling the inside of a memory and carrying with it the earthbound secret of death and Adam's history.

The last of his infant breath dies. I am dizzy again and cling to the cool railing for support. My soul rises to meet my understanding and I fall toward my name and the voice calling me forward.

Chapter Forty-One

I stand among tall grass, crying, not great, gut wrenching sobs but quiet tears that fall in a slow, single line down both sides of my face. They fall onto my neck and I don't bother to wipe them away, instead they baptize my skin with the truth as I know it now. But I am tired and it is with difficulty I move through this tangled garden and toward my final destination where he waits.

Years have passed. A glance at the house behind me confirms this. The balcony upon which I observed events moments ago has long fallen away, leaving the front open and dangerous. The two remaining side pieces are buried now, hidden below a cover of dark ivy as is the rest of the house. I can only assume it lies beneath, sleeping.

Only the windows are visible. The French window shut now against the world and minus the lace covering resembles a gaping hole, suggesting I could move through it again, should I dare.

Tufts of grass and other assorted plant life have attached themselves to the roof. Dandelions in particular clustered like miniature sunbursts among the deep greens and what remains of the blackened tiles make for yellow speckles among the wild foliage. I have no desire to see anymore, I have taken from there what was needed.

My steps continue, cutting through ribbons of mist hovering above long thick stems and I realize night is softening at last toward dawn. Ahead lies Adam's tree, a memoriam to the orchard that stood here years before anything. Before shipping merchants and industrial magnates cut half of it down to make Orchard Road and the immense Orchard House upon which it stands.

Through the shadows of night and half dawn a figure leans against the gnarled trunk, waiting.

It is harder to walk here as I approach the tree at the far end of this vast walled garden, neglected long before the house and everything else was forgotten. And I know why, know of the secret buried within the dark earth. Know of it now as more than a story told to me by Taliesin, my eternal Storyteller.

I am part of everything, the dark wreckage that is this garden, the ruined house behind it and the history within its walls.

The pink sky rises before me and it is raining. I watch each drop wash the white mist to nothing and I am terribly thirsty. I want this rain, want it to take the heat from my skin and the deep burn within my throat.

I want also this figure moving toward me and I take the tips of each gloved hand, his fingers connecting with mine at last. Absent from the familiar dark cloak and hat, he stands as he appeared within the house, protecting Evelyn from the insane truth.

What is to come, I must have. The thirst is unbearable and I can barely stand from the fever of my understanding. Knowing this he leaves his neck exposed, accessible above the loosened collar of his white shirt. Taliesin's blood.

It is needed to steal my thirst and feed my soul, my core with its life.

Already, his strength and magic pushes through my veins, its sudden rush into my blood throws me to my knees, the power of this, transferring magic into me because I have knowledge and can be trusted. I need no instruction, I am thirsty, it is that simple, and I drink and drink, drawing strength from his eternal presence until I am pushed away gently and pulled to my feet once more.

Slowly turning around I see him, Adam.

We stand, the three of us at the foot of his grave, beneath the still canopy of blossom and leaves. He appears exactly as he came to me all that time ago beneath this tree. Although I have seen him since, as a youth beyond the infancy in which he was murdered, this is the first time since understanding my connection to everything.

He smiles slightly, recognition perhaps, then turning, walks toward the house. I want him to wait; there are so many questions I wish to ask. Yes, I am wise to my past, but of him, Adam there is more still to know.

But instead I remain silent, watching as he cuts through the tangled garden, marked by time in his white breeches, long black riding boots and black Victorian riding jacket. Impeccable, polite, as I know only Taliesin, his guardian and mentor could have taught him.

There is magic within Adam's soul too, eternal, indestructible by fate and made stronger by the evil that befell him. I observe his walk toward the house, away from his burial and the apple tree; watch as the grass lies smooth before each stride. Where I struggled to move forward, fighting against each blade and bramble, he lays a smooth path before him.

I realize, in these simple things, there is still much for me to learn.

The house too changes to his approach. The dark reach of ivy transforms into a flush of carmine roses stretching and climbing the walls, the fullness of each bloom framing the windows into works of art. The balcony too, is restored, and the French door, flung open, embraces the rising spring sunshine.

I marvel as an early breeze shifts the lace curtain through the opening, and I believe I see Adam standing at the threshold between door and balcony, watching. Then he is gone and the rain has stopped and I am standing alone with my angel once more.

I am tired, this I am told, the play of Taliesin's hands through my hair, pushing in that familiar way, delivering the rest that must come. Sunlight streaming through the heavy branches touches my face, making it warm and I am glad Adam moves beyond here, his spirit restoring what was taken.

"Sleep, Evie,"

Taliesin's voice, soft, breathing against my face. Through half closed eyes I watch the descent of a single blossom shifted by a light rustle through the young leaves and feel my soul rise to meet it.

*****

Retrieving the pen from the sleeping girl's hand, Mariott Ambrose gathered some hundred or so hastily scrawled pages from the bed, securing them inside his black leather briefcase. In the privacy of his office he would sort through them, certain a breakthrough had been made while unsure what exactly it might be. He liked having answers but frankly had none, other than the certainty that perhaps he had the most interesting case he had ever encountered.

Pushing back his chair and returning it to the corner of the room, Mariott, for the first time in his life felt it necessary to sneak a glance over his shoulder, which being very logical and he argued, 'a man of science' he refused to do.

Instead, very quickly he walked toward the door, and chasing the names of Adam, Taliesin and Orchard House from his thoughts inhaled the fluorescent light and the evening noise pouring into the corridor beyond the reach of Evelyn Edern's room.

Chapter Forty-Two

Already, where lavender once grew street lights illuminated the fractured earth.

It hadn't taken long, barely six months into 2000 for around twelve dozen red brick houses to crowd the soft earth. Now, what life remained in the four acre meadow either slept beneath dark grey paving stones or lay squeezed into tidy little gardens struggling to survive the six narrow streets.

Such was life at 126 Eden Road in the unassuming district of Eden Park, twelve months on.

Evie had been reluctant to leave the hospital, if for no other reason than during her eight week stint both herself and Mariott put the collection of stories Taliesin had given her into some sort of order.

"You have written a little book, a novella of sorts." Mariott told the girl when handing her the complete copy. She held onto it now.

Simple, handwritten pages crumpled and taped together after being torn to shreds by her mother, inserted at long last into a dark green binder. A white label on the cover announced the contents, *Among Other Edens*. Now Evie's index finger traced the outside corner of the label, picking at it so the soft edge folded upwards. She would have to tape it back down it later.

For at least a week, to those around her at least, Evie appeared completely unresponsive. Inside her head, however the girl was aware of everything. The tests, including a brain scan due to a simultaneous bleeding of eyes and nose, the questions, unanswered, and then the conclusions.

Each diagnosis as elusive as the last; psychotic depressive, manic depressive, and her personal favorite the one even Taliesin laughed at. Given Evie's transition between the personalities of Taliesin, Adam and herself, the girl possessed a multiple personality disorder.

All this of course heard while within her head, Evie sat on the moonlit banks of Edern where she had remained since leaving Adam at the beautifully restored Orchard House, unalarmed at the drugs she might have stuffed down her throat or jammed into her arm.

No longer did she care, her thoughts were so far from the so called real world existence that no matter what they threw at her, she couldn't be touched.

Physically, the journey into her past had been exhausting. Not only did Evie become ill from the depth of Taliesin's feed and the truth of her history as she stepped through it, but emotionally she was left drained, witnessing events from a useless distance as they unfolded around her. Eve, Adam and Evelyn's inevitable helplessness, not to mention Taliesin's fury, all took a hard toll.

Indeed, as with Chris, Evie fully expected Taliesin to throw himself into acts of vengeance. When pressed for a response Taliesin replied that Evie must wait for this to happen, and that it would indeed happen, but not on her terms. Thinking that totally weak Evie said so, but her Storyteller leaned into his favorite oak tree unphased. Pulling the edge of his hat further over his face, signaled the subject was not up for discussion.

It didn't matter anyway, Evie had no intention of pursuing anything. Peace was everywhere and inhaling deeply took it into every cell, holding the sense of calm against her soul before taking it even deeper. For hours she lay like that, aware of little more than the cool grass touching the surface of her skin, and Taliesin several feet away, patient, watching.

Peace and the headache.

In spite of Edern's calm, everything ached, every muscle, every sinew. Even in this place of healing there was no escape from the pain. Making an unwelcome request for Evie to stand, the girl's quest for relaxation appeared to be over and touching the ends of her entity's fingers, Evie reluctantly managed to stand, leaving the soft comfort of earth beneath her.

"Follow me."

Wishing Taliesin would do something more useful such as cure the dreadful headache instead of giving her orders, Evie moaned at her entity.

"I thought I'd be okay by now."

"Patience Evie that will come."

He spoke into her thoughts gently and with compassion, so not to create any more noise in her head. "Truth and knowledge are what made you ill that is all."

Leading the hesitant girl along the river bank they stopped after a short while, facing the water's edge. Gently Taliesin pushed the girl forward.

Without shoes Evie leapt back, already the cold stung the ends of her toes. This was liquid ice! He must be joking.

"You must be an idiot If you think I'm going in there." Teeth chattering, Evie refused another step forward and confirming this, sank both heels into the soft mud. It was far too cold.

Laughing softly, Taliesin's voice rolled across the water, returning as a murmur and breaking against the bank.

"Your obstinacy Evie is my eternal amusement. Always though, you shall do as I ask because you trust me and I have never let you down."

The water became luminous and in its becoming transformed into a deep emerald green, the rich color floating across the still surface. The river's flow ceased suddenly, capturing the green clarity in a single sheet.

The moon also had shifted, sliding from behind Taliesin's favorite oak and settling into a new position on the other side of the bank. Intact as always, throwing its yellow light into the river's core and forming a perfect circle, a ring in the center of a crystal jewel.

"Go forward."

"Where? In there? You've gone mad!"

Slowly, Evie felt the edge of his fingers trace the nape of her neck, brushing the dark length of hair in a single, fluid movement.

"Trust this."

Floating against her skin, his voice came soft, clear, so that she no longer wished to question but instead dissolved against his touch, falling into the warmth of each word.

Lulled by the easy cadence, Evie watched silently as the simple cotton dress slipped toward the damp earth where it lay, a pale invasion in the dark grass. And his fingers, tracing the length of her back encouraged a single step forward. Again cold water floated against the edge of Evie's feet.

Mist rising from the surface of the emerald river lifted toward the low slung moon then swooped down to the green surface. Still moving it reached toward the figure hesitating at its edge, until warm vapors kissing her skin eased the girl's journey forward.

Taliesin, Evie realized, had gone.

Everything now was suspended, the tide in the river, the golden moon and the ethereal mist rolling across the silent figure. Evie felt the diminutive drops of mist run across her skin, pure, clear. Taking another step forward she moved at last into the river.

No longer cold, her skin lay wrapped in the same camisole and petticoat Evelyn wore while imprisoned within the nursery at Orchard House. Long to the waist, Evie's hair yielded to a light breeze, blowing soft to both sides of her face. Placing one foot carefully before the other Evie discovered the top of a stairwell.

On either side of the stone steps, the wall of crystal water rose to a perfect arch above her head. Stretching forward it formed a liquid tunnel along which Evie traveled further beneath the river.

That the steps had been there at all came as no surprise, when Evie's feet struck the first stone she knew then that they should be there. And as her head disappeared below the surface, knew also there was no need to fear drowning, that the wall of emerald water would not sweep her away in a massive crystal tide.

For this had been shown to her once, in a time too far away for her soul's memory to fully restore. Aware also that at the foot of the one hundred and twenty sixth stair, the passage threw itself open to the mouth of a deep cave from which hung a thousand stalactites, each droplet imprisoned within the flow of its age where they remained suspended, captured by the time in which they fell.

No mystery either, that hidden among these stalactites lay an emerald crystal and that Evie should discover it hidden, safe, where in a hurry and in the darkest of times it was left, should the coming of others invade this secret place. Entering the mouth of the cave, Evie moved through the soft green light, instinctively seeking, then touching the precious mineral, retrieving it without a second thought into the palm of her hand.

She turned then and walking toward the amber steps clutched the delicate object.

Taliesin she knew, waited.

Evie questioned none of this. Deeper than memory, the knowledge of every footstep and gesture bound to the reflex in each sinew, she had simply known. No fear then when the tunnel of water began at last to liquefy, as Evie knew it should, returning to the river from which it came, sweeping the steps away and carrying her toward the shore. Reaching the shallow edge at last as though she had been lifted slightly, Evie rose to her feet and stepped onto the bank where Taliesin, in his infinite patience waited.

Changed, he no longer wore the familiar black cloak and hat, but stood instead, as a knight, the moonlit sky capturing his silver armor, as he had, recalled Evie during her escape from Chris.

Ungloved, Taliesin's right hand extended forward, urging Evie to release the crystal into his outstretched palm. Luminous, it lay nestled within his touch.

Then it changed, returning to water and caressing his skin for a moment before disappearing into the flesh. Taking his hand Evie accompanied him along the river bank.

Her clothing was completely dry, so that it might never have touched the water.

But something had changed and it took a moment for Evie to realize what it was. The darkness no longer seemed quite as dark, and even though the moon lay before them illuminating their path, no longer was it set against a backdrop of thick blackness, now instead, it threw a beautiful deep blue violet into the forest at Edern.

They stood again at the edge of the small clearing within the forest and at the foot of Taliesin's tree. Examining his hand, Evie traced it with her fingers, marveling at how the crystal turned to water and disappeared.

"Your willingness to understand your truth and to accept my words returned a little light at last into my soul and into Edern."

He seemed content, his words drawing Evie further toward him. She was warm now, so deliciously warm and light, and aware of the subtle movement of the Storyteller's hands across the center of her back. Arching inwards, Evie pushed closer, making it inevitable that he knew she wanted him.

Chapter Forty-Three

Nose pressed against the window, Evie took the cold into her skin. She still liked that sensation, the numbness taking possession of her face and the tingle shooting into her spine afterwards.

The street lights came on an hour ago, except the one outside that new house where her oak tree stood squashed into a tiny back garden. All that did was flick a faint strobe of orange light lasting two seconds and occurring every three.

It took everything not to run to Taliesin and beg for the shelter of Edern once Evie realized what happened. Instead, she recalled that change was inevitable, that life was constantly in shift and she need not see it as a threat.

Mariott's words, not Taliesin's but Evie listened anyway. Since she was in Mariott's office, she might as well. Besides, he had at least gone to the trouble to make her feel comfortable, even lighting a fire in defense of a November afternoon.

Sitting on an overstuffed burnt orange sofa with her legs tucked beneath her, Evie now wore clothes from home. Her jeans and that pink sweater, the cursed rape outfit she always seemed to end up wearing. At least it was better than the hideous hospital gown.

Her now waist-length hair was swept into a thick dark brown ponytail, secured with a practical elastic band by that nurse Flipp who still told Evie she should model her beautiful eyes.

Playing with a loose thread on the side of the sofa Evie thought that what Mariott lacked in interior design, he had at least made up in retrieving the contents of her writings. She could see them now, perched on top of a desk strewn with papers, pens and documents in manila folders. A crystal green paperweight prevented their drift into an underworld of forgotten files and phone messages weighed everything down.

Evie actually liked the mess. It helped her feel safe, relaxed. Staring toward the roaring fire it reminded her of that other fireplace hewn from amber stone, throwing warmth and flickering shadow toward the delight of her repose with Taliesin.

Evie had lain quiet, transported to the place of solitude during the first fall into Taliesin. Quiet among the opulence of soft pillows and velvet coverings, she's known contentment.

Beyond the little windows, stars pressed against a midnight blue sky. Cocooned within the dark shadows of the castle chamber, they might have been all that remained alive and she didn't want to leave, didn't want to risk the destruction of herself out there, among real things.

"But Edern exists within your heart." Taliesin whispered. Delicately, he traced the outline of her heart with the edge of his fingers, making her rise to meet his touch. Knowing he would probably read her thoughts Evie stared at him now, his green eyes, brighter than she could recall. Moving closer, he continued, whispering into the space between them.

"You know who you are, reality cannot touch that. And the waters," he added carefully, "you have their protection. You rose from the waters of Edern, holding in your hand what I had sent you for. You knew what to retrieve, it was my hope that you would. I wished for your soul to know.

"And you were right to believe there is more than this. Everything that has happened is merely the beginning of something larger than yourself; there still is much for you to learn. But that will come, there is time for that."

She wanted to press for more information, but rolled against him instead. To question was pointless.

"Yes it is." Slowly claiming every outline with the tips of his fingers, he ensured Evie's inability to speak.

"My Evie, ever curious, but you have learned enough for now, taking all that is needed to go forward, enabling your return."

"No! What are you saying?"

"I have prepared you for this, there are things you must do in that existence."

"But I want to stay here with you! They think I'm crazy anyway, sometimes the things they say bleed through and I hear everything. I'm catatonic, they said so, they're not even sure if I can recover. Taliesin, I can stay like this forever, it would be so easy.

There are no expectations of me. I can stay in Edern with you and we can live in this castle, you can show me the rest of it, we can even create it. We both have powers; you can teach me so much more. Taliesin, please, I don't want to go back there, into reality, I'm begging you!"

Clutching his shoulders, Evie dug her fingers into her entity's skin, forcing his presence to remain against her. Already, tears threatened. Her throat closing against anything else she might say, strangled all efforts to speak.

"What was the point in understanding my powers of sight and magic, of my connection to Adam and discovering you if I cannot see you again?"

A deep sigh shuddered against the castle walls as he withdrew from her grasp. "My God, I have failed."

"No, no!" She screamed at him. "You haven't failed! You taught me everything I know. Because of you I accept that I See things others can't, I even create images at will if I choose, holding them to myself for hours at a time. You taught me to escape my mind, Taliesin, my life, all of this I owe to you, how could you possibly have failed? Why can't we just stay here forever? Why don't you want me to stay after everything we have been through?"

Positioned at the hearth, he stood, clothed fully minus his cloak and that black hat he wore tilted over his forehead. Over the top of his shoulders, his hair had fallen loose, adding to the shadows seeking his company.

But the biggest difference lay in the cast of desperation pressed against his face, marking an expression of deep, haunting loss.

The curve of his mouth, once sensuous now showed only misery. And his eyes, had surrendered most of their penetrating glow to intense sadness.

Yet in spite of their pain they fastened steady onto her and it was to this Evie responded, absorbing the sadness into her soul through his eyes. He wrung his hands, something else she had never seen.

The air fell bitterly cold and despite the perfect fire accompanying Taliesin on the other side of the room, Evie shook violently.

"No, I am not making this happen." His voice slow, suggested a reluctance to speak. "It is fear that harms you now. I cannot protect you from that, remember?" He sighed, "But why, after all I have shown you, do you remain afraid?"

"I'm afraid I will never see you again, this place, or Orchard House. I have seen Adam there, haunting its rooms, turning them into something beautiful and I want to go back, want to know every corner, every painting hanging against its walls. I have known only death in that place, now memories are needed and I wish to create them."

"But Evie..." Dragging his fingers across his face, Taliesin paused for breath then continued, restrained impatience stalking the edge of his voice.

"Evie, there is more to this than what you See, than the images you are able to create, this you know. Yet fearing your return you fight the inevitable."

"You're not listening to me! It is not the return I fear, it is never seeing you again, not having your feed inside my head, not having you help me understand everything. Your job is done Taliesin, the mystery is over, I know the path I was dragged from over one hundred years ago and the path it set my family on. Yes, there are questions still but it doesn't take a wild imagination to know what happened to Eve. Left at the workhouse, you gave me the image, the rest falls together itself. Of course you killed the trio who murdered Adam, hung them too for all I know, like you did with Chris. It doesn't matter, the point is, Adam's death will have been avenged."

Waiting for Taliesin to speak, Evie observed his solemn expression. He remained by the fire despite the air loosing some of its chill. Turning into profile, he selected a previously absent poker from the hearth and picking it up stabbed furiously at the blackened firewood. A single flame leapt toward the opening, threatening his arm, undeterred Taliesin remained at the open grate.

"Why would he do anything else, he can't be harmed", thought the girl stiffly and she continued, no longer waiting for his response.

"I know who I am, I'm a Seer, you have taught me well and I know what to do when I return. I just don't wish to, I'm not ready yet."

A practical distraction to the empty pain burrowing into her soul, Evie wrapped both hands into the bed sheets. Catching Taliesin's shift toward her and fearing he might speak Evie rushed ahead.

"I cannot imagine your absence. It is that which I fear, my survival apart from your presence. So you see, you have not failed, instead, perhaps you succeeded too well." She didn't say anymore, there seemed little point.

Soundlessly, Taliesin moved across the large chamber and sitting beside her gently unraveled the sheet from Evie's hands, taking each one into his own.

For several moments, he didn't speak, staring instead at the backs of her trembling hands. Evie wanted to touch his face or the long strands of hair falling forward. His touch moved beneath her skin, slow, perfect, claiming the fresh tear in her soul to himself. Eased forward Evie leaned into him, inhaling the warmth of his skin into the final cold choking her throat.

"I love you more than my heart can stand," he spoke at last, the breath from Taliesin's voice stroking the side of Evie's face. "But you must return. It is I who will mourn your departure, for once you return into yourself, you will have little desire for my presence. My feed will be inconvenient and as you move toward your purpose, you will forget about me. At best I will become a vague memory, until even you will question the realness of Edern, of Orchard House, of Adam and this place. This I know Evie, do not deny it is possible, I have foreseen what will happen. Remember, my powers still are much more powerful than your own."

He stared at her then, fixing his gaze against her face, tears flooding the surface of his eyes, breaking her heart. He continued. "Imagine it Evie, questioning my existence." He traced the curve of her neck.

"No! I won't have it, I will not accept what you say, it's impossible. How could I forget about you?"

275

Pulled to her feet, she followed him toward the window, the solitary beat of Taliesin's boots striking the stone floor, detracting from anything else that might have been said. She wished for the sound to continue endlessly.

Staring across the castle grounds, the familiar moon illuminated the sweep of meadow beyond, dark green beneath a display of stars pinned against a quiet sky.

"See this Evie. Take it into your thoughts and hold it there for as long as you are able, and remember when you are least able to believe, that you dwelt here once and that you will again."

"So this is it?" Cracking against Evie's throat, the question was more than she could bear."

"For now."

They fell quiet, the air from the simple statement hanging between them. Already it seemed to force them apart. Determined to fight against it Evie stepped away from the window, pressing tightly against him.

"It is no good. Your desires do not change anything." He was already mourning her, his voice suggesting he wanted this to be over.

"But what will you do?" Eyes closed, Evie couldn't to look at him.

"As before I shall watch until it is time for you to know me again."

"When, ten years, twenty?"

"That is not for you to know."

Dissatisfied, Evie chewed the inside of her lower lip tasting the bitter blood that followed.

Ignoring her response Taliesin backed away from the girl and paced across the castle floor, every step puncturing the silence between them. When the steps stopped, she didn't turn around but suspected he stood several feet away. Needing answers, Evie waited for him to continue, he obliged.

"You will be told I do not exist and you must accept what they tell you."

"What? No! I'm not going to lie." Turning from the window, Evie faced her Storyteller. He was standing in the middle of the room, hands at his sides, already aware of everything she would say next.

"Why am I going to lie, after all you told me about understanding my truth? It goes against everything you put me through. I will not be dishonest. I won't do it! They can think what they like, but I'll tell the truth about you."

"Listen to me Evie! You must understand what I have to tell you. There are those who will believe you are mad, I have told you this before, to not mention my name and tell no-one of my existence. This you did however, and although I have long forgiven your indiscretion, it began a chain of events leading to those who would question your sanity. Let insanity be your diagnosis and you will never move into who you are. Think of it Evie, nothing will be possible from there."

A fast vision swept across her eyes, a small room and herself, strapped onto a metal bed, staring, blank. He continued.

"I do not care what powers of magic you possess even you are not strong enough to stop that!"

He lay his hands upon her shoulders. Quick, she hadn't seen him move. This was serious. Beneath Taliesin's stare Evie read the desperation behind every word he uttered.

"I understand your confusion and the hypocrisy that seems to come from this. Know your truth, understand the path to your existence but keep the nature of this knowledge to yourself. Believe me, there are those who will seek you out and destroy you for it. You must know who to trust and for now, with words, how to protect yourself."

His voice softened and his hands, although still against her shoulders played across their surface, bringing her to him as they always did.

"Do not fear this. I will remain watching and from time to time, you will feel my presence, the scent of lavender, the occasional touch or word, but less so eventually. Please Evie, do not cry." Softly, he traced the flow of tears with the ends of his fingers.

"You have no idea of the pain I already know within my soul, withdrawing from you, your responses, my feed and deep invasion into your core. That I must separate myself from you is unthinkable, but I have no choice. Believe me when I tell you, I have no decision in this.

"But I will come again I promise and stronger than you have known. You will need me then, even before you are aware and for that I forgive your reluctance in advance, and the resistance I must then push through. I will need you also, for reasons you cannot know or understand at present, so do not be tempted to ask.

"This was your final journey into Edern, and no matter how you try, you will not return. Instead you will be immersed in the reality you create for yourself. No more shall it be considered your enemy, your antagonist. Come now away from the window, I feel the shiver beneath your skin. Do not make misery for yourself here, instead walk with me toward the fire."

As one experiencing a complete loss of life force, Evie took Taliesin's hand and followed him silently toward the fireplace. Inside, the fire had grown larger than she remembered, with thick orange flames licking the back of the stone chimney.

Shadows, stealing away from the fire moved steady against the flames, bringing their own life into the silent chamber.

"I love you." He said simply, leading her gently toward the amber hearth.

She faced him, the heat from the fire warming her face as slowly Taliesin, Evie's beloved entity and Storyteller stretched his hands toward her, pulling her forward.

Together they forged a shadow dance of heat and flame as moving closer, Evie inhaled the sense of him one last time.

Chapter Forty-Four

"What are you thinking Evie?"

Mariott's voice jolted Evie from the activity within the fireplace. She was sitting on that orange sofa hosting a new addition of yellow cushions scattered across the top. Clutching one against her chest now, Evie surveyed Mariott's untidy office. *Among Other Edens* lay on his desk amongst a pile of assorted papers. The emerald green paperweight balanced precariously on top.

"I've been watching you transfixed by those flames for almost half an hour. Does it remind you of somewhere else?"

"No." Evie lied quietly. She had been staring into the fireplace at her Enchanted Castle moments before returning to the clinical walls of the psychiatric ward.

"Tell me," prompted the personable Mariott. "Were you thinking of Taliesin?" He was so soft spoken, she could have cried. It made her think of her entity even more.

"No." Another lie and Evie wondered, if Taliesin were listening, would he be pleased or disappointed? The betrayal pushed the sadness deeper, making Evie feel sick.

"Evie." The voice kept prompting, "you can trust me."

She knew that was true. It was the last thing Taliesin had said in the soft aftermath of the cashmere blanket he held her in.

"Where is he now?"

A wry smile played across her mouth and Evie hoped that in the firelight of Mariott's office, he didn't notice.

Where? Edern, The Enchanted Castle, the dark stillness of the Waiting Place or haunting the empty rooms of Orchard House with Adam. She could take her pick.

"He doesn't exist." She could have choked on the dishonesty. "I made it up, everything. Everything I wrote was a lie."

"Is that what you want me to hear?"

A thread hung from the cuff of Mariott's navy blue sweater, crew neck with his shirt collar sneaking above the top. Never had he looked more human, flawed.

"I like to write, I make up stories, I've done it for years." That much Evie could say with complete honesty. That part of the truth she could mention without the fear of a quick lobotomy or a fast pass to shock treatment. She continued while the words still came. Afterwards she would cry for the lies she told. Instinctively Evie reached for Taliesin, her thoughts pushing toward Edern, but as predicted found nothing.

"Look, I made Taliesin up, Adam, all of it. I created a world for myself because it was better than this one. It went too far that's all."

She was looking him right in the eye as Taliesin had told her to. Taliesin who had not spoken to her for an agonizing seven days, and who might be watching now, feeling her isolation and saying nothing.

Expecting Mariott to reply, Evie returned her gaze toward the flames, recalling how, in those final moments when she had known it was over, Taliesin held her close enough for each to be inside the other and she felt the painful sadness of every breath shudder against his soul.

He mentioned something about how the flames in the fireplace merged together if you stared long enough. It seemed such an inconsequential thing to say and so she did just that, staring into the pattern of light and flame until she no longer thought of Taliesin and their threatened presence within the castle but of the heat against her skin and the separation of light from darkness.

She had blinked then, a quick reflex sealing in the memory of room and warmth only to open them to the sterile misery of the psychiatric ward.

It had taken her a moment to understand what had occurred. She could only lay there, trapped in dizzy confusion, staring at the cold reality of a grey tile floor. Someone had been here recently, scraping their chair along the tile leaving a black mark. In that moment she understood the reality of her situation and the abandonment she was left with.

Vaguely she realized that night was falling. She lay there unable to move, silent. She felt nothing, but could feel the nothing sucking her insides into a bleak vacuum, its effect leaving her too sad for tears. How could it be possible to feel nothing? But she did.

Off in the distance a cry pierced the quiet of the corridor and the urgent din of stampeding feet followed. Had she tried, she couldn't have cared any less.

Motionless, Evie continued her silent vigil of the shiny floor and when darkness had at last swept toward her, could not be sure that she slept, she had no recollection of doing so. Instead she recalled how slow shafts of light folding into dark, graduated the previous day into the present.

"Well, Evelyn Edern, welcome back."

She could do without the fake-friendly sarcasm. These were the ones Taliesin warned her about. She felt the presence of each word and gesture crawl across her skin.

They would smile in her face, offer refreshments, evaluate everything right down to the way she held the glass, then stick a needle in her arm the minute she said 'Adam' or mentioned the 'T' word.

Looking at Mariott now and listening to his questions, Evie wondered what he thought of her. Quiet, withdrawn, pale. A liar.

Convincing him Taliesin's existence was nothing more than a work of fiction, when all along he was there, in her veins, her blood and in every breath delivered into her core would be her greatest deception.

She must get out, decided Evie. If Taliesin had been a sickness, in his absence, she was no longer ill. She would tell Mariott whatever he wanted, articulate a future for herself in a way that sounded neither conflicted nor confused and leave this hell hole for good.

Chapter Forty-Five

Already there were stars. An abundant layer stretched across a blue-black sky. It made her think of Edern, then Taliesin and the small hole remaining in her heart. Quickly Evie scanned the pages of Among Other Edens, not for anything in particular, simply for the sake of itself.

Thirteen months had passed since tracing the Storyteller's inscription, "Your Dreams Are My Survival" and imagining who he might have been, once.

A little over a year to understand and possess courage enough to journey into her truth. Now at twenty-one she chose her own destiny and did so, largely under the name Taliesin gave her, Eve.

Still missing Taliesin and her partial existence in Edern, Eve had done exactly as her entity asked and refrained from looking for him. Once she tried and got only deep blackness and a headache for her efforts. After that she took the hint and didn't bother.

Neither did she speak to Mariott of her powers, the blossoming of her abilities as a Seer, her flash-thoughts, or the spirits known since childhood. Sure, she could trust the guy but only in the solid world of teapots, tables and the psych' books strewn across his desk.

During one discussion, just prior to leaving the hospital Mariott confirmed a series of neurological tests. Evie recalling how during her time resting in the forest at Edern, reality had sent her into some sort of tunnel where an image of her brain was captured.

"Inexplicable," they said on finding nothing wrong.

"The migraines," Mariott continued to explain, "are, something you may have to live with." He made a few recommendations then concerning painkillers and the like.

"The blood from your eyes and nose though," lowering his tone Mariott demonstrated obvious concern, "had us very worried. We believed you might have been experiencing a brain hemorrhage."

Swallowing hard, Evie recalled Taliesin's warnings about not taking her too far, that she wasn't strong enough. She remembered also the method to his kill, Chris's ruined corpse, swinging against the night sky, thin carmine trails haunting his ears, eyes and nose.

"But we believe it was brought on by severe stress." He added brightly, splintering the memory, "your blood pressure became considerably elevated."

Yeah, from over a century of lies. Evie felt like adding.

"One other thing. You can't replace one Edern with another." Chastising softly, Mariott might have read her thoughts. Her mother and Cell-Phone Pam were downstairs and he quickly summarized.

"If you're not careful the imagination can act a bit like a vampire, feeding from your ideas, gaining strength, tempting you further from reality. You must be very careful Evie."

The journey home had been awkward and mostly silent, Evie in the back of the car wishing for the comfort of Taliesin's presence. Only once did she have anything to say.

"My name is Eve now. I won't answer to Evie ever again."

The declaration was met with a duo of blank stares. Since no-one knew what to say, they didn't bother saying anything at all.

Things hadn't fared much better on returning to the sanctuary of her old room, empty of lavender and Taliesin for the last eight weeks. What was once Evie's meadow with spring flowers now lay bare to the soil and served as a temporary parking spot for tractors and trucks positioned at jagged angles. Where March daffodils once bowed and danced to their spring partner, wooden stakes impaled the soft earth, killing the heart of Eden.

But in some things life ticked along exactly the same as before. There had been no millennium meltdown, no catastrophic failures, no-one defaulted back to 1900 and washing machines still worked.

Cell-Phone Pam, disappearing with the last millennium firework, possibly from embarrassment that nothing did happen, was never seen or heard from again. For all the chaos the woman injected into the tiny Edern household, it was as though she never existed. Not that Eve shed a tear.

There were other things to consider.

Most likely, Eve could turn things back to 1900 and further, if she tried.

Turning to the past as it lay written on the page of the little red history book given to her all those years ago. The one that had made her See things, resulting in beating by the now Dead Uncle Colin, Evie breathed the image as it shifted slightly.

Tremendous noise and the deafening roar of many voices, all of them shouting. Smoke rising from the valley, the appearance of an ancient sword and the rapid thunder of hooves, charging. Breathing slowly and holding everything against her core in a way that felt deeply familiar, Evelyn Edern began to write.

EPILOGUE

April 30th 2001

My Dearest Eve,

It has been two years since our departure from Edern and I have watched your activities daily since then, and although you will never feel my presence until I wish for it to be so once more, I remain close to you always.

My grief at our separation was deep and I am afraid I behaved rather badly afterwards. Stalking the deep corridors of the hospital until I discovered the perfect mind to take, the most delicious feed and a worthy death I might add. His future, I must say was doubtful. I saw his path as I entered his thoughts. A life destined to collide with your own and at a time not far from this, so I thought it best to act in advance.

I am sure in this case, you can forgive my intrusion into the future of things and if I sound rather contrite, it is because I wish only to see you happy and true to your destiny.

You will be pleased to know that the sky in Edern remains violet blue the way you left it after returning the crystal emerald into the palm of my hand. Never again will it know such darkness and I wait now for the light your return to the waters of Edern some day will bring.

Adam waits also, haunting Orchard House, guardian of the tree beneath which he was buried alive. The blossom is there and always, the petals fall like soft rain toward the warm earth beneath. And although I walk alone mostly, the loneliness sometimes is more than even I can bear, his company on these journeys providing a welcome distraction to the emptiness that claims my soul.

Think of me occasionally and the places we visited, and the way the tips of my fingers float beneath your skin. That is all I ask, until my presence nudges the threshold to your reality once again.

Meanwhile, my love, move forward into life with the grace and dignity that becomes you.

> An evil shifts the dust.
>
> The darkening of a New Age.
>
> Let us return to the Beginning
>
> I wait.
>
> The Storyteller. 2001

About the Author

Born Jennifer Anne Hargreaves, Guinevere Edern *(the pseudonym was chosen after a particularly stressful life event)* grew up in Liverpool England and trained at the *Elliott Clarke Theatre School* as a professional actress and dancer. *Among Other Edens* is the first in *The Legends of Eden* series. An urban blend of supernatural fantasy, madness, betrayal, and murder.

After living dangerously in many countries, Guinevere Edern divides her time between Virginia, Florida and Liverpool. While in Liverpool, Edern walks Evie's Forbidden Path....

Visit, *Among Other Edens* blog at:

http://guinevereedern.blog.com/

To read an excerpt from the forthcoming novel *Strange Heaven* by Guinevere Edern go to www.AmongOtherEdens.com

Breinigsville, PA USA
10 June 2010
239574BV00001B/8/P